THE NIGHT LAWYER

THE NIGHT LAWYER

ALEX CHURCHILL

Red Door

Published by RedDoor

www.reddoorpress.co.uk

ISBN 978-1-913062-26-2

Cover design: Clare Connie Shepherd
www.clareconnieshepherd.com

Typesetting: Jen Parker, Fuzzy Flamingo

Printed and bound in Denmark by Nørhaven

To Paul, Francesca and Katya
David, Freddie and Rosie

'We shall not cease from exploration
And the end of all our exploring
Will be to arrive where we started
And know the place for the first time.'

Excerpt from 'Little Gidding' from
Four Quartets by T.S. Eliot

PROLOGUE

'You'll be all right here on your own?'

Chris, the night editor, looks at me, coat and briefcase in hand.

I nod and turn back to the screens on my desk.

He hesitates a moment longer, then walks away. I can see his stocky figure reflected in the window; a ghostly outline overlaying the city lights outside. He walks with a rolling gait, like a cowboy or a sailor, although as far as I know, he rarely leaves the office except to go home and sleep. I hear the faint electronic echo announcing the lift's arrival, followed by the silence of an empty building.

This is my eyrie. I have a hawk's view of London, outlined in circles, boxes and towers of lights. Random patterns of white, yellow, red and green mark out the roads, the traffic and the landmarks up to the darkness of the horizon. Pinprick aeroplane lights inch across a wide arch of black sky. You can't see the stars but an occasional tiny satellite hovers brightly.

I work at the centre of the hub, 'on the bench', sitting next to the night editor so that he can consult me for an instant decision as the papers go to press. He always wants to know exactly how far he can push a story before it becomes libellous. Sometimes he even steps over that line.

The section desks stretch out like spokes from the editor's desk – features, news, foreign affairs and, in the far distance, the magazine and lifestyle sections. I work here on Friday evenings, after my week in court, arriving at seven o'clock in the evening when most of the journalists are still working at their desks. But as it gets later, the lights go off at desk after desk as computers are closed down and journalists leave, until the room is lit only by the eerie glow of the giant news screens up on the walls and the city lights outside the huge windows.

Just before midnight, I sit in the only pool of light left in the vast office, scrolling down my screen, trying to make sense of what is happening to my life. I follow the online trails, carefully going through the second, third and fourth pages of Google, burrowing deeper down the rabbit holes of information than I have ever gone before.

Everything seems clearer up here. I can think. I feel more real. For a moment, I just sit and watch cars move along the roads like brightly lit ants. The London Eye has halted for the evening, outlined in a circle of red light. I go over and over the words I'd heard in the robing room that afternoon, picking them apart for explanations. I run Theo's name through various search engines. He's been in hundreds of cases and been interviewed many times by small legal publications and blogs, so there are thousands of hits on his name. Every now and then a different Theo Frazer pops up too; one that is too old or too young.

Sometimes I go down dead ends, or get distracted, straying down the tunnels of my subconscious, following words and phrases by instinct rather than by reason. I don't find anything I hadn't known before. I'm just beginning to think that it is all gossip, nothing more.

I send an email to Lydia Brennan to ask her what she had meant, rewording and deleting it dozens of times. Eventually, I just click 'send'.

I jump as my mobile phone echoes shrilly in the silence. I look at it. Not Theo.

'Yes?' I half drop it trying to answer, catching sight of Philip's number flashing up. 'Philip? Aren't you asleep?'

'I'm sorry to disturb you.' Philip sounds tired, as if he hasn't properly woken up.

'No, no. It's fine. I'm at the paper.' I watch a tiny light inch across the vast black horizon outside the windows.

'The police have just called. It's Adam Harris.'

'Who?'

'Harris,' he says. 'The case at Bullingdon you turned down. He's escaped from prison. A guard's in hospital and lucky to not be dead.'

Hundreds of online references to Theo are still on one of the screens in front of me and tweets roll down on the other screen, along with headlines about Uganda, the President of the United States, a baby scandal in the North of England and an incident involving refugees in Europe. At both ends of the room, there are eight giant screens, most silently tuned to different news programmes. One records how many hits the online paper got for each story, and how long people spend reading that story. This is a continually changing leader board, so we can see what people are interested in on a minute-by-minute basis. It is fairly quiet at this time of night, and the order remains unchanged for minutes at a time.

I am practised at sounding calm. But in reality, I am just as capable of feeling panic as anyone. It drenches me in white hot fear and the room temporarily seems brighter and sharper, tilting temporarily as my world destabilises. But we professionals know we must keep these things concealed. It's what gives us our edge. Fear is not weakness. Fear is survival. And when you forget that, you are truly in danger.

'There's nothing up about it yet, oh, no wait, here it is.' I read aloud. '"Escape from Bullingdon Prison. A prisoner,

Adam Harris, 32, got hold of a razor..." He'd have needed more than a razor, surely, to get out of a secure prison? Oh, I see, he seems to have escaped while being transferred to court. "...with two other men, who have been recaptured. The public is advised that he's extremely dangerous".'

Adam Harris's prison photo comes up. His dead, penetrating eyes stare out of the screen at me.

'They think he's coming to find you,' says Philip.

'Me? Why?' I remembered that I thought I had smelt cigarette smoke and heard the sound of footsteps behind me when I'd emerged from the Tube station that evening. But I'd forgotten about it by the time I reached the office.

'When they searched his cell, they discovered some notes. All about you. And I have the prison psychiatrist's report here. There's a credible diagnosis of erotomania as well as psychosis and a few other things.'

'What?'

Philip clears his throat. 'Apparently he told one of the other inmates that you'd turned his case down because it wouldn't be ethical for you to represent someone you were in love with.'

'I turned his case down because he's a violent rapist who tried to burn his last victim to death, and who expected me to say that he was innocent. There's a ton of forensic evidence against him. There was no way I could defend him. He must be mad.'

'I think that is rather the problem,' says Philip. 'He's mentally unstable and very violent. The police are going to visit you tomorrow about providing security at home, but they wanted me to advise you to be very careful tonight.'

I look up from my desk, through all the chest-high glass partitions that mark out individual workstations to the big glass double doors to the lift. 'I'm in a newspaper office, with about three levels of security between me and the outside world,' I remind him. 'I really couldn't be anywhere safer. Anyway, he wouldn't know I worked here.'

'A man who can get out of Bullingdon can probably get into a newspaper office,' says Philip. 'Be careful, Sophie. Just be very careful.'

I forget about Adam Harris and stop listening to him, as an email from Lydia lands in my inbox, with information about Theo. I say goodbye to Philip without hearing anything else he says, so that I can open the email and study it carefully. When one woman tells you something about your husband, you expect it to be about sexual betrayal – he's seeing another woman, you have a rival. But this was quite different. It was worse.

I'm not ready to accept her words. I'm a barrister and you always test the evidence before believing an allegation. You don't condemn someone on hearsay. But this email cuts through the protective shield of what I believe about Theo, like a sharp fragment of glass from a broken mirror.

Theo and I had made a sanctuary together, or so I thought. I take off my glasses and rest my head on my hands. My eyes are gritty with tiredness and I close them for a second. I haven't slept properly for several days.

The room is so dark I can barely see. Candles flicker, illuminating the dull gold of the icons in the corner. It is so quiet in here that I can hear the scratching of a branch against the low windows, but it is cold too and my feet are bare. The moon slips out from behind a cloud and I can see that the room is filled with flowers, cascades of roses and lilies, their smell pungent and underlaid with something sickly that sticks in my throat. I see the coffin on the table, and the white shroud of the body but I can't see who it is. I start to walk towards it. I am cold and afraid but my curiosity is stronger than my fear.

'Oh no, she is sleepwalking again... Take her away! Don't wake her. Don't let her see...' The whispers surround me like a mist, and I am lost.

I jerk awake, my heart thumping and my blood icy with fear. I know this nightmare. I've had it before. But not recently. Not for many years. Each time I creep a little closer to the coffin, closer to seeing who is lying there. And once my heartbeat returns to normal I know that, in a strange way, I value this dream. It's my equivalent of a smoke alarm. It tells me that there is something wrong in my life – that something is seeping silently in, curling itself around me, choking the oxygen out of the air. But I also know it's not about Adam Harris. In the law, we meet people like him every week. They are violent and cruel but they do not penetrate our dreams. They are our work, not who we are.

No, the dream is about something more dangerous – to me personally. It tells me that I'm not looking in the right direction, and that something is behind me or ahead of me, where I least expect it. And something has woken me. I think I can hear someone, but the flooring is soft and noise-absorbing. And surely anyone walking across the office would activate the lights as they moved?

I don't turn round. If there's someone here, I don't want them to know that I have seen them. But I look at the reflections in the windows, stretching down the length and height of the room. I can see my own reflection, in jagged fractions, a slight, insubstantial ghost sitting at a desk. If an intruder could see me, they wouldn't expect me to fight back. And there is nothing in the office I could use as a weapon. But maybe they would think I'm just another trick of the light. There is so much reflected in the windows and outside.

And there. A man, a Cubist impression of a man, in layers

of reflections against the darkness, stands very still by the entrance to the office. Unmistakably taller and stronger than I am. He is between me and the way out. Just as I convince myself again that I'm imagining things, he moves, and the light above him goes on.

I realised that however careful you are, however often you check your locks, however much you protect yourself and follow the rules, and however hard you run... sometimes you still overlook the real danger.

'Hello, Sophie,' he says.

CHAPTER 1

THREE MONTHS EARLIER

When I woke up at five, I instinctively put out a hand to touch Theo, only to find his side of the bed cold and empty. Of course, I remembered, he was in Birmingham on what should be some profitable commercial work. So he had passed me a case at Bullingdon prison. It looked unpleasant, but no more so than many of the other cases I had worked on. It had come to us via Philip Meadowes, a solicitor Theo worked with who handled both high-income commercial cases and cases on legal aid. Theo rated him and I was looking forward to meeting him.

After showering and drinking a coffee made on the expensive coffee machine that Theo had insisted on buying, I left the house in a hurry. But before I got to the bottom of the front steps, I realised I had forgotten my passport. It would be needed as ID at the prison. I rushed back in, and took it out of the desk drawer. It wasn't until I was on the underground, heading for Paddington, that I realised I had forgotten to look in the mirror when I left the house for the second time.

My father always said it was bad luck to not look in the mirror if you had to go back into your house when you had forgotten something. But he was Russian. He came from a world where superstition was sometimes all there was to protect you. Random terrible things happened every day, people disappeared

1

from the streets and were never heard of again. People made up rules to help themselves feel safe. I'd found it irritating when I was younger, but now it just reminded me to ring my parents if I had a moment. I found a window seat and watched the rain as we jolted out of the station. The mud meadows and leafless trees of the Oxfordshire countryside sped past.

I opened my laptop and scrolled through Philip Meadowes' instructions. The defendant was one Adam Harris. He had been arrested two months ago and charged with rape and attempted arson. It seemed very little progress had been made and I only had the prosecution case without any of the defendant's comments. On the face of it, the evidence against him was overwhelming.

In September, the victim, Juliet Monroe, a sex worker, had been found by her landlord after he had broken her door down. He had smelt petrol fumes coming from her flat and she had not answered his knocking. When he broke in he found her lying on the floor, bound and gagged. She had been raped.

The entire carpet had been soaked in petrol and a pile of spent matches were found by the letterbox. Clearly someone had tried, and failed, to set the apartment alight. Harris had two previous convictions for assaulting women. He had found his victims travelling alone on public transport and tried to chat to them. In both cases the victims had ignored him and he had lost his temper and hit them. Harris had been captured on CCTV following Juliet at three in the morning. About half an hour later, a neighbour, a shift-worker, had spotted him acting suspiciously outside her flat.

The scene of crime officers had picked up DNA and debris from the flat and identified the type of petrol that had been sprayed around. Using facial recognition software and a photofit description given by the victim, the police had identified Harris from the CCTV, matching him to an arrest twelve months before. Results on the DNA had not yet come back but spots of petrol had been found on his shoes and trousers when the police searched his flat. They had also recovered a picture of the victim's bedroom from his mobile phone. The case seemed hopeless.

Philip was waiting in a car for me when I reached Bicester station, as he lived near Milton Keynes. Although I'd never met him, I knew he was well respected for his meticulous criminal work as well as being highly rated as a commercial solicitor. But he wasn't ostentatious – his neatly trimmed beard, well-fitting dark grey suit and white shirts were reassuringly plain and understated. I had never done work for Bravos, the firm he worked for, so this would be my chance to work for a significantly more high profile firm of solicitors than my usual high street ones. Although the public could now talk directly to a barrister in some cases, most of our work was still channelled through solicitors. The client approached the solicitor, and the solicitor contacted the barrister's clerks. The clerks passed the work to us.

It was a system that had developed over centuries. Barristers represented their clients in court, forging the arguments that would make their case in front of the judge. Solicitors dealt with the contracts and the legal work behind the scenes. The lines were blurred now, and solicitors could represent their clients in some courts.

He got out of the car and offered me a handshake. 'Philip Meadowes. We've heard good things about you.'

I smiled and walked round to get into the passenger seat of his car, a Mercedes that smelled of leather. He drove off, expertly negotiating the traffic. 'The reason we haven't got anywhere is because Harris sacked his previous legal team,' he said. 'He gave a "No comment" interview, and refused to give any instructions.'

'Oh shit,' I said. 'So it's a complete hospital pass.' To

use a sporting phrase, it was a ball I could catch, but would undoubtedly injure me.

'I'm afraid so. In fact I was quite surprised that you agreed to the con.'

'Well, Lee chose not to tell me the whole story.' Neither did Theo, I added to myself silently. 'OK, let's see what we can do.'

When we arrived, Philip parked and we both looked with glum resignation at the squat, grey shape of Bullingdon Prison. Philip looked at his watch. 'We're early. Coffee?'

We found a small café near the prison and bought takeaway coffees to drink in the car. This was not a conference I was looking forward to. As I sipped from my disposable cup of coffee I looked around Philip's car, noticing a child seat in the back and a scattering of crisp packets in the footwell. It surprised me as he looked so immaculate. At last our watches showed 9.30.

'OK, Sophie. Let's go. Onwards and upwards!'

The reception area was as grey and unwelcoming as the rest of the building. Philip and I were asked for our IDs and I obediently surrendered my passport to a young prison guard whose neck was covered in angry acne. He picked up my passport and stared at my picture and then looked again at me, deliberately taking his time. As I stood there under his cold gaze I felt another wave of unease break over me, although I was used to these endless checks. Usually they didn't bother me, but today I felt frayed and out of balance.

The institutional setting, the sour smell of sweat overlaid with cheap aftershave and the guard's hostile scrutiny felt horribly familiar – a chilling reminder of how powerful and intractable the state can be if it's not on your side. The memory of the guards in Red Square tugged at the edge of my consciousness, like a dark shape moving under water. I started to feel claustrophobic.

4

The feeling passed when Philip gently put a hand on the small of my back and steered me towards the lockers where we had to leave our coats, bags and mobile phones.

We followed the next guard down echoing corridors and through doors, which were locked and unlocked as we passed, until we arrived at a small, windowless conference room furnished with a table and four chairs, which had all been bolted to the floor. As always, I chose the seat nearest to the door and checked the location of the 'Affray' button. We sat and waited. I noticed that someone had scratched a message into the desk-top: 'The number of the Beast is 666, the number of the police is 999. That is all you need to know.'

I was wondering whether the Beast came from the Book of Revelations or The Apocrypha when my thoughts were interrupted by the sound of footsteps and the clang of metal doors, followed by the rattle of keys. Adam Harris was escorted in. I stood up and held out my hand. When I look back, I often wonder if this was the moment at which I could have done something different. Could I have walked away?

The first thing I noticed was how very tall he was. He had a strong face, almost handsome, with stubble. As a remand prisoner he was allowed to wear his own clothes and he was dressed in dark brown corduroy trousers and a startlingly white shirt. As with all prisoners, he was not allowed a belt or shoelaces, and his trousers sagged slightly. He hesitated and then shook my hand. I looked up at him and I was struck by his eyes. They were as dark and flat as a shark's. A predator's eyes.

'Good Morning, Mr Harris. My name is Sophie Angel and I am here to represent you today.'

'I was expecting a man. Someone who's been around the block a few times.'

'Yes, well, I have had to take over this case. That does

5

happen quite a lot with legal aid. Mr Frazer sends his apologies, but please rest assured he has spoken to me at length about your evidence.'

In fact, I wasn't sure that Theo had even read it properly, and I certainly hadn't had any advice from the barrister, who had had the case before him, the one that Harris had sacked. After some shuffling around, all three of us sat down. The room was small and overheated and Harris spread his legs and stretched them, pushing into my space so that I was forced to squeeze closer to Philip. Did I imagine it or had Harris also thrust his hips towards me?

'I know this prison has a reputation – how are you coping?' I began.

'All right. I keep my head down, stay away from the drugs – especially the spice shit they're all on.'

'Good. I know you've been through the evidence with Philip and I'm afraid I have to say that the prosecution case seems very compelling. I see that you did not supply your previous legal team with any instructions. Would you like to take me through your defence?'

Harris crossed his arms across his chest. 'Look, I didn't do it, OK. They've got the wrong man.'

'Very well,' I said. 'Let's go through it bit by bit. What do you say about the CCTV?'

'I was there, walking home. I wasn't following the prossie.'

'Do you mean the sex worker? The victim.'

'Of course. The prossie.'

'Did you know at the time she was a sex worker?'

'Who else is going to be walking about at that time of night in those clothes and all that slap on her face?' I decided to let that pass.

'And the photo on your mobile?'

'The police put it there – Photoshopped it or whatever.'

6

'Right. In my experience, it would be very difficult to persuade a jury of that,' I countered.

'Well, that's what you're paid for, isn't it?'

I took a breath and looked over at Philip but decided to move on. I flicked through my papers to the statement of the scene of crime officer, and then to the forensic reports.

'Do you own a car or a motorbike, Mr Harris?'

'No.'

'So, no reason for you to buy petrol then?'

'No. So what?'

'There are five major brands of petrol in the UK. They all contain different detergent additives. The petrol found on your boots by the forensic officers matches the petrol found soaked into the carpet in the victim's flat. You don't own a car or a motorbike so how do you explain the petrol on your boots?'

Adam Harris touched his mouth again and he gave me a long, flat stare. 'I must have walked across a station forecourt.'

'I see, I suppose that is possible. But there is only a one in five chance that it would be the same brand. And how do you explain the spots of petrol that were found around the bottom of your jeans?'

He exploded. 'Fuck you! Whose side are you on?'

I struggled to hold on to my temper. I felt I was being toyed with.

'I am only asking you what prosecution counsel is bound to ask you at trial,' I said, as calmly as possible.

'Well, I'm not going to give evidence! You won't get me into that fucking box.'

'In which case you are bound to be convicted. The jury will have to hear an explanation from you.'

'You think of an explanation! That's what I am paying you for.'

'That is not my job. I am here to put your case across to

the jury as well as possible, and to test the prosecution case. I am not here to invent a defence. Anyway, you are not paying me. The Government is paying me,' I said more sharply than I meant to.

His eyes blazed briefly, but he didn't reply. He just kept on looking at me with that flat stare.

I took a deep breath. 'I'm here to help you, but I would be failing in my duty if I didn't point out the weaknesses in what you say. The evidence against you is overwhelming, and your previous convictions for attacking women are likely to go before the jury. Both Philip and I are advising you that you have no realistic prospect of an acquittal. These two charges can both result in life sentences. On conviction after a trial you would probably spend the next twenty years inside. The only mitigation that would sway a judge would be an early guilty plea. The judge would be obliged to discount some of your sentence to reflect that. We are trying to help you here.'

'Yeah, well you're not fucking helping me. You're helping yourself to a big fucking fee just like the last lot! You're a useless fucking bitch!'

'Right, I think we're done here.' I closed my file. Philip pressed the bell for the prison officer. The three of us sat in an awkward silence. We all stood as Harris allowed himself to be cuffed to the officer. We jostled as the men moved to let me out of the small room first, and Harris and the officer followed, while the same agonisingly slow pantomime of locking and unlocking commenced in reverse.

Harris was looking at his feet but he seemed to be smiling. 'You don't even remember me, do you?' he said, in a low voice as Philip and the guard spoke to each other.

I hesitated. There was something familiar about him, but I couldn't put my finger on it. I looked at his mocking face again. 'You defended me the first time I got nabbed,' he said. 'You got me sent down. I did time because of you. Five months.' He laughed.

I thought back to my earliest cases. There it was. The magistrates court, many years ago, when I was doing a pupillage in a different chambers. So it was hardly surprising that there was no record of my having had any dealings with him before. I identified a memory of a younger Adam. He had been hunched in a corner, with a skinhead crop, picking his nails, saying he had been attacked, he was only defending himself. I had believed him, but the magistrate hadn't.

Philip asked the prison officer something. They were both turned away from Harris, whose gaze trailed up my legs and across my chest. He opened his mouth and flicked his tongue from side to side.

I held his gaze. As a prosecutor, I had helped send men like him away for ten-year stretches. The prison officer and Philip were still talking. Harris moved a little closer to me and whispered in my ear, 'So what if I fucking did it? What if I made her scream? I bet I know how to make you scream.'

I turned away without replying and decided not to mention it to Philip – women have enough trouble getting briefed for serious cases – but Harris had unnerved me. I was used to dealing with men who had been violent, but it wasn't often that such simmering rage was directed at me. On top of that, today had been a complete waste of time. The early start, the long journey, the hours of preparation had all been for nothing. The clerks would be cross because the case would now go out of chambers and, far from getting a fat brief fee, I would probably not get paid at all.

CHAPTER 2

Three women barristers clattered into the courtyard behind me, their heads bent against the wind. Their wheeled cases, full of documents, rumbled across the cobbles. When I first arrived, I etched every detail of what other women wore at the Bar into my mind. I mentally filed away the exact point at which their black knee-length skirts ended and how high their heels were. I studied every black jacket and every hue of black or skin-colour tights. I assessed the odd flash of colour in a striped shirt. Yes or no? Discreet or no jewellery? These women were at home here. They belonged.

That was seven years ago, when I walked into chambers as Theo Frazer's new pupil. Medlar Court was a square of flat-fronted Georgian buildings with an exquisite little seventeenth century garden at its heart, surrounded on all sides by towering walls and with soft, pale stone underfoot.

Now I, too, often walked through the imposing streets and darted through the pale stone arches without even noticing the ancient brickwork. I hurried past the Round Church thinking of what I would cook for supper or the minutiae of a case, rather than thinking that here I was, Sophie Angel, outside the ancient birthplace of Common Law. But deep down I knew that, although I now looked like those other women, I didn't truly belong anywhere. I was a child who was born in one country and brought up in another, never quite fitting in.

But, as that hesitant new pupil, I'd raised my head and pressed the entry buzzer firmly, knowing I'd been offered a chance and that I had six months to prove myself as Theo Frazer's pupil. My nerves had ebbed away as soon as I looked up into his open, friendly face. 'Tell me, what on earth made you want to join the impoverished criminal bar?' He sounded as if he really wanted to know, looking at me directly.

My flatmate asked me to describe him later, and I couldn't manage anything more than, 'Well, you know, sort of average. Brown hair. Nice face. Tall-ish.' He was fifteen years older than me, and possessed of an easy, comfortable confidence I had never seen close up before. I'd read up as much as I could before my first day at Medlar Court, so I knew he handled high-profile white-collar crime. But I hadn't expected him to be approachable, interested and funny. When he smiled at me, I knew that everything would be all right.

I discovered that he had a brilliance in court that outshone most of the other senior members of chambers, that he was good at explaining things and that he was unhappily married. When his wife Louisa finally left him, he became my lode star, my true North, the anchor in the shifting seas of my restless, anxious mind. We had made a sanctuary together, that was almost, but not quite, impervious to our ghosts.

Now, racing back from court after another busy week, I had barely twenty minutes in which to change for my Friday evening libel reading at the paper. I tapped in the code on the door of 3 Medlar Court, and paused before climbing the stairs from the lobby. I could never resist stopping, just for a second, to read my own name, painted in copperplate cursive script, on the board at the entrance. Theo's name was fifth from the top. My name was near the bottom, just above that of the barrister with whom I shared a room; Augustus Gladwyn.

The walls were hung with expensive modernist oil paintings and there was a plush sofa in the hall. The subliminal message was 'Trust us. We're this plush because we're so successful.

11

We'll help you win'. None of these furnishings came by way of those with a practice like mine in legal aid. They were the trophies of the privately-funded work that chambers covered: the corporate banks, the cheating industrialists, the expensive contested divorces, especially the wives from the Middle East and Russia who kept a flat here in order to benefit from our more generous divorce settlements and our incorruptible judges.

I risked chambers' antiquated lift because I was weighed down with an armful of lever arch files. As it slowly creaked up to the first floor, I caught sight of my face in the mirrored glass, and pulled out the pins that held my court chignon in place. I looked older with my hair tied back and my face was strained with tiredness. I had inherited hooded Russian eyes from my father, probably from the distant past when Russia was ruled by the Mongolian hordes, and they always looked worse when I was tired. Old and tired was fine in court – good, in fact, because clients trusted an older barrister more, especially if you were blonde and female. But not on a Friday night. I shook my hair out, and returned to my actual age of thirty-four.

As I went into the clerks' room, I was nearly knocked flying by Lee, our head clerk, carrying a bundle of papers.

'Speak of the Devil! Hello Miss. Here's your brief for Monday. A nice little firearms. A submachine gun found in a hole in your bloke's garden, wrapped in an oilcloth, with his DNA all over it. Still, I'm sure there is a good explanation! We'll need a defence case statement pretty quick. You'll turn it round in no time.'

He thrust the papers into my hand before I had a chance to reply. Lee knew I welcomed any extra last minute briefs he could push my way. Theo and I had a large mortgage on a small house because Theo had given so much to his ex-wife and I had no money. He had recently taken an important step up, but it had a price. He'd been made a Queen's Counsel, and would now be charging clients much higher fees. However, clients who were prepared to pay those higher fees would prefer a QC with more experience. A newly-appointed QC would pay a higher rent to their chambers, but rarely saw an increase in income for the first few years. In fact, they were more likely to see a considerable decrease. It was up to me to keep us afloat until he had established a steady income again.

I changed in a hurry, behind the door of my room in chambers, into jeans, a soft suede jacket and biker boots. I used to go to the newspaper offices in my court clothes, but after years at the Bar I was weary of the repetitive round of subfusc; the careful charcoal grey, the black, the navy blue. It sometimes felt like being an undertaker, or a nun. No one dressed smartly at the paper. I had never even seen Chris in a tie.

Thirty minutes later, overtaking straggling tourists and leaping up steps, I arrived at the newspaper's reception desk – a long counter of pale limestone, situated centrally in a vast glass-topped atrium – and slapped my lanyard on the turnstile to get in.

'What fucking time do you call this, Blondie?' Chris swivelled in his chair as I walked into the huge, open-plan office. Several journalists lifted their heads above the low desk dividers. Watching Chris savage people was the nearest thing they got to entertainment. He had a nickname for everyone.

I looked at my watch. 'Six forty, Chris, and I don't officially start till seven.' The heads dropped back to their screens. Blood sports were off for the time being. A juicier victim would be along soon.

'Never mind about that. Fucking day lawyer went half an hour ago. Toothache or some such fuck-awful Friday excuse.'

I sat down beside him and logged in. 'So what's the panic?'

'Panic? I don't fucking panic.'

I smiled. Chris lived in a state of perpetual adrenalin-fuelled fury. If he stopped, I thought he would probably collapse, like a punctured balloon.

I dealt with his queries in quick succession, one after the other. The trick with Chris was never to show fear or indecision. When he had finished, I began scrolling through the other stories: the rise of the Far Right in Germany, historic child abuse committed by a group of nuns, the latest royal visit, floods in distant countries, a sports star accused of rape, ethnic minorities fleeing persecution, the return of jihadists... I sighed.

The lead story on the third page caught my eye. I skimmed through it. It was a piece about an increase in violent attacks on women. The story led with the most recent, but it was the last of three other recent cases that were also mentioned that made me catch my breath. A sex worker had been raped. Her rapist had then poured petrol over her and tried to set her on fire. She was seriously injured. There was a photograph of the rapist, Adam Harris. His flat eyes stared back at me and I heard the echo of his whisper again.

I ignored it, and looked again at the wording. Something didn't quite make sense, so I queried it with Chris, reading the story out loud to clarify it to myself and him.

'The police have told us that the owner of the building where it happened is running a brothel. Is there any suggestion that the landlord is involved too?'

This story was getting complicated, and that's where the unspotted libel was likely to creep in. The newspaper needed the police for information but sometimes the police used this channel to flush someone out, and fed fragments of 'news' designed to create a reaction. Sometimes those slivers were little more than a theory held by an over-ambitious detective.

14

Those were the slivers that could land us in court. It was my job to prevent that.

'He's been questioned,' said Chris. 'We're using the word "alleged". What?!' The last word was shouted at a young reporter who had crept up to ask him something in a whisper.

'Don't be a fucking idiot!' The reporter, blushing crimson, scuttled away. He looked up. 'Yes, now what?'

One of the columnists sashayed towards us and draped herself over Chris's desk. 'Chris, darling, what's the latest about the paper being sold?' She nodded briefly in my direction. She was one of the journos who thought night lawyers were beneath her and treated us as if we were dreary little bureaucrats making trivial objections to a great work of art. She could be charming but would switch off like a light as soon as someone more important came along. She manoeuvred herself so that I was facing her back, and I could only hear their conversation as a murmur. At one point, Chris looked over her shoulder at me. 'That rumour's been around for fucking months.'

I concentrated on my work. I had no intention of getting involved in the politics of the paper. This woman was a toxic influence in the office, always suggesting to Chris that other journalists had hidden agendas or that they weren't doing their jobs. But every office had troublemakers. Even the pleasant collegiate atmosphere of a barristers' chambers, made up of self-employed professionals, was undermined by the constant scrapping over work. So I forced myself to focus on the story about the violent rapes, untangling what Katie, the chief crime reporter, had said from the vague insinuations of the police.

I read the piece twice, turning to Chris. 'It's two separate stories. The rapist raped and set fire to a sex worker. The building he tried to burn may be a brothel. This wording conflates the two.'

Chris rubbed his chin, where greying stubble was just

beginning to break through. 'Maybe the landlord was a rapist too. Maybe this Mr...' He peered at the spelling, and decided not to try to pronounce it. 'Well maybe he won't exactly want the publicity of taking us to court.'

'I wouldn't bet on it,' I said.

That's what Chris's job was – to bet that the sales from an important story would outweigh the libel damages.

The columnist's eyes flickered over me, always calculating how much of a threat I was to her. 'It's Kylie, isn't it?' she asked.

I smiled at her. A British smile. Not a real Russian one. 'Sophie. Sophie Angel.'

She moved a little closer to me, invading my space. 'So, what juicy stories are you telling us we can't print? I always think one of the best things about being on a newspaper is knowing the news behind the news.'

I flinched. 'I can't talk about it, you know that.' She sloped off, creating a backwash of unease as she passed the rows of desks. I turned back to my screen to tackle a story about a police sniffer dog that had accidentally eaten a stash of cocaine. The dog had gone mad and savaged the drug dealer who owned the cocaine. The man had died of his wounds. His family were claiming police brutality.

But when there was a brief lull – when it looked as if the paper might be ready to go – I called up the story which featured Adam Harris again, and looked at the photograph. I have always been fascinated by what people's faces say. I have a Russian father and an English mother and spent the first six years of my life in Moscow. We came to Britain in a hurry, in the middle of a school term. Straining to pick up the meaning in the chatter around me in the playground, I realised that faces and movements were a completely different language too. Muscovites don't smile at strangers. Smiling at someone for no reason is a sign of insincerity, or even stupidity. But in my new British school I was seen as impolite and unfriendly and soon learned to smile without meaning it. Being thrust into a different world was confusing to a six year old and I learned to watch carefully.

I try not to get involved. But I couldn't resist going over to Katie McKenzie, the chief crime reporter, who was just pulling on her coat to go home. Katie was tall and angular, all sharp elbows, pointed chin and glossy black hair, and she took enormous risks to get a story. I liked her. She bothered to talk to the lawyers, to get their opinions and suggestions on what she could say and how far she could go.

'Katie, that story about the violent rapes...'

She stopped and rolled her eyes. 'Oh, no, don't tell me you...'

'No, it's fine. No libel, not now. But I wondered if you had any more detail on one of the cases. Adam Harris. Only if you remember it, I don't want to hold you up.'

'I could have written the entire story about him, except you'd never have let me. The police told me that he's got a lot more form than you can see from the story I wrote. I spoke to one of the detectives from the case, who told me that he'd been picked up in the past for a complaint from an ex-girlfriend who never followed it up, and nobody ever heard any more. The detective said he'd been a bit worried about her and had made a few enquiries but she just seemed to have disappeared.'

'Disappeared? Left...?'

Katie shrugged into her coat. 'You tell me. I'd have thought they might have started a murder hunt, but apparently she'd talked about going away after it all happened. She never turned up for the second interview at the police station.'

'Didn't someone try and find out what had happened to her?'

Katie shrugged. 'Not enough manpower, maybe. I don't know. All I know is that the case never came to court because there wasn't enough evidence without the victim's testimony.'

As I returned to my desk, I reconsidered my view of Adam Harris. I'd pegged him as a low-level thug. He'd left so much forensic evidence behind. But maybe he was cleverer than he seemed.

Our email system is set to silent, but you can always tell when an important email has arrived. I was just making a suggested adjustment to the wording of the drug dog story when the air moved differently. Journalists swung round in their chairs. Others ended their muttered telephone conversations quickly.

'Shit!' said Chris. 'Jesus fucking Christ!'

I wouldn't normally take any notice of Chris's swearing because he did it all the time, but I, too, had a message on the bottom right hand corner of my screen, announcing that the paper had been sold to American tech billionaire Robert Brennan. A new owner inevitably meant a new editor. And a new editor meant new section heads, as new journalists brought their former colleagues with them. And that was without the innovations that a tech billionaire would inevitably impose, all of which were likely to mean job losses. The higher you are when there is a change of management, the further you fall. But I didn't believe it would affect me as a night lawyer. To most of the management, we were just faceless bureaucrats, minor irritations who kept them out of trouble. Or so I told Theo when I eventually got home late that evening.

'Robert Brennan?' he repeated. 'You know he has a Russian wife?'

'I don't know anything about him at all,' I said. The rest of the evening was chaotic. Everyone had a story or a rumour about the new owners. Getting the paper out was a nightmare.

No one was concentrating, so I had to. We could have been sued for libel ten times over.

'Perhaps you could be friends with her. You speak Russian,' said Theo, when I got home. He could spot an opportunity the minute it came up, and was always suggesting ways I could 'get on', as he called it.

'I can't imagine why a humble night lawyer would even set eyes on the boss's wife, let alone talk to her.'

He looked at me, smiling. 'Now, don't give me your escalator face. I can see through it.'

'Escalator face' was the blank expression that Muscovites wore in public places. They were a people who had learned that betraying emotion gets you into trouble with the authorities. 'I'm entitled to my escalator face,' I said, smiling at him.

I lived in three separate worlds. The first was my childhood home, with my Russian father and English mother. The second was as a barrister who swapped the collegiate atmosphere of chambers for the combative one of the courtroom as easily as I took on or off my wig and gown. The third world was the newspaper, where, as 'the night lawyer', I was anonymous to most of the people who worked there. Now the newspaper was to be bought by a man with a Russian wife. It was only a tenuous link between my worlds but I strove to keep them separate.

Or maybe I was just concerned, like everyone else at the paper, about redundancies, new technology and distant owners who would make decisions without giving any thought as to how they would affect our lives.

'Time for bed.' Taking off my glasses, Theo gently took a lock of my hair between his finger and thumb, twisting it round with an almost imperceptible tug. He kissed me gently on the lips before heading up the stairs.

I am in Red Square. The tall buildings loom through the snow and it is crowded. I am small and lost and very cold. I look everywhere for a sight of my mother's pink coat but there are so many people and I can't see her anywhere. I feel panic rising and my breath hitches in my chest. I'm trying hard not to cry. There is a tall man walking a few feet ahead of me. He is wearing a uniform, He must be a soldier or a policeman. He could help me find Mama. As I get closer he turns around slowly and, although I can't see his face clearly, I know that it is Kiril. I know that he will find Mama for me. I call his name and hold out my arms. He stops and turns towards me and says my name. Then he bends down to pick me up but I realise that something is terribly wrong. His skin is waxy and grey and as his fingers grasp my shoulders I see that his eye sockets are empty.

'Shh! Shh! Sophie, it's all right. It's a dream. It's a dream. You're OK. You're safe with me.' Theo was holding me, rocking me in his arms. The panic slowly subsided as the dream fragmented and the familiar outlines of our own bedroom swam into my consciousness.

A few minutes later, he detached himself with an absent-minded kiss. 'Are you all right now, darling? I'm sorry, but I really have to sleep. Court tomorrow.' He rolled over and pulled a pillow over his head. I was wide awake though, and knew that sleep would be a long time coming. I quietly got up, walked into the kitchen and put the kettle on. I hadn't had that dream for so long, I'd almost forgotten about it. The memory, like so many others, was locked away in a part of my unconscious that I tried never to revisit. It came from that terrible time. The year we had left Moscow forever, when nothing made sense.

I watched the sun come up, sitting out on our tiny terrace,

huddled in my old coat for warmth, watching the steam from my tea curling up into the air and disappearing into the cold air, vanishing like a dream. A thrush sang on the old Victorian garden wall and the early morning sunlight rose quietly behind the row of houses at the back of us, silver and clear.

I am six years old and my parents have taken me to visit the Armoury in the Kremlin. I am so excited to see the throne of Ivan the Terrible and the Imperial Crown. The entrance to the museum is guarded by two young soldiers who are searching visitors. They are bored and cold. My mother hesitates when they ask for her handbag and one guard snatches it from her hand. There is a brief struggle and the bag springs open spilling its meagre contents onto the ground.

'How dare you!' Mama shouts.

The guard has pale eyes and a slight rash of pimples above his wispy moustache. He turns his back and picks up a telephone and starts shouting into it. I look around desperately but the other people in the queue are shuffling and looking at their feet. Are the guards going to arrest us? The guard puts down the telephone and shouts again in my mother's face, and then pushes her in the chest. Her mouth drops open in a perfect circle of surprise and then, almost in slow motion, she topples backwards. I catch a glimpse of pale flesh and a grey slip before she lands heavily at my father's feet. I feel my cheeks burn and I start to tremble. My mother is gathering herself to shout another protest but my father grabs her hand and pulls her up roughly.

'I am so sorry, sir!' he says. 'Please forgive my wife. Many apologies. We'll be going.'

He drags us both away, my mother making a show of rubbing her elbows and glaring at the guards. We walk in silence for a moment and then my mother says, 'Well we could still go and visit Lenin's tomb since we are nearby, no need for the whole day to have been wasted.' Her voice sounds false and uncharacteristically chirpy.

My father stops walking and pulls my mother into an alleyway, turning to face her. I have never seen him so angry. He looks around carefully, to make sure no one is in earshot, then speaks in Russian as he only does when he is upset.

'You stupid, bloody woman! How could you draw attention to us like that? Don't you realise the danger of drawing attention to yourself? What with Kiril's behaviour... you and Kiril will get us all killed.'

My mother shrugs. 'For God's sake stop being so paranoid. Nothing happened!'

'You understand nothing, nothing! Would you do that sort of thing – shout at a guard – outside Buckingham Palace? Of course you wouldn't.'

'A guard outside Buckingham Palace wouldn't push me over. I could report him if he did.'

My father makes a sound like 'Pah!' He says, 'No one shouts at the guards outside the Kremlin and no one shouts at the guards outside Buckingham Palace. If you do, you go to jail and you don't know when you get out. It's the way the world is.'

'It isn't like that in England,' says my mother. 'Really.'

My father doesn't believe her. 'Don't ever do that again.' He marches ahead and we scuttle after him. I don't understand what Kiril has to do with it. He isn't even here.

We travel home in silence. But, even after we have closed the door to our apartment and Mama has made me a hot chocolate, I feel afraid.

Back in London, the thrush finished his song and flew away. I threw the dregs of my tea onto the roots of a rose I'd planted to climb up the garden wall. It was nearly 7.30 a.m. There was no time for daydreaming – I was due at the Inner London Crown Court at ten.

CHAPTER 3

Two weeks later, I went to the paper on a Tuesday, clutching an invitation I'd received to a party, hosted by Robert and Lydia Brennan to introduce themselves to the staff.

'Here for the party?' Marek, the security guard, smiled at me as I swiped my lanyard through the turnstile. 'Or is it Friday already?'

I smiled back at him. 'Don't worry, Marek, it's still only Tuesday. Yes, here for the party.'

'You have a good time, then.' He sounded cheery enough, but I could see that even Marek was anxious. Since the announcement, the smell of fear had been in the air. The paper had been struggling against competition from the internet for several years. What did Brennan want a failing newspaper for? Rumours said that he had bought the newspaper to get the building, that he would close the paper down. But if that was the case, surely the security guards' jobs would still be safe? But someone only had to mention robotics... Brennan Corp was big on robotics.

The glass lift arrived, I stepped inside. Everyone would be going to this party, to see if any of the rumours were true and to make a good impression on the new owners. I had arrived early, so the lift was empty, but just as the doors were closing, Katie squeezed through.

'Hi, Sophie. Here for the party?' Below us the limestone flooring and reception desk on the ground floor dropped away, and the internal glass walls of other offices swept past as we rose.

I nodded. 'You?'

'Unmissable! Have you heard? They're saying we're going to switch to rolling twenty-four-hour news with video cam in all the offices. Live video at all times when we're out. And that the newsroom staff will be cut by half.'

I raised my eyebrows. 'You've already been cut by half, several times over.'

'Maybe we're going to rely on citizen journalism. You know, nutters tweeting conspiracy theories and people emailing in on the technological equivalent of lavender notepaper.'

So Katie, too, was thinking about her job. 'You'll be all right, though,' she said. 'Companies always need lawyers.'

'Unless Brennan has developed a legal artificial intelligence.' I was only half joking. Along with robotics, AI was a big part of the Brennan portfolio. It wasn't too much of a stretch to imagine a programme designed around the British legal system, created to spit out libel judgements. We stepped out of the lift and into a huge glass room, fourteen floors up, with no furniture but small, high, round tables, dotted around to take glasses. Two or three nervous-looking executives hovered by the bar, but I didn't know any of them.

'Always worth getting to a party like this early,' muttered Katie, pushing her mane of black hair over her shoulder. 'It's when people actually talk.' She looked around. 'Perhaps the Brennans bought the paper for this room. To give parties in.' We both ordered white wine and sipped it, waiting for something to happen.

'At least, it won't matter if they do get in AI to do the legal work.' She returned to the topic of the day, eyeing the empty room over the top of her glass. 'You lawyers earn so much anyway.'

I knew it was pointless to explain that even a big case on legal aid paid very little and paid it very late. Meanwhile, I had my chambers rent to pay, and my mortgage. I needed my job at the newspaper as much as everyone else needed theirs.

But I tried. 'The story you need to be covering is about the way the legal system in Britain is collapsing. Digitisation is having problems. There are savage cuts to legal aid. Many of us think that the government is trying to get rid of the independent Bar and move us towards the American system with poorly paid public defenders employed by the state.

Katie listened to me carefully. 'Mm. Not very sexy. No beautiful grieving mothers and wives. No lives destroyed almost before they've started…'

'Well, there will be if innocent men and women end up in prison because the only person they had to defend them was an overworked lawyer whose loyalty to their employer, the state, takes priority over whether their client is guilty or not.'

'The trouble is,' mused Katie, 'most people think that anyone who's been arrested must have done something wrong. There's just not much sympathy for criminals. Let alone lawyers.'

'Well, that's not even the worst thing about what's happening now. Chronic lack of funding for the police and the Crown Prosecution Services means that sometimes the guilty walk free because disclosure isn't made or cases are underprepared. The case worker might be covering two other courts, which may not even be in the same building, so they're running between different courtrooms. The CPS has just too many cases for the amount of money the government spends on it.'

'Mm, I'm not sure who really cares about whether the government is spending enough money on the CPS.'

'Well, they don't care until they're the victim or the wrongly accused person and…'

'OK,' said Katie, as her eyes flickered towards a few groups of people edging into the room. 'Let me do some digging and we can talk about it again.'

The new group looked like youngsters from advertising or sales, and their eyes swept over us as they looked for someone more interesting. But there was a rumble of interest when a woman swept in, followed by an escort of young executives. She was small and delicate, dressed in red, with short blonde hair swept back to frame her face. It took a lot money and effort to make bouffant look so natural. One of the executives hurried to the bar and returned with a glass of champagne for her.

'Fuck me,' said Katie. 'It's Lydia Brennan herself!'

A small group of people entered the room, led by a woman. I had heard that Robert Brennan's second wife was Russian, but otherwise nobody seemed to know much about her. She looked as if she might be in her fifties, although beautifully preserved. I saw her murmur to the staff around her and survey the room, obviously deciding where to start. Her gaze fell on me and Katie and she headed towards us, presumably because we were the nearest people to her. She walked with the grace of a dancer, and had high Slavic cheekbones. As she faced us, her hand extended for us to shake, I saw the jewellery – heavy diamonds on each ear, and a sparkling brooch on the red lapel.

'I'm Katie McKenzie, chief crime reporter.' Katie's long, bony hand shot out as if to intercept her before she could sweep past us. 'And this is one of our libel lawyers, Sophie Angel.'

Lydia Brennan retained her grip on each of our hands for a moment. Chunky rings dug into my flesh and I looked down into blue eyes.

'Really, how interesting. So you are the one who will keep us all out of jail?'

'Well, only if you're committing libel on a Friday. I'm one

of the night lawyers, so I'm only here for one shift a week. I'm a practicing barrister for the rest of the time. You have full-time lawyers during the day as well.'

'And what do you practice in?' I could see Katie fidgeting to get some attention out of the corner of my eye.

'Oh, rape and murder and things like that,' I said. Although I had yet to get a big murder trial, so it was a slight exaggeration.

'Sophie is absolutely brilliant,' said Katie. 'If you want to know anything about the law in London, she can tell you. And she's half Russian.'

'So, Sophie Angel,' said Lydia, enclosing my hand in both of hers. 'You are a brilliant barrister and you are also half-Russian. What a beautiful and unusual name. But it is not Russian. It must be your mother who is Russian?' Lydia spoke virtually accentless English, but I presumed that her command of the language wasn't quite perfect because it seemed rather an odd thing to say. She smiled at me, but her face reminded me of something.

'No. My father's Russian and we came back here for me to go to school. His name was Andreyushkin, but I couldn't say it, so he changed it to Angel.' I trotted out the well-worn story, part of the amusing furniture of my half-suburban, half-exotic childhood.

'How extraordinary,' said Lydia, her grip tightening on my hand before she released me. I thought I saw a spark of something like recognition, before Lydia recovered it with a bland smile. 'To change your name so that your child can pronounce it.'

People had said this before, and I had always laughed. Papa would do anything for me, and he had wonderfully eccentric ways. But now, looking down into the shrewd blue eyes of Lydia Brennan, I realised that it really was strange. Suddenly, the story no longer felt true. My core shifted uncomfortably and I was embarrassed, as if I had been caught out lying.

'So do you speak Russian?' She spoke in Russian and I answered her in the same language.

'We spoke Russian at home, and I lived in Moscow for the first six years of my life. But it's a bit rusty.'

'Andreyushkin was a very talented musical family when I was young in Moscow.' She studied my face. 'Are you by any chance related to them?'

'My father was the pianist, Vassily Andreyushkin.' Her stare suddenly became almost hostile and I stopped. I didn't want to mention my uncle, Kiril Andreyushkin, and be asked prying questions to which I had no answer.

'I see.' She reverted to English. I wondered if I'd said something wrong. Lydia's eyes bored into me, raking my face for my innermost thoughts. There was recognition somewhere between us, an awareness of a dark place that most people in this room would never know. And where there is darkness, there are secrets. And where there are secrets, there is betrayal.

I became aware of the roar of the party around me. A girl with a friendly smile touched my elbow, obviously recognising me from the news desk. She shouted in my ear, but the party was building up to a roar and I couldn't catch it. I smiled at her. Lydia whispered something to one of her escorts, and detached herself from us. The respectful little group around her was soon swallowed up by the crowd, as it parted for her to make her way across the room.

'You obviously made a big impression,' said Katie. 'Oh, there's the Shadow Home Secretary. I must try to catch her.'

'There you are.' An arm went around my shoulders. I flinched until I saw who it was. 'Theo!' I looked up to see my husband, running a hand through his dark, springy hair as he scanned the room. It was an unconscious gesture he made a hundred times a day. Several women looked up, acknowledging his presence.

'What are you doing here?' I couldn't help smiling as he kissed me.

'I thought you shouldn't have to get yourself home alone on a cold, dark night, and Marek agreed with me.' He winked, and went back to scanning the room over my head. All doors opened for Theo, even electronic security gates manned by trained guards.

'So who's here?' Completing his scan, he returned his attention to me. 'Anyone we know?' Theo could work a party, exchanging cards and smiles, handshakes and kisses with men and women he had barely met.

'Katie's just gone off to talk to the Shadow Home Secretary,' I said.

'She'll be lucky.' Theo grinned. The Shadow Home Secretary was famously adept at evading journalists. 'Are the new owners here?'

'I talked to the wife.' I was oddly conscious of not wanting to tell anyone, not even Theo, about Lydia Brennan and the effect she had had on me. Something dark and terrible had stirred briefly in my subconscious.

'And?' Theo knew me very well, and he was listening now. 'You didn't like her?'

'Not so much didn't like, just that… oh, I don't know. This whole thing is so unsettling. We all need our jobs, and new management, well…' I was trying to justify my feelings to myself. It almost worked. No wonder I was concerned by the arrival of new owners at the paper. My weekly libel reading fee was the only payment I could rely on arriving in my bank account, month after month. It was my security.

'So what did you think of her? Is she a model? A blonde bombshell?' Theo looked around quickly again, in search of such a person in the now packed party.

I checked the room to make sure she wasn't anywhere near. 'No, they've been married for thirty years apparently, although she is his second wife.'

'Interesting. An American billionaire who doesn't trade up to a younger model every decade.'

'Or down. I'd say getting a younger wife was trading down, wouldn't you?' I teased him.

'Did you mention Russia to her?'

I hesitated. I sometimes thought that Theo didn't like the Russian side of me, that he wanted to keep me in the here and now, in London's crowded, jostling streets, as if he were jealous of the birch woods of my childhood. But on the rare occasions that I remembered that the dark forests had starving wolves in them in winter, howling with hunger, Theo kept them away. He held me tight, in our big bed in South London, far away from the glittering domes of Moscow and the dank underground tunnels beneath the streets, where desperate people grasped at you and tried to seize your bag.

I was beginning to feel slightly dizzy from two glasses of wine on an empty stomach. I had had to miss lunch in order to get across town in time for a conference with a client in prison. Once I got there, there hadn't been a guard available to escort the prisoner, so I had waited over an hour before going back to chambers. That meant a whole day wasted, with no fee. I spotted a waitress with a tray of canapés and I edged towards her, but just before she got to me, someone else grabbed the last morsel. She turned away, struggling to make headway, manoeuvring her tray through a thicket of elbows, backs and shoulders.

'I'll have a quick look round before we go,' said Theo. 'See if anyone's here.' I watched him work his way through the crowd, his dark suit easy to spot. He looked like a raven amid the bright plumage of the flock of journalists. There was no dress down for Theo, not while he had to convince the world that he was successful.

It was an investment. As he so often said, 'You have to speculate to accumulate.' That was why our credit cards were up to their limits. He believed a QC had to be seen to be successful, in hand-tailored suits and a cashmere coat. Theo always drove cars with impressive brand names and new licence plates – but he leased them and paid a large monthly fee. His gleaming Audi was better value, he argued, than my clapped-out third-hand VW Golf, which cost a fortune in needing to have parts replaced all the time. Sometimes I agreed with him, especially when I found myself standing at the roadside, phoning the AA, late for court, seeing the morning's fee disappear.

At first, I had no doubt that Theo, with his fifteen years' extra experience, knew better than I did. But one day I accidentally opened a letter from the Inland Revenue. It was a final demand for an unpaid tax bill. I questioned him. We had a terrible row, and our marriage was bruised for weeks afterwards. And I asked his advice about the law less and less after that. Money was still a dangerous topic between us.

So I didn't object when he phoned for a taxi, even though we could quite easily have got home by underground. 'I've talked to everyone I needed to see.' He shot his cuffs. 'And you look tired. Shall we go?'

That was the difference between me and Theo. He could take a party like this for granted. For him, fitting in was effortless, but I was always the girl who never quite belonged.

When we got back to our tiny, flat-fronted house in Clapham, I checked that the front door was double-locked with the chain across and did a quick patrol of the rest of the ground floor. The eyes of an urban fox glinted in the back garden, but he sloped away into the shadows, slipping over the garden wall with a flash of his tail.

Wiping the make-up off my face with cream, I wondered how old Lydia was. And why did she seem familiar? Perhaps it was just that she was photographed with the celebrated and newsworthy in the newspapers.

'You're very quiet. What's up?' asked Theo thirty minutes later, as we settled in bed.

'Long day, that's all.'

'Sure? I thought you seemed rattled when I first saw you at the party. Did something happen?'

I shook my head. 'Nothing.' Nothing I could explain anyway. I'd met a woman who seemed somehow familiar. She'd spoken to me in Russian.

He kissed me gently on the lips and I reached towards him, folding into the warmth and strength of his arms.

'Not too tired, though?' he whispered.

'Never,' I whispered back, as we melted into the familiar movements. Later, I lay in his arms, listening to him breathe. I stared into the darkness. Something wasn't right, but I couldn't put it into words.

CHAPTER 4

Over the next few weeks, I had a succession of poorly-paid bail applications and sentencing hearings that barely covered my travel. Then a three-day drugs trial collapsed because no interpreter had been provided, leaving me with a week almost completely without paid work. I took my own sandwiches to work, but I didn't dare fork out for the expensive coffees in the cafés outside the courtrooms and the government had closed the barristers' messes. Fortunately, Chris needed a night lawyer for a Saturday night at the last minute, so at least that helped.

So far, not many changes had been made at the paper, and everyone's jobs seemed, for the moment, intact. There had been a flurry of indignation when Lydia was appointed editor-at-large and given a small private office on the top floor, next to Human Resources. But the only journalists who saw her were those on the social and gossip pages and the paper seemed to be carrying on as usual. I was only slightly interested, being more concerned about my clients, and about Theo, who had not been given a major case for six weeks.

The next Monday, I sat in the small cubicle in Isleworth Crown Court waiting for my video link to Wormwood Scrubs prison. Video links had been introduced to save prisoners being driven across the country for short hearings where they would only be in court for a few minutes. But there was often a muddle either at the prison or in the court and prisoners did not get to where they needed to be. Or there was a technical problem with the connection.

My new client, Devon Pinnock, had been charged with grievous bodily harm. I had spent the best part of Sunday trying to untangle his role in the complicated choreography of a street fight involving two rival gangs that had ended in three stabbings. Trying to match the grainy CCTV footage to the witness accounts had been like untangling wet spaghetti. We were listed that morning for a preliminary hearing and this was the first opportunity I had had to talk to the defendant. He hadn't given any proper instructions yet, and I needed to establish if we had any defence before we went into court.

In front of me, a live image flickered of an empty chair somewhere in the Scrubs. I could hear the heavy tread of footsteps and a door slamming, but there was no sign of my client nor of a prison guard.

'Scrubs? Scrubs?' The small, empty room gave my voice a tinny echo. I looked at my watch. I had a fifteen minute slot here, from ten to ten fifteen. Then we were straight on in Court 3, where the case was listed.

'Scrubs?' Another five minutes passed.

'Hello?' At last. A prison guard in a crumpled uniform appeared on the screen.

'Good morning, I'm counsel for Devon Pinnock. We have a con booked. Do you know where he is?'

The guard leafed through a sheaf of papers. 'Yeah, he's in A wing. He should have made his way down here by now.'

'Well, can someone fetch him? We're on in ten minutes.'

'No way, Miss. I don't have the manpower. They're supposed to fetch themselves down. I guess he didn't feel like coming.'

I cut the connection and swore under my breath. The tannoy was summoning me to Court 3 already. I left the cubicle, walked down the corridor, and pushed through the swing doors to take my place in counsel's row. In each court there were huge television screens where the video links were displayed. On the screens, I could see the same guard and the same lack of Devon Pinnock. The clerk called on the case, and the judge raised an eyebrow at me.

'Your Honour, I apologise on behalf of Mr Pinnock. It seems that there was no one available in Wormwood Scrubs this morning to escort him to the video link. I have been unable therefore to have any sort of conference with him.'

The judge addressed the prison officer on the screen. 'Is that right?'

At that moment the screens flickered and died, the connection lost. The judge sighed. Presumably this sort of thing happened to him even more often than it happened to me.

'Well, Miss Angel, it seems we won't be able to hear you this morning.' My heart sank. 'I have a jury waiting and I already have another case to interpose at one o'clock. I will hear you at 2 p.m. Hopefully the technical problems will be resolved by then.'

I got to my feet. 'Your Honour, that will create a difficulty for me, I have a conference in chambers at 2.30 this afternoon. Might I request that we put this case over until tomorrow?'

'No, Miss Angel, I am not prepared to do that. We have, as you know, a huge backlog of cases at this court. If you are not available this afternoon I am sure you can arrange for someone else to cover for you. Right, I am going to rise now.' He leaned over to speak to his clerk. 'Jury in fifteen minutes please.' The clerk nodded and picked up the telephone in front of her.

We all rose and bowed and I struggled to keep my face emotionless. I doubted that the clerks had anyone available for 2 p.m. If this case went out of chambers, I would probably never get it back. I would not get paid for today if I left now, nor for all the preparation I had done over the weekend, but there was no way I could cancel my con – which was how we referred to conferences – this afternoon. Ferocious Frankie, the instructing solicitor, would never forgive me.

Frankie McKenna ran her own small but busy firm in Kent. She was a property lawyer whose practice also picked up a surprising amount of crime and she was well known across the Bar for her filthy temper and capriciousness. I didn't know the details of the case she had sent over except that it concerned a young woman charged with child neglect. The clerks had struggled to get her to instruct me in the first place but no one else had been available so she had very grudgingly given me the brief. Unusually, she had decided to attend the con herself, just to make the whole situation even worse.

I went to the robing room, took out my phone and rang chambers.

'What the fuck, Miss! How did that happen?' It was Lee.

'The video link went down,' I said. 'We knew it was a risk, taking this case and the con.' There was no point in reminding him that he had badgered me into it.

'All right, come back then. Your papers have just arrived. I'll see who I can get to cover. Oh, and Frankie has put the con forward to 2 p.m., so you better get here sharpish. She doesn't like to be kept waiting.'

Damn, damn, damn. That shaved another crucial half hour off my preparation time. I didn't have time to eat, and Frankie arrived at 1.45, intent on living up to her reputation. She was a rhinoceros of a woman, in her mid-fifties, crammed into a straining but expensive jacket and bulging black trousers. She pushed into my room ahead of our client, and dumped a large bag with designer logos all over it on the floor.

All of the conference rooms were occupied so we had to have our meeting up in my own room. It was the room I shared with Gus Gladwyn and it was usually a sanctuary from the world. As Frankie looked round for somewhere to sit, I caught her disdainful expression as she took in the shabby sofa, the chipped desk piled high with files. It was a mahogany partner's desk, and had been at Medlar Court for most of the previous century. Under Frankie's designer shoes, the worn rug was embellished with tea stains. While the common parts of chambers looked smart, Gus and I had furnished this room ourselves from Gus's family's discarded furniture and second-hand buys funded by our legal aid income. It showed. With a grunt and a toss of her obviously dyed-red hair, she sank down into Gus's chair, which was the only comfortable one. 'Weren't there any meeting rooms available?'

The client hovered, indecisive and meek, as if uncertain whether to sit, stand or run away. Frankie looked at me through narrowed eyes. 'Get me a cuppa, would you, darling? I'm completely parched after that journey.'

I thought about how to play this. I knew she would never like me, but she needed to respect me. I ignored the request and stepped out from behind my desk to greet my new client.

'Hello, I am Sophie Angel. I'm your barrister. You must be Liya Abebe – is it OK if I call you Liya? Please make yourself comfortable.' I indicated the only other spare chair in the room, and she gave a tiny nod, sitting down nervously. After we were all seated, I rang down to the receptionist and asked her to bring up a pot of tea.

Liya, an Ethiopian woman according to the brief, was dressed in a worn T-shirt, jeans and a dark blue hijab. She hunched over a huge but empty shopping bag, which she held on her lap. Her voice was low and hesitant, and at times I had to strain to hear her.

'My parents made me marry Yonas,' she whispered.

'That's her husband,' Frankie interrupted, clearly under the impression that I was unable to read the papers in front of me.

'He's a friend of theirs…' Liya twisted her hands round the bag. 'They said the family…' She looked at me, clearly terrified that I would judge her. 'Honour,' she murmured into her lap. Frankie snorted.

'So you have just one child?' I checked my notes to see if she had any others.

Liya nodded, her head still bowed. 'I… my mother-in-law… she came to live with us when my father-in-law died, and she…' She looked up at me with frightened eyes. I knew that it was sometimes a tradition for the older woman to take over the running of the household and treat the daughter-in-law like a slave. Although Liya was clearly nervous of criticising her, even here, she mapped out months of abuse. 'Then…' her voice broke. 'Then they were going to take Zala back to Addis Ababa during the school holidays.'

'Your daughter?' I checked my notes again. 'And she is now six?'

'They were going to have her circumcised,' boomed Frankie.

'I told our doctor,' said Liya. 'And then…'

'He reported them all to social services and now the police have charged the whole family under the Female Genital Mutilation Act 2003.' Frankie cut across her.

'Has Zala been taken into care?'

Liya shook her head. 'My mother-in-law… she and Yonas… they lock me in the house when they take Zala to school. I'm afraid that…'

Frankie sighed loudly again and looked at her watch. I was determined to help this young woman who was being terrorised by her partner. I spoke over Frankie's interruptions and tried to get her to see that far from conspiring to hurt her child, our client had done all she could to protect her.

We wrapped up the conference at five, and I opened the

door so that Liya could precede Frankie out of the room. Frankie paused on her way out, speaking to me in a low voice. 'Get the Defence Case Statement done tonight. I don't believe in wasting time that won't be paid for, and this is legal aid so there's not much in it for either of us. Now, where is that gorgeous husband of yours?' She looked up and down the corridor as if he might suddenly appear.

While Frankie prowled the building in search of Theo, I gave Liya a list of useful addresses of women's refuges, charities and helplines. I kept it updated and often gave it out to clients who needed more help than I could give. Liya looked terrified, but stuffed the piece of paper in her pocket.

I was packing up my papers, tired and hungry, when Theo put his head around the door. 'There you are. I've just dodged Frankie, thank God! You know we're deciding on the new tenant at six?'

'Sorry, what?' I vaguely remembered having had this conversation before. We hadn't taken on a new tenant for four years. As a chambers, we simply didn't have the work. If anyone new joined, it would be because they had work to bring with them. That meant they would have to bring in contacts with solicitors that we didn't have.

'You know, we discussed it. Now that old Farrell is finally retiring – and not a moment before time, in my view – we can actually take someone on who might bring something in.'

'Yes, I remember that – I just didn't know we were ready to take a decision. I'm due at the paper by seven.'

'I did tell you.' Theo sounded impatient.

Too busy. That was one of the things that had gone wrong in Theo's first marriage. Louisa was a primary school teacher, and was always involved in some bake sale or end-of-term play. She felt overwhelmed by the bright, articulate barristers so didn't go to chambers events. By the end, they had had nothing in common. I had always resolved that I wouldn't allow that to happen to us. Sometimes I heard colleagues complaining about their partners, how they were lazy, careless or didn't listen. I would nod and smile sympathetically, but I hugged my relationship with Theo to me like a secret. He understood me like no one could.

My father, Vassily, always told me that living life was not like walking through a meadow. His sayings and stories wound through my childhood memories. I understood those stories better now that I was older. They had seemed brutal and almost random when I heard them as a child. Like the story of Snegurochka.

It was a Russian fairy story about an old man and woman who wanted children but they weren't able to have any.

The story was that one bitterly cold morning, an old woman went out to feed her chickens. The sun was shining but the air was glittering with snow crystals. Suddenly, by the edge of the woods, she saw a tiny figure created from those crystals. It was a beautiful little girl with blonde hair and big blue eyes.

She was Snegurochka or Snow Child. She was the daughter of Father Frost and her mother was Spring, and when spring came every year, she had to go back to her father.

Snegurochka was very beautiful, but she couldn't feel love, because if she did, its heat would melt her. The old couple warned her to stay away from men, but she fell in love with a shepherd boy. And when she kissed him, she melted away.

I had always thought it was a cruel and pointless story. Now I thought I understood. When you fell in love, you melted into the other person. The old you is gone. I tried to focus on the subject of the new tenant, rummaging through my mind for any memory of a conversation about it. 'So, who do you think we should take?'

'Polly Chan is the obvious one. She's been here as a pupil

for three months – you must know her. She previously worked as a solicitor for Braithwaites and requalified to become a barrister, so she's got some experience. Not to mention some very interesting contacts.' He smiled at me.

I rummaged through my memory. We were all out of chambers most of the day, and it was quite easy for someone to be here for months without meeting everyone. 'No, I don't think I have met her? Whose pupil is she?'

'Simon's.' He smiled. I loved Theo's smile. It was relaxed, as if everything in the world was going to work out just fine. When dealing with difficult clients, he often leaned back and smiled at them. You could almost see the clients' shoulders drop and the tension drain out of them. Theo's smile said that he was in control, and everything would be all right. Even if what he was actually telling them was that they didn't have a case and would have to settle or plead guilty.

Simon was a good, steady barrister and specialised in commercial work. 'You said she had some good legal contacts?' I queried.

'You know,' he said. 'Chinese contacts.'

'Tongs and triads? That could be useful.'

He smiled again. 'Not all Chinese crime is to do with tongs and triads. I think Wei Chan, Polly's uncle who's a solicitor with a big practice in Birmingham, wants me for his corporate work, mainly.'

'So, well paid.'

'Very.'

I jumped as my phone vibrated. It was the head clerk. 'Hello, Lee.'

'Hello, Miss. Somebody wants to see you tomorrow. They said it was urgent. And it's a private brief fee.'

It was rare for me to get a privately funded case and they were usually far better paid. 'OK. I've got a con at five, but I'm

42

just working on papers any time up until then.'

'Thought so. I've booked them at two. A Mrs Brennan and a Mrs Hanbury, with Henry Hanbury and a solicitor from Bravo's.'

Out of context, I didn't recognise Lydia Brennan's name at first. 'Do you have their full names?'

There was a pause as Lee checked. 'Lydia Brennan and Cornelia Hanbury. It's Mrs Brennan who's paying the bill.'

My gut clenched, as if I had been punched. I took a deep breath. 'Did they say what it was about?'

'No, Miss, just that it was urgent. And confidential. Very confidential, Miss, they're very worried about that. They said it three times.'

'All our work is confidential.' A prickle of excitement overrode my initial unease about meeting Lydia Brennan again.

Theo smiled when I put the phone down. 'If you don't want to come to the meeting this evening, shall I vote on your behalf?'

I nodded. I hadn't put any thought into it, and he clearly had.

He kissed me and left. I decided that I could at least do some basic checks on this Polly person, if she was going to have my proxy vote, so I pulled my laptop towards me and called up the name Polly Chan. I found the right one almost immediately. There was a head-and-shoulders shot of dark, gleaming hair and a confident, inviting smile. She was twenty-eight and had been working for Braithwaites for five years after leaving Imperial College, London. I thought Theo was probably right. She was clever, cosmopolitan and attractive. I wondered if she was single. Maybe she would be good for Gus. He hid a fine brain behind a stuttering, gangly exterior, and I was always looking out for someone who would appreciate him.

And I wondered why Lydia Brennan had decided to consult me as a barrister. It could hardly be a coincidence, could it?

CHAPTER 5

The following day, I hoisted my pull-along suitcase up the stairs to our room.

'Hi, Soph.' We had worked in the same room for nearly six years, and Gus addressed me in much the same way as he spoke to his sisters. I inhaled the smell of dust, papers and furniture polish. It was the scent of solid reassurance, even comfort. The sofa's springs had gone but, if I was working late, it was a very comfortable place to take a quick break. Sometimes I curled up on it to work too.

'How was your mother last weekend?' Gus had a difficult and demanding mother, who appeared to be slipping into early dementia. Gus, his father and his two sisters all took turns to field her, and Gus's stories about her mishaps were both funny and heart-rending. As Gus recounted the latest, I cleared a space on my desk for the current file, balancing papers and boxes on top of each other in an order only I understood. I fished around under the desk for my work shoes, peering at them to see if they needed polishing. They didn't but they weren't going to last much longer. I sighed.

'Are you OK?'

'I'm fine,' I murmured.

He looked at me as if he didn't quite believe me. 'You've been a bit distracted for the past few weeks. Are you worried about Theo not getting enough cases?'

I was briefly surprised at Gus's perspicacity. Or were the rumours about Theo's lack of work circulating around the feverishly gossipy Bar in spite of his tailored suits and smart car?

'No.' I was determined to be loyal to Theo. Then I remembered that this was Gus, my friend. 'Well, not really. I'm sure it'll be fine. Theo is brilliant.' I sighed. 'I just thought that the work would have picked up a bit by now, I suppose.'

Gus nodded.

'And the paper has new owners. No one knows what they're going to do with it.' I wondered if Gus would think me silly if I told him that what had really rattled me was a woman I had met for five minutes at a party.

'I met the owner's wife,' I added. 'She spooked me a bit. She's Russian, and seems perfectly nice. Now she seems to be bringing me a case. And I don't know why.'

'She probably asked the legal department at the paper for a recommendation and you were the barrister they knew whose experience was the most relevant for whatever the case is.'

'Yes, I suppose that would make sense. How are things here?'

Gus leaned back in his chair. 'There's a new tenant...'

'Did they decide on Polly Chan?' I slid my feet into the retrieved shoes, and came back up to see what Gus thought. 'Theo told me about her yesterday. Do the clerks like her?'

Gus grinned at me.

'I'll take that as a yes, then shall I? Do you like her?'

Gus rocked back and forth on the chair. It would break if he kept doing that. Eventually he spoke. 'No.' He seemed quite definitive.

I sat down on my chair. 'Gus! You never not like anyone. Why not?'

'Maybe I'm not being fair...' He began looking through papers as if the matter was closed.

'Gus, I can't imagine anyone fairer than you. What is it?'

But Gus just grinned at me again, and shrugged.

I didn't have time to question him and besides, I knew that if Gus didn't want to tell me something, he wouldn't. He was nervy – even eccentric – but he was surprisingly stubborn. It was what made him a good barrister. He was determined on behalf of his clients. A friend once told me that Gus lost his mild diffidence in court. You didn't often get to see fellow members of chambers in action, so I hadn't seen him 'on his feet', as we called it.

One of the clerks rang to say that the papers for my conference with Lydia Brennan and Cornelia Hanbury had been printed out and were in my pigeonhole. I went to the badly-lit tenants' room, where we collected our papers and post from a wall of pigeonholes, then walked slowly through the Temple towards the Library. As I wandered past the pale stone buildings, my footsteps slowed, feeling the weight of my bag, heavy with documents. Although many of my briefs were delivered electronically, I always liked to have a paper copy, in case my battery went flat in court or if the Wi-Fi went down in the building. So I always asked Holly, one of the juniors in the clerks' room, to print out my papers. She tied them up with the scarlet barristers' tape that is traditionally called 'a pink ribbon' – the colour of blood, I always thought.

In summer, there were roses blooming here. Fountains played in the small squares set between the barristers' chambers, but today no roses were blooming, and no fountains were playing. The Temple was grey and without shadows. I hurried up to the library to get out of the cold, pleased to see that my favourite spot was vacant. The desk overlooked the Temple Gardens, across smooth lawns and down to the Thames. The library was decorated in shades of blue and gold and lined from floor to ceiling with leather-bound copies of law reports. It was lunchtime and the room was almost empty. I set down my iPad and slid the pink ribbon off my bundle of papers.

I still felt a small jolt of excitement whenever I opened a new brief, even after so many years. Sometimes I prosecuted and sometimes I defended, and doing both had alerted me to the tricks of the other. I had, I hoped, sent bad men to prison and saved good ones from an immeasurably terrible experience.

But the thought of sending an innocent person to an over-filled, under-staffed jail horrified me. Many of the older prisons had integral lavatories in the cells. They weren't screened off and were often missing lids. The beds, crammed into tiny rooms, were just inches away from those lavatories. I had been told that some cells were infested with cockroaches and rats. The windows were often cracked and let in rain and cold in the winter but were stiflingly hot in summer. Savage staff cuts could mean that men were often left in their cells for twenty-two or even twenty-three hours a day. They ate and slept next to the open lavatory.

I looked down at the Henry Hanbury papers. I opened the folder up, smoothing the paper down under my hand, flattening it against the desk. Everyone deserves to be listened to, whether they're victims or accused.

A collection of photographs held together by treasury tags slipped out of the bundle. Gathering them up, I looked at each one carefully. The first was a photo of a woman's blouse, torn across the front with one button dangling. There was another of a ripped pair of tights. This must have taken some force. I frowned.

I turned the photos face down and flicked back to the front of the bundle to read the case summary. The complainant, Eva Scott, a freelance public relations specialist, had gone to her local pub in Dalston. She was with a group of friends and had been there since about 7 p.m. She thought she might have consumed four or five glasses of wine, as well as two margaritas.

She had been smoking outside the back door of the pub, when a young man had tripped, falling against her and spilling her drink. He had bought her another, but they only exchanged a few words and he went back to the bar. Eva had returned to her friends, but also came across some work colleagues in the pub, and spent the rest of the evening moving between the two groups. She had very little memory of the latter part of the evening, but remembered talking to the barman at about 10.30 p.m., and then someone holding her elbow and helping her to leave the pub. She thought it was the young man who had bought her a drink. That was her last clear memory. The rest of the evening was a complete blank. She had awoken in her own bed at around 5 a.m. Her skirt was crumpled up at the end of her bed, her pants hung around one ankle and her tights were ripped and lying on the floor. She had felt sore all over and had vomited several times. She had spent that day in bed, so tired and achy that she could barely move.

She had answered the phone at around 6 p.m. It was Melanie, one of the friends who had been with her in the pub. Melanie had been annoyed that Eva had left the pub without saying goodbye, but said she had assumed that she had left with her work colleagues. Eva had told Melanie that she could hardly remember anything, that she felt sore and sick with a pounding headache, with flashes of memory that quite clearly indicated she had been raped. Her friend had suggested she might have been 'roofied', a slang word meaning to have your drink spiked without your knowledge. Eva had called the police, who had visited her flat for a preliminary interview. They had advised her to go to a Sexual Assault Referral Centre or to a doctor, but Eva refused.

The following morning, Eva didn't feel well enough to go to work, but went to a Sexual Assault Referral Centre, where she told them what happened. She consented to an internal examination but halfway through told them she couldn't cope and asked them to stop. The tests hadn't revealed any DNA, but there were traces of Rohypnol in her urine, and also a trace of condom residue. At this stage, Eva had said she didn't want to pursue the matter any further.

Two weeks later, after visiting a psychotherapist for insomnia and anxiety, she went to the police to make a full statement.

I put my pen down and rubbed my eyes. Outside, the weak winter sun glinted on the windows, and I checked my watch. I had just half an hour to go through my client's side of the case before Lydia Brennan and the Hanburys arrived. I sympathised with Eva. Although things were better than they were, it took huge courage to stand up in a courtroom full of strangers to give humiliating and embarrassing details about your own body. I wondered what my client's story would be.

I turned the page to find out. He was Henry Mark Hanbury studying for a PhD in medical biosciences at London University, and was involved in developing a new strain of resistant antibiotics. Or he had been until this had happened. The university had had no choice other than to suspend him until after his trial. I sometimes thought the principle of 'innocent until proven guilty' did not seem to apply except in the courtroom itself and the defence barristers' offices. The 'cab rank' rule meant that we were obliged to take cases we were offered if they were appropriate to our experience. If barristers refused to represent people who had been accused of certain categories of crime, they were in effect subverting the role of the jury. So I had sat in cramped conference rooms with religious maniacs, paranoid schizophrenics, bigots, misogynists and even psychopaths. Often they had been charged with such abhorrent crimes that just reading the case made my stomach churn.

But sometimes the people in front of me were completely innocent of the crimes they had been charged with. Which category did Henry Hanbury fall into? I began to skim it, looking for the essentials I needed to know before the meeting. Part of the fascination of the criminal law for me was that I was parachuted into another life, another crisis. Those lives generally had a tragic similarity – the pinched existence lived out in a tiny flat next to a flyover, the fruitless visits to the job centre, the greasy kebabs eaten alone on a park bench, the drug deals, the fractured relationships.

But not this one. This one was different.

CHAPTER 6

Medlar Court had a series of modernised pale-grey conference rooms in the basement, with frosted glass doors and expensive modern paintings on the walls. Unlike the rest of the building, they were air conditioned, so they were always freezing. There was also Room 4, a smaller, rather stuffy room on the ground floor, which looked as if it hadn't changed in a hundred years.

'Which conference room am I in?' I asked Lee, putting my head into the crammed, untidy clerks' room. Another clerk, Trevor, was swearing at someone while eating a takeaway. The clerks could rarely leave the phones, and they wore earpieces all day.

For a moment, I thought Lee hadn't heard. He was scrolling through the court lists for the following day. 'You're in four,' he said, without looking at me. 'It's not as if it's a ten million pound fraud trial, Miss, is it?' He looked up and bared his teeth to indicate that he was making a joke.

Although some of the other barristers felt demoted when they were allocated the old-fashioned and cramped Room 4, I liked its sense of history. There was a giant Victorian portrait of the founder of chambers, Ebenezer Awmsham, in 1867. It was comfortably ramshackle. Instead of gleaming surfaces, there was an old electric fire plugged in in front of a pretty fireplace that had been there since long before Ebenezer's time.

Lydia Brennan walked in, followed by another woman whom I assumed was Cornelia Hanbury, and the solicitor. Lydia's expensive perfume filled the room. I thought I recognised it as Shalimar. The second woman followed more hesitantly.

Lydia introduced her as Cornelia Hanbury. She wore a Chanel-style suit of the type that used to be sold in little boutiques all over the Home Counties. It hung loosely on her, as if she had recently lost weight. The sinews of her neck strained above her collar. 'Cornelia's son, Henry, is one of my own son's greatest friends. We've known him since they were at Oxford together, and I know he would never do anything so terrible. So when Cornelia phoned me...' She trailed off, and I wondered, not for the first time, why she was paying the legal bills.

'It's so kind of you to see us at such short notice,' Cornelia said.

'It's a pleasure.' I motioned for both women to sit, but Cornelia moved across to the window, pressing the flat of her hand against the pane, almost as if she were restrained against her will. 'Do you know if my son's arrived?'

'The clerks will send him in when he gets here.'

'What a charming courtyard.' Cornelia sounded as if she might break down in tears.

'Well...' I got up to join her beside the window, hoping to distract her. 'It's called Medlar Court because it really was where they grew medlars in Elizabethan times,' I explained. 'Nearby, in Middle Temple, Shakespeare's troupe gave the first performance of *Twelfth Night* in 1602. Shakespeare himself was in the cast and Queen Elizabeth was rumoured to be in the audience.'

We looked out into the autumn mist dampening the flagstones of Medlar Court and I saw it through Cornelia Hanbury's eyes: an institution with quaint customs and intelligent people, which fought for justice, to make things better. Then I turned away from the window and saw Lydia's face, accentuated by her high Russian cheekbones, so like my own. Neither of us really fitted in to this traditionally English environment. Perhaps I would never belong anywhere.

Two men strode into the courtyard. One was Philip Meadowes. The other man loped alongside him with an ungainly stride. He turned his head to look up at the window, and Cornelia waved frantically.

'My son,' she breathed. 'Oh, dear, this is too bad. He absolutely promised me he wouldn't be late. I don't know how someone can be so clever, but also so...' she sighed as words failed her.

He smiled up at her and waved, as if he were on a jolly outing. I wondered if perhaps there might be an issue with Asperger's or autism. It was a possibility – the brilliant scientist who couldn't understand people. I turned back to her with a smile.

'Ah,' said Cornelia, in a soft sigh. 'Do you have children, Miss Angel?'

I shook my head. 'No, I don't,' and thought again that Theo and I should have this conversation soon. We had been together for four years, but after his experiences with Louisa and the failed IVF I was reluctant to open old wounds. There was still time. I wasn't quite thirty-five and although Theo was older at forty-eight, he was fit and seemed physically much younger.

'Seeing your child accused of something he hasn't done and not being able to help him is the worst pain you can imagine,' said Cornelia.

I saw a lot of pain in courtrooms. Desperate people being damaged even further by the system.

'Is there any chance that we'll be able to keep this all secret?' she asked. 'I'm so afraid for his reputation in the future, that this will always hang over him.'

'I promise you that everything that happens in these buildings remains completely confidential,' I said. 'You can trust our clerks not to say who has booked an appointment.'

Cornelia shook her head sadly. 'I'm sure they're totally professional. But what about these Facebook thingies and...' She waved a hand across the room to indicate a new world she didn't understand.

Lydia looked at me and I saw that stare again. The one that said to me, 'If you do anything wrong, someone will find out about it. You will be betrayed.'

I had seen that stare before, and the fear that surrounded it, but I couldn't remember where or why. When I blinked, the mist cleared and she was smiling pleasantly. I must have imagined it.

CHAPTER 7

The receptionist tapped on the door. 'I've got Mr Henry Hanbury and Philip Meadowes of Bravo's here for you, Miss. Would you like some tea?'

'I'd simply adore some,' said Lydia Brennan. 'And Cornelia, my dear, you must keep your strength up. Tea for us all would be wonderful.' Her accent was almost faultless, cut-glass English. But not quite.

The receptionist stood back to allow the two men to enter the room. I looked briefly into Henry's direct blue eyes before he dropped his gaze to his shoes. Or possibly my shoes. One of his shoelaces was trailing undone. There was something gangly and uncoordinated about him.

'Henry, darling,' said Cornelia. She stood on tiptoe to kiss his cheek.

Henry submitted to the kiss, and we all sat down, Henry wrapping his long limbs around a chair and knocking the chair next to him over. Philip picked it up, as Henry was looking embarrassed and clueless.

'Uh, sorry.' He took a pen out of his breast pocket, and dropped that too, his head disappearing under the table while he rootled around to find it.

The receptionist tottered off on stacked heels, returning ten minutes later with six mismatched mugs, a white milk jug and a plate of plain biscuits on a tray. I wondered if Cornelia and Lydia expected porcelain cups and saucers.

'I can't believe this has got so far,' said Cornelia, her eyes fixed on Henry. 'I promise you, Miss Angel…'

'Sophie, call me Sophie,' I said.

Henry Hanbury was a clever, somewhat geeky young man, who had come from an apparently secure and comfortable background. He lived in the suburbs, had gone to a well-regarded local school and then on to study biomedical sciences at Oxford. His father, now dead, had been a civil servant. Henry was bailed to a suburban-sounding address; the family home near Guildford. There was nothing I could see to suggest that Henry Hanbury had ever had any other contact with the law, not even any speeding tickets or cautions. He ran marathons to raise money for medical research and he had been selected to be on a team researching ground-breaking treatment for a new strain of antibiotics.

By the time a defendant found himself facing a serious charge in the Crown Court, he would usually have accumulated a smattering of more minor offences involving theft, burglary, street violence or cruelty to animals. But Henry had no such history, although there could always be exceptions.

Lydia urged Cornelia to take a biscuit. Cornelia looked at the plate of biscuits with faint astonishment and shook her head. I smiled and sat down, opening an A4 notebook. 'Shall we start at the beginning?'

Henry cleared his throat. 'I've been charged with rape.'

'He didn't do it,' said Cornelia. 'He…'

Henry looked from me to his mother, and back again.

'I was at the pub that night,' he said. 'I drank less than one pint and left early because I was tired. I'd been working all day and had gone to the pub just to get out.'

I studied the CCTV photograph from the bar. It was blurry and taken at an angle and showed a tall man, with his back half-turned, with a shock of dark, wavy hair, part of which fell over his face. I flicked back to the original description: 'tall with short, darkish hair'. Personally, I wouldn't have described Henry's hair as short. It seemed relatively long to me, touching his collar at the back, but people were notoriously bad at descriptions. Short hair meant different things to different people. You couldn't see his face properly, but you could see that he wore heavy-rimmed glasses.

'There's nothing in this woman's accusations. Not a scrap of truth,' said Cornelia, her voice rising.

Lydia patted Cornelia on the arm. 'Of course, there isn't. Sophie here will sort it all out. You don't have to worry.'

Clients often started in the middle, with everything spilling out of them in a jumbled mess of fear and indignation. The innocent ones were the most incoherent; the guilty ones more likely to have a script. Theo cautioned me to be methodical. 'Let them tell their story. Try not to interrupt. You may throw them off and miss an important detail.'

'Can we start with some background?' I said. 'I need to be clear about what you do, and what you were doing at the time of the allegation.'

'I'm doing research into a particularly interesting line of treatment for a new antibiotic.' He sat forward. 'You see, nobody's doing any research into antibiotics now because, although we desperately need completely new treatments, not just variations on the ones already in use, there's great pressure on doctors not to prescribe them unless they're really necessary. Which, of course, is right, because otherwise you'd get resistance building up again. But it means that there aren't the profits from antibiotics that you get, say, from an anti-arthritis drug that someone might be prescribed for years, and...'

'Darling.' Cornelia placed a hand on his arm. 'Sophie doesn't need to know about antibiotics; she needs to know about what you were doing that evening.'

He paused, as if surprised to be reminded why he was here. 'That evening?'

'The one where that girl...'

'Oh, *that* evening. Look, it's going to be fine. I only met her for a few moments. I bumped into her on the way into the bar and spilled her drink so I bought her another, and I'm sure she knows that. It's all just a misunderstanding because the police are being too...' He trailed off. 'But I've had to stop my research. The whole project's on hold, and the sponsoring charity is considering withdrawing funding if it isn't sorted out soon.'

'We need to go back to the beginning of the evening,' I said.

'Henry's been suspended,' said Cornelia. 'They've just taken this... this *girl's* word for it.' She twisted her hands.

'Mum.'

Lydia and I exchanged glances.

'You see, it isn't just Henry who will suffer if all this gets out.' She leaned forward urgently. 'I mean who might die in five years' time because they don't have a critical antibiotic? We all know a terrible epidemic must be on the way.'

'We just need to stick to the facts,' I said. 'Try not to think about the future.'

'Do you think we've got a chance, though?' asked Cornelia. 'Is there any likelihood that *anyone* will believe her? Even her friend, Melanie, says she was drunk that night. Will that help?'

'If she was drunk when she was claiming rape, that might make it worse. She wouldn't have been able to give consent.'

'There was nothing for her to give consent to,' said Cornelia. 'It's all a fantasy.'

Cornelia was unravelling fast and I realised that we were never going to make any headway with her in the room, so I suggested that Lydia take her outside for some fresh air. Henry might be able to speak if his mother was being safely marched round Medlar Court.

Lydia rose. 'Cornelia, dear, I think that's a wonderful idea of Sophie's. We can walk round that absolutely charming courtyard, and Henry can explain everything to lovely Sophie.'

Cornelia stopped at the door. 'Henry is a good young man, Sophie. I know every mother thinks that, but I *know* it.'

I smiled at her as the door shut behind them, and opened my laptop, preparing to type. 'Let's start with when you first met Eva Scott.'

He thought he had arrived around 9 p.m., maybe a few minutes earlier. He had taken some antihistamines because he suffered from hayfever, and after drinking barely half the beer, had felt overwhelmingly tired and left. As a result, he had gone to bed shortly after 10 p.m. and slept through to 8 a.m. the next morning. There was no activity on his computer or on his phone, and he had spoken to no one. He lived on his own in a small studio flat rented from a friend of the family. The walk from the pub to his flat was mainly through back streets and there was no CCTV to confirm his story. There was one camera he should have passed, and the film had been asked for, but not received.

There was, however, one CCTV camera in the pub, focused on the till. Henry had bought two drinks, not one, at around 9 p.m. The police had shown Eva the CCTV from the pub, and she had identified Henry as the man who had bought her a drink when he'd spilled hers. When they told her his name – they had identified him from the credit card payment – she thought it sounded familiar.

I sipped some tea. It was the colour of a muddy puddle and thick with tannin. With Cornelia gone I was able to get a reasonable timeline of the evening. There was one part of Henry's story that really concerned me, which was the spilled drink, and the fact he had originally told the police that he had only bought one drink. I asked him to explain it in detail.

He hesitated. 'Look, um, I didn't say I only *bought* one drink, I said I'd only *drunk* one pint. I didn't think the other drink mattered. They were asking me lots of questions about what I did after the pub, and all that, but they didn't say anything about a girl, or rape or anything. I didn't even remember the spilled drink until they showed me that photograph.' He pointed to the picture of Eva on the desk.

When I first started at the Bar, Theo had told me to stay very calm and still when hearing the client's story for the first time. 'Focus on your client completely. Look at their eyes while they're speaking. Make them feel listened to. Keep your questions open-ended.'

So I looked at the nervy boy sitting beside Philip. 'Tell me more about the spilled drink.' The police sometimes liked to question in a way that would get specific answers. I believed in finding out what had happened first.

'I, er, came in the back way of the pub, through the smoking area and she was on her own, smoking.'

'Was she sitting at a table?'

He shook his head. 'No, she was just at the entrance to the bar, smoking and holding a glass, and I tripped on the step and jogged her elbow.' He paused. 'She was nice about it, didn't make a fuss, and I asked her what she was drinking and she said it was a margarita – that pub is famous for its cocktails, you see. So I said I'd get her another. Then I bought my pint and a margarita and I couldn't initially find her because she'd gone back inside, but I found her with a group of friends.'

'Did you speak to any of them?'

He shook his head. 'I don't think so. I just handed her the drink, and went to sit on my own.'

'What did you say when you handed her the drink?'

'She just said thanks. And smiled at me.' He nodded his head vaguely. 'Nice girl.'

'Can you remember anything about the group she was with? Were they men? Women?'

He screwed up his eyes in thought. 'It was very crowded. Not easy to see who was with who. No, I don't think I noticed.'

'What happened then?'

'I went over to the bar where there was a spare stool and drank on my own. I just wanted to get out for a bit, that's all. Then the noise got to me, and I felt kind of tired, so I left.'

'Did you pay by cash or card?'

'I used a card.'

'So your card will show that you only bought two drinks.' It was a slight help, although the prosecution would be able to argue that he could have bought other drinks and paid for them in cash. I made a note to find out whether all payments were at the till or whether someone could buy and pay for drinks without appearing on the pub CCTV.

I noted it down. 'So, our case is that you did not have sex with her at all? And that the CCTV showing you as a tall man matching the description of the rapist is a case of mistaken identity? Is that right?'

He took his glasses off and began to clean them with the edge of his shirt, as he looked directly at me. His eyes were the most astonishing blue and he was, in fact, really quite good-looking. But his social awkwardness would not play well with the jury, and a skilled prosecutor would make the most of that.

'Um, er, yes,' he said.

Like any good solicitor, Phillip had said little so far, letting the barrister lead the meeting, but he raised his pen. 'If she had been drugged, then she's unlikely to remember anything about the person who took her home. The fact that Henry bought her a drink at 9 p.m. and left just after 9.30 p.m. when she seemed fine, is somewhat helpful to our case. The effects start within twenty to thirty minutes, and peak within two hours.'

But we had no proof that Henry had indeed left an hour before the drug took effect. I looked at the portrait of Ebenezer Awmsham. Ebenezer looked back. 'Be thorough. Be clear,' he seemed to say. 'This case may not look very strong, but there may be something you haven't thought of. Henry may be telling the truth. But he may not.'

When we received evidence from the prosecution, their main case came in the form of the primary disclosure, where all the evidence and witnesses that the Crown intended to rely on were revealed to us, the defence. But they were also obliged to pass on evidence that might harm the prosecution. This was often buried in a mountain of otherwise irrelevant paperwork, known as the Unused Material. Sometimes evidence isn't passed on at all. I always checked the Unused Material very carefully. I looked down at my notes again.

'Can you get them to allow me back to work?' said Henry. 'The research I do is at an important stage. It's not just something they can put someone else on, so it's on hold while I'm under investigation. I can't do anything, and I was meant to be going to an international conference in Singapore.'

I continued to ask him questions for an hour and a half. Eventually, I shook Henry's hand, and wished him goodbye. 'There's a lot here we can work with,' I assured him but he didn't seem worried, and I had the sense that I had lost his attention about halfway through. He shook my hand and smiled, but I could see his mind was already on other things.

Cornelia and Lydia were waiting in reception. Cornelia jumped up. 'Is it going to be all right? They always say that if you've done nothing wrong, you've got nothing to fear, don't they?'

I refrained from saying that 'they' might say that. But 'they' weren't always right.

Philip shook my hand, too. 'Look forward to speaking to you. We'll send all the paperwork on to your clerk.'

They left the building, stepping back to let a young woman in. She glittered at them, swinging her dark, shiny hair in a thick chunk across her face, then back again.

'Philip! How lovely to see you. What a treat.' She kissed the solicitor on the cheek and fluttered her fingers at Henry Hanbury, dipping her eyes briefly in acknowledgement of a man. He looked faintly alarmed and stumbled on the top step.

'Polly!' said Philip. 'What are you doing here?'

She smiled. 'I've just been taken on as a tenant. So exciting. So I hope we'll see lots more of each other now.'

Philip muttered a reply and hurried after Henry, who was drifting in the wrong direction across Medlar Court. I saw him take Henry's elbow and redirect him back towards his mother and the car park.

'Hello, I'm Sophie Angel,' I said, when the front door had closed behind them. 'Welcome to Medlar Court.'

'Oh, I've been here for ages,' said Polly. 'You must be Theo Frazer's wife. He's been so helpful. It must be so useful being married to someone like him.'

It seemed a slightly odd thing to say, but perhaps Polly was more nervous than she looked. 'Maybe we could have lunch in the Temple one day when we're neither of us in court,' I suggested, wanting to be friendly towards someone new to chambers.

'That would be great,' said Polly. 'And let's get Theo along too. What was Philip Meadowes doing here?'

'Oh, Bravo's just wanted advice about something.' I had the sense that this Polly Chan didn't acknowledge boundaries.

'Oh, well, they should ask Theo if they want advice.' Polly began to climb the winding stairs. 'My uncle is so pleased he's working with us.'

She smiled down at me from the turn in the stairs. 'Still, having you is almost like engaging Theo, isn't it?'

'Except better,' I said with a smile. Polly looked taken aback. Her shoes – shiny patent leather with spiky high heels, I noted – disappeared up towards the clerks' office. The cream paint covering the old panelling and skirting boards seemed lumpier and bumpier than it had that morning against the high gloss of her shoes. I heard an exclamation of frustration as Polly passed the door.

'Oh, fuck,' shouted Lee. 'Effing Mr Stanley hasn't got his speech in in Woolwich. We need somebody to cover his sentencing at Reading tomorrow.'

'Hello.' Polly's clear tones floated down the stairs. 'I'm the new tenant. I'm happy to volunteer for anything.' The clerks would love her.

I went back to my room to read over what Henry had said. The room was a mess: stacks of paper were almost falling off the desk, ceiling-to-floor bookcases were crammed with leather-bound copies of law reports and lever arch files. But a tidy-up would have to wait. Henry Hanbury was a man whose life had been ripped apart. Even if he hadn't noticed what danger he was in, his mother understood it all too well. As so often in the case in a rape allegation, there were no direct eyewitnesses, no forensic evidence and barely any CCTV. It was just his word against hers.

I sighed. Did Eva Scott have any reason to lie? Or was she being led down a particular road? I knew that once the police had a suspect, they often focused everything on that person and 'clearing up the case', rather than looking for alternative explanations. They simply didn't have the staffing levels to do otherwise.

Once the juggernaut of the legal process starts advancing, it acquires its own momentum and becomes almost impossible to stop. It is especially difficult for a victim to admit that they might be mistaken. And although, when they got to court, they were better protected than they had been, a rape trial was still a deeply wretched experience.

CHAPTER 8

I rushed back from chambers via the supermarket. Theo was back late, so I had invited Katie over for supper. I looked at my watch. I had an hour before she was due to turn up. I decided to concentrate on Henry's testimony.

I put the DVD of Eva Scott's interview into my laptop and a slightly fuzzy picture of the interview room came up on the TV screen, with a digital clock counting down the seconds, minutes and hours in the upper left quadrant. In the upper right quadrant you could see the interview room from above.

I picked up the transcript to follow it along with the interview. It ran to nearly thirty pages. I fast forwarded through the familiar introductions as the interviewing officer identified himself, the police station, the date, explaining that they were being both recorded and watched, and telling Eva where the cameras were. 'Could you now identify yourself, and tell me how old you are?' Her face came on the screen and I paused the interview to look at her face. She had an upturned nose and mid-brown hair, pulled back in a ponytail. There were dark circles under her eyes and she looked pale.

'My name is Eva Scott and I was born on 28th January 1993 in Cardiff. I'm twenty-two years old. I want to tell you about the night when Henry Hanbury...' She began to sob.

'Take your time.'

She blew her nose, and the interviewer steered the conversation back to the night in question. 'When he spilled my drink, I thought he seemed nice enough. He was perfectly polite to me – not like some men who treat women as if they were… well, you know…'

'Tell us about the spilled drink?' The interviewing officer's voice was sympathetic.

'I was in the pub, just standing outside the door for a quick smoke. None of my friends smoke, so I was on my own. He bumped into me and I spilled a bit of my drink, so he offered to buy me another.' Eva crossed and uncrossed her legs and took a sip of tea. 'In fact, Melanie thinks he probably targeted me and spilled my drink deliberately…'

From what I had seen of Henry Hanbury, I suspected that if he had deliberately tried to bump into a woman, he probably would have missed.

'Did you speak to him after that?'

'He came back with the drink and then he went off, and some more friends came in, and then I also saw some people I work with and I talked to them for a bit. I can't remember much after that.' Eva bit her lip and looked as if she were about to cry.

'I'm specially trained and I'm used to having these conversations, so I hope you feel you can be open and frank with me,' said the interviewing officer. 'It's important that you're completely honest. If you can't remember something, just say so.'

Eva nodded, her eyes brimming with tears. 'Melanie and I looked up being roofied. Apparently they don't try and talk to you, they just monitor you, then slip something into your drink, and then move in when they think it's taking effect. So it obviously wasn't any of my friends, was it? I know it was the man who made me spill my drink and bought me another. The one we saw on the CCTV.'

The interviewer smiled and moved on to the next question. Eva was obviously an intelligent woman but she was trying to solve the case herself. I sympathised, but it was dangerous. Wanting to find the person who hurt you can lead you down some very twisty paths if you're not used to sifting evidence and looking at it clearly. I tracked the interview with the transcript, rewinding and fast-forwarding, in search of discrepancies. I was surprised that the interviewing officer had even referred to being 'honest' as it could be interpreted that he thought she might be lying. Before the terrible revelations came out against Jimmy Savile, the attitude of the police had been one of scepticism and complacency towards complainants. Now interviewing officers were trained to work on the assumption that the allegations were true.

Eva looked small and fragile in the armchair, clutching a huge yellow cushion to her, as if it were a giant teddy bear. I made another cup of tea, and stretched. They had got to the point in the interview where Eva had left the pub. 'I don't remember that,' she said. 'Melanie said I didn't say goodbye. She thought I'd been talking to my work colleagues in the other bar, but they'd already gone when she checked.' She looked puzzled. 'But I don't remember anything about any of that.'

'But I do think I can remember someone talking about a party.' Eva sipped her tea and looked up at the camera again. 'Or it might have been me. It is as if I was watching a film…'

I underlined the words on the transcript with a magic marker pen. I kept a selection of different brightly coloured pens for marking transcripts, so that I could find things quickly. Eva looked around the interview room, and fiddled with her hair. 'I can remember walking with a man and my arm being held. And being pushed onto the bed. Not being able to breathe… but it's all in snatches.'

I made a note on the margin of the transcript. 'CCTV on the walk home?' I must remember to ask the prosecution if they had any more. In most cases, it was the Crown Prosecution

Service that gathered the evidence – from the police, forensic laboratories, CCTV and Automatic Number Plate Recognition. The defence, on the other hand, rarely even had the funding for a solicitor's clerk. It was you on your own, up against the full resources of the state.

On top of that, once the case got to court, you often had to deal with the sly interruptions of a prosecution-minded judge. You had to learn to take tough decisions, to understand when to object to the prosecutor's questions and when to let them go and when to take huge gambles, never forgetting that someone else's freedom was on the line.

Even though the Hanbury family was probably financially more comfortable than most of my clients, there was very little we could do. By the time your solicitor sees the police case against you, the evidence is too old. Witnesses may have gone away, forgotten or may even refuse to see you.

On screen, Eva clutched the cushion tighter. 'Melanie said she was warned, at uni, at the beginning of her first year. You can't give consent to sex if you're drunk.' She started crying again. 'Everyone says you have to report a rape. Otherwise they get away with it. But it doesn't have to go to court, does it? They're horrible to women in court, everyone says.'

'I can promise you that no one is allowed to treat you badly in court,' said the interviewer. 'There are very strict rules around how victims and witnesses can be treated in these types of cases. What happened next?'

'I can remember snatches. I think. I have a sense of not being able to breathe, of someone heavy on top of me. Then another bit as if I was floating, like I was in a movie. But I... there's just a big blank. Mainly. Except I woke up hurting everywhere the following day and...' There was a pause. The only sound was Eva's sobs. Then she looked up to the camera and spoke clearly. 'I was sore, you know, down there.'

The interviewer pushed a box of tissues towards Eva, who took them and sobbed quietly again for a few moments.

'May I ask – was he wearing a condom?'

She swallowed, touching her throat with her hand. 'Sorry, can I have a glass of water?'

The interviewing officer poured a glass of water out and handed it to her. 'Tell me when you're ready. There's no hurry.'

As she drank, her eyes flickered about. 'I can't remember.' She hid her head in her hands. 'And I don't want to remember.'

I paused the tape and studied Eva's face. She looked very nervous, her eyes flickering from left to right and back again, as if searching for something, for a tiny scrap of memory that would help. I rewound the tape and paused it again. Eva's frozen expression stared back, her mouth slightly open and her eyes searching for answers.

After scrutinising the screen for a few minutes, I put my pen down. I was tired. My eyes hurt. I would go over the interview again tomorrow. When you're defending, you sometimes felt as if you had to fight with one hand tied behind your back. So you have to fight hard. You couldn't overlook a single detail. My eyes felt dry from reading documents all day. I went upstairs to take my contact lenses out, and put on my glasses. I blinked at myself at the mirror. As a child, my parents had called me Sova, not Sophie, because Papa thought I was like a little owl.

'My Little Owl,' he says, the day I come home from school, crying because I'd been teased for peering at my books and holding them very close to my face.

'My Sova, what's wrong?'

'I don't speak good English,' I say. 'I don't understand. And I can't read the board. The other children say I'm stupid.'

I'm still not used to speaking English all the time and the blackboard seems very blurry. When I open my mouth to *explain myself, nothing comes out. I can't get past the first letter of the first word I am trying to say.*

'S-ss-s-Sophie. SSS-S-Sophie...' the children taunt.

'Don't take any notice,' says my mother, from behind a pile of books and pans. She's making Peace Candles. 'Children don't tease if you don't react.'

But my father makes an appointment with the optician.

'You're my Little Russian Owl,' says Papa, taking my hand as we walk to the bus stop together.

'I don't want to be a Russian Owl,' I say. 'I want to be English like everybody else.'

'You are English.' Papa squeezes my hand. 'But you're Russian too, and you must never forget that. You don't need to be like everyone else.'

Being different hurts. Grown-ups don't understand.

'In Russia, we think of owls as birds that see the bad things coming. In England, owls are wise. So you can be my little English-Russian Owl, my Sova? Yes?'

I still wish I was like the other children, but I adore my father's stories of the Russia he had loved and left. There is always wistfulness in his voice when he talks about the long, cold winters and the brief hot summers of his homeland.

'Short-sighted,' says the optician, prescribing me glasses.

'My little Sova,' says my father, proudly, as if short-sightedness is a great achievement. 'My Little Owl.'

In South London, aged thirty-four, I put on my glasses and looked at myself in the mirror. The doorbell rang in two staccato bursts. It would be Katie. I could do with a drink and a laugh. Katie stood at the door, clutching a bottle. 'As Chris would say – you look so fucking brainy with glasses on.'

We both laughed.

CHAPTER 9

Katie loped past me, shedding a coat, scarf, gloves, hat and several bags in a trail before coming to a halt in the middle of the kitchen. She reminded me of a wild animal sometimes, the way she ranged restlessly round my kitchen, picking things up and asking random questions. 'What a dreadful day. Have you heard? The new boss's wife is sitting in on editorial meetings for both the gossip pages and the culture. I mean, are we going to end up being edited by the chairman's wife? She's calling herself Lydia Kuznetsov, the name of her first husband, the Russian oligarch, ostensibly so that people don't realise she is who she is, which is ridiculous.'

'Drink?' I had no intention of mentioning anything about my own recent contact with Lydia.

'Oh, if you've got a beer somewhere…' Katie flung herself down at the kitchen table where I had been sitting. She looked at the open laptop, and began rifling through the papers. 'What's your latest case?'

I could have kicked myself for leaving everything out. Katie was voracious. I grabbed the laptop and the papers and bundled them into a corner of the room.

'Sorry. Confidential.' As she knew.

'Sorry.' She laughed. 'Reporters report, it's what we do. We can't resist a bit of nosing about.' She had once smuggled herself into a hospital by 'borrowing' a white coat that had been hanging up in a staff room, then interviewed a patient and had written about it. She was shameless. I opened a bottle of beer, plonked it in front of her, and poured myself a glass of white wine from a bottle left over from last night.

She took a large swig. 'You'll never guess who I've got a bit of gossip about.'

Katie had the most encyclopaedic knowledge of people I'd ever come across. She knew everyone, remembered everyone and absorbed little details apparently through her skin. The first sip of white wine hit my veins, warming me, and I said, 'No, I don't think I can guess. But let me get this on the table first, and then tell all.'

The pinger went on the oven. Time to remove the ready meal luxury fish pie and drain the peas. Katie paused while I passed her a plate and offered her salt and pepper.

'Your husband,' she said, once we had both taken our first mouthful of fish pie.

I'd forgotten what she was talking about. 'Theo?'

'Well, not so much Theo, but his ex. Wasn't she called Louisa Frazer? Primary school teacher, very keen on art.'

'Art?' I wondered if my brain was shutting down. None of it made any sense at all. How on earth had Katie come across Louisa?

'Well, I do a life painting class on Monday evenings, and the person who teaches is marrying someone else in the class, a primary school teacher called Louisa Frazer. And the class say that her first husband was a barrister called Theo and an—' She stopped suddenly.

'An what?'

'An up-and-coming name in the law.' I wasn't convinced that that was what Katie had originally intended to say.

I had never completely believed that Louisa would ever let Theo go. And he still felt responsible for her. She played on that, hooking him back in whenever she could manufacture a crisis, playing on his good nature.

'They're getting married next Saturday. The class had a round of Prosecco to wish them well in the last lesson, which is where I found out that she used to be married to Theo. I'd never have connected the dots otherwise.'

Relief washed over me. 'Oh, I'm so pleased. And Theo will be, too.'

Katie looked at her glass, and I got the feeling that there was something else she wanted to say to me. I imagined Louisa spreading lies about Theo, blaming him for everything. Everyone in the painting class would judge him, and although I knew he wouldn't care, I did. I hated it when people were found guilty without the chance to defend themselves.

'You know his marriage to her was completely over by the time we got together,' I said. 'Apparently she behaved very badly. He ended up giving her the house. He came away with almost nothing.'

Katie hesitated for a few seconds.

I continued. 'Really, Theo is generous – maybe too generous. He's always buying me lovely presents, like these earrings, even though we can't really afford them.'

Katie peered at them. 'Oh, yes, they're lovely. You two do seem so well suited, and this art teacher seems perfect for Louisa. And everyone has their difficulties.'

I smiled. 'So, tell me, what's the latest at the paper? Any more news?'

Katie realised that I didn't want to talk about Theo and Louisa. 'Any juicy leads for me?'

I shook my head. 'I don't do leads, Katie, you know that.' I whisked away our plates and put out a miscellaneous collection of leftover chocolates and slightly withered tangerines, which was the closest I could manage to dessert.

Katie picked over them. 'Oh, well, you can't blame me for trying.'

I had a sudden inspiration. 'Actually there is one story I could help you with.'

'Go on.'

'It starts with the CPS...'

'Never a good idea to start any story with an organisation that's referred to by its initials,' said Katie. 'Start with people.'

I ignored her. 'People call it the Innocence Tax.'

Katie looked much more interested at the prospect of a good headline.

I continued. 'In my opinion, what I see in the courts suggests we're moving towards a position where the CPS thinks, 'Well this or that allegation could be true... let's put it in front of a jury and see what it thinks'. Particularly when it's a sexual offence. It seems to me that they are prosecuting these cases now at any cost, in order to make up for catastrophic failures in the past.'

Katie nodded slowly. She was prepared to concede that one. The paper had had to pay out a couple of big libel awards for precisely that reason.

I continued. 'This increases the risk of genuinely innocent people finding themselves in court. But the cuts we're seeing to legal aid mean that people can't afford lawyers to represent them.'

I could sense Katie's attention span starting to drift, so I leaned forward and arranged the salt and pepper pots on the table to represent people. 'Supposing you are a teacher married to a nurse with a small pension pot between you. And you are wrongly accused of something dreadful, say by a disaffected pupil or a bonkers patient. Violence, sexual assault, theft... something. Your career is on the line, your freedom, your marriage... whatever. Your joint incomes mean you're excluded from getting legal aid, but also you are entirely innocent, so you pay whatever it costs to win your case. You instruct a solicitor and a barrister and maybe even an expert witness privately at a market rate, which is far higher than what is paid under legal aid. The bill comes to tens, maybe hundreds of thousands. But, thank God, you win. Your reputation is restored.

'But now you want your costs back. Not so fast. The state, having forced you into this position by wrongly accusing you in the first place and then refusing you legal aid, now refuses to reimburse you. They will only restore to you a token amount. You'd find yourself deeply in debt and may even have to sell your home. And there would be absolutely nothing you could do about it.'

Katie made a note. 'Yup. That could fly. But I do need this theoretical teacher and nurse to tell their story in person, and they need to look attractive in photographs.'

She wrote something down, missing the amazed look I gave her. We gossiped about the subs desk and whether the travel editor's assistant was having an affair with the features editor, but I thought I had planted a spark of interest in her brain. Just as she was about to leave, she dived back into the kitchen. I stood, holding the front door open, as the wind gusted a few leaves into the hall.

'Sorry, just looking for my phone,' she called from the kitchen. 'It was in my bag all the time,' she said, reappearing a few minutes later. 'Honestly, I'd forget my head if it wasn't screwed on.' She stopped, as if trying to decide whether to add something.

'Forgotten something else?'

Katie shook her head. 'No, just thanks for a great dinner.' She surprised me by hugging me, for longer than I felt comfortable with, as I mumbled something about 'only ready meals' into her coat.

Just as Katie reached the bottom of the front steps, she turned round. 'You know, everyone at the paper really appreciates what you do. So don't hesitate to… well, let us know if anything… well, anyway. We're your friends, Sophie, not just colleagues. There, that's me embarrassing myself enough for one evening.' She strode off towards the Tube station before I could respond. I watched her disappear round the corner. What had she really wanted to say? Nothing good if it came from Louisa.

I knew Theo would be on his way back from a day in court in Leeds, so I called him to tell him about Louisa's marriage. He didn't seem to react. 'Mm. Good, good. Sorry, what? Darling, it's not a good time to talk. Send flowers or something. If you think we should.'

Should you send flowers when your husband's ex-wife remarries? It was a tricky piece of etiquette I felt ill-equipped to decide on my own. Theo didn't get back until I was asleep. I woke up to find him crashing round the room, bumping into things. 'Sorry,' he said. 'Trying not to wake you up.'

'Just switch on the light.' I burrowed down under the duvet, but couldn't get back to sleep.

CHAPTER 10

Three weeks later, I pulled into the car park outside the Inner London Crown Court. Wind and rain lashed the grim stone building and it looked even more forbidding than usual. I locked my car, and sprinted to the steps, to join the shuffling queue waiting to pass through security.

'It's supposed to be sunny today,' grumbled the security guard as he opened my pull-along suitcase and checked. 'You wouldn't think, would you?'

I murmured agreement. I could see a mud splatter on my tights, where I had hurried through a puddle, and my hair was wet. Five minutes later I walked into the ladies' robing room and started putting on my wig and attaching my bands.

The room was the usual mess of papers and used coffee cups, smelling faintly of damp bricks and stale perfume. There was an overflowing wastepaper basket and on the floor beside it lay a pair of laddered tights and some crumpled tissues – both had clearly been thrown away but the thrower had missed the target and never bothered to pick them up.

I was sorry that there was no one else there. I appreciated the camaraderie amongst the smart, clever women who talked casually but knowledgeably about the law and their families or their love lives as they adjusted their wigs and changed their shoes. Theo and I were always too busy to have much of a social life.

I hung up my coat and unzipped my small pull-along suitcase, taking out a blue patterned bag, embroidered with my name. It held my black gown and my wig box – a black tin also with my name on it, painted in gold. I dressed carefully, putting on my professional armour, and checked myself in the mirror. The wig made me look older. Less blonde and soft. Good.

People often ask whether barristers feel as if they are wearing fancy dress when they don their wigs and gowns. The truth is that it is more like a soldier's armour. It is the uniform of the doctor's white coat or the police officer's stab vest. It says, 'I am the expert here. I can ask the most astonishingly intimate questions, and you will be able to answer them, indeed, you must answer them, because you know that that is what I do.'

In medieval England, the gowns were green and violet, according to the seasons, but when Charles II died in 1685, they changed to black because the court went into mourning and have remained black ever since. The ruffs were replaced by plain bands at the neck. We still have the little pouch on our hoods attached to the back of the gown, into which people in the distant past dropped coins to keep a barrister talking.

I unzipped the suitcase again, and took out the papers, checking that they were in order before putting the ones I needed first in the front pocket. Had I forgotten anything? I felt that shimmer of anxiety that I got before a big case, that cold, deep pit that warned me to check, check and check again. It always fell away the minute I walked into the hush of the court room and the doors swung closed behind me.

I took one last look in the long mirror, adjusted the gown again, and smiled at myself. I would get justice for Henry Hanbury. The door opened and I was pleased to see it was Millie Knight, a tall, beautiful Jamaican who was an old friend from my student days. 'Hi, Sophie! Long time no see. How are you?'

'Oh… good… yes, really good actually. I don't suppose you are prosecuting the case of Hanbury in Court 9 by any chance?'

'No such luck. I'm part heard in a GBH in Court 4. Been here a week already.' Millie went over to the mirror and adjusted her wig. 'By the way, I see you've taken on Polly Chan as a tenant. She was with us for a while as a pupil. I'm glad she found somewhere.'

'I didn't realise you knew her. Why didn't your chambers take her?'

Millie turned back to the mirror and I couldn't see her face. There was a pause and then Millie said thoughtfully. 'A few of us had some reservations, and there was a rumour about her and our head of chambers… but you know, people will say these things.' I waited. Millie sounded as if she were going to say something else. 'Anyway, she hates to lose. That's, I think, on the whole…' She trailed off, but recovered herself. 'I haven't seen her in court myself, but it always sounded as if she would do anything to win, and that must be good for chambers.' Whenever I saw Millie, I was reminded of how much I liked her, and how I wished I had more time to spend on friendships.

Millie smiled at me. 'Anyway, how's Theo? Is he still away a lot? Didn't he have to do a lot of circuit work outside London?'

'As you know, it's always tough when you first take silk. But Theo seems not to mind.' We laughed. I adjusted my own wig and went out to reception to find Henry.

Henry and Cornelia were side by side at the reception desk. Cornelia glanced nervously around, looking out of place in a smart suit and a string of pearls. I was surprised to see that Lydia Brennan was with them again, a reassuring hand on Cornelia's back. 'Hello, Sophie.' She took my hand in both of hers in a warm handshake, and her blue eyes searched my face.

She seemed to be very intense, not the socialite that everyone at the paper mocked behind her back. I liked the way she was making such an effort for a woman whose link to her appeared to be no more than that their sons had known each other at university.

Beside them, an enormous man with a neck festooned in tattoos was shouting into the face of one of the security guards, who was calling for assistance on his radio. Lydia seemed oblivious to him, but Cornelia flinched every time he drew breath. I shook her hand and noticed that the thin, beringed fingers were trembling. Henry stood beside his mother, looking slightly puzzled, as if he wasn't quite sure how he had got here. I gently steered them towards a vacant conference room. It was small and neutral, with a table, four chairs and an old-fashioned radiator. When they were all seated I began.

'Nothing very exciting will happen today,' I told them. 'The hearing should only take ten or fifteen minutes. All you have to do is enter your plea of not guilty. I and the barrister for the prosecution will do the rest. We will set out a timetable for the trial and flag up any points of law to the judge that may arise, and things like that. Now is there anything you want to ask me?'

Cordelia swallowed hard. 'Will we be in the press? After all, it's not as if we're important or anything? Except maybe Henry's award...' Henry was apparently the youngest student ever to be awarded a prestigious grant from a major medical company, and it was this that was funding his PhD. But I didn't think it was likely to be big news. On the other hand, I didn't want to give them false hope. 'It may get into the papers, at least, the local ones, sooner or later, but we may be lucky today. There's a high-profile sentencing case in one of the other courtrooms, a soap star who kidnapped his own baby from his girlfriend, so I think that will keep the press busy.' I smiled at Cordelia, hoping to reassure her. 'We'll be in and out very quickly. You and Lydia will sit in the visitors' gallery, so you'll be able to see everything, but it's important that you don't actually say anything.'

I led them along to Court 9. It was in the newly-built block at Inner London and, unlike the Victorian courts, it had no natural light. That was courtesy of various bombing campaigns and terrorist threats. Working under a harsh artificial light, with the hum of the air conditioning in the background, you were constantly aware that you weren't breathing fresh air.

Our case was one of a dozen that afternoon and they were dealt with briskly. Henry formally surrendered to the dock officer, who climbed into the dock with him. The door to the dock was locked, and Henry sat behind the tall glass screen. There was a quivering intake of breath from Cornelia, and I saw Lydia take her hand.

Henry entered his not guilty plea in a slightly uncertain voice. I would need to coach him before the case came up. He was bailed to the family house in Guildford and asked to surrender his passport. I made a mental note to remember to impress on both Cornelia and Henry that he would not be able to sleep anywhere other than his home address until he was tried. There would be no dossing on a friend's sofa after a party. No festivals or family weddings at the other end of the country.

'You're also to have no contact with the complainant in this case,' said the judge. 'Nor are you to go within one mile of her home. I rose to ask if the case could be heard soon. The prosecution said that the witness would not be available until November. A trial date was fixed for November 17th, more than two months away. As I had predicted, the press bench was empty. I left them on the steps of the court, Lydia hailing a black cab and bundling Cornelia and Henry into the back.

As I drove back to the Temple in the sluggish traffic, I thought about the weaknesses in the Crown's case, the lack of any definitive forensic evidence, the complainant's vagueness about what had actually happened. Thrown onto the scales on the other side were Henry's social awkwardness and his inability to take this seriously, which could be a real problem with any jury who might be inclined to think anyone slightly odd must be guilty.

And if Eva Scott believed he had raped her, even though she admitted to having no memory of the actual event, then shouldn't she be believed? Why would anyone want to destroy a young man at the beginning of a promising and valuable career?

I reviewed the options. The first possibility was that Eva was telling the truth and Henry was lying. The second was that this was a genuine case of mistaken identity and Eva was being railroaded either by the police or the prosecution because they wanted to improve the rape conviction statistics. And Eva, obviously so traumatised, so willing to help, so anxious to do the right thing, was going along with everyone else's vested interests. Like most people, she wouldn't have known that once the CPS juggernaut starts rolling, it's very hard to stop it.

I had the feeling that they were both telling the truth. I had to brake suddenly to avoid bumping into the car in front. The traffic had come to a complete standstill on Blackfriars Bridge when my phone vibrated. I checked it. It had been on silent and there were several missed calls as well as a message from Theo.

You are all over Twitter and so is your client! Call me!!

As we weren't moving, I also listened to the voicemail message that had been left for me.

'Sophie,' It was Katie. 'I know you're really careful not to disclose anything about your clients during a trial, but I've got the editor on my back on this one, so we can come out as soon as any 'guilty' verdict is announced. Could you just give me a bit of general advice about what the issues might be at this stage? You know it's much better to be the one who talks to the press, all the signs are that the media want to hang, draw and quarter arrogant young men who think that having a double first from Oxbridge allows them to help themselves to anything they like in life. I'm sure that between us, we can stop that happening? I see from the rota that you're in tonight, so we'll speak then. Off the record, of course.'

CHAPTER 11

I couldn't waste time finding out more about what Twitter said because I was late for the paper. I hurried into the newspaper offices, swiping my lanyard to get through the turnstiles. Marek gave me a cheery wave from behind the reception desk. The night sky, dotted with the red and white lights of moving planes, twinkled seven floors above me in the giant glass-topped atrium. One of my father's Russian sayings echoed in my mind: 'Don't tell me the moon is shining. Show me the glint of light on broken glass.'

It was Chekhov. Papa had explained that it was about the value of detail. 'If you are writing about something big, you will paint a better picture by focusing on something small.' He would pinch my cheek affectionately as he bent over my homework, stabbing his finger at the page: 'So many times it is detail that matters. Detail.'

It would certainly be detail that mattered if I were to save Henry Hanbury from an unjust conviction, and the ruin of his life. And it was detail that Katie was looking for to add colour to her column. The glass lifts were busy, so I waited longer than usual before one arrived to take me up to the eleventh floor. They swished up and down, with an electronic 'ping' when they stopped at a floor. I often wondered if the receptionists and guards dreamed of that noise. Ping. Ping, ping. Silence. Ping. Ping. A set of doors slid open.

I got into the lift, watching the reception desk fall away beneath me, and people scurrying out of the building. The atrium emptied fast in the evening between six and seven, and after eight the lights were dimmed and only the guard was left. My phone vibrated again. This time it was a call from Cornelia Hanbury.

'Everyone knows.' She sounded close to tears. 'It's all over social media. The medical company is closing down the project – Henry's research, that is. What can we do?'

'I'm really sorry. I can't discuss the case with you, because you're not, strictly speaking, my client. I can give you general advice, which is to get Bravo's to put out a statement on your behalf. I'll help them work on the wording if Philip asks me to.'

'Now that it's out there, everyone will think he did it, won't they? They'll say there's no smoke without fire.'

'I'm constantly surprised and reassured by how sensible juries are,' I said. 'They really are twelve ordinary people who think very carefully and take matters very seriously.'

'My son is a good man,' said Cornelia. 'He really is. I know he didn't do this thing. Are you married?'

'What?' I wasn't quite sure why she was asking. I didn't like to discuss my private life with clients, however innocently.

'Are you married? Because if you are, you know your husband, don't you? You know exactly what he would do and what he wouldn't do. And with your child, it's even stronger. Henry... well, he has always been a kind boy. He was kind to his sisters, even as a young child. I remember when he was just five. I took him to the dentist after school. We passed an old man huddled in a doorway. He wanted to know why the man was sleeping there, and why he didn't have a home. He made me go back and give him the money in my bag. Even at five, he said that we had more, that we didn't need the money as much as the man in the doorway.'

I decided not to point out that, although this was a charming story, the law courts were full of wives, husbands and parents who hadn't known what their nearest and dearest were capable of.

'I need you to believe me,' said Cornelia. '*We* need you to believe *us*.'

I hesitated. 'It doesn't matter what I believe. It only matters what the jury believes. It's not the role of a barrister to make judgements, only to make sure that every possible avenue has been explored.' I thought of Cornelia's gaunt face and bony hands. 'Really, though,' I added, 'if it helps, I do believe you.'

I don't like to use the word 'instinct' because I've seen people dragged through the court system on little more than a 'copper's instinct'. But I realised that in this case and based on little more than instinct, I did believe Henry. There was a sigh from the other end. 'Thank you. Thank you. It's not being believed that is so terrible. I'll ring Bravo's now. Thank you.'

The offices felt deserted. Everyone had gone home except for the news and city pages. I strode past rows of deserted desks towards the brightly lit hub and Chris. He swung round as I approached. 'Well, well. Sophie Angel. What can you tell us about Mr Henry Hanbury?'

'Nothing.' I sat down and called up my screen. 'As you very well know.'

I had been terrified of Chris when I started as a night lawyer. He swore and raged around the newsroom like an attacking dog. But he was ethical and ferocious in his determination to defend the right to free speech.

He grinned. 'We're planning a background piece on privileged young men who rape.'

My heart sank. I met Chris's eyes and held his gaze. 'He's not that privileged. His father was a civil servant. He went to a state school.'

'And Oxford. Where his best friend was the son of a certain half-American, half-Russian young man called Yevgeny

Brennan, the son of our own Lydia Brennan aka Kuznetsov.'

Chris waited for me to say what I knew but I said nothing. Eventually he swung back to his desk. 'OK, OK, but when the case is over...' It was a delicate situation. No paper could claim to be independent if it spiked an article because of the influence of the owner's wife. And Chris would want to be seen to be independent. Even Robert Brennan would want his editor to be seen to be independent. They would have a battle about editorial independence one day, but – I could see that Chris had decided – not tonight.

'When the case is over, Mr Hanbury will decide what he says and to whom.' I hoped that Chris would continue to tread carefully because Lydia was a family friend of the Hanburys, and that the newsroom didn't ultimately decide to prove itself by going in unnecessarily hard on Henry Hanbury.

Chris glared at me. 'Very fucking ladylike, I'm sure.'

Katie came over from her little patch of light on the news desk. 'Let's have a coffee, Sophie.'

'Yeah, have a coffee,' said Chris. 'There's nothing for you to check just yet.'

I sighed and followed her to the coffee machine. 'There really is nothing I can tell you, Katie. And there's very little that you can actually say.'

'You know how it goes, Sophie. I can't sit on this one, not even for you.'

I remembered closing my laptop sharply just before supper, when Katie found it open. But not even Katie could have read anything in the time it took me to stride across the room and stop her nosing around. So I didn't reply, and picked out a herbal tea from the box in front of me. Katie folded her arms as the coffee machine frothed and whirred.

'He's had to halt some very valuable research,' I said, unable to stop myself. 'And for what? How does that benefit anyone?'

The machine stopped spurting its pale frothy liquid, and Katie edged the disposable cup away carefully. 'Most of our readers won't care if some over-privileged privately-educated moron has to change his course and delay his degree by a few months,' she said. 'At least, that's what they'll say.'

'He isn't privately...' I started to defend him, but realised it would be dangerous to say anything at all.

Katie folded her arms. 'You've got to be realistic about this. There is no public sympathy out there for young men like him. The line we'll be taking is that this is a young woman's life we're talking about. Every other newspaper can suggest that the shifting sands between men and women mean that signals aren't clear, that men are just as much victims in the war between the sexes as women are. But we don't buy it.' She took a sip of coffee and studied me. 'Sorry.'

'Henry Hanbury didn't rape anyone, Katie,' I repeated. I hoped that was true.

Katie tried again. 'Even if he is innocent, let's just call it collateral damage. If it makes even one man think twice before he gropes or tries to kiss a woman when she doesn't want him to, then it's a price worth paying. Women have got to start fighting back.'

'Your collateral damage. His life. You've never sat in a cell with an innocent man waiting for a jury to come to a verdict that might mean he spends ten years in jail and loses his wife and child.'

'Come on, Sophie. A twenty-four-year-old man buying a girl he's never met before a margarita in a pub! You can't tell me he's not after a leg over.'

I suppressed anger. 'Katie. Henry Hanbury is a real person. You're a brilliant journalist because you really care about getting things right. Please don't drag his name through the mud until, or unless, you actually know he's done this. Which you don't.' I went back to my desk.

'You're looking a bit pale. Eaten a duff oyster or something?' asked Chris. 'If you're going to chunder, make sure you hit the wastepaper basket. I hope you're not fucking pregnant.'

'No.' It was most unwise to show any sign of weakness, even basic human emotion, on the news desk. I forced myself to start scanning copy. But I was angry. Did Katie really care so little about justice? Didn't she realise that a country without justice is a country where no one is safe? Not journalists, not anyone. Especially not journalists. I raised my head to look at her. She smiled and waved, and I went back to my screens. They were all pretty well educated about libel on the news desk, so it was headlines I needed to watch, and the accidental libel.

I found one almost immediately. 'Chris, you know that story you published recently about the Secretary of State for Energy having been a member of the British National Party when he was younger?'

'Yeah, yeah, we got it wrong. We're apologising for fuck's sake.'

'But the way you've worded this,' I pointed it out, 'makes it seem as if membership of the BNP is a crime. *They* could sue for libel.'

'It is a fucking crime in my book,' he said. 'But, yeah, I get your point.'

That was what Papa would have called the glint on broken glass. The detail.

I forced myself to go through the stories and not to think about Henry Hanbury, Twitter or whether my job at the newspaper was safe. The sub-editors no longer checked facts as carefully as they did. They checked grammar, added headlines and cut stories, but several years of successive redundancies meant there just wasn't the manpower for extra fact checking. It made my job much more difficult. Everyone makes mistakes.

'I don't give a flying fuck about the government line, just

give me someone to fucking talk to.' Chris slammed the phone back into its holder.

I had become used to the steady ejaculation of curses beside me. The phone on my desk rang. I picked it up, expecting a legal query.

'It's Lydia Kuznetsov here.'

I found my grip on the phone tightening. I found the way Lydia crossed the three boundaries in my life – the Bar, the paper and my Russian childhood – disconcerting. 'Oh, hello. How are you?'

'Well, I'm very well, except, of course for this terrible gossip about poor Henry.'

'I must stop you there because I can't discuss the case with anyone except my client, and that's Henry himself, and Philip, the solicitor from Bravo's.'

'I understand,' said Lydia. 'That's not what I was calling about. I wanted to invite you to one of my little lunches – in my role as editor-at-large. You probably know I sit on the committee for a charity on international justice, and I want to use my position on the paper to do good, to change things for the better. So I've got a few influential people coming to lunch next Thursday, and I'd really value your input, both as a rising young lawyer dealing with the current legal system, and also as a night lawyer for a major newspaper. It seems to me you combine two very important aspects of how justice is actually delivered these days.'

'The Hanburys won't be there, will they? It wouldn't be appropriate for me to be socialising with anyone on the case.'

'Of course not, my dear. Poor Cornelia is almost a nervous wreck, and Henry is bailed to sleep every night in the family home. He can't even see his friends or go to a party unless he can be sure of getting back that night – which is very hard on a young man, don't you think?'

Not being able to go to parties was the least of his problems, but I didn't say so.

'Well, I... the thing is... at the moment, I could come next Thursday, but if the clerks at the chambers give me a case, I'll have to drop out at the last minute.'

'Really?' Lydia's voice was cool. 'Surely you can tell the clerks you'll work on another day? You barristers are self-employed, I understand?'

'Well, it's an odd relationship between us and the clerks, and when you're a junior tenant like me, you can't upset them by turning a case down.'

The power of the clerks was that they booked our cases and collected our fees. A good clerk would have a feel for the type of cases you would be best at. They could get you the right kind of work in front of the right judges. The clerks could make you as a barrister but they could also break you. My relationship with Lee was based, I thought, on mutual respect. But if I fell out with him, he would be as capable of cutting off my supply of work as easily as a plumber cuts off the water from the mains.

'Sorry Miss, that firm didn't seem to like you' or 'Sorry Miss, the whole of chambers is quiet right now. Perhaps you should look elsewhere – somewhere that does more fraud/rape/family work?' Or worst of all: 'Ever thought of a career in the CPS Miss? Regular income, even a pension?'

But I couldn't explain all that to Lydia, and my work as a night lawyer was also very important. I didn't have anything booked in for next Thursday, so I decided to risk it, and pray that I didn't suddenly get a big case on Monday or Tuesday.

'I'd love to,' I said. 'I haven't got a case booked in, so I'll be there.'

'And do you have any advice about these latest allegations?' she asked. 'I know you can't talk about the case, but I feel so sorry for poor Cornelia. It's all lies, I'm convinced. I know the family very well. Is there anything I can do to help?'

I turned away from Chris and lowered my voice. 'I really can't say anything specific to the case, except what I would say to anyone in *any* case, which is that Henry must make sure that his solicitor is with him for every interview with the police, and that it's the solicitor, not Henry, who makes any public comment to the press. It's too easy to say something that can be misinterpreted.'

'I'll tell Cornelia that. She thinks that the sooner everything is explained properly, the sooner it will all go away.'

'I'm afraid that's not the case,' I said. 'I will say this, and then I shouldn't say anything more. It has been known for the allegations to change to fit the accused's account. That's why it's so important to have a lawyer with you, whether you're innocent or guilty. The police are under huge pressure to improve their conviction statistics, so it's not unknown for statements to be changed.'

'I know all about that sort of thing,' said Lydia. 'I am just surprised to hear that it goes on in England, too. And it's why I want you to come to lunch on Thursday.'

As I put the phone down, I realised that somewhere in that conversation, I had glimpsed the real Lydia, beneath the mask of the confident socialite.

Chris swung his chair round. 'You really can't give us anything on Hanbury, then?'

'I really can't. And Henry Hanbury is a young man. Even if he's found not guilty, his future will still be ruined. Every time anyone googles him, all they'll see is "rape".'

'He'll survive. Yup. What?'

I realised that the last question hadn't been for me. A reporter murmured something into Chris's ear.

'No, not yet. Find out more facts. You're meant to be a

journalist, for Christ's sake. Right, Miss Angel, you'd better not be too angelic here. We're a fucking newspaper.'

He indicated the chair next to me, picking up the phone as it rang. 'Yes? What? No. I'm going to see what the fucking lawyer says. We've got Blondie right here beside us.' He slammed the phone back down again and winked at me.

'After Cliff Richard, Leon Brittan and Paul Gambaccini, I'd recommend being very careful,' I said.

'Very careful doesn't sell fucking newspapers. Anyway, it doesn't matter if someone sues us for a hundred grand because we'll get that back in sales.' There was a lull, punctuated by Chris's swearing. At one point a young woman journalist retreated in tears.

'I never think I've done a decent day's work unless I've made someone cry,' muttered Chris. 'I don't want to get soft in my old age.'

I decided to do some research on Henry Hanbury. His Facebook profile was locked down tight. All I could see was a group photo of blurred youngsters on a ski slope, with their arms around each other. Three girls, four men, all smiling and so muffled up with hats and scarves as to be unrecognisable.

He was on Twitter and Instagram, but it was all about his fundraising. He ran marathons in aid of medical research. There were a few photos taken on finish lines, and thanks to everyone who had donated, but no real sense of the man himself. But the online abuse on Twitter about him was vicious: 'I hope you get raped to death in jail.' Even the milder tweets were worrying as they added to the noise around the case and could distract a jury from listening to the hard evidence: '"#hanbury Don't let rapists win", "Only 8% of rape cases in court lead to a conviction in the UK", "Time to get proper angry".'

Where did people get these figures from? I checked online. The actual figures from the Crown Prosecution Service showed that 57.9 per cent of rape cases going to court got 'guilty' convictions. Unless the case was dropped, Henry Hanbury was statistically more likely to be proven guilty than not. The eight per cent conviction rate was the number of convictions achieved as a percentage of rapes reported, not of rapes tried. I put my head in my hands. Why couldn't people just check before they tweeted?

'Hello hello.' Chris was scrolling down his screen. 'What do we have here?'

He swung round in his chair to face me. 'Your client, Mr Henry Hanbury.'

'Yes?' I reminded myself how important it was to give nothing away. I didn't want to find myself up in front of the Bar Council.

Chris rubbed his hands together. 'What do you know! He's only gone and done it before.'

'What?'

'It's on Twitter: "#hanbury #rape He runed my life. Attacked me when I was only 15". I think we can take that as "ruined", don't you? It's been re-tweeted over two thousand times. People are outraged.' Chris loved outrage. It fed the newspaper and its rolling social media output. 'Mm,' he said as he scanned down the feed. 'They're really challenging the police to make sure they take this seriously.'

CHAPTER 12

I was exhausted when I reached home. Theo met me at the front door and folded me into his arms. I sighed deeply and let myself sink into his warmth. 'I've made you some smoked salmon sandwiches,' he whispered. 'I bet you haven't eaten.' He was right.

'It's impossible to know what to believe,' I said, still overwhelmed with the amount of hatred directed at a gangling young medical researcher.

'He may have done it. You have to face that. Come and sit down.' Theo led me through to the back of the house, and poured me a glass of wine.

'You're like my father.' I smiled. 'You think everything can be sorted out with food.'

Theo smiled back. 'Oh, it can.'

He waited until I had had my first few mouthfuls. 'So what are the latest allegations?'

'It's basically one woman on Twitter at the moment. But her tweets have gained a lot of momentum so the police will have to take it seriously. ' I handed my phone to Theo, and he scrolled down.

'Mm. "#rape #hanbury I was only 15", "#rape #hanbury It's time to tell the truth", "#rape #hanbury he runed my life" – I think she must mean "ruined".'

'She's probably after victim's compensation. Either that or it's true.' Theo took a sandwich.

'Don't be so cynical,' I replied. Once I had eaten, my brain

96

started working again. I put my plate down and said to Theo, 'I started off being sure that Henry hadn't done it, but now I'm beginning to wonder.'

'We're not there to decide whether someone's guilty or not,' Theo reminded me. 'We're just there to make sure that the prosecution case really is watertight by testing it thoroughly.' He took my hand and gently rubbed my thumb.

I sighed. 'And now we're dealing with a historic allegation as well as the current complaint. Lord knows what people are going to suddenly start "remembering".' I wiggled my fingers in quote marks. I took a last mouthful of sandwich and thought about Lydia and her phone call. Eventually I decided to discuss it with Theo.

'Lydia Brennan – she called herself Kuznetsov – called me today to ask me for lunch.'

'Great,' murmured Theo, through his own last mouthful of sandwich. 'Good contact.'

'It's just that the conversation had an odd impact on my own memories.' I paused. Was I making sense? 'You know how there's been some useful research in the Journal of Neuroscience on Decay Theory – into the way memories are stored and retrieved, and how they fade over time, particularly if you don't actually think about the event. It bolsters the case against recovered memory?'

Theo nodded. 'But what does this have to do with Lydia Brennan?'

'This might sound off the wall.' Theo and I had often used the science of memory to show the weaknesses of a witness's testimony. I knew where the holes were in memory, and how our minds can invent something that can seem so real, which is why I'd originally ignored something that had flashed into my mind suddenly as I stepped down into the underground. But it wouldn't go away.

'I left the office shortly after her call, and went home the way I always do, down that subway to the underground. And subways have often reminded me of living in Moscow. There were tunnels under the roads so you could cross safely, but I used to hate leaving the bright, clear air by the river to go down into them because they were so dark. I remember squeezing my mother's hand tighter and how beggars pushed their bowls into your faces and the fetid smell was overwhelming.

'So as I was going down into the subway near the paper, I thought about those Moscow subways, because I often do, and I remembered going down into the subway when I was a child, with my mother, and my uncle Kiril and another woman... Tonight I just suddenly got the sense that that other woman had been Lydia. We'd started running, all four of us, and we came out of the subway into the sunlight and then we went over a bridge. It had the most amazing ironwork, and elaborate street lights that looked like chandeliers. It looked like a fairyland. And there were domes, some red, some gold. It was what Muscovites called a "grandmother's summer" – a week of blue skies and sunshine, late in the year. And this other woman and Uncle Kiril were laughing. But looking back, I don't even know if there really is a subway that comes out near a bridge. Or whether I'm remembering one event or whether this was a journey we often did. Or why my memory has suddenly decided to tell me that this other woman was Lydia Kuznetsov.'

Theo didn't look convinced. 'She knows who your parents are. Don't you think that if she'd known them, she'd have said so?'

'That's why I thought it was odd. And I can hardly ask her if she remembers walking with a little girl in an underpass over thirty years ago. It would sound nuts.'

'You could ask your parents.'

'I will.' I thought about it. 'But not on the phone. I'd need to see their faces. They talk about Russia all the time, but there are definitely questions they won't answer. They go all vague and tell some funny or dreadful story that I've heard dozens of times before. An image flashed into my mind. It was the worst winter we'd ever had. There were blizzards and bitter winds, and I could hardly breathe in or stand up in the street. And there was snow everywhere, over everything.'

I remembered curling up in bed, and not wanting to get up. Every morning all the windows in our flat were crusted with frost flowers. I used to scrape the ice off with my finger, making patterns or writing my name in it. One day we were woken by an enormous explosion. There was a horrible man who lived on the ground floor, called Yaroslav. The diesel used to freeze in cars, and he tried to defrost the pipes in his van using a blow-torch. The explosion shook the whole building. We thought we were being bombed by the Americans.

There are whispers in the back of my head, and half-remembered snatches of conversation. I hear my mother's voice say, 'Well, personally I don't care if that Yaroslav is dead. You could call it comeuppance.'

'What's comeuppance?' I ask.

My mother jumps slightly, 'You mustn't gossip, darling.'

Then she explains that Yaroslav had told the police things about people in the flats.

'But if people do something wrong, don't the police have to know?' I reply.

My mother waves her hands vaguely. 'Well, yes, just not like that.' The woman she was talking to laughs, and says, 'There are no flies on her. Isn't that what you English say?'

'No,' I say, firmly. 'There aren't any flies on me. There aren't flies in winter.' Both women laugh again and I feel foolish.

Who was that woman? I felt as if Lydia Kuznetsov's face had imposed itself all over my memories.

'Maybe your mother was friends with another woman called Lydia,' Theo suggested. 'It's a very common name in Russia. It's a bit beyond coincidence to think that someone you knew in Moscow thirty years ago has suddenly popped up in your life now.'

I didn't entirely agree with him. 'Well, if you think about the size of London and the size of Moscow and how many people there are in them both, yes. But if you consider the number of people who have lived in both places and are now currently in London, that's a very much smaller number. And there would be a number of links between them all and ways they might meet.'

Theo yawned. 'I suppose so. I can't count the number of times I've been in some remote place and someone I've been to school or shared a flat with in uni or something like that pops up.'

Now I wondered if Yaroslav and the explosion had anything to do with why we had to come back to England. Although it didn't seem like "coming back" to me because I'd never known anything except Moscow. My mother had told me I was going to my grandparents' house, and I didn't really understand she meant my English grandparents, because I'd never met them.

I remembered being disappointed at the end of the long, frightening journey, looking up at my mother. Her face was as expressionless as stone. Instead of Dedushka and Babushka, there were two elderly strangers, looking down at me as if I was a problem they had to solve.

I longed to be back at my real grandparents' dacha in the countryside. It was even colder than Moscow. The clear air sparkled with frost crystals on sunny days, and at night you could hear the wolves howling in the forest. I would snuggle down under my blankets with my grandfather's dog sleeping by my feet. I always felt safe, until the whispering started. People either whispered or they shouted at each other, but it always stopped when I came into the room.

I came back to the present. One day I would find out what the whispers were about.

Theo got up and stretched. 'Well, whatever the science of memory might have to say about it all, I think we can safely conclude that even if we do find out that Lydia Brennan was once a friend of your parents in Moscow, the chances of you having an accurate memory of running in an underpass with her when you were five, are very, very small.' We both laughed. It did seem ridiculous when you put it like that.

I came back to the present. 'I've been thinking about how the Hanbury story got out.'

'It's time to forget about the Hanburys. You need a good night's sleep.' Theo began kissing gently down the side of my neck, parting my hair gently. 'And I know exactly how to make you relax…'

A thought struck me suddenly and I pulled away. 'Katie!' I jumped up and began to pace around the kitchen, re-enacting to myself how Katie could have seen the papers about the case. 'My laptop was open, and then I put it and the papers here.' She could have got a look at them. Easily. She spotted my work the minute she came in, but I shut it down immediately and stuffed the papers in my bag so I know she didn't get a chance to read it then. But she was in the kitchen alone for at least five minutes, I was so stupid to let her be in a room with my bag.'

Theo said irritably, 'I've always told you never to trust a journalist.'

'Oh God!' I wailed. 'I remember what Katie said to me at the paper this evening. She said, "Don't tell me that a young man buying a margarita for a woman in a pub isn't after a leg over." There's been nothing about it being a margarita in the first hearing, or on Twitter, or anything. It could only have come from someone who saw my paperwork.'

'Or someone at one of the solicitor's offices, or a clerk at the CPS or even the police, who are as leaky as a sieve,' said Theo. He looked at me with something approaching exasperation. 'Even so, I've told you not to trust anyone at the paper. I don't know why you're even surprised.'

'Because Katie is my friend.'

'Barristers and journalists spend a lot of time together. It's a symbiotic relationship. We both feed off each other, but sometimes you'll be the food.'

I was suddenly too tired to argue with him. 'I'm ready for bed.'

'Why not go on up? I've got a few emails to deal with.'

As I fell asleep, an image of my uncle Kiril drifted into my half-dream. He was laughing. He had seemed very tall to me – a giant of a man with blonde hair, a blonde beard and astonishingly blue eyes. I thought he was trying to warn me about something, but the thought slipped away and I slept.

CHAPTER 13

Theo and I visited my parents in Kent every other Saturday.

Theo drove us down. I relaxed back into the leather seats and allowed myself to luxuriate in the sense that he was in charge.

'Thank you for coming with me,' I said. 'I know you've got a lot on with the new work in Birmingham.'

He glanced sideways at me. 'You need someone on your side. Otherwise your father will criticise you for working too hard and your mother will want you to demonstrate against nuclear power or fracking or something.'

'Papa doesn't criticise me. He's just anxious. And his emotions are always on the surface. So everything that comes into his head comes straight out of his mouth.'

Theo smiled. 'Just keep your father focused on the old days in Moscow. Don't give him a chance to ask any questions.'

'I have been wondering if they knew Lydia Brennan. I get the feeling she knows something about me. She's always trying to steer the conversation round towards when I was in Moscow.'

'You were six when you left Moscow. Surely she can't expect you to talk about it as if you'd been an adult?'

'No.' But I could see something shadowy, like a ghost in the birch woods with the moon behind it. Ever since I'd met Lydia Brennan, it had been calling to me, whispering things I didn't want to hear.

The traffic slowed down and the car came to a halt. 'Damn,' said Theo. 'Tell your parents we're going to be late.'

I could hear the phone ringing and imagined my father, Vassily, in his cosy kitchen, swearing in Russian as he struggled to locate it.

'Da! Da! Who is this?' His voice sounded faint.

'Papa! It's me, Sophie. Papa, hold the phone up. I can't hear you.'

There was more swearing, but at last I could hear him clearly. 'Sova, my little one, is that you?'

I felt a catch in my throat. 'Papa, we're going to be late. Are you and Mama busy?'

'Who's that?' I heard my mother, Elinor. She would be cooking, slicing garlic and chillies, with her faded grey hair twisted up on her head with a pencil, tendrils hanging loose.

'If my little owl is going be late, of course that is not a problem.'

'I've got a yoga workshop this afternoon,' said Elinor, in the background. 'Sophie can join in. It'll be good for her.'

'Sophie doesn't need to yogi at her age,' said her father. 'It's for old ladies.'

'Papa!' I shouted before my parents could get diverted into one of their usual arguments. 'We'll be with you as soon as we can.'

'I'm making piroshky,' he said. 'Your favourite.'

My mother was singing when we let ourselves into the Victorian semi that had become my home when we fled Moscow. It had seemed large, dark and frightening when I first saw it, but I now loved its red-brick solidity, its stone doorstep and high ornate ceilings.

Theo was always amused by the suburban street they lived in. 'This is the way the world ends,' he would say, 'not with a bang but a whimper.' Or 'I measure out my life in coffee spoons...'

I decided not to point out that TS Eliot might have had a very different view of English suburbia if he had lived in a cramped flat in a Moscow tower block, with windows that didn't open.

'It's so marvellous to see my Sova.' Papa rolled the word 'marvellous' around like an oak cask of claret across cobbled stone. The word sounded rich and foreign on his tongue. Home wrapped itself around me like a familiar blanket. It smelt of cooking and flowers, and my father's old-fashioned citrus cologne.

My father pinched my chin between his fingers, lifting my head. 'My little Sova is working too hard. And you are so skinny, not good! I am making you your favourite piroshky.' It was my father's philosophy in life that no trouble, however great, could not be soothed by chai and piroshky.

'You need yoga,' said my mother. 'Not piroshky. All that gluten. Scientists have proved a link between anxiety, depression and gluten.'

'Ah, scientists!' my father started pulling ingredients out of cupboards. 'They know nothing.'

And they were off. Theo and I exchanged glances. 'Give us a job, Papa. We need to make ourselves useful.'

After many protests, my father agreed that the hedge needed trimming. 'Your mother no longer allows me to climb a ladder. She says I am too shaky. Me, shaky!'

'You'd break every bone in your body, given half the chance,' said Elinor. 'Theo is much safer on a ladder.'

Theo stripped down to his shirt and worked deftly to trim the garden hedge, while I raked and bagged up the clippings. The manual work was soothing, and the winter sun warmed my back.

Later, Papa opened the door of the Aga and proudly laid the piroshky, delicious flaky pastries stuffed with cabbage and carrots, on a plate in front of us.

Butter oozed through the pastry and my mouth started watering. My father watched us.

'So,' he said, 'is the very famous barrister Theo Frazer still representing terrorists at the Old Bailey?'

Theo laughed. 'Not terrorists, this time. I've got some Chinese clients at the moment.'

'Bloody anchovies. They should be on their knees with gratitude to be safe in this country.' He pummelled his chest. 'This country gave me shelter and asked for nothing in return. It is a debt I can never repay.'

'Anarchists, Papa, anarchists, not anchovies,' I said, after I had worked out what my father was saying. 'And the Chinese aren't anarchists.' My father's ability to mangle the English language knew no bounds, and I suspected that sometimes he did it on purpose to cheer me up.

He looked at me from under beetling brows. 'Anchovies, anarchists, pah! They are all bloody communists, aren't they?'

'Papa, did you know a woman called Lydia Kuznetsov in Moscow?' My parents exchanged glances.

'No, I don't think so,' said my mother, too quickly.

'Kuznetsov? Kuznetsov? That's like saying "did you ever meet someone called Smith in England?" I met lots of Kuznetsovs. Kuznetsovs everywhere in Russia. And Lydias, too!' He glared at us all. 'It is like saying have you met an Anne Smith?'

'Although, oddly enough,' said my mother, 'I don't think we ever have met an Anne Smith. You'd think that if Anne or Smith were considered to be common English names, you would know lots of Anne Smiths. But we don't know a single one!'

'She's called Lydia Brennan now. She married an American tech billionaire,' said Theo. 'But she was in Moscow around the same time you were, and she's a very cultured woman, a real lover of the arts.'

106

My father stared at his plate, and began to attack his piroshky.

'I like the name, Anne,' Elinor added. 'I rather wish we'd called you Anne instead of Sophie.'

'So you don't know a Lydia Kuznetsov?' I persevered, as my mother was never as daft as she made herself out to be.

'How's your job, darling?' asked Elinor. 'You haven't said anything about your work. I want to hear everything. I do hope you aren't defending anyone dangerous.'

'Well, in fact, I'm defending a young man called Henry Hanbury, which is how we've got to know Lydia, and she asked if I was related to the famous musical Andreyushkins.'

My mother turned to Theo with a sigh, laying a hand on his arm. 'Oh, the Andreyushkin boys. They were so handsome. Oh, I was so excited when I saw Vassily in that restaurant in South Kensington. I recognised him immediately. Our eyes met, and…' She raised both hands. 'That was how we met. Strangers across a crowded room.'

I exchanged glances with Theo. He leaned back and allowed my mother to reminisce, although we had both heard the story hundreds of times.

'There we were. I was with a friend, and there were these handsome Russian musicians. That was very exotic in those days. Oh, dangerous and exciting. A Russian lover! A communist. I knew my parents would be outraged.' Elinor stretched a hand out, and laid it on my father's arm. 'Vassily had just finished a triumphant tour of Britain, and they'd just done the last concert at the Royal Albert Hall. It was early spring in 1985, and Gorbachov was in power in Russia.'

Papa placed his gnarled hand on my mother's. 'We didn't know how we would stay together after the tour ended.' He sighed, deeply. 'You cannot understand how things were then.'

'He couldn't defect, you see,' said my mother. 'It would

have ruined Kiril's career.' My father sighed and got up to clear the plates.

My mother continued brightly, enjoying Theo's attention. 'We were so frightened of the secret police. They would harass foreigners and bug our homes. I remember once they broke into our flat, and made sure we'd know they'd been there. The window was open. Everything in the larder had been thrown to the floor… and when I looked out, there was a young man wearing a leather jacket in the street making no effort to hide the fact he was watching our floor.'

She fiddled nervously with the rings on her fingers. 'The secret police accompanied us on our tours, always watching. They would try to mingle at the receptions people gave for the orchestra. Ha! They looked so uncomfortable in their borrowed dinner jackets.'

'Elinor, you talk too much,' said my father. 'These young people don't need to hear stories about the old days.'

'I'm interested,' I said. All my life I had had to piece together the past from my parents' reminiscences, usually my mother's. She told the same stories over and over again, but sometimes a new detail slipped in. I never knew, however, whether it was a real memory or whether my mother had invented it.

My father slammed down a plate.

'I thought it was exciting,' said Elinor. 'Even in that tiny little flat we had, on the third floor, overlooking Tverskaya Ulitsa, it seemed as if the sun shone every day. We were happy, weren't we, darling? In spite of the secret police. And that funny little fellow who used to inform on everyone, what was he called…?'

She turned to Theo. 'We were so short of things, even though Vassily was well paid. So if someone managed to buy a bottle of vodka, everyone would drink it, then we'd all start dancing, either in our flat or in Kiril's, which was next door. It wasn't like here, where everyone plans their parties months in advance. All our friends were musical. And at weekends, we took a train into the countryside, where Vassily's parents lived on the edge of the woods.'

I had a sudden memory, of running across the soft floor of the woods, and the bright shafts of sunlight. I could almost hear Kiril's voice: 'I'm coming to get you…'

'We used to play hide and seek in the woods with Uncle Kiril, didn't we?' I said.

My mother looked blank. 'I don't remember that. I didn't realise… well, never mind.' She got up and began getting her yoga bag together. 'Actually, now that I think about it, we did know a Lydia, Vassily, didn't we? Wasn't she that very pretty girl we hoped would marry Kiril? Well, until we realised he wasn't the marrying type.'

'She was not called Kuznetsov.'

'That was only her first husband's name. She would have been called something else then.'

'If we don't know her name, how would we know her?' My father put the plates down and walked out into the garden.

I hurried out into the garden to find him standing in his beloved vegetable patch, sobbing. I put my arms round him. 'Papa, it's all right. It's all over now. Nobody is watching us anymore. Nobody is judging us.'

'It was our fault,' said her father. 'They were so suspicious of us because I married an Englishwoman. If…'

'What was your fault?' I saw the birch woods again around my Russian grandparents' dacha, where I had played as a child, and the memories slanted against the sunlight. There was one memory there, a bad one I didn't understand. Kiril was thirty when he died. That had seemed very old to me when I was a child. Uncles died when they were old. But now I suddenly realised that I was now four years older than Kiril had ever been.

My father blew his nose, and took my hand in his. 'All that matters to me, my little Sova, is that you are happy with your Theo. Because one day,' he patted his chest, 'this old ticker, as you say, will stop.'

'Don't say that, Papa.'

'I must say these things, my darling. I must.' He patted my hand. 'So tell me, all is well?'

'All's well, Papa. Theo… he's wonderful. I know I can always rely on him. We are very happy.'

I squeezed his hand, and let it go. I hoped he wasn't going to mention children. 'Good. That is good. At least I know my little Sova is safe.' He began to walk back to the house, blowing his nose on a handkerchief he extracted from the depths of a baggy trouser pocket.

I followed him.

'Why is this Lydia in touch with you?' he asked, stopping with his hand on the door. 'What does she want?'

I hugged myself to keep warm. A cloud slid over the sun, shutting off the warmth. The edge of a bitter wind nipped at my nose and hands. 'I don't know what she wants. I think she is a good woman. At least, she seems good to her friends.'

'And are you her friend?'

'That's what I don't know.'

'Then don't trust her,' said my father. 'Whoever she is, she's come back to us from a bad time.'

'We need to get going,' said Theo, opening the door before my father could turn the handle. 'We should try to get back before the traffic builds up. I've got a case to prepare.'

Later, in the car, he said he thought my parents weren't managing in the house.

'It really is time to get them into sheltered accommodation

before it's too late. And I think your mother might be showing the early signs of dementia.'

'I thought she was being evasive, rather than vague.'

Theo didn't reply and turned the radio on to get the latest match results.

CHAPTER 14

'The police have interviewed Hanbury again.' It was Philip Meadowes calling.

'Do we think there's anything in it?' I asked, walking briskly towards the door of Harrow Crown Court while taking the call. The front steps were littered with cigarette ends, and a man paced up and down outside, smoking.

'It's an allegation from someone called Shelley Bartlett. She says Henry raped her when she was fifteen. She says she remembered it clearly because it happened on the first of July, which was a month before her sixteenth birthday.'

'How credible is she?'

Philip's voice was measured and calm. It always was. 'She obviously saw the news on Twitter or in the papers. She was at a day school in Birmingham at the time. Henry was seventeen and in his last term at a school in Guildford. It's difficult to see how they could have met. Shelley said that he made friends with her on Facebook and she was really impressed by him. So he borrowed his father's car and drove up to Birmingham, took her to a local park, and raped her.'

'Do the police have the Facebook records?'

'Yes,' said Philip. 'She wasn't even on Facebook in 2010. There's no other sign they were ever friends. She can't keep a job for more than a couple of weeks. She blames Henry Hanbury for the way her life has turned out. She says she doesn't trust anyone anymore.'

I sighed. 'Have the police dropped the charges?'

'No, but this doesn't feel like a real complaint.

It worried me. 'Do you think the police will just keep him hanging on this one? I've had clients who've spent years reporting on bail every month after being arrested, but never being charged.'

'Me, too. We need to deal with this one as quickly as possible,' admitted Philip.

'They took his laptop away, didn't they? And his mobile phone? Have you heard whether they've found anything on them?'

'I haven't heard anything at all.' Philip rang off, promising to let me know.

I ignored the lift and ran up the wide staircase, pushing my way through the swing doors to the robing room. I sat down at a desk to scroll through that day's listings until I found my case.

I was slightly startled to see that Polly Chan was my opponent. I paused for a moment, my fingers hovering over the keyboard. I had never seen Polly 'on her feet' conducting a trial. It would be interesting to know if she lived up to the hype surrounding her.

I heard the tinny noise of the tannoy warning all parties to go to Court 4 immediately. Grabbing my wig and laptop, I headed for the stairs. As I drew level with the courtroom I saw Polly standing next to the large swing doors. She was immaculately dressed in a black trouser suit and very high heels. The heavy wings of her dark hair were pulled back by a floppy velvet bow.

'Ah, there you are, Sophie! At last. Judge Maddock is getting quite steamed up!'

'Why?' I looked at my watch. 'It's only 10.15.'

'Didn't you get a message from the clerks? We were supposed to be sitting at ten. You're late.' Polly gave a tight little smile: 'Good luck with Mad Dog.'

I hadn't checked my email before leaving. I should have done. Judge Maddock had been christened 'Mad Dog' because of his ferocious temper. He had been an unfair prosecutor and now he was an unfair judge, constantly throwing his weight against the defence, puncturing carefully planned cross-examination and summing up for a conviction. Universally loathed by the Defence Bar, he was coming up for retirement in a few months and would not care much if his rulings were overturned on appeal. I swore under my breath. I had already irritated him and I hadn't set foot in court yet.

My client was a Croatian mother called Bodmira. She shared custody of her two children with her ex-husband Josef. He had accused Bodmira of attacking their ten-year-old son, breaking his front tooth and then waving a knife at both children threatening to kill them. The main prosecution witness was their fourteen-year-old daughter who had witnessed the whole episode. Social services had become involved and the children had been taken away from Bodmira. She was now only allowed supervised access.

Bodmira had told me in conference that the allegations were ridiculous. She adored both her children and found the separation agonising. Josef's solicitor had taken out a non-molestation order that prevented her going within a hundred yards of Josef's house. She had not contacted the children but had dropped a card through her husband's door on her daughter's birthday. Bodmira had recently been shocked to be told by a neighbour that her husband was involved with a Croatian woman and that he planned to marry her and take the children to live with them back in his old home in Croatia.

Josef came across as an aggressive bully. The prosecution case collapsed completely when their daughter broke down under cross-examination and, through her sobs, admitted that her father had forced her to lie on his behalf. Her little brother had broken his tooth trying to climb a wall and her mother had never hurt or threatened them. The jury took less than an hour to return with an unanimous acquittal.

I rose to my feet. 'Your Honour, may the defendant be discharged?'

Polly stood up swiftly. 'Your Honour, I have an application to make before your Honour discharges the defendant. I am instructed to ask for a restraining order against the defendant. Even though she has been acquitted of the more serious charge, she did breach the non-molestation order by dropping off a card for her daughter, thereby going within a hundred yards of the matrimonial home.'

I could hardly believe Polly's lack of judgement. We both knew that Josef had lied. The judge twinkled down at Polly and made the order, disregarding my objections, then he swept from the courtroom. Bodmira was bewildered. 'I don't understand,' she said. 'They proved it was all lies. Why cannot I see my children?'

'Because of the birthday card,' I said. 'You shouldn't have pushed a birthday card through the letterbox when you weren't allowed to go near the house. I will appeal, and it will be overturned, I promise you. But you can't see your children until I do.'

'I no understand. Where is this British justice we hear about?' Bodmira shook her head and stumbled towards the door.

Polly was checking herself in the mirror when I got back to the robing room.

'God, these wigs aren't exactly flattering, are they?' She pursed her lips, and reapplied some lipstick. 'Well done, Sophie, for getting her off.'

'I didn't get her off. She quite clearly didn't do it.' I stood behind Polly. 'She was an innocent woman who loves her children and they obviously love her. She hasn't seen them alone for five months, which is a long time in the life of a ten-year-old and a fourteen-year-old, and who knows what damage this latest order is doing to them?'

'It's a pretty dysfunctional family anyway.' Polly shrugged. She applied another dark red slash of lipstick, pressing her lips together. She stowed the lipstick in her handbag and packed the wig away in its tin. She zipped up her pull-along case and began to head out of the door. Talking to her was like swimming in a very choppy sea – every time you tried to draw breath, you found yourself choking.

I moved ahead of her and stood in front of the door. 'What were you doing, Polly? That poor woman has already suffered so much. Your witness was a lying bastard who has tried to ruin her life.'

Polly put a hand on the door knob, although she had to step sideways to do it.

'Don't get so wound up, Sophie. You can get the order overturned in a couple of weeks. You know how hard it is to get briefs from the CPS. I can't go back completely empty handed. I bet five years ago you would have done the same. Not all of us are married to QCs who make sure work gets directed our way.' She turned the door handle and pushed past me, turning round with a smile. 'There are boxes to be ticked if you want to be instructed again.'

'No, Polly, it's not about ticking boxes. It's about justice, not a conviction at any cost.'

Polly laughed. 'I don't suppose Theo thinks that, does he? You can afford your principles because you've got a successful QC behind you. Those of us who have to make our own way in life have to be a bit more realistic.' As she left, she passed a barrister called Sadiq Patel, who always cheered a robing room up with a joke.

'You look as if you've been mugged by the delicious Polly.' He closed the robing room door behind him.

I shook my head. 'I just don't believe it. I can't understand how anyone can be so...'

'Ruthless?' suggested Sadiq. 'One wonders why people take an instant dislike to her?' He raised an eyebrow at me. 'It's because it saves time in the long run.'

I laughed. 'I'm glad it's not just me.'

'Normally, I'd say she wasn't getting enough, but I gather she's getting rather too much. Have you heard? She's having an affair with someone in her chambers.'

For a moment, my heart stopped.

'Some upper class twat, apparently. Gus somebody or other?' Sadiq began robing.

'Gus Gladwyn? He's not a twat. He's actually very sweet, and an excellent barrister. But I didn't think he even liked her.'

'Sorry, Sophie, I didn't know he was a friend of yours.' Sadiq touched my shoulder in apology. 'I gather the lovely Polly fancies being part of the British aristocracy, and Gladwyn's part of all that, isn't he?'

Polly would eat Gus alive. He had no confidence with women, and if Polly had decided to make a play for him, Gus had about as much chance of escape as a tethered goat had of evading a tiger. But Gus was my friend. He and I had shared a room in chambers ever since we were both taken on as tenants. I wanted him to marry someone who loved him, not a social climber on the way up.

When I arrived at the newspaper offices that evening, there was a huddle around the bench, with Chris in the centre. He nodded at me as I hung my jacket over my chair.

'Blondie, can you join us in this?'

I swung my chair round, and the group parted to let me in.

117

I nodded at David, our news editor, and Katie, who was pacing restlessly up and down as Chris frowned at the screen.

'We've got quite a lot of material,' said Chris, 'but no real proof.'

'We've got info on a ring of bent solicitors linked to people trafficking,' said Katie. 'Pregnant women are trafficked, or women who are trafficked get pregnant, and no father is registered. Then when the woman is sold on, the man who buys her registers himself as the father of the child, thus gaining legal control of that child until he or she is eighteen. It really is slavery.'

I thought of the child I might have one day, and imagined it born into a world where she or he was only a commodity to be bought and sold. 'So what have you got?'

'Mainly the usual suspects,' said Katie. 'We're getting tips that many of the big organised crime groups are getting into this. They need bent solicitors to create the identities and show them loopholes. Our strongest lead is a group of Chinese businesses linked to several firms of solicitors in the Midlands.'

I decided not to mention that Theo had just started taking work from a Chinese solicitor in Birmingham. There would be hundreds of Chinese solicitors in the area and most of them would be straight, I told myself. There's a percentage of bent ones in every community. I reassured myself that Theo was careful enough not to get involved, even accidentally.

Katie emailed the story to my screen, and I read it carefully. It sickened me. I swung my chair round to Chris and the group after reading it. 'I'm sorry, there's nothing you can use. It's all libellous in the extreme, and there's not enough proof.'

They went back to discussing how to take the story forward, on the limited budget that newspapers had for investigation these days, and the risk of libelling a company or group rather than an individual.

These babies, born into slavery in a world where people thought it had been abolished, suddenly felt like my own. I couldn't see them, hear them or feel them, but I knew that their little hands would look like starfish and that they were crying, alone in empty rooms, waiting for someone to save them. I wanted one in my arms and to keep her safe forever.

CHAPTER 15

My diary remained empty for the week of Lydia's lunch. By midday on Tuesday, I had nothing to do, so I texted Theo that I was going home, and gathered up my things. The phone rang. It was Lee. 'Can you babysit a jury for Mr Gladwyn, Miss? He's got to start a case at Croydon.' That meant I had to be in the building while the jury were out, for which I would be comparatively well paid. It was one of the better last-minute jobs to get.

I hurried into the Great Hall at The Old Bailey, feeling its oppressive hush settle around me. The green and white marble walls contrasted with the black and white geometry of the floor in a display of Victorian opulence. Above me I could see aphorisms painted on the vaulted ceiling. 'The Law of the Wise is a Fountain of Life,' read one. 'Poise the Cause in Justice's Equal Scales,' exhorted another. I had always wondered exactly what that meant. To my right stood a statue of Elizabeth Fry, gazing sightlessly at the never-ending procession of lawyers, defendants and victims, who had passed this way over the centuries – each and every one with a story to tell.

As I rounded the corner, I saw two barristers standing close together, and realised that one of them was Theo. I stopped. He was talking to a dark-haired woman, who was standing very close to him, looking up at him. I'd seen that adoring body language from young female barristers before, but Theo always laughed when I suggested he was being idolised. The woman picked something off his shoulder, brushing him down in a proprietary way before turning and walking towards me. It was Polly.

I stepped back into the shadows and she walked past without seeing me. I hurried after Theo. He turned in surprise. 'I thought you'd gone home.'

'I'm babysitting a jury for Gus.' I studied his face to see if I could spot signs of guilt, but he seemed unconcerned.

'Good, good.' He checked his watch.

'Was that Polly Chan you were talking to?'

'Yes, didn't you say hello? She must have walked right past you.'

'I… didn't have time.' I looked at his coat. 'Did she manage to pick all the fluff off your coat or shall I have a go?'

Theo threw his head back and laughed. 'You saw that, did you? She stands too close, invades your space and before you know where you are, she's adjusting your tie. Or worse, if you're not bloody careful. Now, you have a jury to babysit and I have a case to defend.' He kissed the tip of my nose. 'See you tonight, and stop worrying about women picking things off my coat.'

I got into court just in time to appear before Judge Connelly, who swept in two minutes later. He settled himself, fussing with the arrangement of his pens and dwarfed by the vaulted cathedral ceiling of the courtroom. The clerk of the court sat at a desk in the middle, flanked by an usher. They whispered to each other and the great empty spaces above their heads swallowed their murmurings. The imposing height of Judge Connelly's dais elevated him to an almost godlike level. Even the benches where the barristers sat and the dark wood panelling of the jury benches seemed to have been designed to intimidate. There was a hushed reverence about everyone in the courtroom. It made my concern over Theo and Polly seem very small and trivial. Theo hadn't expected to see me there, but he didn't seem worried about it or guilty either.

I hoped that the fee I had earned this afternoon wasn't going to be my only income this week. I thought of asking Chris for some more evenings of night lawyer work, but it was a risk. If I had a case out of town or a late conference with clients, I might not get to the paper in time for the evening shift. Theo was spending more time on Wei Chan's work, but we weren't paid for paperwork and nothing had actually come to court yet, so no money was coming in. And even then we had no idea when the fees would actually be paid. Not all solicitors paid their barristers' fees punctually. Legal aid fees took a while to come in, too, often after considerable wrangling.

As I left the court, Philip phoned. 'Adam Harris has been in touch.'

My stomach did a small flip. 'What! But he hated both of us. He said I was useless, and he pretty much admitted he was guilty.'

'I know, but he appears to have changed his mind. He particularly wants you.'

'I don't want to take it, Philip,' I blurted out. 'I know we're not supposed to turn away briefs, but we are not allowed to represent people we *know* are guilty as if they were innocent either. He nearly murdered that poor girl.'

'Well, we don't know for sure.' Philip sounded uncertain. He was a decent man. I felt sorry for him. He probably didn't like Adam Harris any more than I did.

'He told me to think up a defence for him. You know I can't do that. I'm really sorry, Philip, I can only represent him if he's prepared to plead guilty.'

'I know you've been under quite a lot of strain recently.' Philip sounded sympathetic. 'Look. I'll see what I can do.'

'Remind me, when is Harris listed for?' I asked.

'It's a fixture for the first week next month.'

I thought for a minute, 'Well, I can't do it anyway. I've got a case in the warned list at Snaresbrook that week. By the way, do the clerks know he has come back to us?'

'Er, possibly. Someone from my office might have contacted them after I left this morning.'

I braced myself for a battle. The clerks wouldn't want me to turn down the defence of Adam Harris because it was a case that would get chambers publicity. 'Even so, I can't do it unless he pleads guilty. I'm sorry, Philip,' I said again.

'Whatever you think best, Sophie.' Philip started to say something else and then seemed to change his mind. 'You know I'll always support you.' I wondered what he meant by that.

Almost as soon as Philip rang off, Lee called, with the news that Adam Harris wanted me to represent him.

'Changed his mind, Miss. 'Spect he fancies you.' Lee chortled.

My heart chilled at the memory of his flat stare. It was all very well for me to tell people at parties that all evidence has to be challenged in order to make sure it's safe and true. That justice can only happen if everyone has a reliable defence.

'You've got a three day warned list in that week,' said Lee. 'But I can give that to someone else, no problem.'

'I don't want you to,' I said.

'Well, it would be taking a risk to try to do both.'

'No, I don't want the Harris case, I want you to say that I am already booked.'

The explosion that vibrated through the phone would have been comic if I had not been so nervous. 'You don't want it! What the fuck...? It'll be all over the press, a better brief fee than you usually get, lots of forensics, huge page count. What do you mean you don't want it?'

'I can't do it, Harris admitted to me that he was guilty. I would be professionally embarrassed.'

'Maybe you misheard it, Miss. Mr Meadows said nothing about any of that. Anyway, if all my guvnors thought like that we'd all be out of a job. You can't afford to have that kind of a conscience, not in the work you do.'

'He threatened me. He's mad and dangerous.'

Theo stopped making coffee and was listening to our exchange.

'This is the Criminal Bar, Miss. Welcome to the real world. Just about all your clients are going to be one or the other!'

'Look, we've both read the Bar Handbook, I'm entitled to turn it down.' I would not be bullied into breaching the guidelines on ethical practice.

Lee sighed. 'All right, I'll try to keep it in chambers. Philip Meadowes won't be pleased though. No guarantee your other case will come into the list that week, either, so you may find yourself out of court altogether.' The phone went silent. I had been dismissed. Lee's threat had been veiled but clear: you don't get to pick and choose your cases.

That evening Theo agreed with me completely. 'It's obviously far too much for you,' said Theo, scrolling through evidence on my laptop. 'The man is clearly a psychopath, and guilty as hell.'

'It's not that I'm frightened,' I told him, determined to convince myself as much as Theo, 'although he's a really nasty piece of work. But you know that we're not in the job of inventing defences.'

CHAPTER 16

The clerks didn't have anything else for me for the next two days, which at least meant I could go to Lydia's lunch. Katie was waiting for the lift when I arrived at the newspaper offices. 'What are you doing here in the middle of the day?'

'I wish I knew. Some lunch that Lydia Brennan is hosting.'

Katie's eyes sharpened. 'People think that Robert Brennan bought the paper for her, that she's got some bee in her bonnet and wants a newspaper rather than a wardrobe full of designer handbags.'

Another man joined us as the lift arrived, disgorging several stressed-looking people. 'Katie,' he nodded to her.

'Tim.'

'I hope you know the rumours aren't true,' Tim said, as she pressed the button for the fourteenth floor. 'Graham wasn't made redundant because of any impropriety. Everything's completely above board.'

Katie smiled. 'Not what I heard, but I take your point.' When the lift stopped on the fourteenth floor, Tim scurried off. Katie stepped out of the lift, scrolling down her phone. 'Bound to be on Twitter whatever it was.' She grinned. 'I hadn't heard any rumours. I must be slipping.'

I put an arm out to stop the doors closing. 'More redundancies?'

'Always,' said Katie. 'Five were banged out of the news desk yesterday, to be replaced by three trainees who will rewrite stories they find on social media.'

I sighed as the doors closed on her. 'Banging out' was an old Fleet Street newsroom tradition. When someone from the news desk left, the remainder banged their desks until the leaver reached the door. It started when printers banged their desks with their hammers to serenade retiring employees or when apprentices graduated. Now it was a drumroll of doom, marking repeated rounds of redundancies. Five lots of banging out must have made for a grim afternoon.

The executive floor was above the editorial department on the fifteenth floor. I had rarely needed to go up there. Instead of the vast open-plan hub, it was a warren of offices. Lydia's secretary led me round a confusing maze of corridors and into a dining room, which had one vast wall of glass, through which could be seen the miniature city spread out far below with tiny houses and streets. I could see the birds circling between us and the view. The table was laid for ten, and there was a bottle of white wine and one of red on the sideboard.

Lydia greeted me with a kiss on both cheeks. 'I'm so delighted you could make it. You have told those clerks that you are in charge of your diary, I hope.'

'I wouldn't dare!' I laughed, imagining Lee's face if I did any such thing.

'Sophie Angel is a very famous up-and-coming barrister, and one of our most valued night lawyers.' Lydia introduced me to a thickset man with a ruddy face. 'James Black of James Black Ltd, the leading firm of accountants for charities.'

I wondered if James Black's introduction was as exaggerated as mine, but we shook hands. Lydia continued to introduce me to people whose names I barely caught – a recently retired and knighted senior diplomat, a taut, tired-looking woman with dark hair called Marina Sokolova whom Lydia described as 'one of Russia's most respected dissident journalists' and, from the paper, 'Our top columnist, Jess Edwards – you know "The Voice of a Common-sense Mother".'

I had always considered Jess Edwards' writing one of the most irritating columns in the paper, but as she was on a freelance contract, I had never had to meet her before. Her opinions veered wildly from one end of the political spectrum to the other with no logical underlying thread to them. The day lawyers usually handled her columns, but on the rare occasion that her work had coincided with one of my shifts, I had discovered the very few facts she bothered to include were incorrect. When I marked them as libellous, she asked Chris to sack me because I was, successively on different occasions, a 'Tory apologist', 'ridiculously biased towards the left' and then 'absurdly politically correct'. I didn't think she remembered any of the encounters, but only offered me the tips of three limp fingers to shake, before kissing everyone else in the room.

The waiters set tiny, exquisite salads in front of us, and we all, with the exception of Jess, refused the wine they offered. Lydia called us to attention. 'I've invited you here today because each of you is highly influential in your own field. And because I think you all believe in justice.'

'Except the lawyers, of course. We all know you're only interested in money,' quipped Jess. 'Otherwise, why would you defend someone when you know they're guilty?' She took a swig of her wine. Her face was flushed.

I should have ignored her, but I couldn't resist it. I got so sick of this particular thoughtless criticism of what I did. 'If someone actually tells me they're guilty but still expects me to say they're innocent, I am ethically obliged to withdraw.' My voice bounced against the plate glass window, a tiny noise against the vastness of the city beyond. I should just smile and change the subject when this old chestnut came up, but I felt it was worth challenging carelessly-held views.

'But defending guilty people is all such a waste of public money.' Jess slugged back another mouthful of wine.

I leaned forward, wanting to get my points across. 'I think I should add that legal aid for work in crime has been slashed to the bone by successive governments to the extent that junior barristers are paid so little that at times we are actually paying the government to be allowed to work for them.'

Jess cut across me. 'Not that old song again. No one cares, Sophie! All barristers are perceived as fat cats. You won't get any sympathy from my readers just because you have to trade your Audi down to a Ford Focus.'

I turned on her. 'That's bollocks! Perhaps you'd like me to explain.' I took a deep breath and consciously dropped my voice. 'A young criminal barrister coming to the Bar would probably already be saddled with over £75,000 of debt and would be working sixty hour weeks for around £5 an hour. Who will want to come into criminal law? The public needs good lawyers – we all do – or the system doesn't work.'

'No one gives a toss. That's not going to sell newspapers.' Jess flicked her eyes at her phone, as if surreptitiously checking her messages. She looked straight at me again. 'And it doesn't justify you defending a rapist or a murderer.'

'It's not up to me, or to you, or even to the police, to decide who's innocent and who's guilty.' I ploughed on. 'It's for the jury to decide after a fair trial. Police and prosecutors make just as many mistakes as people in any other profession.'

'This goes to the heart of why we are meeting,' said Lydia. 'I...' She corrected herself. 'The principle is that everyone who lives under a democracy is entitled to a fair trial. And I believe that right is under threat and is gradually being eroded.' She paused and looked down at her hands for a moment. 'I think I am perhaps better equipped than others around this table to recognise what is happening because I come from a country where jury trial was abolished altogether under Soviet rule and even today is rarely used. In the end it is juries that stand between the citizen and a tyrannical state. In Russia, once a case gets to court, the conviction rate is close to a hundred per cent.'

I thought of my father. Was that why he had left? I had always assumed, as most people did, that escaping to the West was the obvious thing to do if you found the opportunity. I had never heard anyone actually ask him why he had done it, and it had never occurred to me to ask him. But now I was old enough to understand that he had loved his country and been famous and respected. He had even been relatively privileged. I felt a prickle of unease. Looking at Lydia, barely a decade younger than my parents, and also a Russian, I had a sudden sense of my parents as people rather than as part of the comforting blanket of home – people who, in some ways, I barely knew.

Lydia had paused, looking around the table at each of us in turn before continuing. 'Without a jury, it is hard to challenge what the police say. If you're accused of a crime, you have to prove you haven't committed it to just one man, one judge, who is employed by the state.' Lydia's neck was flushed. 'How much easier it is to bribe, to corrupt, to threaten just one person rather than twelve.'

Everyone looked at me, and I wondered why Lydia was so personally upset about this. 'And our criminal justice system is falling apart,' I said. 'The police are under-resourced so they make mistakes. The Crown Prosecution Service is under-resourced, so they are more likely to make mistakes. The Defence Bar is under-resourced, so they're often doing two people's work at once.'

Jess looked at me over her wine glass. 'I still don't think my readers really care about legal resources.'

'Well, do they care about the fact that the murder rate is

the highest it's been in ten years, and that prosecutions for serious crime are down twenty per cent? There's never been a worse time to be a victim.'

Jess scribbled something in her notebook. 'Ooh, I could use that phrase as a starter for my next column.' She was clearly doing one of her 180 degree turns.

The accountant, James Black, leaned forward, drumming one finger nervously on the table. 'At the moment, innocent people are being tried and found guilty by social media before they even get to court. Personally I think that is the biggest threat to getting a fair trial at the moment. Judges get their decisions abused on Twitter and on Facebook, by people who don't have the faintest idea what the real issues are. It's putting the judiciary under quite intolerable pressure in some cases.'

Lydia re-established a grip on the conversation. 'And that is why I want to set up this charity,' she said. 'I want to use the influence of the paper to stop justice from being eroded until we all wake up one morning as virtual slaves of the state. We will fight individual cases, giving them publicity and raising funding, working with other charities like Journalists Without Borders and Amnesty International.' She looked at each one of us in turn.

'We must think about the world our children will grow up in,' said Jess, now switching sides completely. 'I have mothers writing to me about justice all the time. They're very worried about what's going on on social media. Bullying, for example.'

I could see Lydia flashing Jess a brief puzzled look, before carrying on. 'I have a case here, which would make a good beginning. Matvey Orlov is an investigative journalist. He'd been investigating the embezzlement of public funds by a construction company employed on a government project. He received threats by phone telling him to stop but he persisted. In 2016 he was arrested and charged with extremism.

'There was no evidence to substantiate these charges at the time of the arrest, but he was held on remand for two years. His case is due to be heard before a judge and two lay assessors, but no date for trial has yet been set. It won't be a trial by jury because that is still very rare in Russia, so he is very likely to be convicted, no matter what the evidence.'

She let this sink in before going on. 'The allegations against Orlov keep changing. His lawyer has been intimidated into withdrawing, so now Orlov is without any legal representation. And the prosecutor is asking for a prison sentence of five years.'

'But isn't it the sort of thing that goes on in Russia all the time?' asked Jess. 'How can we stop it?'

'We can talk about it,' said Lydia. 'In the press, on social media, when we meet, and also we can talk about what is happening to justice in this country. We need people to start to think about what justice really is, and what it means to them.'

'Exactly,' I said. 'And the reason why all this is so dangerous is that if juries start to mistrust the justice system, they will fail to convict people who should be convicted. And juries, who in my experience are very sensible, do usually throw weak cases out. But that doesn't stop the defendant's life being damaged, sometimes irreparably.' I had seen an increasing number of cases which should never have come to court, while real criminals walked free. I thought of Henry Hanbury. Even when I started at the Bar, ten years ago, I don't think he would have been charged.

A few minutes later, I realised that the conversation at the lunch was carrying on without me, and that Jess had promised her support for the venture. There was a general murmur of agreement around the table, and Lydia was noting down names for specific tasks.

'Have you thought about a name?' asked James. 'It's

important for any cause to have a name, so that people know what they're talking about.'

'Yes,' said Lydia. 'Although, of course, we can all vote on whether we would like it. I would like to call it the Kiril Trust.'

CHAPTER 17

I wasn't sure if the name was significant. Kiril was a common Russian name, and there was no reason why it should have any special connection to me. But I felt as if the ground beneath me had shifted – just fractionally – and found it hard to concentrate for the rest of the meal. When everyone got up to leave, Lydia held on to my hand. 'Can you stay?'

I hesitated.

'I want to talk to you about remuneration. I know it's difficult for young barristers to establish themselves these days, and I wanted to say that you won't need to be doing the Kiril Trust on a pro bono basis.'

I wasn't in a position to refuse.

'Come through to my office,' she said, when the last guest had kissed and smiled their way out of the door. She led me through a door that had been closed throughout lunch. The office behind it wasn't large, but it had a plate glass window and spectacular view of London. On Lydia's desk, there was a matryoshka doll, which reminded me of one I had had as a child. She sat herself down behind the desk and, indicating that I should take the chair in front of it, opened a dossier set out for her.

'Vassily Andreyushkin was one of the Soviet Union's most celebrated concert pianists in the 1980s,' she read. 'And his brother, Kiril, was equally famous as a violinist. Vassily was the hard-working sensible older brother, and Kiril was the younger rebel, coasting on having so much talent. They studied at the

Moscow State Conservatory together.' She closed the dossier, clasped her hands together, and leaned forward towards me. 'I was there, too, you know.' She saw the question in my face, and continued. 'When I married, I no longer had five or six hours a day to practise and, anyway, by then I'd realised I was never going to be the best cellist in the world. So I gave it up.'

Then, speaking with the assurance of one who knows she isn't going to be challenged, she said, 'I hope you'll forgive me – but when I met you, and you told me about your name, and that your father had changed it, I wanted to discover if he had been the Andreyushkin I studied with.'

'There are a lot of Andreyushkins in Russia. What made you think he might be the same one?'

'A pianist who escaped to the West with his English wife and child? There are not so many of those.' She was watching me carefully. 'It was a very great shock to meet you at that party,' she said. 'I was a friend of your uncle Kiril's. And I had been hoping to trace your father and see him again.' She gave a short, humourless laugh. 'I have always thought, maybe, in England, I would bump into him, but England is a very big place. Not so big if you are looking for a Russian, perhaps, because we often know each other.'

'My parents don't seem to have many Russian friends.'

She nodded, as if she already knew that. 'Do you know how many times I've asked someone, when I meet them in London and they have Russian connections, if they know a Vassily Andreyushkin? I even... well, never mind. You are here. It seems extraordinary that we came to be in the same room together, but don't they say 'these things are meant?' She wiggled her fingers to indicate quote marks.

Lydia did not strike me as a woman who believed in that sort of thing. 'Why did you want to see him?'

'Oh, we were old friends. You all left very suddenly.' She

stretched out a hand to me across the desk. 'Now, tell me how your papa and mama are. I remember them well. And I remember you, when you were a little girl. You were too young to remember me, I think?'

Looking into Lydia's hard, blue eyes, I had a memory of a woman with blue eyes, holding my hands, just like this, and whispering. And I thought of the young woman running through the underpass, laughing with Kiril. 'Yes, I think I do remember you. But not... very well.'

And why had my parents been so vague when I asked them if they knew a Lydia? I was about to say that I could give her their number, but I realised that I had stepped back into a world where you couldn't trust anybody. A world where you didn't give away information because it could be dangerous. Certainly my parents hadn't seemed keen to reconnect with anyone called Lydia. Perhaps Lydia remembered them better than they remembered her. Or perhaps they didn't want to be found, for some reason.

She filled in the silence. 'I tried to contact them. I asked musicians who travelled to the West to look out for them. Of course, I didn't know about the name change. You should think about that, and ask yourself why they did that.'

My childhood story, the one about my not being able to pronounce Andreyushkin, seemed thin and unlikely.

'You know your father was part of the elite,' Lydia said, 'as was I. We were trusted, in so far as anyone was ever trusted.'

'And what about my uncle Kiril?' I couldn't help my curiosity. My father spoke so little about that time. He told me fairy stories and memories of Moscow, the midnight sun in St Petersburg, the concerts by the lakes – but the faces and names were blurred and indistinct.

'Kiril was always a little different. I'm not sure the authorities ever really trusted him. He and your father were

135

so very competitive when they were younger, but they adored each other. At least, I thought they did.'

'They did.' I tried to imagine my father as a young man, and to remember the shadowy face of Kiril.

'We often toured together,' she added. 'Your father and I, or Kiril and I. We were trusted that much – but Kiril and Vassily were never allowed out of the country at the same time. And when we were away, we always had a member of the secret police with us, night and day. When anyone left the country, the authorities always insisted that a close family member stay behind so that you'd fear what might happen to them if you defected. The ballet dancer, Rudolph Nureyev, had defected just a few years earlier. They were afraid we would go too. Kiril wanted to. But Vassily...'

'What are you saying?' I could sense the blame now, the accusation.

She searched my face for some recognition of what she was talking about. It was ridiculous to feel afraid in an office in the middle of a city. But I could feel a pulse beating at the base of my neck. A sick, cold sensation churned the food I had eaten. 'I need to know,' said Lydia. 'I need to know what happened to your uncle Kiril.'

I was bewildered. 'But that's public knowledge. He died when he was very young. He drowned in the Moscow River when he was drunk. It was a tragedy. My father has never forgotten it. He still cries on Kiril's birthday.'

'Kiril did not drink. I do not believe this story. It was put about by the authorities as a cover-up.'

I was beginning to wonder if Lydia was a conspiracy theorist, seeing malicious state intervention everywhere, but she saw the doubt in my eyes and leaned forward over her desk. 'Have you ever even asked yourself how your father got away while Kiril died?' She picked up the matryoshka doll, briefly running her fingers over its bright peasant patterns, and pulled it apart to reveal the doll beneath.

I had left my matryoshka doll in my bedroom in Moscow. We had left everything. My mother and I had walked, hand-in-hand, with just a handbag and a school satchel, to the nearest underground station and then to the British embassy on a cold, dark morning, our hurried steps slipping in the snow.

'Let me tell you what we musicians believed,' said Lydia. 'Your father betrayed his brother. To the police. He told them that Kiril was involved in anti-government activities. That was the price he paid to be allowed to leave.'

'Papa would never do that. And if we were allowed to leave, then why did we have to go so suddenly?' I pointed to the doll. 'I had to leave my toys behind.'

'Hurry or no hurry,' Lydia dismissed my theory, 'Kiril was easy to betray. He was gay, and that was illegal until 1993. Even now many Russians don't like gay men, and your father was a typical Russian man, in that respect at least.'

I opened my mouth to say that, of course, Papa was not prejudiced. But it wasn't quite true. He never liked to talk about Kiril. And when my mother's earnest gatherings included gay men, he often withdrew to another room. My mother alternately teased him and reproached him. He always denied he had any views and pointed to something urgent he had to do. But I don't think my mother was fully convinced.

'My father doesn't talk about homosexuality much,' I admitted. 'But whenever he has said anything, he has simply said that everyone has a right to a private life and that we shouldn't judge. That doesn't sound very homophobic to me.'

'Perhaps he's changed since he tried to persuade Kiril he was wrong and should change. I was there. They shouted at each other. I thought your father was going to hit Kiril.'

'My father would never hit anyone. He believes all physical violence is wrong.'

Lydia shook her head, with a little laugh. 'Ah yes, maybe now, after thirty years in a peaceful, safe country. But he grew up in a place and time where it was considered acceptable to rape and murder someone for their sexual orientation. It was also acceptable to denounce your own family or friends. You would be rewarded. One day, Kiril disappeared. He was found in the Moscow river, like so many drunks. But he never drank. They said he was battered on the rocks. He was probably beaten. Badly. By the police. Then you and your mother were gone, Kiril was dead and your father went on tour, and never came back.' Lydia took the next doll out and revealed the doll inside that. 'What am I supposed to think? It was dangerous for me too, you know, because I knew them so well. Luckily, I had some influential friends.'

'You're wrong,' I said. 'Family is the most important thing to my father. He would never have betrayed Kiril, no matter what. Anyway, if that were true, he could have defected any time he went abroad, even if Kiril was still in Moscow.'

Lydia hesitated. 'Yes... I too have thought that. But there isn't another explanation that makes sense. Someone betrayed Kiril, someone from his own family, that is what everyone said.'

I had a flash of memory. Or was it a fragment of a dream? And I could smell lilies, but there weren't any flowers in the room. Perhaps it was Lydia's scent. I thought about the shadows in my father's face. He felt guilty about Kiril.

That much I did know. But maybe that was just because if he had listened to Kiril from the start, then they would both be alive now and have found some way of defecting together.

'Your father believed in communism, that the West was decadent, and the communist way was fairer,' said Lydia, taking the third doll out and placing it beside the second.

'He doesn't anymore.'

She shrugged. 'It took him too long to see things Kiril's way.' She tapped the matryoshka doll, still with one tiny doll inside. 'So you really don't know any more than I do?'

'I know that Papa would never have betrayed his own brother. He always tries to do what's right. He didn't just lose his country and his family, but he lost all his idealism about everything he'd believed in since he was a child. All he was left with was a passionate sense that governments shouldn't be allowed to trample over freedom and justice. You have to be able to ask questions and get answers.'

'And that's why you're a barrister?' She patted my hand. 'For your father.'

'No, I did it for me...' But it was true. He had wanted me to become a lawyer. My parents wanted me to have a career I could use anywhere. In case we had to run again. I used to hear them talking. 'Everyone always needs a lawyer,' my mother would say, 'even if she has to retrain in a different country.' And my father would murmur agreement. 'Or a doctor?'

'Sciences?' my mother replied. 'Not her strong point.'

'I did it for me,' I said. 'I want to make things better.'

Lydia smiled. 'Perhaps so. And what does your charming clever husband say about that?'

'I don't know, I haven't asked him. Why?'

She took the final little doll out and placed it on the desk. 'Just curious. It's not easy being the wife of an alpha male, I know that myself.'

I was surprised. How did Lydia know anything about Theo? 'Well, he may be an alpha male sometimes but he's not difficult.'

Lydia's hand tightened on the doll. 'Oh. I'm sorry. I assumed...' Lydia's phone rang and she picked it up. '*Da?*' I heard her tell someone in Russian that she would call them back immediately. She looked flustered for a moment. 'With your work, you must come across some treacherous people?'

The words sounded awkward as if Lydia was stumbling over her English, not quite able to say what she really meant. But people often asked me if I was afraid of my violent clients. 'There's the odd threat, but I mainly do defence work, so if anyone's at risk it's more likely to be the prosecuting barrister.' I wondered where she was going with this.

'But you take precautions about your safety, yes? I feel, somehow,' she placed a hand on her heart and spoke haltingly, 'that you are… in jeopardy.'

'Jeopardy?' I was puzzled.

'I'm sorry. I apologise. Perhaps I should not have said it like that. Sometimes it's hard for me to use the right words.' Her Russian accent, usually almost undetectable, became more pronounced. 'I did not mean danger. You understand – yes? That sometimes how you think in English is not how you think in Russian?'

I did. Even now, although I hadn't lived in Moscow for nearly thirty years and considered myself in many ways English, a Russian word would occasionally insert itself into my brain in place of its English counterpart. 'If there's anything you think I should know,' I gathered up my bag, and prepared to leave, 'please do tell me.'

Lydia stood up, and I put my hand out for her to shake. For a moment, I thought she was going to say something more. She hesitated, wrapping my hand in both of hers.

Perhaps I should have let her speak, just standing there until she formulated her thoughts. A good lawyer knows when to stay silent. But I fluffed it, uneasy at the situation I found myself in. 'Thank you for lunch. And if you need a lawyer for the Kiril Trust, I'm happy to take on the work or to recommend someone else if you prefer.' I took my hand away, grasping my bag nervously. I couldn't afford to turn down Lydia's offer, but I was beginning to feel like a puppet as her money and power insinuated itself into all three areas of my life – the paper, the Bar and the Russian side of my family.

She smiled. 'No, I won't be asking you for another recommendation of a lawyer for the Trust. You will do an excellent job, I know. Give my regards to your parents.' Just as I opened the door, she added, in Russian. 'Be careful, Sova, *berezhonogo bog berezhot.*' It was one of my father's sayings – God keeps safe those who keep themselves safe.

That night I dreamed about a child's drawing, and the icy waters of the Moskva River. I woke up with my heart pounding and my legs tangled in the sheets. The bed beside me was empty. Theo had gone. I couldn't find the light switch because I wasn't sure which room I was in. Was it my childhood bed? I inched out of bed, and felt around the room, eventually feeling the curtains. I drew them back and moonlight illuminated the room. Theo's mobile had gone from his bedside table. I didn't feel like searching the house for him, so I curled up back in bed, with moonlight and streetlights creating a yellow and shadowy daylight, my ears straining to hear any unusual noises, trying to shake the nightmare off. Theo opened the door quietly.

'Theo,' I whispered.

'Hey.' He turned the light on. 'Hey, hey, hey.' He must have seen something in my face, because he looked surprised. 'What's wrong?' He climbed into bed beside me, and put his arms round me. His skin felt cold against my cheek.

'Where have you been?'

'I went downstairs to get a glass of water.'

'Your mobile was gone.'

'I had left it in the kitchen. Look, here it is.'

My brain fogged over. I was sure it had been on his bedside

table while he was in the bathroom brushing his teeth. It had pinged. Maybe I dreamed it, and I certainly couldn't be bothered to pursue it. And I hadn't told Theo what Lydia had wanted to talk to me about. That minor, indigestible secret burned in my throat. I sometimes sensed that Theo disapproved of my parents. So I didn't want to give him any more ammunition until I was sure Lydia was wrong, but I could at least mention the Trust. 'Lydia Brennan asked me to that lunch today, to set up a new charity. She knew my uncle Kiril, the one who died when he was young,' I said. 'She was a really good friend of his and wanted to talk to me about it.'

'What did she say?'

'Oh, nothing really. Just that he was very talented, and that it was a tragedy. That sort of thing.'

Theo propped himself up on an elbow and studied my face carefully, as if deciding whether to believe me. 'Let's go away,' he murmured. 'You've been working too hard, and so have I. We should take a week off, and spend it on our own, just us. We can walk along a beach or climb a mountain. I got a big fee in today from that case I did last year.'

I nodded and murmured, 'Just us.'

But as Theo slept beside me, I wondered whether we could afford to spend Theo's fee on a holiday. I knew the way he operated: when he worked on a case with a big fee, he would buy something 'because I've got the big fee coming in'. Then when it actually came in, often nearly a year later, he would spend it again. And he was so bad at putting money aside for tax and VAT.

Thinking about money was oddly less upsetting than endlessly rewinding the conversation with Lydia in my head. Papa would never have betrayed his brother. Never. I kept thinking of things I should have said to Lydia. And I wondered what Lydia had meant by saying that I might be in jeopardy.

It was such an odd word to use. Whatever the truth about my father and Kiril, I couldn't see why it would affect me now, nearly thirty years later. I knew enough about the life we had lived in Moscow to realise that the system we all lived under made people paranoid, convinced that someone was going to inform on them. That was probably it. Lydia, like my father, saw dangers in shadows that weren't actually there. Including the 'jeopardy' to me.

As I finally fell asleep, I realised she had called me *Sova*. But I thought my nickname had come from my short-sighted days at my first English school, not from Moscow.

Not even that family story was true, it seemed.

CHAPTER 18

We booked a week away. It would be a break before the Henry Hanbury trial. Chris had been grumpy about me missing my night at the paper. 'For fuck's sake! First you want more work, then you don't fucking do the work you're committed to.' Chris didn't seem to believe in holidays, and I had rarely known him take one, which might be why he had survived so many rounds of redundancies.

Lee rang me. 'We haven't been able to get anyone in chambers for the Adam Harris case, so it's gone out. And Philip Meadowes has lost it as well, so you'll need to do the legal aid transfer to another team. They're at Inner London – it won't take you five minutes.' I sighed, but I supposed it was the least I could do.

When I got to Court 9, I spoke to the clerk of the court and explained that I needed to speak to the prisoner for a few minutes before the judge came in. The court clerk phoned down to the cells and five minutes later Harris was brought into the dock, flanked by an overweight prison officer. Harris was dressed in the same trousers and shirt that he had been wearing when we first met but he looked pale with deep shadows under his eyes. I walked to the back of the court and leaned over to talk to him.

'Good morning, Mr Harris, I'm dealing with your case just for this morning,' I said. 'It's just to hand over to a new legal aid team.' He raised his eyes and fixed me with the same flat stare I had seen in the prison.

'Hello, Sophie, I've been thinking about you.' He spoke very quietly so I had to lean in even further to hear him, and I breathed in the smell of stale cigarette smoke that clung to his clothing. 'I'll be out of here very soon, don't you worry.'

I stared back at him. 'I don't think so.' Then I turned and walked back to my seat.

As Lee had promised, the hearing only lasted five minutes, and then Harris was taken back down to the cells. He stared at me throughout. Did he really think that he could be acquitted? Could he be that delusional? I felt a wave of relief that I had turned down his defence and I would never have to see him again.

I went home, but couldn't concentrate on work. I bustled around tiding up the kitchen, hating the silence of our empty house, then made a cup of ginger tea and curled up on the sofa. Within seconds I was asleep. When I woke it was dark. I checked my watch. Half past nine – a good time to call Theo. He would usually have called me by now, but there was nothing on my phone. I dialled Theo's number but it went straight to voicemail. I hung up and phoned the Birmingham hotel where he was staying.

'Hello, could you put me through to Theo Frazer please?'

'Just one moment.' The line went silent. 'I'm sorry but that guest has checked out.'

'Really? Are you sure?' I said.

'Yes, Mr and Mrs Frazer checked out this morning. I remember calling them a cab.'

The words hung in the ether, like a puzzle that made no sense. I disconnected, feeling as though I were falling down a lift shaft, dropping helplessly through the air, knowing that there was a crushing blow coming towards me, that there could only be pain and emptiness when I finally landed.

As soon as I put the phone down on the Birmingham receptionist, I went online to check who was doing what in chambers, and discovered that Theo had only been booked in for one day in Birmingham, not the three he had told me. Presumably he had relied on my not checking with the clerks.

I got up and walked into our bedroom. Theo's suits were hanging neatly on his side of the cupboard. I went through the pockets with a creeping sense of shame, not really knowing what I was looking for. I took one down and held it to my face, afraid that it would smell of Polly's perfume with its musky base note. Nothing.

I thought about where else I might find evidence. Theo would have his mobile and his laptop with him, but there would be texts and emails between them anyway. Theo and I were able to log into each other's email addresses because it was occasionally useful. That's why I trusted him. I pulled my laptop up and typed in the passwords. There were plenty of emails to and from Polly, so it took me a while to read them. Not one of them mentioned anything other than work. They were all completely professional.

I sighed. Where else, where else can I look? I knew from the many cases I'd worked on that people were often very careful about leaving evidence in obvious places – on their phones, their laptops, their homes. But they sometimes forgot about their cars. I pulled on jeans and a T-shirt, went back downstairs and picked up the keys to the Audi. I knew where to look for evidence and how easily our presence at a scene can leave evidence. DNA, skin, hairs, fibres, any contact leaves a trace and every trace tells a story. The car unlocked with a beep and I climbed into the passenger seat, but not before looking carefully for long black hairs on the headrests. I opened the glove compartment and groped inside; again nothing, apart from a small packet of mints and a crumpled up tie. I was beginning to feel more and more ridiculous. I got out and slid the passenger seat back when something shiny caught my eye in the foot well under the seat. It was a tube of lipstick, a brand I had never bought. I took off the top and remembered Polly applying her lipstick in the changing room, re-enforcing the deep slash of dark red across her mouth. The lipstick in my hand was the deep crimson colour of Polly's lips.

CHAPTER 19

I don't know how long I sat there, in the darkness of our kitchen, trying to rearrange the pieces of the puzzle into a picture that made sense. The receptionist could have got it wrong. The clerks might not have filled in the online calendar correctly. I re-dialled Theo twice but there was no answer. I didn't leave a message.

I started when my phone rang. It slipped under my fingers and fell to the floor. Scrabbling around to get it before the ringing stopped, I finally managed to swipe it open. 'Hello?'

'Sophie?' Theo sounded completely normal.

'Yes?' I spoke into the phone as if the slightest vibration might make it explode.

'Are you there?' He cleared his throat. 'The reception doesn't seem very good. Where are you?'

'At home.'

'Can you hear me?'

'Yes,' I said. 'I can hear you.' Theo seemed unreal, as if he belonged in another play, as if I had accidentally switched my life on at the wrong wavelength.

'The case settled. It was just the one day in the end.' I didn't tell him that I knew. I allowed myself a sliver of relief.

'We left the hotel,' shouted Theo, apparently convinced that my lack of response was due to a weak mobile signal. 'We thought we'd be able to cover Wei Chan's work in one day once the case settled. But there's a bit more to do in the morning, so we've booked in somewhere else tonight. Such a nuisance – we should have stayed in the first place.'

'The receptionist told me that Mr and Mrs Frazer had checked out.' It didn't sound like my voice. I couldn't believe that I was actually saying this.

Theo laughed. 'God, she was thick, that receptionist. Polly and Michael were on a different floor from me.'

'Polly and Michael.' The pieces of the puzzle shifted again.

'Michael Chan, Polly's cousin. Wei Chan's brother is grooming him to take over the empire, although probably not any time soon.'

'Are Polly and Michael… um… when you say Polly and Michael, do you mean they're together?' Was he saying what I thought he was saying?

Theo snorted. 'I've no idea. Their room or rooms were on a different floor from mine. They booked themselves in. I booked myself in. And I wouldn't dream of asking Polly about her personal life.'

So that was all right then. The world seemed less distorted, less bright. I could hear the refrigerator jerk itself into action, humming like a train. We would need to replace it soon, I thought.

'The woman called us Mr and Mrs Frazer when she got us the taxi. We thought it was funny, and I couldn't be bothered to correct her. It didn't occur to me you might call. What did you want to ask me about, anyway?'

I tried to collect my thoughts. What had I been calling him about? 'Oh… er… Adam Harris.' He seemed rather unimportant now. Just a horrible man I would never have to deal with again.

'Oh, yes. How's that going?'

'I turned it down, remember? I was just handing him over to a new legal aid team.'

'Good, good,' said Theo, sounding vague. 'I must have half

149

a dozen missed calls from you. Are you OK? You sound a bit odd.'

'I'm fine.' I took a deep breath. 'But I was…' What could I say I'd been doing? 'I was looking for something I thought I'd dropped in your car… one of my little notebooks, it's been missing. And I found a lipstick which definitely isn't mine. Under the front passenger seat.'

'Oh, good, it's Polly's,' said Theo. 'I gave her a lift to court the other day, and she was doing her lipstick in the passenger mirror – horrible habit if you ask me, but there you are. She's been asking me about it. I couldn't find it anywhere. She will be pleased you've found it, I think it was rather expensive.'

I thought so, too.

'One bit of bad news,' said Theo, in a hearty voice. 'That week of holiday is off. I've been offered a big case, probably the biggest so far, and it runs across the time we were going away. I can't pass it up.'

I was so relieved that there was a perfectly logical explanation to both the lipstick and the receptionist's comments that I didn't mind. 'You can't pass up a big case. Of course I understand. We'll go away when we're both free. We could go last minute, couldn't we?'

'Good, good.' He sounded distracted.

'What about a weekend? I could book it if you don't have the time.'

'Why not?' Theo sounded relieved. 'I'll leave it to you. Off to bed, then. Tuck yourself up tight and have sweet dreams. I'll be back some time tomorrow. Any time from tea time onwards, but it might be quite late.'

CHAPTER 20

Beautiful blue-green eyes, the colour of sea glass, look into mine.

'Come, little Sophie, follow me, I'll take you to him. I know where they have hidden him.'

'Who?' I try to get up but I can't move. There is a deep sense of fear and dread.

Outside the tall schoolroom window, the birch trees sway in the sunlight, beckoning me. Anya stands by the door, her hand held out. I can hear someone crying. Is it me? 'Where is he? Where?'

Then the bell starts to ring to signal the end of lessons, growing louder and more insistent.

The dream began to fragment and drift away like smoke. Who was Anya? She seemed so real, so familiar. I must have known her once.

I groped out a hand from under the duvet. My iPhone was vibrating beside my pillow. I struggled to find my glasses but failed.

The bedroom was washed by pale morning light and Theo was already gone. He must have gone for a run. Or was he in Birmingham again? What day was it, anyway?

I squinted at the screen on my phone and pressed the green accept icon. What time was it? I must have overslept.

Last night my insomnia had returned. I was so tired, but every time I closed my eyes I felt completely awake.

'Hello.' I struggled to focus and shake off the fug, but the feeling of dread from the dream remained.

'Good morning! Heavens, you sound like I've woken you up. I thought you'd be on your way to court by now.'

My heart sank. Jamie, Theo's brother. He didn't like me and I didn't like him. He had stayed friends with Louisa, the first wife, and had made it clear that I was to blame for the end of their marriage. His voice oozed out of the phone, sticky and dark like treacle – the last person I wanted to talk to.

'No, no, I'm not in court today.'

'Oh good, because I really need to talk to you.'

'Jamie, I'm sorry, this is really not a good time. I have a con in the Scrubs at two and I have to get through a mountain of forensics before then. Can I call you back this evening?'

Relentlessly Jamie ploughed on. 'It'll only take a minute. A really good friend of mine is in desperate need of your help.'

I found my glasses and padded towards the kitchen in my pyjamas to make myself an espresso, switching the phone on to loudspeaker. I was used to friends ringing for help. I wondered if plumbers and electricians got the same sort of calls from people who just 'needed a moment of their time'.

'OK, Jamie. Has he been arrested? Is he in custody? Go on.'

'Oh God no! Nothing so sordid. It's a she. She was stopped for speeding outside Stevenage and she could lose her licence. She was clocking over a hundred.'

'Sorry, Jamie. Are you asking me about a road traffic offence?'

'Well, I thought you were having a bit of a dry spell workwise, and that you'd help me out. I thought you could just pop along to the magistrates court and do the mitigation for her. It's so straightforward you could do it in your sleep.'

I felt a wave of irritation wash over me.

'Jamie, I haven't set foot in a magistrates court for five years, I don't do that kind of work. I've forgotten everything I ever knew about road traffic offences years ago. There are lots of perfectly able pupils in chambers who would be happy to cover it for a private fee, but it's not my kind of work anymore.'

I wanted to add that I wasn't having a 'dry spell'. I had marked out the following week to catch up on my research and do my skeleton arguments.

'Basically, I am booked up from now until Christmas.' There was an ominous silence. 'What about the week when you were going to France?' Jamie retaliated. 'Theo said you'd be needing something to do.'

'When did he say that?' I hadn't meant to ask that question, but he had caught me on the raw.

'Last weekend. When he came to see Caspar's football match.'

I tried to understand why Theo hadn't told me that France was cancelled earlier if he already knew about it.

'Not that he saw much of it,' grumbled Jamie. 'He only stayed for about five minutes, and now that I'm divorced the children do need some support from family, you know. Well, this is very awkward for me, I sort of already promised her you'd do it, and she can't afford to pay.'

'Well...' I was puzzled. Surely Theo had been out for quite a lot of the day.

Hadn't he said he had had lunch with Jamie? But I could have imagined it. I'd been rushing about myself, on a series of errands – picking up the dry cleaning, and travelling miles to find a particular kind of light bulb that had apparently been abolished. I didn't know exactly when he had left the house or when he had come back.

'So you will do it,' coaxed Jamie. 'Just once? I promise I won't ask you again.'

'Jamie, really. I haven't done road traffic offences for years. I'm not the right person to help your friend. Who is she, anyway?'

Jamie paused. 'She's my new girlfriend, a yoga teacher, actually. I am sure I could arrange for her to give you a free session.'

I tried to think of a compromise. 'I can ring the clerks for you, and see which pupil might have a morning free next week. Maybe they could do it for a reduced fee.'

Jamie's voice hardened: 'Please don't trouble yourself. I ran into Theo with such a nice Chinese barrister the other day, and she was obviously such a good friend of his. I'm sure she'll help.'

I clicked the phone off, refusing to demean myself by asking where Jamie had 'run into' Theo and Polly. I was sure that Jamie was hinting of something untoward about Theo and Polly being together. It was even possible that this whole conversation was intended to alert me to it. I wondered how someone as charming and clever as my husband could have such an infuriating brother.

I sipped my coffee and stared out of the window, feeling furious with Jamie. He should have known that it was completely inappropriate to ask me to do work of that calibre. It would have taken most of the day, once I had read up about it, and travelled to the magistrates court. A precious day, which I needed for my own cases and for finding things like light bulbs and places to spend a romantic weekend with my husband. Theo and I needed the time together. Being so busy made Theo happy, but we hardly saw each other. I missed him. I understood about work – I would never be one of those wives who saw work as a rival – but I missed him so much it was like an ache.

I tried to reassemble the fragments of my dream but

nothing came to me. The feeling of dread persisted. I thought about the mysterious Anya. Was she trying to warn me about something?

CHAPTER 21

We were allocated one of the grander downstairs meeting rooms this time.

Chambers' clerks like high profile cases that get into the news. I could almost imagine Lee rubbing his hands together at the prospect of more work every time a tweet about Henry Hanbury went out.

Philip was sitting next to Henry and Cornelia at the end of a long conference table. I was surprised to see that Lydia was accompanying them. Since the lunch, I had had a few emails about the Trust she was setting up, but I hadn't seen her in person. She kissed me on both cheeks, which was, perhaps, not very professional.

I hadn't decided what to do about her suggestion that Papa might have betrayed Kiril. I could never ask him. I could never believe it. But I hadn't been able to speak to him. He would hear there was something wrong in my voice.

Philip cleared his throat. 'Henry hasn't been charged, but he has been asked to attend the police station for a further interview. And they've disclosed details of the evidence they've got.'

'We've gone through all our records, and can absolutely prove that Henry's innocent,' interjected Cornelia. She seemed to have lost even more weight and her complexion was grey.

Henry sat like a polite schoolboy, one knee twitching up and down. He looked different, as if the life, the eagerness to learn and some of the puppyish clumsiness had been crushed out of him. Cornelia said the family had tried to keep the social media abuse away from him, but he looked profoundly shocked. He had shaved and it made him look younger. He stared at the desk and said nothing.

Lydia put a hand on Cornelia's arm. 'Let's hear what they have to say.'

Philip read out the evidence. 'The Crown have let us know the identity of the complainant.'

'Complainant!' said Cornelia. 'Liar, more like.'

I exchanged a glance with Philip, who rustled the papers in front of him.

Cornelia looked embarrassed. 'Sorry, Sophie. I really will let you get on with it, Philip.' She tried to smile. Henry looked down, jiggling his knee so hard it was shaking his whole body.

'She's called Shelley Blake, and she was at school at the time. She says Henry borrowed his father's car and used it to take her to a deserted piece of woodland. She's given a detailed description of the car, a Mercedes.

'We never had a Mercedes,' said Cornelia.

Philip continued. 'The Crown alleges that the complainant was only fifteen. She remembers vividly that it was a month before her sixteenth birthday. The assault happened in the first week of July, during the first week of Henry's school holidays. As the complainant was at a school in a different county, her school term had not yet finished.'

Henry fidgeted. 'I remember that year. It was after my A levels and seven of us from the year group went to stay in Corfu. One of the guys' fathers had a house out there, and they lent it to us for the week. After that, I joined the rest of the family in Cornwall.'

Cornelia looked hopeful, but I was still worried.

Philip rustled his papers again: 'The Crown has also admitted that the complainant suffers from severe psychological problems. We... er... have pursued this angle vigorously and have forced the Crown to disclose notes made by a psychotherapist who saw Shelley two years ago, when she was training to become a nurse but suffered a breakdown.' Philip passed me a scrawled manuscript entitled *Employee Care Session Case Notes*.

I read it out loud: 'Client feels she is fragmenting. Delusional disorder. Episodes of psychosis. She reports obsessing about a rape which allegedly took place when she was a teenager. She has trouble distinguishing fantasy from reality. She has previously accused two other men of the rape, an electrician of fifty-nine and a taxi driver in his late thirties. Neither case came to court. She is aware of presenting different selves to others. She accepts that nothing happened with either of them. We explored her feelings of anger and resentment. Theoretical interventions used... cognitive behavioural therapy... to prepare coping strategies for returning to work etc., etc...'

Cornelia sighed. 'You see! Surely that must be an end to it.'

I laid the case notes on the table. 'I'm sorry, Cornelia, but this only ends when the Crown says it ends. Once the CPS start an enquiry like this, it becomes very reluctant to drop it.'

'But that's so unfair.' She was close to tears.

'On the whole, in the light of this report, combined with the timing being completely off, I doubt they'll charge Henry.' I looked at him to check that he understood there would be no easy answers, no quick way out, even though no jury would ever convict on this one.

He seemed almost afraid to look up. 'Thank you,' he said, to the floor.

'We very much appreciate the efforts you've both made to establish his innocence,' said Lydia. 'I never expected this sort of thing to happen here. I thought... well, never mind.'

But it was clear that Cornelia and Henry both believed that

all they had to do was to explain everything, and it would all go away. 'The police have a habit of keeping an investigation open for months,' I said. 'Sometimes they don't do anything to progress it one way or the other. But at least now we know what we are dealing with.'

'And it's very unlikely that the Crown would want to join it to the indictment for the other rape. It's so weak, it would probably undermine their case as a whole,' added Philip.

I tried to clarify the situation to them both. 'The law regarding sexual abuse changed some time ago. It's no longer necessary to have corroborating evidence – the word of the victim can be enough to convict someone. And there is sense in that, because most sexual offences take place between two people without anyone else present. But it does make it harder for everyone – for the CPS to decide when a case is in the public interest; for the jury to decide who to believe; and for the defendant to remember what he or she was doing when the offence was alleged to have taken place.'

Cornelia looked anxious. 'I don't understand why we can't just explain. Why don't they believe us? Isn't there a presumption that you're innocent until you're proved guilty? Henry has never had so much as a parking ticket before.' She pulled at a loose thread on her jacket.

I said, 'It's the job of the police to find enough evidence to get a case to court. It's the defence's job to find enough evidence to test their case, to find out if there are doubts or things that don't add up, and to expose them.

'Then the judge, and the jury, who haven't been involved with the case before it gets to court and who aren't invested either way, can compare the two accounts. Innocent until proven guilty is for the courts. It's up to them to decide which is most credible and which makes the most sense.' Henry nodded.

I spoke as gently as I could. 'I think Shelley's allegation will turn out to be an irrelevant sideshow that won't go any further. However, we need to try to limit the damage being done on social media.'

Philip raised a finger. 'We also have to deal with several photos of naked children that the police found on Henry's computer.' He pulled up his own laptop and turned it towards them.

Henry frowned. 'That's me and my brother in the bath. Mum asked me to digitise the family photo collection to keep it safe.'

'I took these,' said Cornelia, her voice trembling. 'Everybody took photos of their children in the bath twenty years ago. We had them developed at Boots the Chemist. Nobody raised an eyebrow. I asked Henry to make sure we had copies.'

I believed her. 'Firstly, we'll inform Twitter and any other social media companies that Shelley's comments are defamatory. They're obliged to go back to the person who tweets the allegations and ask them either to take them down or to substantiate them. If they fail to do so, Twitter has to take the tweets down.'

'How will they find them all?' asked Cornelia. 'How does it work?'

'You set up a search on certain words, such as Hanbury, and we see what comes up.' We would certainly be able to get some tweets taken down, but who knew how many misspelt allegations were out there which would slip through.

'I'm so sorry, Mum, I'm so sorry.' Henry looked exhausted and embarrassed. He had finally realised that he was caught in a trap, and that all his brains, intelligence and education were not enough to spring him free.

Lydia touched his shoulder gently. 'It's not your fault. You haven't done anything wrong. These things can happen to anyone.' She met my eyes over the table, and I nodded. Her words and her voice triggered off a flash of memory.

There is the sound of knocking, of shouts, and a scuffle further down the corridor. My father and mother exchange glances but she carefully concentrates on peeling potatoes. 'Shh, darling,' my mother says, when I tug at her skirt and ask what is happening. She puts down the potato and the knife, but not before I see that her hand is shaking.

CHAPTER 22

Gus was working at his desk when I returned from the conference. He smiled at me. After we'd exchanged a few pleasantries, I asked him about Polly.

'Someone told me you'd been seeing Polly Chan?'

Gus put his pen down and sighed, pushing his chair away from the desk and stretching his lanky frame out as far as he could manage. 'I have absolutely no idea what you're talking about. Don't people have anything worthwhile to think about?' He looked perplexed. 'Oh, there was one thing someone could have seen. She was in the café down the road at the same time as I was, and asked if she could join me. The woman is made of Velcro, every time she comes anywhere near you, she sticks to you. I've never drunk my coffee so fast, but in about ten minutes, she'd managed to rearrange my hair, invite me to Paris for the weekend and straighten my collar.'

I laughed. I could just imagine Gus, who was always polite, trying to fend off all Polly's suggestions. There was a tap at the door and Theo put his head round, thrusting a bunch of flowers into the room. He kissed me. 'Darling, I've been neglecting you lately.'

'No, no, I understand.' I was slightly embarrassed in front of Gus, who tucked his chair back in and bent his head down over his laptop.

'So I'm going to make it up to you. We're going away for the weekend now. I've packed your case.'

'But we're booked for tomorrow, at The Wife of Bath...'

162

After Theo telling me how busy he was, our weekend away had shrunk to a Saturday night. I had researched online for the perfect little place, close enough to London so we didn't have to spend all our time travelling. According to the reviews it had atmosphere, comfortable beds, good food and a great wine list.

'I've cancelled that,' Theo interrupted me. 'You deserve something better. Doesn't she, Gus?'

Gus mumbled assent.

Theo didn't require an answer. 'I've got your case in the car. I know what you look beautiful in.'

It took me back to the early days of our relationship. A year after we had started seeing each other, Theo had swept me off for a surprise long weekend near Nice, having first cleared my diary with the clerks and then secretly bought me everything I needed. In the right size.

It was there he had proposed to me, in the restaurant of one of the most idyllic hotels in the area. The whole restaurant had applauded, the maître d' had brought champagne and a band had struck up with a rendition of Al Green's Let's Stay Together.

His romantic gestures had been wonderful when we first met, but now I was more concerned about whether we could pay the heating bill and whether we could insure the cars properly. He handed me the flowers, which were exquisite.

'You put these flowers in a vase, so they're here when you get back.' Theo took my folders and laptop from me and firmly locked everything away in my desk drawers.

'Bye, Gus. Have a good weekend.' He seized my hand and Gus's head twitched up again.

'Er, bye.'

'Honestly, they only allow these upper-class twits into chambers because they've got connections,' muttered Theo. 'Talk about dead from the neck upwards.'

I heard the front door close and someone came up the stairs. It was Polly. Theo and I had to flatten ourselves against the cream-painted wood panelling as she clattered past. 'Have a good weekend, Polly,' said Theo, smiling at her, still holding my hand.

She wasn't looking at me, and didn't seem to hear my reluctant 'hello'.

'Polly wasn't as good as she makes herself out to be in court the other day,' I said, once we had buckled ourselves into Theo's cream leather seats and he had nosed the car out into the traffic.

'Funnily enough, that's what she said about you.' Theo gave me an amused sideways glance. 'She said you were late, and got on the wrong side of Mad Dog, then failed to get your client access to her children even though it was perfectly obvious to everyone that she was completely innocent.'

I nearly jumped out of the car in fury. But there was no point in taking it out on Theo. And there was some truth in Polly's accusations in that I had been late.

'I'm sorry. I thought you'd want to know,' he said. 'To be honest, I think she's jealous of you. You being a rising star in chambers and all that.'

'Am I?' I hated these arbitrary labels. 'You're only as good as your last case.'

He laughed. 'Of course, you are. And she might think you've got an unfair advantage with me to help you.' He touched my knee affectionately.

I swallowed. I didn't want Polly to intrude on our perfect weekend.

'And, darling, I know you don't like criticism,' he added. 'But if you're going to have a problem with Polly, it's important to remember that you're senior to Polly, so anything you do or say might be construed as bullying a new, vulnerable member of chambers.'

164

We inched through the Friday traffic. The last thing I wanted was an argument with him.

'I'm only thinking of you,' he added. 'So please don't sulk.'

'I'm not. I'm just thinking about what you said.'

'Sometimes I think you're a bit of a softy, Sophie. My own Mrs Softy.' He lifted one of my hands and kissed it.

I thought it made me sound like an ice cream, but I let it go. Polly's malice could be much more of an issue than I had realised. Was she saying these things to everyone in chambers? And to other people in the law? The Bar was like a whispering gallery, and this sort of campaign was hard to fight. I had known better barristers than me completely destroyed in this way, apparently almost overnight.

'I thought you ought to know something else about Polly,' he added. 'Before you hear it from anyone else.'

My heart turned cold.

'Polly has made it very clear to me that, well, she'd be prepared to confer certain, let us say, *privileges*, if I were to advance her.'

For a moment I didn't understand. 'What do you mean? Privileges?'

'She's made it very clear that she'd sleep with me if I help her,' he added. 'I was lucky to escape with my shirt on in Birmingham once. She's an absolute man-eater.'

'That's awful!' But I was comforted by the thought that Theo was sharing this with me and that if he had something to hide, he wouldn't have raised the subject.

'That's why I made sure she saw we were holding hands,' he added. 'She needs to know that however hard she tries, she can't tear us apart.'

I was touched.

'And, darling, I am so sorry about France. I know you love the mountains, but there's just no way I can take a week off right now.'

'Of course, you couldn't. This is lovely.' I settled back in my seat, enjoying Theo's reassuring presence, watching motorways become A roads, A roads become winding lanes and felt my heart lift as I took in the stone cottages of Dorset mellowing in the falling light. We passed the ruins of an old castle and turned into a narrow drive, which soon revealed a gabled manor house. I pressed a button to roll my car window down, and could smell the salty tang of the sea.

'This is wonderful, Theo. Where are we?'

'It's called The Shack on The Beach, and it comes very highly recommended.'

Theo parked the car and hefted our bags out of the boot. It was hardly a shack, but never mind. We were warmly greeted by our host and taken to our room. Everything was perfect, the open log fire, the quirky furnishings, the huge comfy bed and the bottle of champagne waiting in an ice bucket. I threw myself down on the bed.

Theo lay down beside me, twining a lock of my hair round his finger. 'Just you and me for a whole two days. You know I do love you, I really do. If I don't show it sometimes, it's because I'm under such strain.'

'I understand.' I inhaled the smell of him, that unique blend of soap and starched linen, with overtones of something else clean and spicy. 'But, Theo, are you sure we can afford this?'

'It's a thank you from someone I helped with a licensing application.'

I sat up. 'Theo, that's sailing a bit close to the wind.'

His expression hardened. 'It's not as if I was accepting cash in brown envelopes. It's just like the flowers some clients send you.'

I let it drop, although I would never have accepted a weekend stay in a hotel as any form of thank you or payment. There were professional guidelines limiting what barristers could receive from clients as gifts.

Theo stood up. 'I know it's dark but there's a full moon. Let's go and have a quick walk on the beach before supper.' We changed quickly into jeans, jumpers and coats and strolled down to the shore, the wind whipping my hair around my face.

After London, the breeze felt cold, but Theo hugged me to him and we walked together along the shoreline. We sat on an upturned dinghy, and I spotted a perfect shell. Theo put it in the pocket of his Barbour. 'When we are old and grey I will take this out to show you, and remind you that you once loved me,' he said, with a smile. A sea mist was blowing in, but in the distance we could still just make out the dark hilly outline of the Isle of Wight and its lights. The riding lights of yachts moored off shore were dotted across the water. How well Theo knew me. I was always happiest in the countryside, in the mountains or by the sea. How clever of him to find this place.

As we walked back along the beach, Theo took my hand. 'So are you going to tell me why you've been so distracted for the last few weeks?'

'Have I?'

'Come on,' he stopped and turned me to face him. 'This is me. We don't have secrets.'

Don't we? The sharp comment almost slipped out. I'd often been disconcerted by how observant Theo was. I hadn't said anything about what Lydia had implied about Papa and Kiril, but Theo and I shouldn't have secrets. I told him everything she'd said. It felt like a betrayal of my beloved father just to speak the words. He couldn't have been the one to inform on Kiril. It just wasn't possible.

But Theo thought otherwise. He listened to the whole story, and kissed me. 'I'm so sorry. I know you've put your father on a pedestal, but every pedestal breaks eventually. I thought something like that might have happened. The story of how your father escaped to the West never quite added up, as far as I could see. There must have been something else to it.'

'I just don't know how I can face him now,' I said. 'I've been pretending to be busy, so I haven't gone down there, and if he rings, I text him back.' My throat tightened. 'And I miss him so much. It's as if the father I knew never really existed.'

'Shh,' said Theo. 'You've got me now. It's best not to see him, not to see either of them, until you know what you want to say. Just wait until you feel better about it, then you can have it out with him. But you don't need to go down there all the time. Most people don't see their parents that often.' We walked along in silence, our footsteps sinking into the sand at every step.

When we got back to our room, Theo opened the bottle of bubbly he had ordered. We touched our glasses to each other in a toast, then set them down on the bedside table. There was something about this that felt different, I thought. Such passion that it almost felt like desperation. Later, ravenous from the long drive and the sea air, we dressed and wandered into the dining room where we dined on grilled Dorset lobster and lamb cutlets. Theo ordered us a pudding – tiny pots of something exquisite and chocolatey.

Back in our room, I opened the curtains so that I could watch the moon as it shone down between dark, scudding clouds. As I turned round, I caught sight of Theo moving his hair back with his hand, checking it in the mirror. He had an expression on his face I didn't quite recognise. 'Theo?'

He came towards me. The expression was gone and he dropped a kiss on my lips. As I fell asleep, I felt a burst of euphoria so intense it was almost physical. It looked as if our financial problems would soon be solved, and, away from work, Theo and I were as close as ever. I felt happy. Truly happy.

But when you're happy, you think everything is going to be all right. But I should have been paying attention.

CHAPTER 23

The traffic was heavy on the Embankment as I drove into chambers a week later. It was another bitterly cold day. To my right, the Thames churned like dull pewter under a leaden sky. I swung left before Blackfriars underpass and headed towards Fleet Street before cutting through the winding back roads until I came to the entrance to the Inner Temple car park.

I gave in my name at the gate and the security guard checked the sticker on my windscreen, a symbol of the flying horse Pegasus. He lifted the barrier and waved me through. The car park wasn't full and I soon found a slot near Paper Buildings where I had done the first six months of my pupillage ten years ago.

I needed to buy some new bands – my old ones were looking frayed – and I decided that I had time to dash up to Ede and Ravenscroft, the barristers' outfitters in Chancery Lane. I locked my car and walked up past the Round Church and on to Inner Temple Lane to the old Gatehouse that led on to Fleet Street.

The gatehouse was one of the few buildings that had survived the Great Fire of London and its foundations stretched back to the twelfth century when it had been part of the estate of the Knights Templar. I often made a detour to come this way just to admire the magnificent Jacobean architecture that had been built over the medieval site.

Generations of black-clad lawyers had walked through this arch. How many of them had been anxious and driven like me? Or had they all been like Theo, cocksure showmen who loved being in the spotlight with the eyes of an entire courtroom on them? Lost in thought, I stepped out on to Fleet Street and almost walked straight into Philip. He blinked rapidly behind his steel-framed glasses.

'Oh! Hello, Philip, how are you?'

Philip's eyes slid away from my face. I was surprised to detect an awkwardness between us that had never been there before.

'Oh, have we got a conference? I haven't forgotten something have I?' Heat flooded my face – could I have forgotten a conference?

'No, no. I'm heading for Medlar Court, but to see Miss Chan, actually. Not something you would like, it's a minor fraud.' He sounded apologetic.

We looked at each other for a moment. When had Philip started to brief Polly of all people?

'Philip, I'm sorry I didn't take the Harris case. He came too close to admitting he was guilty – it could have got us into all sorts of difficulties.'

'Are you all right, Sophie?'

'Philip, honestly, I'm fine. Look, would you like to have lunch in hall with me after your con?'

Again Philip looked uncomfortable. 'That would be lovely, but I ought to crack on. Let's have lunch another time, OK?'

He leaned forward and gave me a peck on the cheek, then turned and walked off in the direction of Medlar Court. I stood still, staring after him, puzzled and upset. Why did he think I wouldn't want a minor fraud? I wondered if that had come from the clerks? As a small reminder that turning down cases was a bad idea?

Only the day before, Lee had told me that a case of mine – one I was looking forward to – was going out of chambers 'for administrative reasons'. I couldn't believe he would actually let a juicy case out of his hands unless he really had to, but I hadn't been able to suppress the thought that he was just making excuses, and that this was my punishment for turning down Adam Harris.

Twenty minutes later I was back in chambers, clutching my new bands. I climbed the stone staircase up to the second floor and collapsed down on the worn chesterfield in my room. I had slept badly last night – I always did when I lost work or lost a case – and my eyes already felt tired and gritty; I had the beginnings of a headache. All I wanted was to skive off and go home but I knew the clerks were likely to need me to cover something in court tomorrow so it made sense to stay in chambers until I knew what they were offering. Besides, I needed to speak to Lee to make it clear that I wasn't turning into a diva. I would do any other case. Just not Adam Harris.

With a sigh, I set up my laptop, wondering if I needed to do any of the skeleton arguments that I had to serve on the prosecution in the Hanbury trial. I badly needed a cup of coffee and went into the cramped kitchenette that was next to my room. I opened the tiny fridge and found a carton with a few drops of milk left. As I switched on the kettle I heard voices drifting down the corridor. The door to the room Polly shared with three other barristers was open and I could hear her laughter. I had the sudden unwelcome thought that she was laughing at me, but told myself that my insomnia was making me paranoid.

I went downstairs to the clerks' room. It was infused with the usual manic energy bordering on barely-contained panic. The clerks sat at separate stations spread around the oak-panelled, brightly-lit room with glowing computer screens showing the court listings in front of them, talking or shouting into headsets. It was just past one o'clock, so barristers were phoning in with progress reports on their cases. The clerks resented all but the most senior members coming in and interrupting them but I had no choice. Lee was talking loudly into his headset and scowled as I stood in front of his desk.

'Fucking hell, Sir! You told me you'd have your speech in by Friday. What the fuck am I going to do with the Sheffield case on Monday? No! I have not got anyone else who can cover it. It will have to go out of chambers. All right, all right, I'll email the list office. Call me back at four.' He looked up, his face carefully blank. 'Yes, Miss?'

Now was not the time to talk to him. 'Oh, I was just wondering if…'

I jumped as a soft hand touched my arm. It was Holly. 'Are you all right, Miss?'

'Yes, Holly, I'm fine. Really. '

'Your con's booked in on Friday,' added Holly.

'Great. That's what I wanted to know.' I smiled at her as I left the clerks' room, hoping that Gus was in our room, and that I could talk it over with him.

But Gus was out, and the room looked untidier and more derelict than ever. I cleared a place on the desk to work on what was turning into one of my biggest cases so far. Henry Hanbury. Seemingly, an innocent man. The Henry Hanburys of this world were, in so many ways, more of a worry than the Adam Harrises. Defending someone you thought was innocent was much harder than someone who might be guilty. If they were convicted, it must be your fault. I thought of Lydia.

Outside the window, the lacy outlines of leafless trees cast patterns across the hoar frost. If I half-closed my eyes, I fancied I could see Snegurochka, the frost child, dancing in the slanting winter sun, unaware of the terrible price she'd pay for loving someone.

CHAPTER 24

By the time the Hanbury trial came up, I felt oddly lacking in energy. A trial usually made me feel more alive, but now life seemed foggy, as if I were dragging myself through a dark wood with a heavy burden on my back. I'd seen Lydia once in the lift at the paper and she'd kissed me on both cheeks as if she was one of my favourite aunts. '*Sova*,' she said. 'How lovely to see you.' That night I'd woken with a start at 3 a.m. to hear voices whispering. They died away when I turned on the light to see only our own bedroom, my clothes flung carelessly over a chair and the reassuring mound of Theo in the bed. But when Theo was away, usually overnight in Birmingham, the voices came back the way they used to when I was child. I missed talking easily to my father – I still couldn't face asking him about Kiril and, until I did, there would be a barrier between us. I just hoped he hadn't noticed it.

One day – when I had the time – I promised myself, I would find out what those voices were whispering about. I grew up in a safe Kent town, where people stroll along the beach with their dogs, greeting strangers with a smile. But behind the polite, well-brought-up middle-class girl was a father who had run for his life. Generations of terror. An uncle whose death held too many questions for me. The history of Russia was one of bloodshed. My father often referred to terrible things that had happened to a cousin or an uncle, not because they were criminals or victims of crime, but because they were on the wrong side of the state. But these were people I had never met. It had all happened long before I was born.

So why were they whispering to me?

On the first day of the trial, I queued up outside the Inner London Crown Court, while two thickset men in uniforms fumbled through bags and directed people through the scanner. I sometimes wondered if they took pleasure in making barristers wait. Or perhaps they liked making criminals wait. Most likely, they enjoyed making everyone wait.

I stepped into the building and finally gave my bag to the guard. Once through the scanner, I hurried to the ladies' robing room. For a moment, my mind went blank. The security code? What had I been told? Where was that scrap of paper? I found it in my pocket, punched in the number and pushed open the door.

I hung up my coat and unzipped my small pull-along suitcase. I dressed carefully and checked in the mirror to make sure my wig was on straight.

Then I took out my papers, checking that they were in order before putting the ones I needed first in the front pocket, as I always did. Had I forgotten anything? I took one last look in the long mirror, adjusted the gown again, and smiled at myself, anxiety forgotten. Going into court was a heady mixture of terror and euphoria. Almost addictive. I would get justice for Henry Hanbury and his pale, anxious mother.

At the reception desk, I put out a tannoy for him. A few minutes later, the Hanburys appeared at my side. Cornelia was gaunt and smartly dressed. She fussed at Henry, fixing his tie. Lydia stood beside them, imperious, her hands glittering with rings. 'Sophie, my dear,' she said, grasping both my hands in hers. I was relieved that she didn't kiss me on both cheeks as she had in the lift.

Henry appraised me with his blue, light-filled eyes, as if

searching for an answer I couldn't give. 'Er... hello...' He shook my hand, clinging to it as if he were drowning.

'Is everything all right?' asked Cornelia.

I gave her what I hoped was a reassuring smile. 'We haven't started yet, Cornelia. We're going to do everything we can, and the case against Henry isn't strong. Try not to worry.'

Cornelia drew me aside, taking both my hands in hers. 'Henry's putting a brave face on it, but I'm really worried about him. I think...' she swallowed. 'He won't go out, he just lies in his room in the dark.' Her voice cracked. Cornelia's anxiety was an extra load we all had to carry, and sometimes it was so heavy it threatened to drag us off course.

I turned to Henry. 'How are you?'

'I want to get this over with.' There were dark shadows behind the horn-rimmed glasses, and he was very pale. There was a faint stale smell in the air, as if he hadn't washed his hair. Cornelia had asked me what he ought to wear for court. Should he wear a tie? Surely a suit would be better than casual wear? She had peppered me with questions, barely listening to the answers.

I often advised clients on what to wear for their trial. At first glance, Henry looked smart. He, or more likely Cornelia, had chosen a dark blue cashmere sweater over a crisp white shirt and a tie. But the back of the shirt had come untucked, and his dark hair stuck up unevenly where he had run his hand through it. I sighed inwardly. He looked generally rumpled. While I was always impressed with how much care juries took to be fair, looking unkempt would unconsciously give the jury a bad impression. The courtroom was theatre and clothing was all part of the performance. I exchanged a glance with Cornelia, who murmured that he should tuck the back of his shirt in. He complied.

Henry shifted uneasily from one foot to another. I forced

myself to smile at him. 'We'll go straight along to Court 9. I can explain some of the protocol to you on the way.' They followed me through the gloomy corridors, passing people on benches outside of the other courts. Some looked bored or frightened. Outside Court 3, a man leaned forward, resting his elbows on his knees, with the hunched shoulders of despair.

'You must come up against a lot of dangerous types in your job,' said Cornelia too brightly. I got the impression that she was trying to cover her nervousness with chatter. 'Do they ever... you know... come after you?'

'Not so far. I only do a little prosecution, it's mainly defence work. And I don't see why you would come after your defence barrister. I'm the one who's trying to keep them out of jail.' Sometimes – when I was alone in the house – I did imagine that there was someone there, that a creaking floorboard or a shadow in the street was a person waiting for me. Someone who thought I hadn't done my best. But that's how you think when your work means seeing what terrible things human beings do to each other.

Other barristers walked past, their black gowns fluttering, trailing suitcases or carrying big leather bags full of papers. One smiled at me. I nodded back, as I spoke over my shoulder to Henry. 'You're on bail, so you'll have to surrender to the dock officer when we get to court. Then you'll take a seat in the dock.'

'I understand.'

'I'm afraid it can all take a surprisingly long time. We may not get to the actual evidence before the court breaks for lunch.'

'He just wants to be able to tell his side of the story,' said Cornelia. 'It's all such nonsense. I can't believe it's got this far.'

I didn't reply. There was nothing I could say. I didn't think the evidence against Henry was strong, and I believed in the jury system. But nothing was a foregone conclusion in a criminal trial.

Cornelia grabbed my arm. 'You do believe us, don't you?'

Her hand was surprisingly strong. I looked down at it, and she let me go.

'I apologise,' she said. 'I just feel that no one is listening. No matter what Henry says, or that the claims don't make sense, everyone believes the accusation and no one even seems to listen to him. Not the police or anyone.'

'He will be heard. In court. I promise.' She sighed.

'Don't swear in court,' I advised Henry, walking ahead of him again. 'Sometimes people do. And try not to appear angry, however frustrating the prosecution is. I know it's hard, but it's really important that you don't come across as someone who loses his temper easily.'

'OK,' he said. 'I understand.'

'First, we'll have to empanel a jury. Then the prosecution will open the case. That may take some time, depending on how long-winded my opponent is.'

'Can we object to jurors? Suppose there are mainly women on the panel?' interjected Cornelia.

'It's only in the United States, and in films, that you can question each juror individually and have the right to reject a certain number. Here, the court officials are meant to screen out anyone who's disqualified from jury service, and the remainder are usually expected to serve in any trial, unless there's something obvious, like they know the judge, the defendant or the witnesses.' We walked on in silence, past more courtroom doors.

'But it's not likely that the jury will be mainly women,' I added. 'Even if it were, if you were hoping for an acquittal in a sex case, particularly where consent's an issue, women, surprisingly, are often more often sympathetic to a defendant than men.'

'I expect women are better at telling when people are lying.' There was a tearful edge to Cornelia's voice. 'I think we are better judges of character.'

'Mum,' Henry reproached her.

Once again, I saw myself in Cornelia, and heard Theo telling me that my anxiety was making things worse.

'It may be a couple of days before you give evidence,' I added. 'There may be a discussion with the judge as to what evidence can go in front of the jury. Not everything is admissible and the rules are very complicated.' I paused. I didn't want to tell Cornelia anything that would make her even more hysterical.

'There are limits on what the defence can say about the person making the allegations,' I explained. 'We shouldn't be putting her on trial, only putting forward evidence that indicates that Henry's innocent. So the judge has to decide what's relevant. Then the jury will have to watch Eva's ABE interview...'

'Sorry?' Cornelia almost whispered.

'The police record statements on video now, because it means you can both see and hear everything that goes on. It's to stop allegations of police brutality, which is why it's called an Achieving Best Evidence interview – ABE. I will cross-examine her. She'll be behind a screen, so you won't be able to see her but the jury and the judge will, and so will I when I'm asking her questions. If I score points, the prosecution will try to mitigate any damage to their case by re-examining her.

'I'll have quite a lot to put to Eva and the other witnesses, then there is usually the forensics, and they'll read out the interview of what you said when you were arrested... look, here's Court 9.'

Henry pushed open the large swing doors for me. I caught a whiff of his locker-room stale scent again as I passed ahead of him. The courtroom was modern, carpeted in grey, with comfortable seats and blonde wood panelling.

I greeted the court clerk, steering Henry towards the dock. I showed Lydia and Cornelia the visitors' gallery, before slipping onto the padded bench closest to the jury box.

Before Henry stepped up into the dock, he turned. I smiled at him. For a moment, he looked much younger, and frightened, like a hunted animal unable to outrun its pursuer. He sat down behind the heavy glass, squashed up next to a burly dock officer.

It was already 10 a.m. and there was no sign of a prosecutor. The case was listed for 10.15 and he should have been there by now. There was the running order to sort out, possible admissions to be agreed, and points of law that might need to be discussed without troubling the judge. The court clerk looked up and asked the usher if anyone had signed in. 'Yes, Brian Linton.'

I knew Brian Linton. He was solid rather than brilliant, and he had the high complexion of a frequent drinker.

'Has anyone seen him?' asked the court clerk.

'No,' I said, 'and I'll need time with him before we bring the judge in.'

The court clerk sighed with irritation and picked up her phone, as the doors swung open with a crash. A stout middle-aged barrister with the look of a rugby player gone to seed bowled in. He was carrying a stack of papers and a hefty copy of Archbold Criminal Pleading, Evidence & Practice under his arm. He collapsed onto the bench beside me. I noticed beads of sweat crawling down his brow. Few barristers used books these days; Brian Linton must be very old-school not to have everything digital. But that didn't mean he wasn't up to date on the law. 'Ah! Good morning! You must be Sandra, sorry to keep you waiting. I'm Brian.'

'Yes, we've met. And it's Sophie, actually, Sophie Angel.'

'Whoops, sorry. Look, I'm going to have to ask for an adjournment. This is a really late return. The chap I'm covering is part heard in Snaresbrook and he biked it over to me late last night... I'm really not ready to go on.'

'Well, I'm sorry too, but there's no way I'd agree to that,' I replied. 'This case has been fixed for months. You can raise it with the judge if you want, but I am going to object.'

'I shall.' I saw a flash of dislike in Brian's eyes. Or was it panic?

Secretly, I was delighted. There was no possibility that any judge would allow this case to come out of the list at such a late stage. But Brian would not have had time to pore over the forensic evidence as I had done, let alone the 'unused' material that the CPS had served on us late last week. Amid the stacks of irrelevant facts and long-winded statements, there were often unexpected gems of information. And we were still waiting for the statement from the barman in the White Horse, which the prosecution said they were unable to find.

Before Brian could say anything else, the usher entered: 'Be upstanding in court,' he bellowed.

His Honour, Judge Okonju strode in, with a flourish of his gown, and took his seat. Brian and I got to our feet and bowed. He spent a moment rearranging his desk and then looked down at us from over the rims of his half-moon glasses.

'Now, Miss Angel.' I immediately got to my feet as he addressed me. 'A couple of preliminary matters. Your client may continue to have bail on the usual terms, but he must stay within the confines of the building during the lunchtime adjournment, and he may not leave court until fifteen minutes after we adjourn to avoid any contact with the jury panel.'

'Yes, Your Honour,' I said.

Judge Okonju frowned down at his papers. 'There is also

the matter of a missing statement from PC Nathalie Duggan, who interviewed the barman on duty at the White Horse, Mr Linton…'

'Your Honour, I've made repeated applications for this statement,' I said.

Brian Linton stood up to ask for an adjournment, to give the prosecution time to find the statement.

'The prosecution has had several months to find the statement,' said Judge Okonju. 'I expect it to be on my desk by the close of play today, which will give us plenty of time.' He glared at Brian Linton, and a prosecution clerk scurried off to get the statement.

It was a risk. Only a slight one. If the barman's statement was favourable to the defence, it wasn't unknown for it to be 'lost'. On the other hand, sometimes statements did genuinely get lost, and if so, it might not be in our favour. Cockup or conspiracy?

Henry was listening to these arguments from the dock. He looked pale and blank, staring straight ahead of him. I needed him to look fresh, clean and honest, not traumatised. I knew that attractive, successful men could be rapists. But, for a jury, there was always the unspoken question, 'Why would this man need to rape someone?'

There was a further delay of over an hour as there was a problem with the ventilation system in court, and one of the jurors revealed she had an operation scheduled for the end of the week. She had to be replaced. As the jury were sworn in one by one, I studied their faces as they read the oath. They were the usual mixture of a central London crowd that you might see any day on the underground in rush hour. I just hoped that none of them had come with a personal mission to improve the rape conviction statistics, regardless of what the case in front of them appeared to be. I had met such people and I never wanted them on my jury. At the heart of this trial, there were two people who had done nothing wrong. Henry and Eva. Eva had been raped, but convicting the wrong man would not bring her justice. I had to destroy the prosecution case but without damaging her any further.

I almost jumped as Brian Linton rose to his feet. He took a huge handkerchief from his pocket and blew his nose loudly. 'Ladies and gentlemen of the jury, it's now my opportunity to address you on the facts of this case. Nothing that I or that my friend, Miss Angel, says can be considered evidence. You have to judge the case on the evidence that you hear from the witness box. The burden of proving this case is on the Crown, and remains on the Crown all the way through.'

He blew his nose again and, in a voice thickened by cold, said, 'This is a case of rape. You may find aspects of it shocking and distressing, but in the end, once you've heard all the evidence, I submit that you'll be persuaded that there's ample evidence on which to convict on a count of rape...'

I looked at the judge. He was already looking bored. I hoped Brian Linton would continue in the same congested monotone for the rest of his opening speech. A jury bored by the prosecution was a gift to the defence.

CHAPTER 25

Before we called the first witness, Brian stood up. 'With His Honour's leave, I wish to read out an agreed statement from Dr Alan Jilkes, who is an expert in the field of drug usage and addiction, and who can explain the effects of Rohypnol pills, commonly known as "roofies".'

The judge turned to the jury and explained that this was evidence that was agreed on by both sides and had the same weight as if it were being given under oath before them.

He started to read from a list.

'Point one: Rohypnol is a sedative which is seven to ten times stronger than Valium, and is odourless and flavourless.' He looked up at the jury.

'Two. Rohypnol or generic equivalents cause loss of inhibition, impaired motor control and may cause amnesia. Individuals are often unable to clearly remember an assault, the assailant or the events surrounding the assault. Three. It takes around twenty minutes to take effect and the full effects last around four to six hours. Some residual effects last up to twelve hours later. Four. Its effects are stronger when combined with alcohol, when it can cause loss of consciousness and blackouts. Five. Other effects include dizziness, excitability, lack of coordination. Longer term side effects last for several days and include headaches, nightmares and confusion. Six. The drug is often dropped into an unattended glass.'

He sat down, and one of the clerks at court set up Eva's video testimony. It was the ABE interview, and I had watched it over and over again. So I examined the jurors' faces as they watched. Two of the women shot sideways glances at Henry with open disgust, their arms folded in front of them. Most of the other ten were scribbling notes on their pads, except for one young man who was staring at the ceiling and occasionally yawning. When the ABE interview ended, Brian paused the DVD and rose to his feet.

'Just one supplementary question, Miss Scott. Could you tell His Honour and the jury what effect this has had on you?'

'I can't sleep with the lights off.' Eva's voice trembled. 'I have flashbacks. I keep thinking I'm being pinned down, and I can't breathe. I keep seeing his arm with that big watch on it coming towards my face every time I start to fall asleep.'

'Thank you, Miss Scott. Please wait there.'

I hadn't seen any mention of a memory of a watch in any of the papers – unless I had missed it. And I remembered Cornelia fretting about her son's timekeeping at our first conference. I got to my feet. I took a sip of water, hoping to sound confident.

'Your Honour, I see the time is ten to one. Is this a convenient moment for a break?' Judge Okonju looked down at me. After what seemed like a long deliberation, he looked back up. 'Two o'clock, please, members of the jury.'

I sank down in my seat in relief. I would have one more opportunity to talk to Henry before the cross-examination. And if the police had found the statement, it should give me a chance to find out what the barman had said. Henry was released from the dock after the jury had left, and I followed him outside. We left the building through the swing doors, hit by the usual fug of cigarette smoke. 'Henry, what sort of watch do you wear?'

He looked puzzled. 'I don't. I use my phone if I want to know the time.'

'So you don't have a fitness watch or anything like that?'

He shook his head. A brisk breeze ruffled my hair and I shivered. It was time to go back inside. Was it my imagination or did someone behind me break stride, and move in a slightly different direction? The rest of Henry's family surrounded me outside the court in an anxious circle, their faces trusting that I had some good news.

My mobile buzzed. 'Sorry. It's chambers. My clerk. I need to take this.' It was Lee. 'We've had Bravo's on about your case next week. They need you to prepare the defence case statement by Friday. You were supposed to have it in by last week.'

'What?' I rummaged through my mind. 'I'm in the middle of the Henry Hanbury trial. And I haven't had all the papers yet.'

'I'll check we've sent them over.' He hung up.

'Are you OK?' Henry asked. 'Was that bad news?'

I jumped. 'No, no. It's all fine. It's ten to two. We need to go back into the courtroom.' I lifted the wig on to my head as we went inside again. Theo always says that we're actors and if you're not nervous before going on stage, you're no good. But once the doors of the courtroom swing shut behind me, the performance nerves fall away. I stepped onto the stage, just making it back in before Judge Okonju.

Most importantly, I had to put my case across without destroying a young woman who had already been badly hurt. And I also knew that if my client were found guilty, the real rapist would walk free and could claim further victims.

'Miss Angel?'

'Thank you, Your Honour.' I stood up. The rest of the world hushed and all I could see was Eva's face and the questions I had to ask her. 'So, Miss Scott...' I heard my own voice too high and sharp, and adjusted it. 'I am now going to ask you some questions on behalf of the defendant, Henry Hanbury.' Eva nodded.

Judge Okonju flicked through the bound folder of documents in front of him and adjusted his glasses.

'You said in your evidence that you went to the pub to meet your friend Melanie and a group of others. But while you were there, you saw some colleagues from work, so you also spent some time chatting to them.'

'Yes.' Eva sounded puzzled.

'Can you remember how many people were in the pub that evening?'

'Well, not really. But it was quite full. I mean, I had to wiggle a bit to get across the room. And it was noisy, which was why I was outside smoking for a bit.'

'And you left your drink unattended while you were switching between the two groups?'

She shrugged. 'I can't remember. Probably.'

'So the pub was crowded and you left an unattended drink on a table?'

'Yes.'

'Where absolutely anyone could have slipped something into it?'

'I don't think so. People would have noticed.'

'So can you remember at what point your memory started to fade?'

'I remember one of my work colleagues asking me what the time was because she didn't want to miss her train home. That was... er... um just before ten o'clock, I think. I can vaguely remember talking to the barman after that, but I can't remember what I said. Just snatches, as if I was in a film or a dream.'

It was time to switch tack.

'Now, I just want to clarify this. The first time you discussed the alleged rape with anyone was with your friend Melanie by phone the day afterwards?'

'Yes, she wondered where I'd gone. She thought I might have gone off with my work friends, and was a bit upset that I hadn't said goodbye. Then when I told her that I couldn't remember anything and felt sore all over, she realised I must have been drugged by the man who bought me that drink. She said it was wrong that Henry should get away with it.'

'So was it only when Melanie mentioned it that the idea came into your mind that the man who had bought you the drink was the same man who had spiked your drink?'

'Objection.' Brian Linton rose.

'I'm going to allow it, that's a perfectly fair question.'

'I knew something bad had happened,' said Eva. 'I felt really sore. And I kept thinking I was seeing things and then being sick.'

'I understand that, but it's was not what I was asking. It was Melanie who planted the association with Henry Hanbury, wasn't it? It was not something that you had an independent recollection of?'

'I suppose not.' She said it so quietly that I had to strain to hear her. I didn't press her. It was something I would save for my speech.

My anxiety drained away as my barrister's training kicked in and I gently but firmly steered Eva and the jury to consider other possible interpretations of the evening's events.

I looked at Eva. 'You say that Henry took your arm, led you out of the pub and followed you home. But you said earlier that you can't remember anything clearly after your colleague asked you the time at ten o'clock, so how can you be sure that it was Henry who was with you, and not another man from the pub?'

Eva's voice was firm again. 'It must have been him. There wasn't anyone else it could have been.'

'How can you possibly be sure of that? The pub was

crowded, and you accept you had left your drink unattended?'

I couldn't let her get away with supposition. I was fighting for Henry's life. But already Judge Okonju had leaned forwards towards Eva. 'That is speculation Miss Scott, and you are not allowed to speculate.'

I checked my notes again. 'In your ABE evidence, you described the man who attacked you as tall, wearing a dark jacket and glasses.'

'Yes, that's right, he was.'

'Are you sure about that?'

'Yes.'

'Well, help me with this then, if you would.' I looked down again.

'Do you recall the Sunday, the day after you were assaulted, you spoke to Melanie and then rang the police. Shortly afterwards, you were visited by two police officers, and one of them was a woman?'

'Yes, of course I do.'

'Do you recall that that female police officer had a short conversation with you?'

'Um, no, I can't really remember... specifically. I know we had a chat over a cup of tea.' Eva's voice was hesitant and wary.

'Well, perhaps I can jog your memory.' I put down my notes for a moment and addressed the judge. 'It is on page sixty-three in Your Honour's unused bundle.'

'Thank you, Miss Angel.'

'You were asked for a description of the man who attacked you and you said, and I quote, "He was tall, balding or with very short hair, and wearing a pale grey jacket. I think he was unshaven". Does that help you?'

'I can't remember saying it.'

'With your Honour's leave, I would like to pass Miss Scott

a copy of the relevant page of the officer's notebook, which she has signed.' I held out the piece of paper. An usher scurried over and handed it to Eva.

She looked at it blankly. 'I can't remember saying it.'

I made my voice sound sympathetic. 'Well, it is in the officer's notebook, so I suggest it is exactly what you said. Would you accept that your memory of the event, and therefore your description would have been more accurate at that point – because it was closer to the event – than at any time later?'

'I suppose so, but I still wasn't feeling well.'

'In that first description, you described the man as wearing a pale jacket. Was that a mistake?'

'Well, I suppose it must have been.' She looked across at the police officer behind Brian.

'And you described him as balding. Was that a mistake?'

'I just don't know.' Eva started to look tearful. I knew I had to tread carefully from now on, because upsetting her too much would alienate the jury.

'Would you look please at the defendant in the dock?'

Everyone turned to look at Henry, who blushed a mottled scarlet, and shuffled in his seat.

'It is plain to see that he is wearing thick, horn-rimmed glasses, is it not?'

Eva nodded.

'He was wearing the same horn-rimmed glasses when he was captured on CCTV in the pub. Would you agree that that would also be a distinguishing feature? Strong enough to bear mentioning in a description?'

Brian jumped to his feet again. But the judge interrupted him before he could open his mouth. 'No, Mr Linton! Sit down! These are perfectly valid questions.'

I continued, 'The glasses are, I suggest, such a distinguishing feature that you could not have failed to mention them, if your attacker had actually been this defendant. Would you accept that?'

'He could have taken them off…'

'We have agreed evidence that he is very short-sighted indeed.' I pushed on. 'The reality is that the man you first described did not look like the defendant, that you started to feel the effects of the Rohypnol much later than would be expected from the drink bought for you by Mr Hanbury, and you don't know who accompanied you when you left the pub.' I dropped my voice and continued softly. 'Isn't that the truth of it?'

Eva looked surprised. 'I don't know. I can't remember! And I never wanted to come here and go over it all again. Why should I? Everybody said it was him.'

I sat down. I knew I had done well. Few people realised how notoriously unreliable identifications were, and how difficult they were to recall accurately. Mistaken witnesses often wholeheartedly believed they were right, even when they were later proved to have been disastrously and obviously wrong. I knew I had undermined Eva's recollection in the jury's eyes. But it didn't mean that I had won my case. We had at least one more demanding day ahead of us.

CHAPTER 26

As I walked back into court the following morning, I allowed myself a brief burst of optimism. I felt I had gone quite a long way towards destroying the prosecution's case. And the Crown didn't have much more to throw at me. I looked over at Brian, and noted that he was looking smug, which struck me as odd, given Eva's testimony. The jury had not yet been called in and Brian had told the clerk that he had something to discuss in their absence. As Judge Okonju took his seat, Brian pushed two sheets of paper over to me.

I picked them up and read them in disbelief. Brian was already on his feet, explaining that he wished to call a witness whom they had been unable to track down until last night. I argued as forcefully as I could against allowing them to call a new witness at such late notice. But Judge Okonju accepted Brian's excuse that the statement had been lost, the original interviewing officer had left the force, and the officer in the case had 'strained every sinew' to track down this important witness. Brian explained, 'The witness is Dr Tyzak, a psychotherapist whom the victim consulted after the rape and before she viewed the CCTV footage from the pub or did her ABE interview.'

Judge Okonju frowned, reading the statement. I scanned it quickly. There were two pages of close written manuscript headed 'Session Notes', attached to the doctor's statement. I would have to go through them carefully later. On the face of it, what the notes contained was devastating and seemed to support Eva's testimony that her attacker was wearing a dark jacket and not a pale one, that her assailant was 'tall, with short dark curly hair, heavy-rimmed glasses and a dark blue coat'.

Dr Tyzak's notes supported the prosecution version of events and could destroy our defence. The statement began with the date and time that Eva saw Dr Tyzak, who had been recommended by another patient, her friend Melanie. They continued: 'I have been a practising psychotherapist for five years. My area of expertise involves counselling rape victims and helping them manage the after-effects of trauma. Miss Scott was raped by a stranger whom she spoke to briefly in a pub when he bought her a drink, giving him the opportunity to slip in a date-rape drug, and who followed her home where he raped her. Miss Scott was calm and composed during our interview but in my experience this is often consistent with Post Traumatic Stress Disorder'. The description of the assailant came in an addendum, which also read: 'I should have added that using recovered memory techniques I was able to gain a more accurate description of her assailant.'

Then I spotted that the addendum had only been written yesterday. Someone had been up to something very tricky. Brian was too old school to have been behind it, but I wondered if one of the officers in 'straining every sinew' had overstepped the line.

The statement ran on for another page describing generalised symptoms but I had read enough to know that it could be catastrophic for our case. I thought back to consultations I had had with psychotherapists. I knew how helpful a therapist could be, but now I had a lot of research to do on Dr Tyzak.

There was something off about the timing, too. How convenient that this should come to light now. As a barrister,

Judge Okonju had been a fair, thorough and well-liked prosecutor. He had continued as a fair-minded judge, so he allowed us to rise early so that I had time to take instructions from Henry and prepare my cross-examination based on the new evidence. And he scolded Brian for creating a situation that wasted a whole day of valuable court time by stalling the trial, and murmured something about wasted cost orders against the prosecution. We rose and I took Henry, Cornelia and Lydia into the same airless conference room as before. They sat close together in an anxious huddle. Henry looked exhausted and confused. Cornelia was pale and stricken as she tore a soggy tissue to pieces between her fingers. They spoke over each other.

'Why would the judge allow the new evidence in now? How can that be fair?' Cornelia asked.

'What does it mean for me?' Henry interrupted.

I took a deep breath. 'I know it looks bad, but I'm a little suspicious. Eva virtually accepted under cross-examination that her memory of her attacker didn't match your description properly, so this doctor's evidence seems odd. I haven't had much time, but I've had a quick look through her notes. Firstly, I can't find any evidence in the session notes that Eva said anything about remembering any details of the rape and secondly Dr Tyzak's qualifications look weird. She doesn't have any of the usual letters after her name that I would expect from a properly-qualified psychotherapist. I will do some research tonight and get to the bottom of it. There is definitely something fishy going on.'

Henry looked miserably at his shoes, his shoulders slumped in defeat. The responsibility of his defence suddenly weighed very heavily on me. I knew what prison would hold for an educated but awkward young man: a mix of constant low-level violence simmering below the surface and endless boredom, crammed with two or three others into a tiny cell built for two prisoners, and being strip-searched every time he moved from one place to another. He would be locked up twenty-three out of twenty-four hours, only able to use an open lavatory in front of his cell mates, and always vulnerable to someone wanting to hurt or kill a sex offender. When he was released he would be unlikely to find a job, let alone one that made the most of his experience and qualifications. I looked again at Dr Tyzak's statement. The sooner I got home and started my research the better.

The next morning Dr Anne Tyzak was Brian's first witness. As he stood waiting for the usher to bring her into the courtroom, I noticed he was bouncing on the balls of his feet. I watched her carefully as she was led across the courtroom by the usher to the witness box. Dr Tyzak was older than I had imagined, probably closer to fifty than forty, very slim and wearing thick opaque tights under a very short skirt. She wore no make-up and had long straight hair, which fell to below her shoulders. I wondered briefly how it would feel to sit across from her and unburden myself. Uncomfortable, I decided. She was sworn in and Brian took her through her statement, wisely sticking closely to the script. Then it was my turn to cross-examine her.

I got to my feet. 'You had your first session with Miss Scott at your house, where you practise as a psychotherapist? Is that correct?'

'Yes, I met Mr Hanbury's victim for the first time then.'

'You mean, the complainant, Miss Scott.'

'Mr Hanbury's victim, yes.'

'Forgive me, Dr Tyzak, but this is a court of law and it has not yet been decided who attacked Miss Scott.'

She shot me a hostile glance from beneath her lashes and then turned away slightly to face the jury. 'As far as I am concerned, she is his victim.'

I scribbled a note in my notebook, and then turned back to her. 'Dr Tyzak, I see from your website that your psychotherapeutic orientation is called "person-centred" or "client-centred". Is that right?'

'Yes, that is correct.'

'And "client-centred" is a well-established approach, is that correct?'

'Yes, it is.'

'Is it a tenet of that discipline that the truth is subjective, as we can never truly understand someone else's perspective?'

'Yes.' She nodded.

'Would you go so far as to say that whatever the client believes to be reality should be totally accepted as reality by their therapist?'

'Well, it's more nuanced than that, but broadly speaking that is correct.'

'On your website you say, and I quote: "Awareness is subjective and personal. Your reality is my reality." Is that right?'

'Well, there is a lot more to it than that, but yes, that's my own personal interpretation of the philosophy. How other therapists interpret it is up to them.'

'Do you have a copy of your session notes in front of you?'

'Yes I do.'

'And is it right that those notes were made up by you immediately after each session?'

'Yes they were.'

'Would you accept that it is good practice to note down each important issue at the time?'

'Yes, absolutely.'

'In that case, can you please tell His Honour and the jury where those contemporaneous notes record Miss Scott's description of the man?'

Dr Tyzak put on a pair of green-rimmed reading glasses and peered at the paper in front of her. 'It's in the addendum.'

'Which you wrote yesterday!' I dropped my voice a little. 'Because she didn't say it at the time, did she?'

There was a long pause and Dr Tyzak looked down at her notes again, as if a more convenient answer might magically appear. 'Maybe not in those terms, but when the officer came round yesterday, it jogged my memory and I was sure that she had mentioned a man with dark hair and glasses.'

'Put another way, you were speculating. Speculating because Eva Scott told you that she could not remember what happened that night. That is the truth, isn't it?'

'Everyone's truth is subjective.' Dr Tyzak treated the jury to a condescending smile. 'That is most important.'

I heard a sigh from the bench and looked up to see the judge toss down his pen in irritation.

I continued, 'I see you also practise something called regression therapy, otherwise known as recovered memory therapy?'

'Yes.'

'Did Eva ever say to you that she was able to identify who raped her?'

'Not in those terms exactly.'

'So how did you come to that conclusion?'

'It was part of our therapeutic journey, where I interpreted her dreams to recover memories that had otherwise been repressed because they were too painful to bear. And yesterday, whilst I was speaking to the officer, those fragments fell into place.'

'So the fact that a client has no conscious memory of an event means that you take that as evidence that there is detail at a subconscious level? Which you can intuit as part of the therapeutic journey?'

'Yes, you've sort of grasped it.'

Judge Okonju took his glasses off to look down at her.

I pressed my point. 'Do you accept that regression therapy has been widely discredited by all mainstream therapeutic organisations?'

'Of course, there's always institutionalised resistance to those of us who think for ourselves.'

It was time to change tack. 'You say in your statement that you have been a therapist for five years, what did you do before that?'

'I worked for local government and was a volunteer counsellor in my spare time.'

I paused to allow that to sink in. 'And you have a Doctorate, I see. Are you a Doctor of Medicine?'

'No.'

'A Doctor of Psychiatry perhaps?'

'No.'

'Well, Dr Tyzak, please tell His Honour and the jury what you are a doctor of?'

'I don't see why it is relevant.'

'Please answer the question. I am sure His Honour will stop me if he thinks it is irrelevant.'

'My Doctorate is in Parapsychology.'

I consulted my notes. 'Parapsychology is the study of paranormal and psychic phenomena, including telepathy, precognition, clairvoyance, near-death experiences, reincarnation, and other paranormal claims. Do you accept that definition?'

'Well, I suppose that's partially correct.'

'Ghosts?'

Brian jumped up, his face red. 'Your Honour, I object. Dr Tyzak is here to give important evidence about recent complaint and identification. Miss Angel is badgering her about the minutiae of her PhD. It is totally irrelevant!'

The judge put his glasses back on and glared down at Brian. 'But she has not given evidence about recent complaint or any meaningful identification, has she, Mr Linton? She has given evidence so far that is purely speculation and of no help to this court whatsoever. Furthermore, you may find the minutiae of her PhD irrelevant but personally I have found it very illuminating, as I am sure have the jury.'

Brian sat down, his cheeks flushed with high colour, twisting around to have a whispered conversation with the police officer sitting behind him.

I stood up again. 'Your Honour, I have one final question for this witness.'

'Yes, Miss Angel.'

'Can you tell me when you first googled Henry Hanbury?'

'Not until the officer...' She bit back the rest of her answer.

'Exactly. No further questions, thank you, Your Honour.'

I thought Brian might have re-examined her but he clearly decided it was wiser not to. He rose and said 'That concludes the case for the Crown, your Honour.'

I looked at the jury and sat down. I had made my point. This was the one advantage of representing someone you believed in. I was sure that the description given in Anya Tyzack's statement had not come from Eva. So there was only one other way she could have found out what he looked like.

To my surprise, the judge turned to the jury. 'Members of the jury, a matter of law has arisen, which need not trouble you. So you'll be pleased to know that I intend to give you an early day. Please collect your belongings and we will see you again at 10 a.m. tomorrow.'

The jury members looked delighted, stood up and started to shuffle out. Once they had left, Brian and I got to our feet.

'I need not trouble you, Miss Angel. Please sit down. Mr Linton, I am frankly astonished that counsel of your call and experience would allow such a witness to give evidence. I thought it only fair to warn you that I intend to tell the jury to disregard her evidence entirely. In fairness to you, I am prepared to hear any argument you may put forward after the adjournment. Let it be clear, I am very concerned about the way this case has been run, not least in the late service of statements. I intend to make further enquiries when we reach the end of the trial. There is increasing concern in these courts for the lack of regulation of expert witnesses. You know they're not supposed to be hired guns, brought in to prove one side or the other. And you well know that they should give impartial evidence, not this sort of claptrap larded with dogma.' With that he nodded his head at us. We both bowed as he stood up and left the courtroom.

As I left the courtroom, I could hear Brian and the CPS prosecutor engaged in a low-voiced argument. It was easy to imagine what they were saying. Brian would be telling the CPS that they should never have produced this witness without researching her more thoroughly. It had made them look dishonest as well as incompetent.

But this was a jury who had been fed on stories about Henry being an over-privileged rapist, via both social media and the traditional press. Most of what had been written about him so far was either inaccurate or untrue. I believed they would do their best to judge him on what they heard in the courtroom, but who can escape the slow, seeping influence of public opinion once it has already judged someone and found him guilty?

The judge would have warned them, over and over again, that they must not read about it, research it or discuss it with anyone except in the jury room. But in the real world, how diligently can you really seal yourself off from the media and other people's opinions?

Ten minutes later, when I was just about to go into the robing room, Brian intercepted me, carrying two cups of Costa coffee.

'Shall we have a chat?'

I looked at him with surprise.

'OK, let's go outside to the car park and get some fresh air.'

We both leaned up against a small stone wall and blew on our coffees. Brian said, 'Let's talk turkey.'

'Oh...' I raised my eyebrows. 'You know I'm going to make an application to dismiss.'

'No judge would ever withdraw a rape case at this stage. Not these days.' Brian may have been cynical, but he was also probably right. And he still seemed unnervingly confident. 'I accept my girl was pretty crap, and Dr Tyzak was a fucking disaster, but, by the looks of him, I doubt your boy is up to much either. I'm prepared to offer you a plea to indecent assault and drop the rape altogether.'

'But our defence is that it's mistaken identity. Either he was there or he wasn't – and I can assure you he wasn't.' I looked at Brian in astonishment. I noticed a sheen of sweat on his brow and he smelt slightly of alcohol. So, he knew his case was crumbling. However, he was just calculating the odds in the same way that I was. I thought we were going to win but I couldn't be a hundred per cent sure. And I had no idea how Henry would perform on the stand. I didn't, to be honest, have high hopes of him coming across well. A good defence was always at its strongest at the end of the prosecution case. In my experience, it was once your client was actually in the witness box, being cross-examined, that the case often went downhill.

I took a sip of coffee and studied Brian over the rim of my cup. His ruddy face was more flushed than usual and I could see sweat patches under his arms. 'I'm sure we can come up with some kind of wording between us,' he said.

I spoke, projecting more confidence than I really felt. 'I don't think so!' I took my wig off and pushed my hair out of my eyes. My head itched. 'Are you really going to press ahead with this one? There are no proper forensics and your case is incredibly weak. Even in today's climate, you could drop it altogether.'

'As you know, my dear Miss Angel, rape is the one area of the law where we can prosecute and convict *without* the need for physical evidence.' He smiled at me. 'We can convict on what the victim says. As is right and proper.'

'Complainant,' I corrected him. 'Whatever the outcome, the publicity in this case is going to destroy my client. He is only twenty-four; he is a brilliant biomedical researcher; he's got no form. Where's the public interest?'

Brian snorted. 'I know the CPS would offer a plea of some kind. We could drop it down to indecent assault. Just a fiddle and a giggle. He pleads guilty and – ta da! – no prison sentence. There are ways of doing these things, you know.'

I knew that Brian needed a tally of convictions. A conviction for indecent assault would look a whole lot better for him with the CPS than a not guilty verdict of rape. But would it be better for Henry? This was a very weak case, but nobody can guarantee a 'not guilty' verdict.

Brian looked down at me, his arms crossed. 'You know that no prosecutor can possibly drop this kind of case altogether.'

'Five years ago you would have,' I observed, letting him know that I knew what he was up to.

'As you know, things have changed since then. So, I'll say it again. Your boy pleads guilty to a fiddle and a giggle, and he walks free.'

I have always loathed lawyers who use that phrase. I couldn't believe I still heard it. But there were more important things than semantics at play here. 'He'll be on the Sex

Offenders Register for ten years or more,' I said. 'With all that that means for applying for jobs, travel, having to register with the police every time he spends more than a short time away from home, people abusing him, thinking he's a paedophile...'

'Better than jail. You know the judge isn't allowed to give him less than five years, no matter how nice a young man he is.' Brian treated me to a wolfish grin.

'I'll talk to Henry.' I managed not to shudder at the sight of Brian's nicotine-stained teeth. The coffee was revolting and I threw it into a bin before walking back through security.

I went to see Henry in the little conference room beside the courtroom, Cornelia anxiously tagging behind me, and the more confident click of Lydia's heels alongside her.

'No!' said Henry. 'I didn't do anything wrong, and I won't say that I did.'

'But, darling,' said Cornelia. 'If they don't believe you, you get five whole years in jail, and you'll still be on the Sex Offenders Register.'

He put his arms round his mother. 'It'll be OK, Mum.' She wrapped her arms around him and rested her face on his chest, as he lowered his head onto her shoulder. It was hard to see whether it was a son comforting a mother or a mother reassuring a son.

I turned away, and Lydia followed me. 'They need some time together,' she whispered. We leaned against the wall just outside the room. 'My son and Henry were friends at Oxford,' Lydia said, apparently not realising I knew this already. 'He's called Yevgeny, and he is now twenty-five, just a year older than Henry.' She shook her head. 'After Oxford, he moved back to Moscow so I don't see him as often as I would like to, but when we see each other we hug. He is a loving son, like Henry. I could not bear it if I could not hold my son for five years. But the visits in prison – they cannot do that?'

I shook my head. 'No. The visits are supervised and they have to avoid anything that might mean drugs or weapons being passed over.' I didn't add that lack of funding often left young, able men and women locked in their cells, doing nothing for most of the day. Or that few young men would want to risk hugging their mother in the public visiting space, under the eyes of the other prisoners and guards. There would be consequences. I had to throw off the sudden sense that Cornelia and Henry might not get many more chances to be a mother and son. We had a strong case, but public opinion that rapists and the raped don't get justice was against us. Cornelia straightened up, but she kept her head down and away from Henry, so he couldn't see a tear trickling down her cheek.

When Brian and I got back into Court, I made my application to Judge Okonju, asking him to dismiss the Crown's case. But, as I had suspected, he turned me down. It would have been too easy for the media to interpret such a decision as failing to give a rapist a proper trial. He was going to let the jury make the decision. I only hoped that they would do so fairly.

CHAPTER 27

The next morning started with the prosecution clerk handing me the missing witness statement, as I entered the courtroom. I read it quickly, and remained standing after Judge Okonju came back in and sat down. 'I have here a statement from the barman in the pub, Grant Stockley, Your Honour, so I propose to call him as a witness.'

Brian Linton objected. 'Your Honour, this statement has only just arrived. I would ask for a short adjournment now, so that I may study what it says.'

Judge Okonju took off his glasses and rubbed his eyes. 'This statement has been requested several times over the last three months. That should have given you plenty of time to study it.' He put the glasses back on and looked at Brian wearily. 'Now we've dealt with that, let's have the jury in, and then we can call the defendant. Miss Angel, your client please.'

It was time for Henry to give his side of the story. He walked across the courtroom to the witness box. He stumbled slightly as he stepped up and I saw him covering his embarrassment with a smile. Twelve pairs of eyes were trained intently on him. It was a bad start. Even to me he came across as too cocky.

After a few preliminary questions designed to put him at ease, I went straight to the night that he had met Eva. He told the jury that he had been studying all day, and had hayfever, as he usually did in June. He went to the pub. He thought he would have just one beer to unwind and then have an early night. He described bumping into Eva, which made her spill her drink, so he bought her another.

'Did you find her attractive?' I asked.

'I thought she was nice and very friendly.' He gave a nervous giggle.

When I first met him, I'd wondered whether he was on the autistic spectrum and whether we should get a formal diagnosis. But sometimes that could backfire, as a jury could make unfounded assumptions about even the slightest suggestion of mental issues.

'Your Honour, I have a printout from Barclaycard, the card used by my client that evening. It's on page twenty-three of Your Honour's bundle. The amount he paid, at exactly one minute to nine, matches the price of a pint and one margarita at the White Horse. It confirms that my client only bought one drink for Miss Scott and that he bought it too early for it to have been the drink that was spiked as she first felt the effects of the Rohypnol an hour later.'

'Save your interpretation for your closing speech.' Judge Okonju looked at me severely over his dais.

'I'm sorry, Your Honour.' I turned to Henry. 'When the police originally questioned you about the evening, you said you had only bought one drink. Why didn't you tell them about the drink you bought for Miss Scott?' This was one piece of evidence that worried me, and I had to take the sting out of it before Brian Linton got to question him.

'I said I only drank one drink,' said Henry. 'They didn't ask me how many drinks I bought. They were asking general questions, so I thought maybe it was about something that had happened in the pub after I left, I don't know, pickpocketing or something. I didn't know it was about her until they showed me her picture.'

'What were you wearing?'

'I was wearing my dark blue jacket and a blue jumper.'

'And do you always wear your glasses?'

'Yes, I'm very short-sighted and my eyes are too sensitive for contact lenses.' I asked the usher if Henry could take off his glasses and pass them round the jury so they could see how strong the prescription was.

'What happened next?'

'The pint and the antihistamine made me feel very sleepy, so I went home, probably around half past nine, and as soon as I got home I went to bed and slept until eight the following morning.'

'As far as you're aware, did you pass any CCTV cameras on the way home?'

There was a pause as he seemed to be thinking. 'I think there's one by the bus stop, which is near the pub, but most of my walk home is through the side streets.'

'We have asked for that CCTV evidence, Your Honour, but the prosecution have failed to give it to us.'

Judge Okonju asked Brian what the position was on the retrieval of the CCTV.

'Nothing relevant has been brought to my attention, Your Honour.'

Judge Okonju accepted Brian's answer. One of the strengths of the British justice system is that as a barrister you would never deliberately mislead the court. If you lied about something like the existence of CCTV, you would find yourself in front of the Bar Council, facing the risk of being suspended for six months or even disbarred. It was about complete trust within the profession, and it made even a crumbling British criminal justice system the envy of the world.

'Did you have sex with Eva?'

'No, absolutely not.' His mouth worked silently for a moment and I thought he might cry.

I decided to leave it there. 'Thank you, please wait there.'

Henry smiled nervously again. As I sat down Brian got to his feet. He drew the moment out, letting the tension gather in the silent courtroom. He pulled his wooden lectern towards him and, resting his arm on it, faced the jury, as if he were questioning them. I always found this an irritating mannerism and it struck me as typical of someone as old school as Brian. Then he plunged straight in by drawing attention to Henry's slightly odd personality, as Henry smiled nervously at him.

'So, do you think this is a bit of a joke?'

'Er, n-no.' Henry sounded puzzled.

Brian then attacked with his best point. 'You bought a pretty girl a drink and decided to slip a little something into it. Then you lied to the police about it, didn't you?'

'No, well, yes, I bought her a drink but I didn't put anything in it, and I didn't lie.'

'This girl was easy prey, you watched as she got more drunk and succumbed to the drug so you could escort her home when it had taken a full effect. Didn't you?'

'No, absolutely not! I only bought her a drink to replace the one I spilled.'

'When you followed her home, she could barely walk in a straight line, could she?'

Henry didn't fall into the trap. 'I didn't follow her. I don't know when she left. I just went back home.'

'Yet you didn't see anyone you knew? No phone calls? No texts? No email or social media?'

'No, none of that.'

'Are you asking us to believe that a normal young man, at a university, on a Saturday night, has absolutely no contact with anyone, not even electronically?'

I wondered if Brian was trying to make Henry out to be a weirdo. But the more a defence barrister jumps up and down protesting, the more it looks as if you are trying to protect your client from being accused of lying. I decided to let this one go.

'I was tired. I had hayfever. I slept.'

'So you say. I say that you followed or guided Miss Scott home, having slipped Rohypnol into the drink you bought her, pushed her down on the bed and pulled off her top, leaving her naked, and then you raped her.'

'No, no, no. I didn't.' But Henry's voice sounded weak and uncertain.

Old warhorse that he was, Brian ploughed on, landing the occasional blow without gaining any real ground. But slowly, almost imperceptibly, he was giving the jury the impression of a geeky loner who was unlikely to get a girlfriend and a man whose qualifications in biochemistry made familiarity with drugs almost a certainty.

I hoped that my character witness, the female head of his research department, would help to dispel that image. She confirmed that he had always treated all his colleagues, both male and female, with equal respect, and that he was a brilliant scientist with a great future ahead of him.

Lastly, I called Grant Stockley, the barman of the White Horse on the night of the rape. He remembered Eva because she had become very obviously drunk and had asked him, along with everyone else in the pub, 'back to hers for a party'. He thought she had probably been taking something and was concerned about her. 'She kept saying the same thing over and over again. I kept telling her it was my girlfriend's birthday, so I couldn't come.'

'Did anyone seem to be with her?'

'She seemed to be chatting to quite a lot of people. But she was talking to one man in particular, quite tall he was, and getting bald, but I can't remember his face.'

'Balding,' I repeated. I turned slightly to look at Henry in the dock to emphasise the discrepancy to the jury. Then I made a point of scribbling in my notebook to give the jury time to absorb this new evidence. No wonder Grant's statement had gone astray. 'Thank you, Mr Stockley, please wait there.'

Brian Linton heaved himself to his feet for cross-examination. 'How many drinks had you served that evening?'

Grant shrugged. 'I don't count them. A lot.'

'And how many women did you talk to?'

'You can't expect me to remember that!'

'Indeed. We can't. You don't know how many drinks you served, and you can't remember how many women you spoke to. I would suggest that we cannot rely on your memory as to whether it was Miss Scott, or indeed a completely different woman on a completely different night, who invited you to a party. After all, do you have any proof of the encounter?'

Grant began patting his pockets. 'Well, I know it was the night of my girlfriend's birthday and I think Eva – er, Miss Scott – gave me a business card, and scribbled the address of the party on the back.'

'So you took the card, did you?'

'Yes, I did, just to be polite. I might still have it.' He pulled his wallet out of a pocket and began searching through the compartments. 'Yes, look, here it is. She gave one to a man I was about to serve, too.'

The judge signalled to see the card and scribbled a note.

Brian resumed his questioning. 'Indeed! So, who was this mysterious man?'

I tried to keep my face expressionless but Brian was going off-piste. Neither he nor I knew where this line of questioning was going. It was likely to be catastrophic for one of us.

'I don't know.' The witness looked up at the ceiling and was clearly struggling to remember. 'I think he was tall, balding and wearing a pale grey jacket. And he had a big, flashy watch.'

I looked at the jury to make sure they'd got the point, and saw that most of them were making notes.

Brian had made an elementary mistake and broken one of the cardinal rules of cross-examination – never ask a question to which you don't already know the answer. He had allowed himself to get swept up in the moment and must have thought that a corroborating identification had just fallen into his lap. Instead, he had gifted a point to the defence by introducing an entirely new suspect into the frame. He paused for a moment and then recovered.

'How can you possibly recall what he was wearing? You must have served dozens of people that evening.'

'You are right, I did, but I remembered because I was concerned about the girl and I had decided I was not going to serve her with any more alcohol and I got into a bit of a quarrel with the man in the pale jacket. He accused me of short-changing him and I knew that I hadn't. It's a nice pub and that kind of unpleasantness doesn't happen often. He struck me as a bit of a bully, as if having an expensive watch made him better than the rest of us.'

Belatedly, Brian decided to move on, but the damage to his case had been done. He was clearly rattled and his cross-examination faltered.

I asked the judge permission to re-examine Grant Stockley.

'It's right, isn't it, that the CCTV is only in the till area of the bar?'

'Yes.' The barman nodded.

'Therefore it's possible that someone paying for a drink in cash would not appear on the CCTV?'

'Yes, it's a very long bar and the staff often take the cash to the till because there isn't room for customers to move around.'

I was pleased to see how many of the jury were taking notes. Brian's own goal with Grant Stockley had strengthened my case. Finally, all the evidence had been heard and now all that remained were the final speeches and the judge's summing up.

Brian Linton managed to make a speech lasting nearly an hour with the paltry evidence that he had. A couple of the jurors looked at their watches and one of them yawned. One of the women on the jury looked across at Henry. Was there sympathy in her gaze? Eventually, Brian inched towards the end of his closing remarks. 'And so, members of the jury,' he droned, 'if there is doubt in your mind about the defendant's guilt, it will of course be your pleasure to acquit him. But the Crown contends that there is ample evidence on which you can convict, and the proper verdict for you to return is one of guilty.' He flicked out his gown and sat down heavily, creating a breeze that caused a few of the exhibits on the desk in front of him to flutter to the ground. I sneaked a glance at the wall clock and saw with relief that it was already a quarter to one.

No fair judge would make me give my speech in such an important trial before lunch. I had prepared well the night before but was always grateful for a last opportunity to draw together the threads of my argument and deal with points that might have arisen during the prosecution's closing speech. Now Brian had unintentionally given me more ammunition and I could address the jury with an alternative scenario around the man in the pale jacket. The police had closed their minds to any other possibility, once they had identified Henry as buying Eva a drink and conveniently paying with a card so he could easily be identified. And there was still no satisfactory explanation as to why no one had found the CCTV showing either Henry or Eva leaving the pub, which was something I would emphasise in my speech.

The judge addressed me. 'Miss Angel, I would rather you

started your speech after the short adjournment. We will hear your closing remarks at ten to two. I'll rise now.'

We all stood while the judge withdrew. I picked up my laptop and blue notebook and left the courtroom.

CHAPTER 28

There was nowhere I liked to have lunch near the Inner London Crown Court and time was short, so I raced back to the robing room to eat the sandwich I had brought from home that morning. It was full of other women barristers, picking at takeaway salads and gossiping.

I knew one or two of them by sight, but no one to talk to. Since marrying Theo, I had seen so little of my female friends. We both travelled to courts all over the country, often getting important cases quite late in the day, which meant that it was difficult to plan an evening without having to rearrange several times, and often cancel altogether. I sometimes felt people had given up on us.

I picked up a free copy of *Counsel* magazine from a worn leather sofa, and squeezed in beside two other women. I leafed through a discussion of new acts, ads for wig makers and announcements of new chambers taking on tenants, snatching mouthfuls of my sandwich. I stopped. There was an article by Polly Chan on the importance of mentoring in the law. The woman next to me peered over my shoulder. 'Mentoring, eh? Is that what they're calling it these days!'

'Sorry?' I'd never met the woman before.

She pointed to Polly's article. 'Oldest trick in the book, isn't it? Have an affair to get him to get you into chambers. I usually think that we women should stick up for each other, and that we've all found it hard enough without slagging each other off, but that Polly Chan really gets my goat.'

'Marion,' said the woman sitting beyond her, sharply.

Marion took no notice. 'Of course, I blame Theo Frazer as well. He's the living embodiment of the saying, "When a man marries his mistress, he creates a job vacancy".' She laughed harshly. 'Apparently his wife's in the same chambers, too. Talk about shitting on your own doorstep. But he was like that with his first wife, Louisa. I think he's what's known as a serial monogamist. Someone who is absolutely faithful until he isn't.'

I watched Marion suddenly realise who I was and what she had said but I couldn't make my mouth work. I remembered searching Theo's pockets and the lipstick in the car, and Theo's easy convincing replies to my questions. I had found no evidence that he was having an affair. I had let myself believe that no evidence was proof of innocence.

'Actually, so sorry, must have got that wrong, don't listen to me.' Marion jumped up, scrunching up the remains of her lunch and throwing it at the bin. She gathered up her things and left as quickly as she could. Her friend looked at me with compassion, and got up to follow her, touching me briefly on the shoulder as she passed. Everyone else started talking very fast. I felt that a wall had come up between me and the other women remaining in the robing room, sealing me off from normal conversation. I looked for a friendly face, someone I could trust, amongst the awkward expressions and carefully turned backs.

The door opened and my old friend from my student days, Millie Knight, came in. 'Sophie!' She stopped. 'Are you all right?'

I couldn't make any of my limbs, or my voice, work.

Someone murmured a few words to Millie, and she nodded. Then she came over to kneel beside me, and the robing room emptied around us, as people filtered out. 'What happened?'

I pushed myself off the sofa and stood up, dizzy.

'Let me get a doctor,' said Millie. 'You're obviously ill.'

I shook my head. 'Henry... Hanbury. And his mother. His brother and sister. His research colleagues.' I swallowed. 'They need me to do my job.'

Millie stood up. 'Is it Theo?'

I nodded.

'You can deal with him later. You've got a trial to win now. You're the best criminal lawyer I know, Sophie. You can do it.' She rubbed my arm.

I shook my head. She was just being kind. Theo was the good lawyer in our family. At the door, I stopped and turned back to her. 'Millie?'

'Yes?'

'Does everybody know?'

She dropped her eyes. She was too honest to pretend she didn't know what I meant.

I felt as though a fist had closed over my heart. I could hardly breathe. I had to get out of this claustrophobic room. I couldn't stay here a second longer. I opened the door and saw Marion and her friend outside, turning towards me, looking shocked. I held my head up and walked past them, stony-faced. As I left the building for some fresh air, I could hear people talking around me, but I couldn't make sense of the words. They were just a buzzing sound in my head.

I sat in my car and tried to pull myself together. Somehow I had to get through the next hour and make my speech. I couldn't let Henry and Cornelia down. Trembling, I rang Theo but his phone went straight to voicemail. Five minutes later I was back in Court 9. Polly and Theo, Polly and Theo, the hideous refrain went round and round on a loop. The jury filed back in and took their places and I saw Cornelia in the visitor's gallery looking at me anxiously. I realised I held her future, and Henry's, in my hands. I took my place.

'Yes, Miss Angel,' said Judge Okonju with a brisk smile.

I got to my feet and arranged my laptop on the lectern in front of me. As the defence barrister, I sat closer to the jury than the prosecution and I knew that looking directly into a juror's eyes often made them feel uncomfortable, so I let my eyes roam, occasionally focusing on the space between them. My notes seemed to be sliding out of focus. 'Members of the jury. This is my opportunity to address you on behalf of... my client.' A wave of terror pushed through me, as my mind went blank. The judge looked at me over the top of his spectacles. I felt the blood rush to my face and my palms went sticky.

I'm a professional, I can do this, I'm a professional. Breathe, breathe, breathe. It felt as though time was standing still in the silent courtroom. Then my training and self-discipline kicked in. I gathered my thoughts, started my speech, and lost myself in the moment. My only focus was to save Henry and to see justice done.

CHAPTER 29

The jury did not come back that afternoon. The next day was a Saturday so Henry and Cornelia would have to suffer all weekend, not knowing the verdict.

I tried to reassure them and told them that it meant nothing. 'It's very rare for a jury to come straight back with a verdict, and, if they do, it's more likely to be guilty. I didn't like it, though. I thought the evidence was far from convincing, and that ours was exceptionally strong. But the jury could hardly have missed all the press coverage leading up to the trial, the salacious stories of pillars of society and young, talented men who had been convicted of sexual offences. The inaccurate statistics that were bandied around bore very little relationship to the official ones. But often people would rather believe rumours than facts.

Henry Hanbury had been tried and found guilty thousands of times over on Twitter and Facebook. Even Cornelia had been abused, with messages saying, 'I hope your mother is raped to death'. A Facebook page, called Justice4Eva, claiming to have heard from several other girls he had raped, had gone viral, although it wasn't clear who had originated the page.

At 4.30 p.m. I headed home, to my narrow house in South London. Its pale blue front door had always spelt home for me, but now I hesitated before turning the front door key in the lock. Theo wouldn't be there – he was hosting a reception for American lawyers in chambers. And it was Friday so I still had my stint as a night lawyer that evening before I could allow myself to think properly about him.

I listened to the silence inside before stepping into the hall. The air felt different. As if someone malevolent had been there. I shut the door behind me, and sank slowly down. I couldn't stay here, not with Theo coming back after his reception had finished. He would read the knowledge in my eyes, and I wasn't ready for that. And I wanted to run away from the pain. I went upstairs on trembling legs, and packed a small wheelie case with essentials: my black suit for court, the blue silk bag with the gown and wig-tin, contact lens solution, knickers, T-shirts. I stuffed things in carelessly and with little thought. I would tell Theo I had been called away on an urgent case. Or that my parents were ill. I opened the drawers in the desk to get my credit cards and driving licence. I knew how to run away. I remembered my mother, her hands shaking, pulling our passports out of a drawer and looking round the room to decide what else she needed to take. Now, as an adult, I needed my professional identity – as a lawyer, you need identification on you to get through various levels of security.

I rifled through the desk, and pulled the drawer out. I was trembling so much I had to wrench it, tugging and swearing. I turned it upside down. It was a tidy drawer, because it was Theo's drawer. It had various notebooks, pens and pieces of spare paper stacked neatly, as well as the worn black leather wallet where we kept the passports and driving licences. I took mine.

I was going to be late for the newspaper. I rushed upstairs to change out of my crumpled court clothes, hanging my jacket and skirt up carefully and then throwing my tights into the laundry basket. I threw a toothbrush and some make-up into the bag I was packing. I pulled out my favourite pair of worn jeans and a T-shirt. Theo had given me a beautiful Joseph jacket in soft buttery leather as a consolation for a cancelled holiday last year and I laid it out on the bed. My left foot was halfway into my jeans when I heard the front door slam. In the empty house, it sounded as loud as a gunshot.

I froze, not knowing whether someone had come in or left. The bedroom door was open, and my phone was downstairs, in the kitchen, in my bag. It couldn't be Theo – the reception would barely have started. I strained to hear anything above the distant rumble of traffic but could only hear the sound of my heartbeat, hammering in my head. I couldn't stay here immobile and vulnerable, so I pulled my jeans on as silently as I could. Gripping the banister I stepped softly down the stairs, wincing as a board creaked.

Nothing. I opened the door and looked down the street. I could just see the tail lights of a delivery van at the end of the road, but nothing else. I went back inside and closed the door carefully. There was something else, something unfamiliar and disturbing. It took me a moment before I realised what it was; the faint smell of cigarette smoke hanging in the air.

I felt as if I was facing a tsunami, a massive out-of-control wave, drawing back, gathering strength and preparing to smash my life into fragments. But I was imagining things. Just because Theo was having an affair, that didn't mean we were being burgled. I was late for the paper and told myself there must be an explanation. I scooped up my bag, and just before leaving, glanced at the dresser. There had been a framed photo of Theo and me smiling into the camera on a holiday in France. The photograph was gone. I shook the thought out of my head. Perhaps one of us had moved it ages ago. There was no time to worry about that now. I had to be logical. Why would anyone steal a snapshot? Rather than anything more valuable in the house?

As I walked to the Tube station, dragging the wheelie

bag behind me, I couldn't shake off the sensation of being watched and followed. I heard another set of footsteps echoing in the quiet residential street, bouncing off the walls of the tall terraced houses. I watched my shadow as I passed the streetlamps. If anyone came up behind me, I would see their shadow loom up beside mine. Once I got to the main road, I crossed it twice, looking out of the corner of my eye to see if anyone else did so. I wasn't sure. There were so many people now we were out on the main road. Anyone could be following me. Logically, that also meant I was safer. Muggers and rapists didn't like witnesses. But I only finally felt safe when I got to the newspaper offices.

CHAPTER 30

Chris was talking to two of the news team when I arrived. I hung my coat over a chair with a muttered, 'Hello.'

Katie loped in. 'Hi, Soph, what's up?' I wondered if she meant it, or whether that was just something you say. Then she saw my face and stopped. She leaned over the desk, casting a look over to the big screens on the wall where Chris was now shouting at someone, and said quietly, 'You look dreadful. Come into the meeting room.' She ushered me across the room to a glass-walled cubby hole, closed the door and dropped the blinds. 'What's happened?'

'It's Theo. Someone told me that he's having an affair.' I could hear the shake in my voice, and also the last fragments of hope – that she would say, "Nonsense, Theo adores you, everyone can see that". I scrabbled at the tiniest possibility of escape from the place I'd found myself.

Her eyes dropped.

'Did you know?'

Katie shook her head. 'No, but when I met Louisa, she said that their marriage had ended because he'd had the affair with you. That she'd had no idea that anything was wrong. Also she didn't leave him. He kicked her out. Claimed she'd left him when she went to stay with her parents one weekend. She came back to find the locks changed.'

I frowned. 'Maybe she misunderstood? Or she's trying to blame him?' I hoped, perhaps, that an account given by an ex-wife could hardly be relied upon.

222

'She's a nice woman. Really. Quite sensible. A bit nervy, but a good person.' Katie prised up one of the Venetian blinds. 'Shit, Chris is coming back. Look, let me know if there's anything I can do.'

I nodded, too numb to really care about whether Louisa had or hadn't been telling the truth, and went back to my desk.

'Cheer up, Blondie, it might never happen.' Chris sat down with a crash.

I smiled at him, and logged in. I always suspected that Chris was trying to wind me up with his sexist nicknames and building site taunts. I just ignored them.

Chris would have told me to fuck off if I had ever told him that I believed him to be a kind and deeply principled man underneath all the swearing. I didn't think he was anything like as tough as he made himself out to be. We worked together steadily, until he stood up and put on his jacket. He was almost always the last journalist to leave the office.

'You'll be all right here on your own?'

I nodded and turned back to the screens on my desk.

He hesitated a moment longer, then walked away. I could see his stocky outline reflected in the window glass; a ghostly outline overlaying the city lights outside. I heard the faint electronic echo announcing the lift's arrival, followed by the silence of an empty building.

This was my eyrie. I had a hawk's view of London, outlined in circles, boxes and towers of lights. Random patterns of white, yellow, red and green marked out the roads, the traffic and the landmarks up to the darkness of the horizon. Pinprick aeroplane lights inched across a wide arch of black sky. You couldn't see the stars, but an occasional tiny satellite hovered brightly.

The section desks stretched out like spokes from the editor's desk – features, news, foreign affairs and, in the far distance, the magazine and lifestyle sections. The lights had

and rested my head on my hands. My eyes were gritty with tiredness.

The room is so dark I can barely see. Candles flicker, illuminating the dull gold of the icons in the corner. It is so quiet in here that I can hear the scratching of a branch against the low windows, but it is cold too and my feet are bare. The moon slips out from behind a cloud and I can see that the room is filled with flowers, cascades of roses and lilies, their smell pungent and underlaid with something sickly that sticks in my throat. I see the coffin on the table, and the white shroud of the body, but I can't see who it is. I start to walk towards it, I am cold and afraid but my curiosity is stronger than my fear.

'Oh no, she is sleepwalking again... Take her away! Don't wake her. Don't let her see...' The whispers surround me like a mist, and I am lost.

I jerked awake, my heart thumping. It was the dream again.

Something had woken me. I thought it might have been the lift arriving. On the screen, Lydia's email was still open.

I am sorry. Perhaps I should not have said anything. Your husband, Theo, is working with some solicitors in Birmingham who seem to be involved in illegal activities. When I wanted to find out more about you before approaching you about Kiril, I asked my private detective to look into your husband's life too. He is involved with solicitors who are facilitating drugs and modern slavery.

With best wishes, your friend, Lydia.

Perhaps Lydia's detectives weren't as good as she thought they were. Although she was obviously so rich that getting people checked out by private detectives was routine, I was amazed she'd gone to these lengths to find out about Theo, too. I couldn't believe that Theo would risk everything – his career, his reputation, even his liberty – by getting involved in something illegal. The Theo I knew would never have cheated on me – but was he the Theo I thought I knew? I couldn't see into the darkness around the other desks because it was too bright here at the hub. I thought I could hear someone, but the flooring was soft and absorbed noise. And surely anyone walking across the office would activate the lights as they moved.

I didn't turn round. If there was someone here, I didn't want them to know that I had seen them. But I looked at the reflections in the windows, stretching down the length and height of the room. I could see my own reflection, in jagged fractions, a slight, insubstantial ghost sitting at a desk.

And there. A man, a Cubist impression of a man, in layers of reflections against the darkness, stood very still by the entrance to the office. Just as I had convinced myself again that I was imagining things, he moved, and the light above him went on.

'Hello, Sophie,' he said.

CHAPTER 31

It was Theo. He looked different. He looked like someone you could be afraid of.

I wasn't ready for him. I didn't want to talk about anything until I was. I hastily deleted the email before he could see it.

He walked through the dark office towards me, setting off the automatic lights as he moved. 'I heard about Adam Harris,' he said. 'The police arrived on the doorstep to warn you. I waited for you to come home. Then I got really worried.'

'There's been a flap on here.' My voice sounded false. I wondered why he hadn't rung me, and then if he had noticed that I hadn't asked that question. More layers of lies, or untruths, floated between us like an icy fog drifting across a treacherous road.

Theo lifted my coat from the back of my chair, and held it up for me to put on. 'Ready to come home?'

When my arms were in, Theo paused with the coat still behind my back, so my arms were restricted. 'Did you go through my desk drawers? They're in a mess.'

'I thought I'd lost my driving licence,' I said.

'What did you want it for?' His hands dug into the tops of my arms, pinning them behind me. Was he usually like this? He seemed a different Theo, distorted by my new knowledge.

'Oh, you know, we always need ID for this and for that.'

He sighed as he released my arms and helped me shrug the coat onto my shoulders. He affected not to notice, or maybe didn't notice, the wheelie bag I lugged with me. I could have brought cases home, after all. We were silent as he led me down the dimly-lit corridors, into the empty lift and across the cavernous reception area to the dark street. As I put my seatbelt on, I couldn't help looking round. Was that a man in the shadow of a doorway on the other side of the road? Theo crossed my line of vision to get into the driver's seat, and when I looked again, there was no one there.

When we arrived at our door, a small motorbike passed us. I thought it had been behind us for a while. Before closing the front door, I turned to see if the motorbike had really gone, and glanced quickly up and down the street. I could see one of my neighbours walking their dog. Or did people walk their dogs at two in the morning? Was that really my neighbour? The dog walker disappeared round the corner before I could look again.

'Theo?'

'Yes?' He turned round in our narrow hallway. My heart thudded unpleasantly, and I wanted to challenge him about Polly, but I saw a coldness in his look and the words stuck in my throat. He walked away from me and went upstairs. Half of me wanted to race up after him screaming that he'd destroyed our lives but, at the same time, I desperately clung to the hope that the Bar was rife with rumours and that barristers loved gossip more than any other profession. Polly's constant pawing, flirtation and her inability to recognise boundaries could easily be misinterpreted. And as for Lydia's private detective... I needed to clear my thoughts. My years of experience had taught me how wrong people could be. There were always two sides to every story.

Eventually, I went upstairs. Theo was asleep in the spare room. He sometimes slept there if he came in late, but this felt like a cold, silent act of separation. I took a sleeping pill, but it didn't work, and I lay awake until he shook me out of what felt like my first five minutes of deep sleep to tell me that the police were here to talk about my personal protection and Adam Harris.

It was 9.30 a.m. Two police officers, one a man and one a woman, both looking very young, filled the room with the bulk of their stab vests and the crackle of their radios. Theo hovered solicitously, offering us all coffee. They introduced themselves but their names evaporated into the air. We sat down.

They seemed to be talking about Adam Harris. I tried to rearrange the words spoken around me into something I could understand... 'a previous psychiatric report... erotomania as well as psychosis.'

'It's a delusional disorder where the affected person believes that he is in love with someone,' added the woman. 'Often someone famous or otherwise out of reach – and that they secretly return the love through secret signals.'

Theo and I nodded. We knew about such things.

'And, judging from papers found in his cell when it was searched after his escape, it seems that the person he has fixated on is you.'

'I think the problem may be that I represented him when I was starting out at the Bar. He got an immediate prison sentence and I think he blames me for it.'

'We don't anticipate him being on the loose for much longer,' said one of the police officers. 'It's difficult not to leave a trace these days.'

'Unless you can get a fake identity,' I said.

'We believe Harris is a psychotic loner, not a career criminal with access to that kind of support.'

I decided not to point out that anyone escaping from prison almost definitely had access to some kind of help. And that I knew that Adam Harris had been accused of violence against a woman before, but that the woman had disappeared.

They handed me a personal alarm, a small black object that looked like a mobile phone with just one button on it. 'It's for use in the home, and will work to about fifty metres outside. Press here, and the alarm will be silently activated, alerting us to the problem. Theo went round with one of them to inspect all the locks and doors. Once he had gone upstairs, I tried to explain to the woman police officer that I thought someone had been here, but nothing I said seemed to make sense to me, let alone to her.

'I thought someone was here. I heard a bang and the door was open. I was sure I'd shut it...'

Theo came back in the middle of my explanation, proud that his locks and doors had more than passed muster. 'I have to say, sir, that I'd like to see every householder install this kind of set-up. We wouldn't be called out to so many casual break-ins.' The police officer and Theo beamed approvingly at each other. I didn't say that it was me who had insisted on proper security locks.

'Mrs Frazer seems to think there may have been a recent intruder,' said his colleague.

Theo sat down beside me and took my hand. 'My wife has been highly stressed recently. She's in the middle of a big trial, aren't you, darling? And I've noticed that she tends to... well... be even more nervous at such times. I haven't noticed anything.'

'No, Theo, I don't get more nervous. I'm perfectly able to deal with the stress of a trial.' Was this the man who loved me and who had shared my life for four years, or was he a stranger I barely knew?

'Mrs Frazer?' They both turned to me. They weren't accepting Theo's word for it, and I was grateful.

'There was a photo of me and Theo, framed, on the dresser in the kitchen. It's missing...' I trailed off. They all exchanged glances.

'It's probably nothing,' I said. 'Sorry to bother you.' I felt so tired that as soon as they left I went back to bed. I slept for most of the day, drifting in and out, not wanting to wake up and face Theo's infidelity, the possible threat of Adam Harris and my worries over the Hanbury case. I must be ill, I thought. Theo made sympathetic noises and offered cups of tea. But when I woke up, and edged round the house on cotton wool legs, he wasn't there.

At around seven, I showered and made myself some toast, with a long drink of water to clear my head. Theo came back at half-past eight that evening, whistling. 'Oh, you're up.'

I needed to ask Theo two very important things. But once I'd asked them, they could never be unsaid. Everything would change between us. I gripped the side of the kitchen work surface, feeling the hard granite cool under my skin.

'Theo, I need to ask you something...'

'Really?' he asked, raising an eyebrow with a vicious lash of sarcasm. He held my gaze and I looked away. 'Who have you been talking to?' he said derisively. 'My darling brother Jamie? You know he wants to cause as much trouble between us as possible.'

'Jamie hasn't told me anything. I overheard something in the robing room.' He rolled his eyes. 'Well, if someone said something in the robing room, it must be true. And what did you hear?'

I swallowed. 'It's just that, well, it seems to be common knowledge around the Bar that...'

He looked bored and irritated and checked his mobile phone.

'They said that you were having an affair with Polly. And that you and Louisa hadn't even discussed divorce when you and I started...'

'Polly,' he said. 'I should have known it. This is all about

232

your ridiculous jealousy of Polly. For Christ's sake, Sophie, I've told you all about that situation.' He ran a hand through his hair. 'If you don't believe me, you can always go.'

'Perhaps you should be the one to leave.'

'Don't push me. Don't fucking push me. A man can only take so much.'

We stared at each other until he dropped his voice. 'Go,' he said. 'Just go.'

His face was hard and I was suddenly afraid. Afraid of this house, of this new Theo who looked at me like a distant stranger. Afraid of my own heartbeat, thumping so fast that I could hear it. I couldn't ask Theo about the Birmingham solicitors, not when his face was white with fury. The bag I had packed on Friday night was still in the hall where I had left it forgotten. I pulled it out of the cupboard with shaking hands, dropping it twice. My coat was tangled up with a carrier bag, so I took them both.

Theo didn't move. He sat at the kitchen table with his head in his hands. I stopped and looked at him, hoping and half-expecting him to ask me not to leave. But the one time he lifted his head, his eyes were dark with anger.

I opened the door and stepped out into the fresh air, with the sense of having escaped but also having lost something. Standing in the road, looking back at the house, I expected to see Theo at the door, telling me that he was joking. But there was only a man with a hoodie pulled over his head, walking past. He didn't look at me. Eventually, when Theo didn't call and didn't come out of the house, an empty taxi went past. I raised my hand, and got in.

'Where to, love?'

I didn't hesitate. There was only one other option. I went to chambers and spent a restless night on the lumpy sofa in my room, surrounded by the distant noises of the night traffic drifting into the deserted Inner Temple. I had left my security alarm behind, and besides, it only worked in my home. If Adam Harris wanted to find me – well, at that moment, I wasn't sure that I cared.

CHAPTER 32

Sunday morning was bright and fair, with a cold edge to the sunshine. My old VW Golf was parked under a chestnut tree, looking shabby beside the sleek new cars that barristers who specialised in commercial law could afford. Theo always teased me about my car. He said no one would take me seriously in a battered old banger. 'You've got to think of your image.'

But I always thought of chambers' rent, the mortgage and whether my parents might need financial help at some point. 'It gets me from A to B,' I said. 'That's good enough for me.' Theo would shake his head and laugh about how women always failed to see the bigger picture. 'I'm only thinking of you. You'd impress people more if you had a better car.'

The Temple was empty and almost silent. I could hear birdsong and the distant rumble of traffic along the Embankment. A gaggle of tourists, rustling maps and peering at their phones, ventured in, blinking in the sunshine. They photographed each other against the golden stone of the Round Church, and shrieked as their heels turned on the flagstones.

I put my key in the ignition, but couldn't face going back to Theo in South London. I took the key out, and rested my head on the steering wheel. Maybe he was right. Maybe I was being unreasonably jealous, listening to stupid gossip. A flicker of hope fluttered for a few moments.

'Papa,' I whispered. I suddenly longed for home, for my father. It was just past seven in the morning. If I started now I would miss any weekend traffic on the M2 and I could be there in a couple of hours.

An hour and a half later, I pulled into the cracked, overgrown driveway. The garden gate was askew on its hinges, the green paint peeling. As I stepped out of the car I could smell the familiar smell of home, the mulch of fallen leaves, a wood fire and the aroma of my father's cooking. Before I had time to gather up my coat and bag, the front door was open and my father stood there, his arms spread wide in welcome. His face dropped as he took in my crumpled clothes and swollen, red eyes. 'Oh, my darling Sova! What is it? Come in. Sit down. Tea! Tea! Elinor, put on the kettle, our Sova is home!'

'Not now, Vassily, I'm busy. You do it.' My mother's voice floated down from upstairs.

He ushered me into the kitchen and busied himself with the kettle and the Aga, then came and sat beside me. He took my hand in his as his face creased with concern. 'You have had a row with Theo? Don't be so upset. In a marriage these things happen. The rows I've had with your mother! Ach! So many. But in the end they always blow over.'

I shook my head mutely. A tear dripped down my nose and onto the tablecloth.

'It's worse? Something worse than just a row? Nyet, nyet. Not another woman?'

'Polly, in my chambers. People say he's been having an affair for months.' I sniffed.

My father's gnarled hands curled into fists. 'Never mind what people say. What does Theo say?'

'He says I'm imagining it, that I'm driving him mad with my jealousy and the way I go on about things. He says...'

'What?'

'He says I'm stupid to believe the gossip. Papa, he's so angry with me.'

My father jumped up. 'That little shit, that *govnyuk*.' Other Russian expletives followed, only some of which I understood.

'I did not give him my beautiful daughter to destroy in this way. I will rip him apart with my bare hands!'

'Papa, Papa. No. Calm down, you're not helping.'

'I always said he was no good. I told your mother when we first met him – my Sova make mistake. Man is shit; divorced. I never liked him, never!'

'Well that's the first I've heard of it! You never told me you didn't like him,' I protested.

'What would have been the point? You were so headstrong, so in love.'

'So you were pretending when you said you would love him like a son!'

'No. Yes. Maybe. I just wanted you to be happy.'

'It seems everyone in my life is pretending.' I took a breath. 'What else are you lying to me about?'

'I don't know… I don't know what you mean.' But he looked evasive.

Suddenly everything came flooding out. 'What about how we escaped from Moscow and Kiril didn't?'

'What? Who have you been talking to?' He was hiding something, I could see that. My father's face was usually so open and honest. At least, that was what I had always thought.

'Papa, you were always the one who told me that justice was so important. That we all, each of us, have to stand up for ourselves. That if we let lies take hold they will destroy us. But you don't say what happened to Kiril.'

'You don't know how it was. You don't know anything. You were just a child. Kiril drowned in the Moskva river. He was drunk. Many Russians are drunk.'

I shook my head. 'No, Papa, I can see now, that isn't what happened.'

He was an old man suddenly, shrunken over the kitchen

table. 'Don't ask questions,' he said. 'Don't ask about things you don't understand.'

'That's what my job is,' I said. 'Asking questions about things people don't understand. And you encouraged me to do it. You must be a lawyer, you said. You must fight for justice. Why? Why did I have to fight for justice? Was it to ease your conscience?'

Papa looked very pale. 'No, Sova... please...' He put a hand out to me. It was trembling.

I was suddenly angry. The weeks of suspicion and the sudden shock of the discovery overwhelmed me. The rage and hurt rose up in me and looked for an outlet. 'I'm not English, I'm not Russian. I don't belong anywhere. *You* wanted me to be a lawyer to fulfil your dreams of justice, not mine. Life isn't really like one of your stupid fairy tales. It doesn't end happily ever after, not for me...'

My father flinched with each sentence I uttered. I hated myself for hurting him but the toxic words would not stop, pouring out of me like water out of a broken dam.

My mother spoke from the doorway. 'We only ever wanted you to be happy, darling. Your father and I came back here with nothing; poor and frightened. We never wanted *you* to feel like that. A lawyer, a doctor – whatever happens, wherever you go, you can take that with you.'

'Everyone needs lawyers,' said Papa. 'Even dictators, even tyrants. And here we thought being a lawyer would give you a good life, a safe life here, working in a country with proper laws, proper rights for citizen against state.' He looked at me, his face utterly crumpled and bereft. 'We never thought it would make you unhappy.'

'Tell me now, once and for all. What happened to Kiril?'

He clutched on to the back of a kitchen chair as if it were the only thing holding him up. 'Why do you want to know now? It was all so long ago. Nothing good can come of asking these questions. Just let it go, let it all go.'

I picked up my bag and headed for the door. I could hear my father stumbling after me. 'No, no, Sova, come back. Don't drive like this. Wait! Talk! Please…' But I didn't stop. I got in my car and drove off, driving too fast as I plunged down the lane. I glanced in the rearview mirror and saw him standing by the broken gate, forlorn in the falling light.

It was only when I reached the T-junction at the end of our road that I realised I had nowhere left to go. I could not go back home to South London, and I couldn't survive another night on the lumpy sofa in chambers.

I drove to a cheap hotel near chambers, converted from an office block. But when I got there, I realised that my credit cards were in my other bag.

'I don't know what's happened, I was sure I had it with me,' I stammered, but the receptionist gave me the bland smile of someone who has heard such things many times before.

I stumbled out. I had seventeen pounds in cash in my purse. It would have to be the chambers sofa, with only a glass front door between me and Adam Harris, after all.

Not that I had given him a moment's thought all day. Adam Harris was just one of those minor threats that all barristers endure from time to time, which never come to anything. Gus had been threatened twice. Gus. He had a spare room. I rang him, but as soon as I heard his voice, I started to cry.

'Where are you, Sophie?' he asked. 'Wait there, and I'll come and get you.'

I shook my head without realising he couldn't see me. I ended the call and texted him.

See you in a minute.

He was waiting by the front door.

CHAPTER 33

I didn't tell Gus much, but I think he probably guessed most of it.

'You can stay here as long as you like,' he said. 'What do you need for now? I can whip up some bacon and eggs if you're hungry.'

My thoughts were blurred and my head ached. 'Have you got Wi-Fi? So I can deal with any important emails, then bed. I don't need to eat, thanks.'

'Sure? I make a mean bacon and eggs.' Gus helped me set up, and I worked through a fog of pain and tiredness. I just hoped the emails made sense.

As soon as I collapsed onto the bed in Gus's spare room and pulled the duvet up, I was asleep.

Gus woke me the following morning, gently shaking my shoulder. He was dressed in his suit, and holding a cup of steaming coffee. Bright winter sunlight flooded the room.

'Sophie, it's half past eight, do you want me to ring the clerks and tell them you're ill? I'm not in court today, I can easily go down to Inner London and babysit the jury.'

I shook my head, groggy from sleep.

'If it's a conviction he won't be sentenced today and he won't get bail so there is nothing much to do. You looked shattered last night. Why don't you just stay in bed?'

I sat up and tried to focus. 'I must have slept through my alarm. No, Gus, that's incredibly sweet of you but I have to be there. I owe it to Henry and his mother. I have to be there, whatever happens.'

'If you're sure.'

'Yes, I'm sure. I'll easily make it.'

Gus left the coffee for me on a bedside table. I quickly got dressed. My black suit needed pressing but at least it would be hidden by my gown once I was robed. I checked in my wig-tin and was relieved to find that I at least had a spare set of clean, starched bands.

I took the coffee cup back into the kitchen, and stopped to look at some photos propped up on the mantelpiece. There was Gus in a polo team with his arms flung over the shoulder of a minor royal. There was another of him at a beach bar smiling up towards the camera, his legs white and skinny under baggy board shorts.

And then another, in a troop carrier, wearing a helmet and surrounded by soldiers, holding up his thumb with a slightly uncertain grin on his face. So Gus had taken that courts martial brief in Helmand, which the rest of chambers had hurriedly turned down. I remembered him saying something about how important it was to defend the people who were defending us, but he had never mentioned it otherwise. It was strange, seeing this Gus rather than the awkward, clever lawyer.

Barely an hour later, I was walking into the ladies' robing room at Inner London, relieved to see that there was no one there I knew. I put on my wig and gown and went straight to Court 9 to wait for Henry.

By twenty past ten, he still hadn't arrived. I checked my phone again to see if there was a message, but there was nothing. I wondered whether he could possibly be so stupid as to have run away. I was about to ring chambers to see if he had telephoned when Cornelia appeared at the end of the corridor. She looked even more distraught than usual.

'I'm so sorry! Henry had to go back and get something from home. He said he would be on the next train but there's been some major delay on the underground, and no one seems to know what it is,' she said.

I quickly checked the Transport for London information on my phone. She was right. Several trains were cancelled due to an incident.

'It's fine, it's fine. I'll explain it to the judge.' I hoped my tone would calm Cornelia. The heavy double doors swung open when we pushed them. Once everyone was assembled, the judge told the jury to continue their deliberations, as Henry was held up until the trains started running again. The jurors stood up and filed out, some of them glancing over at me as they did so. I tried to read their expressions to gauge their mood, but it was impossible.

I pushed back my seat, and went over to Cornelia, taking her arm to walk her out into the corridor. She was trembling slightly, reminding me of a frightened dog who has been abandoned by his owner. 'What do you think, Sophie? How long will they take?'

'I'm afraid it's not easy to say. Sometimes they can be out for a couple of days.' Her body sagged, and her face seemed to collapse in on itself. I struggled to find something comforting to tell her. 'But probably not that long. The Crown's case is fairly weak, and Henry gave evidence really well.' I was saved from having to say more by my phone vibrating. I saw that it was chambers.

'I'm sorry, I'll have to take this.' I turned away.

'Hello, Miss, it's Lee.' He sounded unusually friendly, which immediately made me suspicious. Everyone always said that you were much safer if Lee was snarling at you. 'How are you getting on? Jury still out?'

Lee's ability to see through walls and know what was

242

going on never ceased to amaze me. 'Yes, no news.'

'Do you think you'll get a result by the end of today?'

'Can't tell, really. Maybe,' I said.

He went to say that my case for next week had settled. 'And I've got you that nice little return from Mr Armitage starting down at Croydon on Wednesday. It's a GBH, two-hander, you're first on the indictment.'

'What?' I suddenly felt desperately tired, as if I might sink into the floor and never get up again. The thought of finishing here, preparing another case overnight, then getting up and down to Croydon on the train overwhelmed me. I had to sort out my marriage before I could think of anything else.

'I'm going to say no to this one, Lee.'

He was already talking over me. 'Well, Miss, it will probably plead. I don't have anyone else to cover it, so if you don't do it, I'll have to let it go out of chambers. The solicitors won't be pleased.'

'Lee. I'm really sorry. But my decision is final.' He hung up without saying goodbye. I made my excuses to Cornelia, told her to listen out for the tannoy in case we were called back to court and made my way back to the robing room.

It was the usual mess of discarded disposable coffee cups and crumpled bits of paper. There was no window and the room smelled slightly of cheap deodorant. I didn't have anything to read, or anything else to pass the time, and found it impossible to concentrate on the paperwork I had in my case. I picked up a discarded copy of yesterday's *Times* from the battered leather sofa and tried to do the sudoku, but my thoughts kept drifting back to Theo and Polly.

I checked the travel news on my phone. Henry's failure to turn up didn't look good, but there had genuinely been an incident. However, two hours after my phone app informed me that the underground was working normally again, there was still no sign of him. Had he run for it? But it made no sense. Could my judgement have been so off? Could he actually be guilty after all? I believed that justice was dependent on every case being argued and that it couldn't be lawyers deciding who was guilty and who was innocent. But sitting on the dilapidated sofa in the robing room, I knew that I wanted to defend innocent parties and prosecute guilty ones. You have to take a case when you're assigned it – and everyone deserves a defence. The evidence must be tested. All these things we tell ourselves over and over again.

'Will all parties in the case of Hanbury please go to Court 9 immediately,'

I jumped. The jury had only been out for an hour that morning, I couldn't believe we were being called back to court already.

I met up with Cornelia and Lydia at the door of the court. Cornelia was white, her lips compressed, and she was clinging to Lydia's slender arm as if she were about to pass out. I looked at Lydia and she shook her head. No Henry. The courtroom was crowded as another case had started and barristers and solicitors were spread across their benches.

'Is it a verdict?' I whispered to the usher.

'No, it's a question from the jury.' She bustled off.

The court was halfway through another trial, so the other barristers shuffled up to allow us to sit down. There was a commotion at the back of the court as the prisoner in the dock from the other case was taken downstairs.

The judge cleared his throat. 'Ah, yes, Mr Linton, Miss Angel, there is a question from the jury.'

'Yes, Your Honour,' we replied in unison, both of us hoping that the query might indicate how the jury's minds were working.

'Yes, well I have looked at this and have taken a view. I am sure you will both agree,' said the judge. 'But I will read the question into the record. The jury would like to know if there is any CCTV of the defendant and the complainant walking back to the complainant's flat.' The judge swivelled in his seat and looked over at the jury.

'Members of the jury, there has been no CCTV produced by either side in this case, except for the CCTV by the till in the pub. The evidence is now closed, which means that neither side may put any more evidence before you. You must decide this case on the facts that you already have. Will you please return to the jury-room and continue with your deliberations.'

One or two jurors looked embarrassed, as they filed out again. Ten minutes later I was sequestered with Cornelia and Lydia in a small conference room. I was now seriously worried about Cornelia and how much more of this she could bear.

'What does that question mean? Is it good for Henry? Why do they want to know?' Cornelia asked as she twisted her hands in her lap. 'And where is he? Why hasn't he called?'

Lydia murmured something about how long it took the underground to recover from 'an incident'. 'If Henry is trying to get here, he won't be able to call.'

'And I think the question is good for us,' I began slowly. 'It means they are thinking very carefully about our defence. They're looking for support for our assertion that Henry left the pub at least an hour before Eva did. In fact, it's a real pain that there isn't any CCTV because it would have supported us. I asked the prosecutor about it and he said they hadn't been able to find it, that there was probably no film in the camera. That tends to be the way with CCTV. Although the whole of Britain, and London, in particular, is bristling with cameras, not even five per cent of crimes are solved by it. In my experience, the camera is usually pointing the wrong way at the crucial moment, or the film has been erased.'

Cornelia was not to be so easily distracted by my lecture on prosecution equipment. 'Where do you think he is?' asked Cornelia. 'The trains must be running by now, surely?'

I checked my phone again. 'I think it's getting sorted.' I tried to smile at her.

'He's not answering his phone. Surely he must be able to answer his phone?'

Lydia laid a hand on her arm. 'He'll be here soon. Try not to worry, Cornelia, my dear.'

We fell into silence after that, but I felt I should stay with her. Cornelia produced a sandwich she had made for Henry, lovingly wrapped in old-fashioned greaseproof paper, and offered it to me. I declined. I saw the clock was inching towards one o'clock, I warned her not to be too startled if there was a tannoy just before one as it would just be the court releasing us until two. At that moment, there was a knock on the door as Philip gave it a gentle rap with his knuckles.

'I just popped up to court to see if there was any news. They are just about to put out a call. It's a verdict.'

CHAPTER 34

After reassembling the prosecution, the officer in the case and the defence, we waited for the jury to be led in. We could hear the murmuring of their voices on the other side of the door. A few of them looked dishevelled and tired, and none of them seemed cheerful. No one glanced over to the dock where Henry should have been sitting, or at me. That was a bad sign. In my experience, acquitting juries often looked over at the defendant, sometimes giving a reassuring smile. The clerk got to her feet.

'Would the foreman please stand?' A young man wearing a T-shirt and jeans got to his feet. 'Members of the jury, have you reached a verdict on which you all agree?'

The foreman took out a piece of paper and held it out in front of him. I noticed his hands were trembling slightly. 'Yes we have.'

'Do you find the defendant guilty or not guilty of rape?'

The court was utterly silent, except for the soft hum of the air conditioning unit. I was sure that the clerk must have been able to hear my heartbeat.

'Not guilty, Your Honour.'

'And that is the verdict of you all?'

I turned to smile at Cornelia but her head was in her hands. She was sobbing. There are few emotions that I have experienced like the rush of winning a case. The adrenalin in my veins, the explosion of euphoria mingled with intense relief that it was over. Even my anguish over Theo was forgotten in the moment.

As we left the courtroom, Cornelia clung to me, as if afraid to lose me in the throng of people hurrying to and from different courts. 'Henry is in breach of his bail conditions,' I explained. 'So he must register with the Court when he arrives or he will be in big trouble.' I strained my eyes, hoping to see a gangling figure hurrying towards us.

When we got outside, Philip standing protectively beside us, Lydia stood away from us. 'This is Cornelia's moment,' she whispered, but her eyes were concerned. Standing on the steps of the court in the sunshine as reporters lobbed questions at us, I advised her to say nothing other than to thank the jury, but Cornelia could not be silenced.

A single news reporter broke free from the gaggle, and ran up the steps, thrusting a microphone at her, shouting a question that the wind whipped away from me. Before I could draw Cornelia away, she touched her hair briefly, as if to neaten it and spoke up, trying to raise her voice over the sound of the traffic.

'This is not a day for celebration,' she took the microphone from the reporter. 'My son has been named and shamed on social media. As a result of all the terrible publicity, all our lives have been damaged. He has been forced out of the university he loved where he was in the middle of important research. That research has now lost its funding. Someone else will probably do that research somewhere else, but the delay may cost people their lives. Our lives, and theirs, will be permanently affected.'

I tried to draw her back, eyeing the street over the reporter's head for a taxi, so that I could get Cornelia into it before she made things worse. 'And as for the consequences on my son's life,' Cornelia continued, 'whenever anyone googles him, the word rape will appear.' Her voice broke and her eyes were bright with tears. 'So, in answer to your question, no there won't be any champagne corks popping in our house tonight.'

I raised a hand and, finally, a taxi halted beside us. 'Thank you,' said Philip, stepping forward and helping Cornelia into the taxi. He turned to face the microphones. 'This has been very hard on Henry Hanbury's mother. I'd ask everyone to respect her privacy.'

I stepped away from the small group of people and went to find my car. I waited to feel that rush of victory again. The feeling of having conquered the world, coursing through my veins, hot and vibrant, like an explosion of sunshine. Winning a case was the best feeling in the world. But suddenly this didn't feel like winning. All I felt was sad. For Henry and Cornelia. And for Eva, who had been raped and then let down by the system, and had gone through all this and yet the man who'd really raped her was still out there. And I was tired. So tired.

'Sophie.' A hand touched my elbow lightly. It was Lydia. She stood beside me, bright and birdlike, dressed in red, her hair carefully styled as usual. 'I think a strong coffee would do you good, don't you?' She waved away a chauffeur, who had appeared in a car to collect her, and steered me along to a small café outside the court.

As Lydia and I walked towards the coffee shop, I caught sight of Brian standing in the main entrance to the court. He was pacing up and down whilst talking into his phone. It struck me as odd that he was still in his robes even though the case was over. As I watched he was approached by two police officers. They were moving with a slow and heavy tread. Perhaps he had another case to deal with but it seemed unlikely so late in the day. Still, it was none of my business and I brought my attention back to Lydia.

'You did well,' she said, surprising me by stirring sugar into her coffee. 'Yes, I know, horrible habit, isn't it?' She nodded towards the sugar. 'So, what's wrong?'

Lydia was the last person I would normally have confided in, but I did. I needed somebody, she was there and she also knew some of it already, or thought she did. I told her everything. 'Theo has accused me of being paranoid, of being so anxious that I'm imagining things that aren't there. And my nightmares about Russia and my childhood have come back.'

She looked at me over her coffee, and I wondered if we were all pawns in some game she was playing. But when she spoke, it was to reassure. 'You have a right to be anxious. You know what it's like to be different. Not to belong.'

I didn't want to answer. I could hear the children teasing me in the playground and taunting me for 'being a communist'.

'Maybe it's time to go back,' Lydia spoke gently. 'Go back and face your fears. We all have to stop running at some point.'

'Back where?' I genuinely didn't understand.

'To Russia,' said Lydia. 'I believe that nightmares are unresolved feelings and experiences that have been buried alive and will come back to haunt you until you face them. Find out more about how things really were then, and what made people do what they did.' She took a deep breath. 'I didn't want to tell you before, but after Kiril died and your family left, I stayed in touch with your grandparents because they were devastated at the loss of both their sons. And after they died, I bought the dacha. Come to the dacha with me – maybe you'll find some answers there. And your uncle Kiril's grave is close by.'

I shook my head. 'I certainly can't upset Chris and my shifts at the paper.'

'Pah! Chris will not be a problem. You will not lose your spot at the paper.'

I thought of the weeks ahead. Having turned down the case in Croydon, I now didn't have any cases for more than three weeks. But I thought of Lee's displeasure, breathing heavily down the phone. 'The clerks get furious if we turn down cases. I need to earn, more than ever, if I'm going to...' I couldn't say the word 'divorce'.

Lydia stirred her coffee, and I could hear the spoon tinkle against the thick mug. I reached a decision. 'Besides, Theo and I haven't really talked about everything yet, so I'm not going to make any final decisions. I still have no real evidence that the rumours are true and that he's lying.' I managed a crooked smile. 'We barristers always say that everyone deserves a defence, don't we?' I didn't add that I hadn't even begun to think about how I was going to tackle the issue over Theo's work with Wei Chan. If he really was doing something illegal, it would ruin his career – perhaps even mine – and damage chambers very badly. I occasionally worried that he sailed too close to the wind but these allegations – of involvement with people traffickers and drug smugglers – went beyond anything I would ever have believed of him.

Lydia started to say something, then stopped. 'Well, if you change your mind about Russia, I'll give you my private number.'

I got out my phone and switched it on. My screensaver – a photo of me and Theo on holiday last year – flashed up. He was smiling down at me. I took down Lydia's number and thanked her but I was thinking about Theo and how there was no actual evidence against him. Suddenly the allegations against him seemed almost meaningless. A few words overheard in a robing room. Something seen by a private detective... I knew how Polly was around men. Anyone watching would think she was having an affair with any man she spoke to. I needed to contact Theo so we could talk, find out what the real truth was and perhaps arrange counselling. I was vaguely aware of a man getting up at the same time as I did, and throwing some money on the table. But I was tired of seeing threats in shadows. So tired.

As I pulled out of the car park, I stopped to let a group of pedestrians cross the road. I recognised them as several members of my jury. One of them saw me and nudged the others, two or three of them gave me a thumbs up and big smiles, and just for a moment I forgot about everything else; I wasn't the deceived and rejected wife. I was a lawyer, and a good one at that. I headed out to Newington Causeway and my heart lifted again as I drove over Blackfriars Bridge. The dome of St Paul's Cathedral glowed with the majesty of history in the late afternoon sun. The geometric patterns of the Gherkin building and the sharper, jagged needle of the Shard shimmered gold in a contemporary reply. This was London. This was my city.

I had just parked the car in the Temple, when my phone vibrated. I didn't recognise the number but pressed the green icon anyway.

'Sophie? It's Brian.' I felt a jolt of surprise. He would hardly be calling to congratulate me. His voice seemed different. It had lost its pompous edge and he sounded gentle and hesitant.

'Can you meet me in your chambers? I need to tell you something.'

CHAPTER 35

As I reached the steps of Medlar Court, I noticed someone hurrying towards me. As he drew nearer, I was surprised to see that it was Brian Linton already. I swiped my entrance card and pushed hard on the heavy oak door. Brian caught up and followed me into the empty entrance hall. He looked haggard, his tie was askew and his jacket undone. In the light of a fading afternoon, he seemed older. In his sixties, I thought.

'What is it Brian? Why are you here? Have I forgotten to sign off on something?'

'Can we go in here?' He nodded towards one of the ground floor conference rooms.

'Sure,' I replied, opening the door and sliding the engaged sign across. As I looked at him, I noticed that he had something in his hand; it looked like a DVD.

'Sophie, this is so terrible – I just had to come and see you personally.'

I suddenly knew with a sickening certainty what was on the disc. I felt my stomach clench. 'Oh dear God, no! It's the missing CCTV, isn't it? The one from outside the pub.'

Brian handed it over to me. I saw him swallow. 'It exonerates Henry – everything he said about leaving alone at 9.30 p.m. is true. And it shows Eva, looking very unsteady, leaving about an hour later with a tall balding man in a pale jacket who appears to be holding her up, or steering her.'

I groped behind me for a chair and sat down with relief.

'This wouldn't have happened ten years ago,' he said.

'These bloody cuts... we don't have the manpower anymore.' He trailed off.

For a moment, I stopped seeing him as my opponent and saw the fundamentally decent man behind the prosecutor. 'And Sophie, I'm sorry...' He shook his head in despair; his face was bleached of colour. Was there more?

'Henry Hanbury stepped in front of the train at Reading station this morning. He killed himself.'

The world stopped for a moment. I stared at Brian, hoping I had misheard.

'I didn't believe him,' said Brian, looking down at me. 'I'm sorry, I really didn't. I guess years of prosecuting make you cynical.' He swallowed again and shuffled his feet. 'We both know that the mischief in all this is that it's the police who decide what should and shouldn't be disclosed. It's up to them. If the officer in the case knew about this and actually decided not to disclose it, I will do everything I can to bring a shit load of trouble down on his head.' He paused, seeming to gather his thoughts. 'But it's probably not even that. We all know how desperately the whole sodding criminal justice system is under-resourced and under-staffed. It's probably just another fuck-up. I am so sorry, Sophie.' He looked down at me and turned back to the door to let himself out.

'But none of that will bring Henry back. If I'd had that evidence at the outset we probably wouldn't even have gone to trial,' I said to the closing door.

I took out my laptop and loaded the disc. And there was Henry, distinct despite the grainy footage. The same awkward gait and floppy hair. He was loping away from the pub, on his own. The time in the corner of the screen showed 21.28. He had left the pub before half past nine. Nearly an hour before Eva first felt the effects of the Rohypnol. I fast forwarded to just after 10.30 p.m. The man holding Eva's arm was around the same height and build as Henry, but he was almost bald. I could see something like a big watch on his wrist.

I stayed at my desk, with my head in my hands, trying to absorb the horror of what I had heard. I thought of the young man who had shambled into my chambers all those weeks ago. His awkwardness, his passion for his research, his curiously old-fashioned courtesy and his naive belief that if you had done nothing wrong, then you had nothing to fear.

A wave of sorrow and disbelief pushed through me. Had we all been so focused on the strategy of the trial that we hadn't picked up on the signals of despair? I knew that the adversarial system only works if both parties really care about winning. It's like a game of chess in that you were constantly trying to out-manoeuvre your opposition with the few weapons you had at your disposal and very little back-up. It was easy to forget that there was a human being at the heart of it all, whose life was being changed forever.

I stayed at Gus's for the rest of that week. He admitted he'd heard the rumours about Polly and Theo because he had first-hand experience of her flirtatious behaviour. 'The Bar is a hothouse for rumours, and I didn't want to say anything unless I was sure.' I barely saw him because he had a three-day legal argument in a terrorism case in the high security court in Woolwich. I managed to get hold of Theo on the phone as he was walking from court to chambers at the end of the day. He sounded aggrieved that I'd believed what other people had said about him without checking with him first, and I almost believed I was the one in the wrong, the one who'd created a fuss out of a few scraps of gossip. His voice was guarded, and it was difficult to assess how we should move forward, but he agreed to counselling. I said I would make an appointment. I didn't want to mention the allegations about him being involved with illegal activities in Wei Chan's practice on the phone. Maybe we could discuss it after we'd been to counselling.

'Good, good, that's great,' he said.

I managed to get a cancellation appointment for Thursday after work. I texted him, and he texted back. 'Let's try it.' Suddenly, I thought it might be all right. I looked down from my window into Medlar Court and felt some sense of peace. All the rumours online about Henry had been false. So it was possible that the gossip about Theo was false too. At least I would have the courage to hear him out. I could plan here, in this room with its beautiful view and shabby furniture. I turned towards my desk and flinched as the door opened. The light was blocked out by a big man standing there.

'Lee!'

'Good morning.' He rapped his knuckles, unnecessarily, on the open door. His paunch hung over his belt, and the effort of climbing three flights of stairs had left him panting.

Normally, he was wedged behind his vast desk with the huge window over the Thames as a backdrop. It was odd to see him like this, slightly incongruous, like a snail without its shell.

'Are you looking for someone?' I asked.

'Yes, Miss. You, actually.'

'Really? What about?'

He looked uncomfortable. 'Well, you know my brother is the senior clerk at that new set in High Holborn?'

'Er, no I didn't actually.' I wondered if Lee was going to ask a favour for his brother, although I couldn't think what it could be.

'Well, it's a good set. Lots of white collar crime, good solicitors, low rent. Really up and coming... but not enough women tenants. They are having trouble covering the sex crimes coming in. Having to return a lot of work out of chambers and such. You know, seeing as solicitors like to brief women to defend the sex cases.' He gave me a heavy wink.

I racked my brain for any up-and-coming female barristers I could recommend. I couldn't think of anyone who would want to change chambers. It was like leaving a family, not like changing jobs. Most barristers I knew stayed at the same chambers for forty years, and some even came bumbling in in their eighties.

'I'm sorry, Lee, I can't think of anyone. But I'll bear it in mind.'

'Thought you might like to move there, Miss, what with what has been going on with Mr Frazer and all. Separating and all.'

'What?' For a moment I was too staggered to understand what he was saying.

'Of course not, Lee. This isn't going to affect my work at all, and, besides, Theo and I are not separating.'

'Mr Frazer said you left him. To go to Mr Gladwyn.'

'I... I... That's not true. I admit I'm staying at Gus's, temporarily, but we're just friends.'

'That's not my concern, Miss. My priority is looking after chambers and this isn't a good situation for anyone. Not for anyone, Miss. Makes us a laughing stock, Miss, and that's not good for business.'

Exasperated, I blurted, 'For goodness' sake, it's not me who's having an affair, it's Theo and Polly.'

Lee shifted. The ancient floorboards creaked under his weight. 'I don't know about that, Miss, but if it's true, there's even more reason why you need to go.'

'You can't just kick tenants out without a chambers vote. It is up to the Head, not you.'

'No, no, Miss. Of course not. I couldn't do that even if I wanted to.' His small eyes glinted at me. 'You need to look at it from my viewpoint. For the way it affects chambers as a whole.'

My mouth was dry. 'And how does it affect chambers as a whole? I am having difficulties in my marriage, and I would support any member of chambers in my position.'

'It's not an easy situation for anyone, Miss, I understand that. Divorce never is. That's why I... we... think you'll be better off in a new set.'

'Theo and I haven't even mentioned the word divorce.' I was having difficulty understanding Lee.

'That's not my understanding, Miss.' Lee faced me squarely. 'He said you'd left the house, gone to Mr Gladwyn and you were getting a divorce. It's been very difficult for him.'

'There must be some misunderstanding. I've been trying to...'

Lee's face told me he had no intention of hearing me. I didn't want to sound completely deluded – the woman who didn't know she was getting divorced – so I looked down at my hands before looking up at him again. 'This is absurd, Lee. You can't push a barrister out of their own chambers because of a bit of completely unfounded gossip. The Bar is full of stories about who's done what, but that doesn't justify something like this.'

'That's as may be, Miss, but it doesn't change anything. My understanding is that you're divorcing Mr Frazer, and that he can't work in the same chambers as you while this is going on. If Mr Frazer leaves, then I am sure he'll take our Miss Chan and several others with him, and we would lose an awful lot of work, an awful lot, out of chambers. And you would not be flavour of the month. With any of the clerks. So, just to make it clear.' He leaned forward to wag his finger. The floorboard creaked again. 'You would not get as much as a single brief out of my clerks' room. OK, you may get work from Bravo's, but not enough to keep you in court every day. Not enough, I'd bet, to even cover your chambers rent.'

'I'll report you to the Bar Council.'

'Of course, you could do that, Miss.' He moved closer towards me, and dropped his voice. 'But, honestly, where would that get you?'

I could smell the fatty odour of chips on his breath. He was right, of course. Barristers' clerks were a fraternity that dated back to medieval times. Even I realised I would be a fool to take them on. Lee would believe Theo's account, because Theo and Polly – between them – were bringing serious money into chambers. I was still an up and coming barrister, without any guarantees as to how much work I might bring in the future.

'But, if you go without making a fuss, I'll make sure you are well set up. I know how good you are, I've clocked your results – don't think I haven't. My brother will take care of you and I'll send some juicy returns over.'

'That set is not even in the Temple.'

'Well now, that's the way of the world these days, isn't it? More and more sets are moving out to smaller premises. What with video links and that, we don't need all these big rooms. There's never anyone in here during the daytime any more. You have to understand, Miss, this is a business, a big business with a turnover of millions of pounds. I can't let anything damage that.'

'And I can't let you damage my career.' I leaned both hands on my desk and faced him.

'Think of it as an opportunity.' He winked at me again and lumbered back down the stairs. I waited till I heard him shouting at the other clerks before I let myself exhale.

I went to see Gerald, the head of chambers. This could be sorted out. His door was open and the top of his bald head was bent over a stack of papers. I walked in.

Gerald got up from his desk and took both my hands. 'Sophie, my dear. *Auribus teneo lupum.* We'll all be so sorry to lose you, but at least Lee will see you right.' Gerald always had a Latin aphorism for every situation, but I had no idea what most of them meant.

'I have no intention of leaving chambers, Gerald. It isn't fair. My private life is my own business, and it won't affect my work. Theo and I haven't even discussed divorce.'

Gerald urged me to sit on the big leather sofa, which was well stuffed, and in much better condition than the one in our room. 'Sit down, my dear, sit down. Now, that's not absolutely true, is it? Theo told me that you walked out, and you're now living with Gus.'

'Well, yes, but only because I had to live somewhere. He's a friend and nothing more. He put me up in the spare room. I could just as easily have turned up on your doorstep.'

Gerald looked startled as the hideous ramifications of that scenario played out in his imagination. 'Well, as you must see, that is *auribus teneo lupum.*'

'I wish you'd speak English, Gerald. It's not the nineteenth century anymore.'

Gerald patted my hand. 'It means literally "holding a wolf by the ears". It means that it's an unsustainable situation, in which both doing something and not doing something are equally risky. But Lee and I must both make decisions for chambers as a whole. You know how fond of you I am... how fond we all are of you... but...'

'It isn't me who's having the affair. It's Theo, with Polly.'

Gerald sighed. 'I'm afraid I have no idea about that. But even if it were true that Theo is also having an affair, then it's even more important for you to leave chambers. We can't have this *per statum rei similum esse.*' He caught my eye. 'Impossible state of affairs,' he translated.

I knew about human nature from the years of working in the justice system. The first person to make the accusation is more likely to be believed. Gus and I often had coffee or lunch together or a drink in the pub at the end of the day, laughing at each other's jokes. For all I knew, there had already been rumours about us. 'Lee has told me to leave. He said I won't get any more work if I stay.'

Gerald stood up and moved over to his desk to fiddle with some papers. He couldn't meet my eye.

'Can I ask you something?'

Gerald nodded, nervously.

'When Theo told you, did he actually use the word "divorce"?' I presumed that Lee had it wrong, that Theo had hinted at our problems and that Lee had put two and two together to make five.

'He did,' said Gerald. 'He told me you had left him and were now living with Gus, and had asked him for a divorce. I was very sorry to hear it, but I understood that it was your decision to go.' He sat down at his desk. 'Sophie, I don't think you understand how Theo has been hurt by this. Theo is a very proud man, like so many of us. And you're with one of his junior colleagues.' He shook his head. 'It really is *auribus teneo lupum.*

'How dare you, Gerald? Look at your own chambers website. Committed to equality and diversity. This isn't equality. You're forcing me out because Theo is having an affair.'

'My dear, I am so awfully sorry. So, so embarrassing. If there's been some sort of misunderstanding, you need to talk to Theo about it. I can't get involved. So very, very bad for chambers. Quite ghastly. I feel for you, really. But *ad summum bonum* – everything for the highest good. That's what Lee and I must focus on, don't you know.'

For a second I had believed him. That it was I who was in the wrong, that I had walked out on Theo. Reality tilted, and then levelled again.

'Well,' I said. 'It will all have to wait until I come back from Moscow.' I resolved to accept Lydia's invitation. I almost didn't realise I'd made the decision until the words came out of my mouth.

'Moscow?' Gerald looked bewildered.

'Yes. I don't have any cases booked in for the next three weeks so I'm going to Moscow. And Gerald…' I paused. 'I've heard some very serious rumours about Polly Chan's uncle's company. I'd strongly advise you to look into them before chambers ends up with a lot more gossip to worry about than a couple of affairs.'

But Gerald's face had the Latin for 'there is no fury like a woman scorned' written all over it. If no one believed me about Theo and Polly, then anything I said about their work in Birmingham would just look like petty revenge.

Engulfed with hot fury, I ran down the wide stone stairs and out into the cobbled courtyard, slamming the door of Medlar Court almost hard enough to break its panes of Georgian glass.

I was able to switch my shift at the paper, after which I went back to our house in South London to get my clothes, my passport and my bank card. There was a copy of the Metro on the free seat next to me on the Tube, and I picked it up. On page three, there was a blurry photograph of Adam Harris, who was described as 'very dangerous' and a hotline number for who to call. I looked up and down the carriage. It was one of the newer ones with bendy, open sections between the cars, so you could see almost down the length of the train. There was no one there who looked like Adam Harris, although my heart skipped a beat when I spotted a tall man, slouching, with

262

a hood over his face. But when I looked again he was gone.

As I stood on the familiar steps, fitting my key into the lock, I wondered what I was doing. Couldn't I step through the door, call out to Theo, then go downstairs to prepare supper? Surely none of this had really happened? I eventually tugged the key in the right direction, and opened the door to find Theo standing in the hall. 'What the hell are you doing?' he asked. His voice was icy.

'Picking up my things. Although I thought we were going to counselling before making any decisions.' I searched his face for any trace of the Theo I knew, the loving, laughing man I'd shared my life with for four years.

'That was before I heard you were fucking Gus Gladwyn.'

'What? Where did you hear that? Gus and I are...'

'I notice you haven't denied it. I've seen the way he looks at you, like a lovesick goat. Is he the only one, or have you been fucking half of chambers behind my back?'

'No, I mean, yes, that is to say, Gus is...'

'Gus is an upper-class twerp, and if you have to humiliate me, you could at least have chosen someone I could respect. I trust you'll have the decency to leave chambers without making us both look idiotic,' he said.

'I'm not having an affair with Gus.' The words finally popped out of my mouth.

'Well, I don't care if it's an affair or a one-night stand.'

'I stayed there because I didn't have any money. I left my card in my other bag. And he's a friend with a spare room, which is where I sleep.'

Theo sighed. 'Oh, for Christ's sake, you can think up something better than that.'

'I'm going to Moscow,' I said. I walked past him and went upstairs. 'We'll have to talk when I get back.' When I had packed, I called to him. 'I'm just leaving.'

He came back up the stairs, and I noticed that he was unshaven and looked tired. 'Yes,' he said, heavily. 'You're leaving. I had grasped that.' I waited for him to tell me not to go, but his eyes seemed dark and hard. For a second, I thought we had connected – that he was going to pull me towards him and say that we should try again, that he did love me. But the moment passed, and he went on looking down at me, impassive and cold.

'I'll ring you when I get back.' I moved past him, and dragged the heavy case down the steps. There was a cashpoint by the Tube station. I took out as much as I was allowed in cash and stowed it carefully in my purse. And then I went back to Gus's empty flat.

CHAPTER 36

The rich are different. For the first time in my life, I really understood what Fitzgerald meant. A 4 a.m. seamless transfer from a chauffeur-driven car at Heathrow into the private jet. No endless queues through security, standing in my socks – we went straight onto a plane with a surprisingly narrow but luxurious interior. We were served a chilled glass of Krug before the sudden and steep take-off, climbing fast and up through the weather to fly above the commercial flights. I looked down to see them – tiny specks of silver, thousands of feet below us. Nearly four hours later, we were landing in Domodedovo airport. Another car was waiting for us. The sun was out but I noticed the slush on the ground and the snow on the roofs. As the car ate up the miles, Lydia handed me a cashmere blanket and I tucked it around me. And as the endless birch forests flashed past the windows, I dozed, comforted by the fact that for the next few days, I didn't have to make any more decisions. I woke up as we passed through a village, but we kept driving through the snowy countryside for another ten minutes until we came into a tiny settlement of wooden dachas, grouped around an old ivy-covered church with a traditional onion-shaped dome. As we drove into the village, a feeling of familiarity washed over me. When the car pulled up outside a green-painted cabin, I felt as if I might weep. I remembered it. I stepped out of the car, stiff after the long drive, and looked around me.

The air was cold and fresh, redolent with the intoxicating

smell of spruce and pine. I closed my eyes for a moment and took a deep breath. Fragments of memory came to me – my grandmother deadheading her flowers in the garden, stopping to point out different species of birds as I played beside her; the dog that followed me everywhere; Kiril and my father singing together in the kitchen; my grandfather, his face wrinkled like an old apple.

I felt safe, as if I were waking from a long dream. The nearby cottages were mostly shuttered, but well kept, each with a small vegetable garden and a leafless apple tree, both now covered in snow. The place was quite deserted. Many of the dachas were shut up for the winter months, ready to be reopened in the summer when their owners fled the pollution and smog of Moscow. The door of the dacha opened and a housekeeper dressed in jeans and a black jumper stepped out. Lydia embraced her and they spoke quickly in Russian. She turned to me. 'Come in, come in.'

We stepped into the cottage. It was almost exactly as I had remembered it. The wood-burning stove in a corner, the painted chairs, the wooden table. Almost nothing had changed, except that it seemed so much smaller.

'Hello, Sophie, I am Marina,' she spoke to me in Russian, too. 'I live in the village and knew your grandparents. Let me show you to your room.'

She opened the door to a tiny bedroom with a single bed tucked under the window. 'This was your bedroom, yes?'

'I... you're so kind.' I sat down on the bed, and everything around me drained away. I just wanted to sleep, to be surrounded by the rustle of the woods, with the echo of my grandmother's singing and the smell of wood smoke. It seemed impossible that Theo, so much a part of me in London, even existed here. I sank down on the bed and fingered the hand-crocheted blanket.

Lydia smiled. 'It's not the one your grandmother made, but it's very similar. All our grandmothers made the same blankets.' She looked at me. 'Are you alright? You're looking pale.'

'I think I just need some fresh air.'

'Let's see the garden,' said Lydia. 'Marina is a wonderful gardener and she can show us what she plans for next summer.'

Marina took us outside to give us a tour of her garden, proudly showing me where she grew redcurrants and raspberries in summer, and turnips and potatoes in the winter. Now the bare branches of the trees were stark against the blue sky, enamelled with snow. We could see our breath in the air, and the faint nausea that had overwhelmed me inside dissipated. There was an old, rather dilapidated shed at the bottom of the garden, half-hidden by the trees and the snow, where I had played hide and seek as a child.

Lydia switched into English to talk to me. 'I've got a box of Kiril's belongings and also a few other things your grandparents left behind. You might like to go through them. When I heard that Kiril had been arrested, I went straight to his flat, but the police had already been there and taken anything they needed as evidence. They'd ransacked it, but I managed to find a few books and things they missed.'

'How extraordinary that anything has survived. We left almost everything behind.'

'I wish I could have saved more. After Kiril died and Vassily left, the rooms were reallocated.'

I must have looked puzzled because she added: 'You know that a lot of people didn't own or rent their homes, then, don't you?' Lydia explained. 'Sometimes you were given a flat for free, depending on your job or whether you'd done the authorities a particular favour. Kiril and Vassily were both given good apartments because they were cultural icons.'

Marina pulled open the door to the shed. Lydia pointed to

a box so Marina picked it up, took it outside and dropped it onto the snow. 'Let's take this inside,' Lydia ordered her. 'It's too cold out here.'

Marina carried the box into the kitchen and put it down on the floor. She knelt down and reached into the box. She picked out my matryoshka doll and handed it to me.

I held it in my hands, gently wiping the dust off it with my fingers until Marina handed me a cloth. All the little dolls were inside, nothing had been lost. I lined them up along the windowsill, just as I used to. Behind me, Lydia picked out some books. She blew some dust off the one at the top as I turned to face her.

I recognised it straight away and felt my world tilt on its axis. I could hear crows cawing and smelt a faint, lingering scent of pine wood. Everything seemed hyperreal. I saw the book in her hands and felt again the inchoate terror that had haunted my dreams, the dark, threatening shape that swam just below the surface. She handed it to me. It was printed in Russian, and I read it with difficulty. They were love poems, from one man to another. I looked at Lydia, and she shook her head, taking the book back again. 'Owning this book could have been enough to get you arrested in Moscow in the 1980s.' She flicked through its hand-typed, blurry pages. 'Kiril was writing it, though, and publishing it. I tried to warn him to be more careful.' She picked two more books out of the box.

'And the other books are worse.' Marina shook her head. 'They would have been really dangerous. Anti-state. Some political. Some personal. Cartoons about the secret police, for example.'

'*Samizdat*,' I said. It was a question, of sorts. The other two nodded.

'I self-publish,' I murmured, translating the term exactly but not in the sense that we mean it now. This had been a dangerous, furtive, illegal process. No one had dared speak up against the communist state for so many decades, but in the 1980s, dissident articles, books and magazines were reproduced crudely on typewriters or secretly at night on printing presses that were otherwise tightly controlled by the state.

'These poems, they are anti-government,' said Lydia, picking up another book. 'They are about the right a gay man has to express himself. But it's not just that. This is so critical of so many aspects of the state. I'd forgotten how far we went, how angry we were...' She shook her head and sighed.

I nodded. I vaguely remembered my parents talking about it, but it had all seemed very distant.

'For a while, under Gorbachov, it seemed as if the state was becoming more liberal. But that was a false dawn and the secret police were still hounding people.' Lydia's face was sad. 'And the Russians have never really accepted homosexuality.'

She turned the pages of the book again. 'I thought he was being more careful. But someone betrayed us. The authorities had discovered what Kiril was publishing...' She opened another book, and briefly read a page. 'Well, this sort of anti-state publishing... It would have been a death sentence.' I held the book in my hand, looking at its insignificant cover, remembering a blonde teacher with her hair plaited in two rings around her ears. She had a smile like a fairy princess, and we all loved to see that smile. 'Even in the 1980s?' I asked. 'Do you mean that people would be executed for writing this sort of thing only thirty years ago?'

'Not executed, nothing so open. But disappeared. Or dead in an accident. And, of course, there were also show trials where the jury were given the verdict before they had even heard the evidence.'

Marina suddenly noticed my face. 'Oh, Sophie, you've gone white. Are you ill?'

'Could you get Sophie some tea, Marina? I'll stay with her.' Lydia led me over to a kitchen chair and sat beside me. I tried to speak but it took me two attempts. 'I recognise these books. I was a child. I was only a child.' I struggled with the words. 'I saw one... here. I found it when I was playing hide and seek under Kiril's bed, and I put it under my clothes. I didn't understand what it was about. I showed it to Anya, my teacher.' The tears came and I could not speak.

Lydia took my hand in hers. I could feel it trembling. I heard Marina leave the room and close the door quietly behind her. 'Now I see,' she murmured, as if to herself.

'What? What do you see?'

'Nothing good can come of talking about this now. It is all over. That's all you need to know.'

'Lydia, you have to tell me. I don't care how much it hurts. I need to know what happened. I need to understand.'

The sun was slipping quickly over the horizon, and around us the light was growing dim. The dacha was surrounded by woods, and I could hear rustling as small animals settled for the night. 'Very well. The book that you took – it was another copy of this one?'

I nodded. 'I remember the cover. I liked it.'

She weighed it in her hand and then stroked it. 'Kiril was part of a group writing poetry, articles, reviews of books and films that were only available in the West. Cartoons too, critical of the state, subversive. Kiril loved Russia, passionately, but he loved freedom more.' Lydia paused.

'Please go on, Lydia. I need to know.'

'Somehow, one of our books got into the hands of the police. We could not understand it. He thought he had been so careful. I tried to find out what had happened.' She sighed and looked down at her hands. 'There were rumours; they said it was a family member who had betrayed him. Kiril was arrested for crimes against the state, and then he was found drowned in the Moscow River.'

'Not my father. Never him.'

'I suspected your father because I thought he had the traditional Russian attitude to homosexuality,' said Lydia. 'And he got away to the West. We thought maybe there was a price to his escape. But now I see I was wrong.'

The forest melted away and I was six years old again. I remembered lying on the floor in my uncle's flat playing with my dolls while the grown-ups were talking in the next room. I'd seen a book wedged under the mattress and had edged it out. I started to read it, but my mother called me to go, so I hid it in my pinafore.

'It was me,' I said, taking the book, remembering Anya's smile when I handed it over. She had taken it quickly, praising me, telling me that she was going to show it to someone important. 'I gave it to my teacher to show her. I wanted to impress her. I didn't know what I was doing.'

Lydia looked shocked and, for a moment, she didn't speak. Then she laid a hand gently on mine. 'You couldn't know, Sophie, you were a very young child. Your teacher, Anya...?' She thought for a while. 'Yes, that would make sense. They gave her Kiril's flat. I went there one day, and there was a blonde teacher living there. Her name was Anya Galkina. Someone told me she had been given the flat as a reward; that before that she'd been living with her parents in one room with her little boy.'

'So I took the book and gave it to Anya and she handed it in,' I repeated, trying to understand the words. Lydia didn't contradict me. We sat, together, quietly thinking about it.

'You were a child.' She spoke in a low whisper. 'You were innocent. And Anya had a small child, and no husband, so maybe she was desperate, just like so many people. Maybe she thought it could buy her a promotion. It probably did.'

So that was it, the terrible thing that I had done. An innocent act – the desire to please my teacher. In Britain, it would have meant so little, but here in Russia it had set off a chain of events that had destroyed a family and resulted in the death of my uncle. It was hard to believe. 'But would the police actually have killed him?'

'Unlike most Russians, Kiril didn't drink. But the autopsy showed a high level of alcohol in his system. They must have forced vodka down his throat when they beat him. Then they threw him into the river.' She squeezed my hand again. 'Maybe it wasn't wholly deliberate, maybe they just wanted to teach him a lesson and didn't care how dangerous it was. We don't have answers to those sorts of questions here. He wouldn't have lasted long – it was winter – and the vodka would have stopped him feeling anything.'

I could barely breathe. The feelings that overwhelmed me were so intense that they had no name, but somewhere in the mix lay guilt, shame and grief, complicated by an intense relief that my father had not betrayed his brother as well as a terrible sadness that two young men – Kiril and Henry Hanbury – separated by thirty years and two different justice systems had been failed by them both, and it had cost them their lives.

I sat beside Lydia in appalled silence, struggling to process what she had just told me.

'I'm so sorry,' she said. 'I must admit that I deliberately picked out that book to show it to you. I wondered if you might remember something your parents had said about it. But I hope you know I would never have done that if I'd even guessed at the truth.'

I waved her apology away. 'I had to know. Perhaps, deep down, I've always known. My poor father, I have to call him. The terrible things I said. I virtually blamed him for Kiril's death. What was I thinking? Lydia, I have to call him. Can we get a signal here?' I checked my watch. It would be early afternoon in England.

'Of course, let's try.'

I walked away a few steps and dialled my father's number. I heard the familiar dialling tone and willed one of them to pick up. On and on it rang. Suppose he wasn't well? He was an old man now. I felt a helpless panic rising in my chest, and then suddenly my father's voice came on the line sounding sleepy and confused. He'd obviously been woken from his afternoon nap. 'Hello, da, da, hello?' For a moment my throat closed up and I could not speak.

'Papa, it's me, Sophie, Papa.'

'Sophie, darling, what's wrong? Where are you? Are you at the station? Shall I come to fetch you?'

'Papa, no, no, I am in Russia.'

'Russia, my darling, that is not safe. Elinor, Elinor, our Sophie is in Russia. Elinor, Elinor...' I heard him calling to my mother up the stairs, and her indistinct reply, before he spoke to me again. 'My darling, what are you doing there? Who are you talking to?'

My mother seized the phone. 'Sophie, what's this? You're upsetting your father.' My usually vague mother spoke with authority. I knew that voice, I knew it meant something bad was happening around me, but that she could use her strength to keep me and Papa safe.

'Mama, I'm in Russia. I needed to come here. It's all right. I've found out what happened to Uncle Kiril.'

'Oh, my darling. We didn't want you to know. You were only a child.'

'Tell Papa I am so sorry, I know everything now. I'm at Granny and Grandpa's old dacha – you know my friend, Lydia, she bought it, and I'll tell you all about that when I see you. I've seen Kiril's books. I remembered what I did all those years ago.'

Her voice softened. 'It isn't your fault. Never think it was your fault. I'll hand you back to your father.' I heard her hand the phone back. 'She's fine, Vassily, everything is fine.'

'*Da?*' His voice sounded so old and croaky.

'I am so sorry, Papa. I was so wrong about you, so, so wrong. Please can you ever forgive me? Those terrible things I said, I am so ashamed…' My voice broke as I pictured him lying on the sofa in our cluttered sitting room in Kent. I looked up at the clear night sky, trying to hold back my tears, up at the cold, distant stars and slowly moving satellites and I wondered which one was carrying my voice from this forest to my father.

'Sophie, don't cry, my little Sova. You could not have known. I always tried to protect you, to keep such a thing away from you. You told your mother you'd shown the book to your teacher, and then we understood why Kiril had disappeared. We never told anybody. We love you, my little owl, there is nothing to forgive. So, when are you coming home? I don't like to think of you out there, so far away. Even now, maybe, for us, Russia is not so safe.'

'Soon, Papa, I promise. I love you, Papa.'

CHAPTER 37

That night I went to bed in the same room I had slept in so many times as a child. A full moon cast shadows through the window and moonbeams played over the knitted bedspread, reminding me of the nightlight my grandmother had always left to comfort me. I fell asleep thinking of my memories, mentally walking through my life before we left.

I remembered the fug of our tiny kitchen in Moscow, with its ancient gas stove and rickety cupboard. There had been a quiet tap on the door. My mother was cooking supper, and there were some potatoes on a few square inches of work space, peeled and chopped for our dinner. One potato still had the kitchen knife stuck into it, but Mama left it there after a hurried, whispered conversation. My eyes grew heavy, as my thoughts mingled with the stories Kiril had told me so many years ago, of forest spirits who hid in the trees, and brave huntsmen who rescued princesses. But perhaps the princess could find her way out of the forest herself. I thought of my brave Mama and Papa.

'Sophie, Sophie, we must go now. Come with me, and be very quiet.'

I am kneeling on the floor of the bedroom I share with Papa and Mama, playing with my matryoshka doll. The littlest doll is bossing all the other dolls about, and I can feel the tiled floor rough against my knees. I hear a low knocking at the front door and a muttered conversation, but it doesn't interest me. My mother comes in and takes things out of her bedroom drawer and stuffs them into her handbag. 'Quickly, Sophie, get up. No, leave your dolls there.'

'Where are we going, Mama?'

'To… to a party, darling.' She clicks her handbag shut and takes her favourite scarf from a peg on the wall.

I jump up. 'Can I wear my party dress?'

'There isn't time. We must go, we're late.'

'But I can't go to a party without my party dress.'

My mother hesitates, and I prepare myself for a battle, but she surprises me. 'Quickly then. But with lots of jumpers, or you'll be cold on the walk there. I'm going to ask Tatiana something.'

I pull my dress on, and a jumper on top. I know about the fearful cold. The flat is so small that I can hear snatches of my mother's whispered conversation with our neighbour, Tatiana: '…just a few days… thank you, thank you.' And she hands over our cat, Chaika.

'Why is Chaika going to Tatiana's?' I ask.

'Shh.' My mother puts her fingers on her lips, and bends down to help me put on my coat, hat and scarf. 'You must be very good today. It's very important. We're going to a party at the British Embassy.'

It doesn't sound so exciting after all. Just a lot of grown-ups hanging around talking. 'Can't I stay with Tatiana and Chaika?'

'No, darling, now you must be good. Please.' Something about the tone of her voice surprises me. As we leave, I see her look round our narrow sitting room, as if counting – the peeling wallpaper, the dining table that is almost as wide as the room, the mishmash of chairs, and the sagging sofa where I love to curl up. The door is open to the bedroom revealing my parents' two single beds, crammed together, with the screen *shielding the third bed where I sleep. My matryoshka dolls are still scattered over the floor. I think my mother will tell me to pick them up, but she seems to be in a dream.*

She sighs, a long, slow exhalation.

'Mama? Are you all right?'

She closes the first door to our flat and then the second – the inner and outer door following immediately after each other, a double layer protecting us from the outside world. 'Yes, darling, everything's fine. We're going to a lovely party.' She seizes my hand, and marches me down the concrete stairs, which smell of urine and cooking cabbage. We walk, as fast as we can in the snow, to the underground, then get one rattling train after another until we arrive at the British Embassy. Mama tells me we're not going back home again. 'But my dolls,' I wail. 'And Chaika? He'll think we don't love him if we don't go back.'

Something woke me and the dream began to fragment. Perhaps a hungry fox was barking, the noise muffled by the snow. Somehow I found myself in the other dream again, the one in this dacha that had always haunted me.

The moonlight is shining through a crack in the curtains. The door is ajar, and I can hear voices downstairs.

I tiptoe downstairs, feeling the grain of the wood beneath my bare feet and the smooth balustrade under my hand. There is a light flickering in the dining room on the right, and the sound of whispering. I push open the door.

The scent of lilies mingles with a heavy, sour smell, lingering in the air. The dining table is in the centre of the room and the whispering echoes in the corners. The coffin is on the table.

I walk towards it. Kiril is there. His face is as cold and lifeless as marble, and rough make-up covers a bruise from his temple to his chin. He doesn't look as if he is sleeping. He has gone. This isn't Kiril anymore. I lay my hand on the polished wood.

    'Goodbye, Kiril,' I whisper. 'I'm so sorry.'

CHAPTER 38

I awoke to the aroma of freshly brewed coffee and baking bread. It was past nine o'clock. I opened the window and breathed in the crisp, clean air of the forest.

Lydia came in, cradling a coffee mug in her hands. 'Let's visit Kiril's grave.'

'Yes, I would like that very much.'

'You need to wrap up very warm. It is only a ten-minute walk but the temperature dropped again overnight.'

I chose a pair of fur-lined boots from a row lined up by the door and put on another jumper before shrugging on my coat and wrapping a scarf around my face. We stepped out together into the biting cold. The sky was a brilliant blue, but the temperature had dropped so low that ice crystals had formed in the air and floated around us like diamond dust. This cold was unlike any I could remember. The fresh snow squeaked under our boots as we trudged towards the little churchyard.

There were only a few graves in the cemetery. One or two had been surrounded by black painted ironwork. Kiril's was marked simply with a Russian Orthodox cross, a small crossbar placed above the main one and a short, slanted crosspiece near its foot. The grave was covered in snow and a small mammal had left a trail of footprints from one side to the other.

I had a sudden vivid memory of Kiril. He must have been younger than I was now, standing under a birch tree, his head thrown back with laughter and his arms stretched wide to catch me, looking as wild and untamed as a Cossack from the history books. I prayed that his spirit still lingered here and silently asked it for forgiveness and then told myself that this was as good a place as any for him to be laid to rest.

'Your grandmother wanted him buried here,' said Lydia. 'Because she said he was happiest in the country. But it was really because she wanted the old ceremonies. There was a priest, and the women sat in her dining room with his body all night. That sort of thing was not encouraged in Moscow. It was seen as anti-state.' She gave a small, nervous smile. We turned away from the grave to walk back, as Lydia started to talk about her memories of Kiril. She told me about Kiril's love of the Russian countryside, his obsession with mountaineering and ice-fishing, how they would spend days together trekking in the wilderness, and sleeping out under the stars.

'He found Moscow claustrophobic. Russia is so vast, he would say. It has eleven time zones, and he needed to explore them all. But he was always taking risks, climbing in bad weather, driving too fast. He was wild and crazy, sooner or later his luck was bound to run out.' She touched my arm as we walked along. 'Perhaps, even if you hadn't given that book to Anya Galkina, I don't think he'd be with us now.'

'Thank you,' I murmured.

'I loved him so much, and he would have wanted me to help you if I could. But also I see a lot of myself in you. I've been where you are now, uncertain and betrayed. Do you remember that Kiril used to tell you the story about the Snow Child?'

'The ice child who couldn't fall in love because she would melt away and die if she met the warmth of love? I thought it was my father who told me the story.'

Lydia smiled. 'Perhaps they both did. When you fall in love, you melt into that other person. That's the joy of it, but also the pain. And if you have to leave them, you have to re-

280

build yourself all over again. That what I felt when I left my first husband, Oleg.'

I suddenly saw how the mesh of my dreams and memories had been woven together, trapping me in a net of guilt and anxiety, unconsciously driving me on, both to be the best I could be, and to choose a man who would betray me. If Theo had indeed betrayed me. I now knew who I was. I was no longer afraid to find out the truth about Theo too now.

We walked in companionable silence. I felt tears in my eyes, perhaps it was the cold wind, and could not find any words of solace. A moment later the dacha came into view, and I caught the sweet scent of wood smoke on the still air. I pushed open the door and knocked the snow from my boots before pulling them off and warming myself by the wood-burning stove.

Lydia followed me in and poured me some coffee that Marina had left out on the stove. 'So, at last we have the truth. This is why freedom is important. A world where a child can betray a beloved uncle by accident is not a free world. It is not a just world. Help me fight for freedom, for people being able to express their views safely, for those who have done nothing wrong not to be imprisoned.'

CHAPTER 39

'You're a bit fucking friendly with the boss, aren't you?' muttered Chris, when I got back into London two days later and took the underground straight to the paper. Everyone obviously knew where I'd been.

I smiled and switched on both screens, firing up my laptop. Tweets scrolled down one side of one of the screens, breaking news along the bottom. On the giant televisions up on the walls and anchored to the ceilings, I could see headlines about a humanitarian crisis in Syria, an earthquake in Chile, a speech being given in soundbites by the US president, some British tourists who had been rescued from floods and a series of charts, which I never took much notice of.

My phone rang. 'Hello, it's Emily from reception. There are some flowers here for you.'

'Flowers?'

'Red ones,' said Emily. 'It's rather a large bunch.'

Curious, I went to collect them. A large bunch of red flowers didn't sound like Theo. It had been a long time since he bought me flowers, I realised. And then they were usually simple posies of hyacinths, tulips or summer roses, albeit from fashionable florists. We had argued once, I remembered, about buying extravagant flowers when we could barely pay our utility bills. Maybe that was why he stopped giving me presents. But I couldn't think who else might be sending me flowers.

The card with the flowers simply said: 'You'll always have

me to watch over you.' I turned it over. 'I can't see who it's from.' I couldn't imagine Theo sending a message like that.

'Maybe it's that language of flowers thing,' said Emily. 'Let me see... red chrysanthemums...' her fingers flew over the keyboard. 'Ah, yes, definitely someone in love with you. Love, passion, desire... red chrysanthemums, oh, that doesn't work...' She closed her screen and looked up brightly. 'It was just obviously sent to you by someone who likes red.'

I looked up red chrysanthemums when I got back to my desk. They symbolised deceit and betrayal. The flowers took up too much space on the desk, and I was going to throw them away until I thought about Adam Harris. A sudden wave of fear washed over me. I had felt so safe in Russia. Could he still be watching me? And would a stalker send flowers? I still had the card of the police officer who had visited my house, so I phoned her. He hadn't been recaptured, no, she said. Probably left the country. May have acquired a false identity. Could anyone else have sent me the flowers? My husband, for example? After a few questions, she asked me to keep the card for their enquiries, although I didn't hold out much hope that those enquiries would be very thorough. I would have to make my own. The red flowers dominated my desk for the rest of the evening, glowing in the monochrome environment of the office until I couldn't stand them any longer. I threw them in the bin, earning a raised eyebrow from Chris.

Most of my work that evening involved checking stories about attacks on the government. The Prime Minister should do this or not do that. Politicians from all parties were accused of everything from affairs to mismanagement and corruption. I had to delete some of the more outrageous allegations and suggest some different wording on others. I thought about the book Kiril had published, which had cost him his life. I had read some of it, painfully translating the Russian and following the lines with my fingers. The criticisms of the government in the book were so mild compared to what I saw every time I worked at the paper and what I read every time I picked up a paper myself.

As the office emptied, thoughts of Theo started to echo around my head. I started to remember little things: the way he was so secretive about money, his subtle criticisms of my parents, how I had lost touch with so many friends. And what was the truth about the allegations of shady dealings in Birmingham that Lydia's detective believed he'd uncovered? I hadn't even begun to work out how I would deal with that side of the situation. So I pushed those thoughts aside for now; somehow we had to move forward. I called him at the end of my shift, hooking my phone under my ear as I wrestled with my coat. 'I'm back,' I said. 'Shall we talk?'

'Not while you're living with Gus,' he replied. 'Do you know what a fool that makes me look? Especially in chambers.' He disconnected before I left the building, swiping myself through and nodding at the security guards. I texted to ask if he had sent me flowers. 'No. Ask Gus,' was his reply. Gus simply sounded baffled. As I rang off, I thought – with a quick stab of fear – that I saw a man in a hoodie across the other side of the road, but when I looked properly, there was no one there.

On Saturday morning I went into chambers to get my things, on the assumption that hardly anyone would be in. A rather snide woman from the chambers next door chased after me as I walked under the great arch and into the Temple. Theo was distraught, she told me when she caught up with me, and he had lost weight. 'Theo's very popular, you know, and some people seem to think you've behaved rather badly. Not me, of course.' She sounded proud of herself. 'Everyone seems to have dropped you but I hope you'll feel you can always get in touch with me.'

I noted that she didn't appear to know anything about Polly Chan or her role in the collapse of our marriage. 'So kind of you,' I murmured, tapping in the code on the door of Medlar Court. 'I'll be sure to remember your words.'

Now I had to untangle the tightly interwoven strands of my life with Theo. Philip had recommended the best divorce lawyer at Bravo's, Ayesha Patel, who I'd heard of but had never met. It was only as I sat nervously waiting in the reception area of Bravo's that the enormity of my situation finally sank in. I would never touch Theo again, never kiss him, never fall asleep with his arms around me. The house in South London would be sold, strangers would wake in my bedroom and drink their morning coffee in my kitchen and someone else's children would play in my garden.

The sense of loss was almost unbearable. I felt dizzy and then nauseous. I suddenly thought I was going to vomit and made a dash for the ladies. I splashed cold water on my face until the nausea passed and then caught sight of my face in the small mirror over the hand-basin.

I looked grey and exhausted; a phrase came into my head from Shakespeare, 'the blue-eyed hag'. My hair was lank and my whole face looked puffy. I turned away and went back outside to wait for my appointment. Philip came into reception and surprised me by giving me a hug before ushering me into Ayesha's office. It was quite small, decorated in shades of taupe and white, with a view far below of a rain-washed Chancery Lane.

Ayesha stood as we entered and stepped out from behind her partner's desk, holding out a hand. She was older than me, with a smiling motherly face. Philip had assured me, however, that she had a fearsome reputation for being a very tough negotiator. As I took a seat, I caught sight of a framed photograph on her desk of her with two smiling children and a handsome man with his arm draped protectively around her. I felt the familiar painful squeeze of my heart.

'Hello, Sophie.' She shook my hand. 'I'm Ayesha Patel. Philip speaks highly of your work.'

It warmed me to hear her say that. But perhaps she was just being polite. I had the sense of my career perched on something high but unstable, ready to topple over and crash to the ground, unless I navigated the next few months carefully. Theo was well-liked and his reputation at the Bar preceded mine by many years. He could damage me if he chose to. Although, of course, I didn't expect he would stoop to such things. But Polly wouldn't hesitate to blacken my name. Perhaps she was putting around rumours even now, and was behind the occasional cool, tight smiles and turned backs that I had encountered in court over the past few months.

We ran through the background to my marriage, my discovery of Theo's adultery, and Lee asking me to leave chambers. She looked at me carefully while I told my story and even managed to look sympathetic, although she must have heard the same tale, or something like it, a thousand times before.

'The house, is it in joint names?'

'Yes, we put in equal shares and divide the mortgage payments equally. It's quite a large mortgage because I just had a small savings pot, and Theo got a bad deal in his last divorce. I'd expect us to do a straight split down the middle. The whole thing should be quite straightforward.'

'Pension? I take it you have one?'

'Er... no, I was meaning to do something about it next year. It is such a struggle to build up a practice, and with chambers rent and the mortgage I never seem to have enough to put something aside on top. Theo always said he was making plenty for both of us and I shouldn't worry. But I wouldn't dream of making a claim on his pension, I'll just have to build my own.' Ayesha sighed. She had indeed heard it all before.

'Right, well. Do you have children?'

'No, no we don't. We had been thinking of trying, but... Polly happened before we could make a decision.'

She scribbled a note on a jotter in front of her. 'I see, well that simplifies matters, of course, unless there is any chance you may be pregnant?' She raised her eyebrows at me enquiringly, but I sensed that the question was just a formality.

The room suddenly seemed unnaturally quiet, I could just hear the distant hum of the traffic far below us. Ayesha stared at me. My heart was pounding so hard I was sure she must be able to hear it.

My breath caught in my chest. Pieces of a puzzle suddenly slid together, like clues in a detective novel. The puffiness, the slight tightness of my court skirt waistband, the metallic taste in my mouth, my constant tiredness. I desperately did some calculations, I had missed my last period but had put it down to stress. No, no, no, not now. Shakespeare's 'blue-eyed hag was hither brought with child'. It had been Sycorax in *The Tempest*.

At some level I must have known. I could not speak, I was so shocked.

'I may be,' I whispered. 'At least, I...'

'Ah,' she said, putting down her pen. 'Of course, that changes everything. You will have to ask for maintenance for both you and the child. I assume you want to keep it? Or is that something you would like a little time to think about?'

'No, I mean yes. I should go... I need to think. I am so sorry to have wasted your time. Please forgive me.' I pushed back my chair as another wave of nausea engulfed me and I ran to the ladies room, pushed open the door and grabbed on to the sink.

Fifteen minutes later, I stumbled down the stairs, out into Chancery Lane, and went into the nearest Boots to buy a pregnancy test. It took me an hour to get back to Gus's house. Luckily he was out. I threw my coat down and went upstairs to the bathroom.

It was five o'clock. If Theo had been in court they would have risen by now and he would either be in his car or already back in chambers, but his phone went straight to voicemail. 'Theo, it's Sophie, there is something I have to tell you. Could you please call me as soon as you get this?' I was going to add something else but he picked up.

'What is it Sophie?' His voice was neutral, as though he were speaking to an acquaintance.

'There's something I need to tell you. I don't want to talk about it over the phone. Could we meet?'

There was a long pause. 'I don't really think that would be a good idea at the moment, do you?'

'Very well then.' He would have to hear it straight then. But I would have liked to see his eyes when I told him. 'I'm pregnant.' There was a long pause.

'I see.' That same chilly neutrality. 'I assume you don't intend to keep it?'

'Actually, I do.'

'And how do I know that it's mine? It could be that upper-class twit or anyone else you've been sleeping with'

'I haven't slept with anyone apart from you.' But my voice sounded thin. Why did the truth sometimes sound so like a lie? 'Ayesha Patel asked me, and I suddenly realised. It's why I've been so tired recently.'

'Ayesha Patel?' he asked, sharply. 'So you're really setting the dogs on me?'

'No, of course not. We'll go fifty-fifty, we'll share everything. I'm not like Louisa.'

'I have to go now, I've got a con starting and they are already downstairs. I'll call you this evening.' And with that he hung up.

I had a bath and made myself a pot of tea. I carried my tray through into Gus's living room and switched on the television but waves of exhaustion engulfed me and I felt myself pulled down into a deep sleep.

I'm in Red Square. It is crowded with brides in their white dresses. I'm trying to find Mama, but the brides kept blocking my view. I call for her but the bells on the Kremlin clock on Spasskaya *tower start ringing, and then so do the bells of St Basil's. She can't hear me because of all the clocks.*

I struggled to wake up and throw off the shackles of the dream, but as the dream dissolved, I could still hear ringing. I realised it was the doorbell. It must be Gus and he had probably locked himself out. I looked at my watch. It was gone ten. I had slept for hours. I stood up, pulled my dressing gown closed and then stumbled to the door.

'Hang on! I'm just coming.' I slid the deadbolt across and opened the door.

Theo stood there. He looked wretched. His eyes had dark circles under them and he hadn't shaved.

He held out his hands towards me. 'Sophie, I need to talk to you, I couldn't do this over the phone. Please can I come in?'

I instinctively held the door more firmly, as if to block him.

He rested his elbow against the door frame and looked down into my eyes. I had never seen him look desperate before. He was always so in control. 'Please hear me out. Don't turn me away.'

I opened my mouth to say something.

'I don't love Polly,' he continued. 'I never loved her, I hate myself for what I did to you, to us. We split up when you left, because I realised what I'd lost. If you give me another chance, I will never, ever do anything like that again.'

I stared at him, unable to understand what he was saying.

'I felt so alone. Your career was going so well and I knew you liked Gus. You were always talking about him. I felt as if you only needed me to help you with your cases... that you didn't love me.' He swallowed, as if the admission lodged painfully in his throat.

I still couldn't reply. The wind ruffled his hair, and I saw the Theo I loved looking broken.

'I could see I was losing you, and Polly got me at a vulnerable moment. Then she threatened to tell you if I broke it off, and I couldn't face losing you. Please don't leave me. For the sake of our child. You can't go through this on your own.'

He took my hand. 'Please come back, I will make it up to you. We'll be a real family. It's what we always dreamed of. Everything will be different now. Please come back.'

I hesitated. 'I can't make a decision like this.' I hovered for a moment, looking into the face I knew so well. Theo, the Theo I knew and loved, was back. But I couldn't let him in, not now. Perhaps not ever. I closed the door and slid down onto the hall floor, where I sat, stunned, until I heard Gus's key in the lock.

CHAPTER 40

Two days later, I left my shift at the paper at 11.30 p.m. I still hadn't decided what to do about Theo. I still loved him, but I wasn't sure how we could ever rebuild the trust we'd had or what would be best for our baby. As I stood on the underground platform, I caught sight of a familiar figure, lounging against the wall, slightly turned away from me, his hood pulled over his face. Harris? This time I was instinctively sure it was him, even though the lawyer in me screamed that it could be a mistaken identification. I felt my heart race, and reached into my bag for my phone to call the police, turning my back to him. But, of course, deep down in the underground there was no signal.

For a moment, I felt trapped, but a flood of students, chattering and shouting in Italian, came tearing down the steps. There were about thirty of them, calling to each other and joking, and what looked like a teacher or a guide desperately trying to keep order. I melted into the group, letting them surround me with their laughter. A train drew up, so although it wasn't the right train, I went with them, like a piece of driftwood swept out by the tide. As it pulled out, I saw the platform was empty. I realised with horror that he must have got on the same train and was probably only two or three carriages away. Luckily, it was an old-fashioned tube train with doors between the carriages, so it wasn't easy for anyone to go from carriage to carriage without attracting attention.

One of the Italian boys jumped up and offered me a seat,

and I took it gratefully. The train was surprisingly full for this time of night and there was even a young couple with a baby sitting opposite me. The father was blowing bubbles and the baby was laughing. The mother took the baby's hand and pressed it to her cheek as the man dropped a kiss on the baby's head. It was done quickly, as if it was all a frequent ritual and I saw them smile at each other.

'This is a Northern line train to Morden,' said the announcement. It was my old train, the one I took home every Friday night from the paper to our house. But it was the wrong one for getting back to Gus's flat. I started to work out what the best thing to do would be. I needed to get to somewhere safe where I could ring the police. The train stopped at Clapham South, my old stop. I read the familiar sign, over and over again, as a blurry announcement said something about the train being held at a red light. I looked carefully along the carriage. Perhaps I could wait until the last minute and jump off, leaving Adam Harris on the train. Then I could race to the convenience store by the station and call the police. I knew the area well, and was sure I could find somewhere safe.

A crackling announcement apologised again for the delay, but offered no explanation or estimate as to how long it would continue. Passengers shifted and sighed, and one or two fought their way off. And then suddenly our departure was announced and the doors started to close. I sprang up and squeezed through the packed bodies, and out onto the platform, not sure if I'd heard the doors open again behind me. Out in the open air, however, there were no shops open. So I walked quickly to our house, turning round twice. Each time the road behind me was completely empty. I knew a few people locally, but as I passed their houses I couldn't see any lights. If Adam Harris was following me, I didn't want to get trapped in front of a door that would never open because the inhabitants weren't at home or were asleep.

Outside our front door, I briefly hesitated. Should I ring the doorbell? But there was no time for thinking. I rang it twice, hard, while digging out my keys in case Adam Harris had indeed managed to follow without my noticing. Rain splashed in a puddle by my feet. Theo opened the door and stared at me blankly, and my heart turned cold. 'Adam H…' I started to explain.

But after staring at me as if he didn't know who I was, he smiled. 'Sophie,' he said. 'Sophie. You're home.' And he folded me into his arms, burying his face in my hair, pulling me inside. 'You're shaking,' he murmured into my hair. 'What's wrong?'

'It's Harris, he's following me. He was on the train.' I shut the door, leaning against it as if it might be forced open again.

'You're home, you're home now, it's all going to be all right,' said Theo. 'You're with me. I'll keep you safe.'

'I need to call the police. I need to tell them Adam Harris is here in Clapham. That he might even be heading for the house.'

'I'll do that. You look exhausted.' He made me sit down in the kitchen, pouring an unexpected whisky. I allowed myself a single sip and felt warmed as my heartbeat slowed back to normal. After a pause, he took my hand.

'Polly's leaving chambers. She's going back to Birmingham. We can be a family.' He looked thinner, with edges and shadows to his face that I hadn't seen before. 'Stay now. Never leave again.'

'I haven't brought anything. And we need to call the police.'

'All your stuff is still here. I haven't changed anything. And don't worry, I'll do it.'

'I'm so tired, Theo, so tired.'

'Let's get you upstairs,' he said. 'Just sleep. We can talk later.

We have our whole lives to talk. I'll call the police, and I've got a few things to get straight for tomorrow. I'll be up soon.'

'Don't forget to put the deadbolt on,' I said, pausing in the hall on our way upstairs.

He turned the key in the lock and shot the bolt across the door. 'There. In front of your eyes.' He took my hand to lead me upstairs. 'I promise to use every key, lock and bolt in the house to turn us into Fort Knox.'

In the bedroom, my bedside table was clean and clear, and there was no sign of another woman in the room. I ran my hands along the rails on my side of the wardrobe and wondered if I would be suspicious forever, checking towels for mascara marks and looking for credit card bills in Theo's pockets.

But it was home. It smelt reassuring and familiar, a one-off blend of washing powder, an edge of burnt toast and the woody, resinous sharpness of Theo's aftershave. We made this house, Theo and I, painting the walls ourselves when we first moved in, our arms aching as we stretched up to do the ceiling. Every inch had a story: there was that tiny stain, almost gone, where I had spilled the wine we had taken upstairs to bed. Outside I could see the bare branches of a cherry tree I had planted five years ago. How had it grown so big? This house held our memories. I snuggled down into my own bed with a sense that there was now a way ahead, however hard it might turn out to be. But after I turned off the light, I got up again and went to our bedroom window, pinching a tiny corner of curtain aside, to look out into the dear, familiar street with darkness behind me. There was a shadow there, something moving in the wind. For a heart-stopping moment I thought it was a person, but it was just a trick of the light.

I thought of asking Theo to check, but I was too tired. Our windows had locked security grilles, our doors were double-locked.

Just before I dropped off, the bedroom door opened. 'Goodnight, my darling,' Theo whispered into my ear. He tucked my duvet up around me. 'I'll make sure you never regret giving me another chance.'

I slipped into sleep without replying, but jerked awake at some point in the night to the sound of a woman shouting outside and the lower tones of a man remonstrating with her. I wondered if I ought to check, to see if the woman needed help, but she sounded angry rather than frightened and we often heard shouts from the street.

I ignored my instincts and fell asleep again, telling myself it was nothing to do with me.

CHAPTER 41

I knew the noises in my home very well. My ears were quick to tell me that there was something unusual. Over the years, I've learned to classify the sounds: a pigeon landing on the windowsill, the wind blowing a plant pot over and a door swinging in the breeze. Our front gate creaks, with a certain squeaky melody that I would recognise anywhere. But I didn't know what had woken me or what time it was. Theo was snoring beside me. I touched his shoulder. 'Theo, I think there might be someone in the house.'

He stirred. 'Mmm. I've got court in the morning.' He pulled the edge of the duvet over his head.

'I'll go and find out,' I whispered. He grunted. It was probably nothing. I moved as quietly as I could, avoiding the familiar creaking steps. I switched on the light before going down the stairs. The hall was empty. The front door was closed. I checked it. It wasn't double-locked and the bolt was no longer closed. I hesitated. Surely I'd seen Theo lock it myself?

But the sitting room sat in stillness, as if waiting for something to happen. There was no sign of an intruder. I edged down the stairs into the kitchen without turning on the kitchen light, so that I could get downstairs before anyone could see me. The lights from the backs of the terraced houses opposite and a bright moon washed the kitchen in a monochrome play of black and grey. The silence and emptiness seemed to mock me. I stood on the bottom step, facing the glass doors to the garden. There was a glimmer of movement behind my reflection.

I opened my mouth to scream but he was too fast. His huge hand covered my mouth and nose and I couldn't breathe. I could smell the nicotine on his fingers and the stink of stale sweat.

'Now, girlie, you just keep quiet. If you scream, that useless shit of a husband might come down and I'd have to kill him. Now I'm going to let you go, but you be still, nod if you understand. I don't want to hurt you.' I nodded but he continued to hold me. I could hear his breathing, hoarse and fast as my own heartbeat echoed in my ears. His hand slid down from my mouth and skimmed my breast before he stood aside and pointed at a pile of clothes on the kitchen table. I looked at the tumble dryer. The door was open. 'Get dressed. We're going.'

He stood in front of the knife block, holding our most vicious carving knife in his hand. I knew I must not let him take me. I had sat through enough murder trials to know that once your abductor got you into his car your chance of survival plummeted.

'Where are we going?' The longer I could keep him here, the more chance there was of Theo realising something was wrong. He would come down, carefully, I hoped. Without taking my eyes off Harris I began to scan the kitchen in my peripheral vision for something I could safely use as a weapon.

He pointed the knife at me, jabbing the air to emphasise his words. 'I've got it all planned. I've got somewhere we can be very private. Come on, get dressed. We need to go – I've got your car keys.' He pulled them out of his pocket and dangled them at me. 'Oh, yes,' he sniggered, 'you'd be surprised at what drawers I've been opening.'

I would die here fighting him if I had to but he wouldn't get me out of the house. I had to find a weapon that he couldn't easily take and use against me. The knife block was on the run of worktop behind him, and I knew from my GBH cases that it was too easy for a knife to be taken off you by a stronger person. There were three bottles next to it – olive oil, vinegar and a half bottle of red that Theo had left stoppered. I could grab the neck, smash the bottle and it would be difficult for Harris to take it from me without getting severely lacerated in the process.

But the central island stood between me and the wine bottle. The sink and hob were both set into it, and it was cluttered with the mess of our evening's washing up. Theo had offered to do it but, as usual, he'd forgotten. Next to the sink was a bottle of washing up liquid and one of bleach. There was a kettle but I doubted Harris would allow me to boil water.

'I had to come and get you. I know you want me the way I want you. It's just your cheating hubby keeping you away. Now, put some clothes on.' I edged carefully towards the kitchen table and the clothes, hoping that it would leave the central island between me and Harris.

But he moved round, so he was still between me and the bottom of the stairs.

My legs were trembling so much that I had trouble dressing, I felt his eyes on me as I pulled a pair of jeans over my nightdress before taking off my dressing gown. I wouldn't give him the satisfaction of seeing me naked. His eyes had the same flat stare I remembered from the prison.

'You know this won't work, Adam. Theo or the police will be here any minute.' I could hear my voice shaking.

He snorted. 'You know I like a challenge, Sophie, but your husband is still fucking that chinky bitch. She was here twice last week and they had an argument on the doorstep tonight. I heard every word. He told her he couldn't afford another expensive divorce and told her to fuck off. I think he'll find it kind of convenient that you're out of the way. He pretty much left the door wide open for me, didn't he?' Adam smirked. 'I thought the days of getting into a house with a credit card and a bit of wire were over, but there's no fool like an old fool. We can start over, just you and me. I've got money saved, you'd be surprised how much. Now hurry up, it doesn't take that long to dress.' He waved the knife at me again, and I slowly reached a hand out for a sweater in the pile of clean clothes. I was afraid to pull it over my head because I didn't dare take my eyes off him for a moment.

I remembered the diagnosis I had seen after he had escaped from custody – schizophrenia and erotomania. I knew that someone going through a psychotic episode could stay awake for days, never relaxing, and also that anything you said could be interpreted to prove their beliefs.

Adam was talking very fast, the words tumbling out. 'For a clever girl you've made a lot of mistakes, Sophie. You fucked up that first time, and it was all your fault I got sent down. I've forgiven you, I love you, but you need to learn a few lessons, so you never forget who's in charge. First, you're going to find out what it's like to be locked up twenty-four hours a day. It's like being buried alive. I've got a little place where no one will find you.'

There was a brief silence as he watched me. 'It's all for your own good. You'll thank me one day. I knew you loved me when you insisted on trying to represent me that day in Bullingdon prison. It was clever the way you tried to hide your feelings in front of that thick prick Philip, but I saw, yes, I saw. I got the message.' He rattled on, the instability apparent in his voice.

'I found a man who supplies passports, and I got us one. Two, even. That was clever of me, wasn't it? I even managed to steal that photo of you and that cheating shit and cut it out for a passport. They're in here.' He patted his rucksack. 'We're married. They won't be looking for a married couple. We'll be through customs before you can say knife.' He picked up the knife again. 'Just in case you were thinking of it, by the way.' He laughed. 'I'm witty, aren't I? I'm a bag of laughs once you get to know me.'

I was glad he was still talking, it gave me time to think and for Theo to realise I had not come back upstairs. My peripheral vision continued to inventory my options in the kitchen, but there was nothing else I could use. I needed to distract him so that I could get to the bleach beside the sink, just inches from me on the counter. Harris stopped talking and the kitchen fell silent, with only the sound of our breathing, and I heard the familiar noise of a stair creaking.

I could not stop myself from turning towards the sound, but Harris heard it too. For a vital second he took his eyes off me and snapped his head towards the stairs leading up to the hall. I could see Theo's shadow, thrown from the landing by the hall light, on the basement stairs. And I caught a glimpse of his pale, naked feet on the landing. I lunged for the bleach bottle, twisted the cap and when Harris turned back to me, I squirted the contents into his face, aiming for his eyes. His head flew back and he roared in rage and shock as he clawed at his face. 'You bitch! I'll fucking kill you!'

I raced round the other side of the central island, snatched up the wine bottle by the neck and smashed it on the granite worktop, almost getting to the top of the stairs, as he bellowed. Then he grabbed my ankle and brought me crashing down.

'Theo!' I screamed, but Harris was dragging me back down the stairs. I twisted round and tried to kick back at him, grabbing the stairs to anchor me, but one of the uprights broke away in my hand and I slithered down a little. I looked up but the shadow had gone, the landing was empty. Theo wasn't there.

For a moment I was distracted, and was dragged even

further down the stairs by Harris, until I was on the ground and he was above me. But I drew my knee back and managed to kick upwards towards Harris's groin. As he gasped, I stabbed his throat with the wine bottle. He seized me by the throat, his whole weight on top of me. 'I gave you a chance,' he hissed. 'Fucking ungrateful bitch.' And he began to squeeze my throat.

It felt as if my lungs were going to explode and the pressure on my neck was so painful that I couldn't scream. My brain started to work in a huge loop and everything seemed to slow down. I saw a curled-up image of my baby as I'd imagined it would be on a scan. I tightened my grip on the neck of the wine bottle and brought my arm up, blindly aiming for Harris's face or neck. It caught him in the throat again and a bright arc of arterial blood shot out covering the wall behind me.

He collapsed on top of me but I pushed his body off and crawled up the stairs, heading for the front door, my feet slick with blood and my vision clouding. I threw open the front door and stumbled into the garden, collapsing by the front gate. I dimly heard people shouting and saw lights going on in the street and the distant sound of sirens. I started to feel very cold and I let myself be pulled down into the enveloping darkness.

CHAPTER 42

I became aware of hands rolling me onto a stretcher. I told them I was pregnant. At least that's what I tried to say, but my throat was burning with pain and I could barely speak. The jolting journey to the hospital felt as if it were happening to someone else. Occasionally people spoke to me or spoke above me. I tried to tell them to be careful about the baby. I don't know if they heard. I heard the word 'surgery' and then 'pregnant'. But I saw my mother's face, and she told me that everything would be fine. I nodded. A voice asked me to count, and then I woke up with a nurse beside me.

As I swum towards consciousness I was aware of the clatter of metal against metal and the squeak of rubber wheels on a trolley. My throat felt as if someone had taken a blowtorch to it. I tried to say 'water', but no sound came out. A nurse helped me sit up.

'It's all right. You'll be fine. Here, just sip this.' She held out a small beaker of water. 'You've just come out of the operating theatre. We've just taken a tube out of your throat so you'll be sore. Don't try to talk. I just need to check your vitals and then I'll let you sleep.'

The nurse attached something to one of my fingertips and then held a thermometer to my ear. I struggled to speak and tried to form the word 'baby' but my throat was too parched. My hand fluttered over my tummy and she immediately understood. 'The doctor will be along to talk to you soon.' I fell back onto my pillow and sleep pulled me down again even before she had finished ticking her chart. When I awoke again, hours must have passed. The light in the room had changed and different shadows fell across the nurses' station. The curtain around my bed was pulled back. The same woman bustled in, followed by the doctor.

I tried to speak but my voice came out in a hoarse whisper. 'My baby...'

He took my hand and smiled. 'Everything's fine. You've sustained multiple injuries, including a broken leg and a shattered collarbone.' He patted my hand. 'You're lucky to be alive. We've operated, but conservatively so as not to give you too long an anaesthetic. You'll need to rest and take care of yourself.'

I felt hollowed out, like a ghost, but at least I hadn't failed my baby.

At some point – hours or days later – another nurse came in. 'You've got some visitors, but they can only stay a few minutes. You have to rest.' My parents. I was relieved to see that my mother, for once, was empty-handed. The catastrophic turn my life had taken was far beyond the help of nettle juice. My father was crying and took my hand in his, distressed beyond words.

'Theo,' I whispered. 'Where is he?' My mother kissed my forehead. They sat on either side of me, each holding one hand.

'My darling, my Sova...' My father tried to speak, but simply held my hand to his lips, sobbing. Eventually he lifted his face to mine. 'My darling, I must tell you. The police found your *malodushnyy* of a husband hiding in the bathroom.'

I knew that *malodushnyy* was an extreme term for a coward, translating as craven, faint-hearted and pusillanimous.

'He did call the police,' said my mother, who always liked to see the positive side.

'From the other side of a locked bathroom door while that

man was hurting my daughter,' snorted my father. 'He should have called the police when he said he would. When she asked him to. They could have picked Harris up and this would never have happened.'

'Ssh, Vassily, you're only making things worse. Sophie, dearest...' She looked into my eyes. 'Theo's coming later.' I could hear disdain even in her voice for a man who had sent his wife downstairs in the middle of the night to investigate a suspicious noise. They talked quietly to me and to each other while I dozed.

'Theo?' My voice was still hoarse.

Theo stood behind them. I saw his face over my father's shoulder. He looked immaculate as usual. He could have been a photograph in a clothes catalogue for checked shirts for middle-aged men. The part of me who had been prepared, however cautiously, to give him – to give us, as a family – a second chance, had died when he left me fighting for my life in the basement, protecting himself in a locked bathroom. I now knew he was a coward and a liar, and would always save his own skin.

'Come, Vassily,' commanded my mother. 'Theo needs to talk to Sophie. Let's go and find some tea.'

'I come straight back, my little Sova,' my father responded.

Theo tried, inexpertly, to rearrange a pillow behind me. I waved him away. His touch made my flesh crawl.

'What happened to Adam Harris?' I wondered how I could ever have loved the man sitting in front of me, with his easy charm and self-importance.

'The paramedics were there almost immediately,' said Theo. 'And he's in hospital, still unconscious – they don't know if he's going to make it.'

He sat down on the chair nearest to the bed, sitting forward awkwardly, and cleared his throat. Dread coiled itself around me and I found it hard to breathe. He passed me a glass of water and reminded me to take small sips.

I put the glass down and looked straight at him. 'I saw you coming halfway down the stairs. Why didn't you come down? I nearly died.'

'I felt it was best to call the police. There would have been no point in getting both of us hurt or even killed.'

'And I gather you only split up from Polly that night on the doorstep.'

He shifted in his chair and looked at me, as if he was trying to weigh the strength of the evidence against him. 'Well, I don't know what you think you might have heard...'

'You having a screaming row with Polly on the doorstep?'

His expression was carefully neutral. 'You've jumped to the wrong conclusions again.'

'You'd clearly opened the door after I went to bed and didn't lock it again. And actually it was Harris who saw you having an argument with Polly on the doorstep that night. Was that true?'

'I was going to tell you,' he said. 'It's only fair. I feel very guilty.'

Theo feeling guilty? If he did, he sounded very smug about it. But I forced myself to look calm. 'Really? Why is that?'

'I'm afraid he was right. Just after you went to bed, she turned up.'

'I didn't hear the doorbell ring. Or does she have a key?'

'You always get so bogged down in practicalities – those sorts of details don't matter.'

So she'd had a key, which presumably had failed to work as the door had been bolted. Interesting. Although she didn't seem to have moved any possessions in.

'I told her that you were back, and that we were going to be a family. That it was my duty to stand by you, and that she and I were finished.'

Duty? Fortunately, he misinterpreted my look of incredulity, and continued to look pleased with himself. 'She started shouting. I had to throw her out.'

'I've had enough of the excuses and lies, Theo. Our marriage is now over.'

'Very well,' he stood up. 'But you needn't think you're going to get any of my money.'

'Get out.' I finally got my voice back.

As he left, I realised he hadn't even mentioned the baby.

CHAPTER 43

Four months later, I walked into the familiar entrance hall of Medlar Court and touched the screen on the reception desk to register my arrival. My name popped up immediately. A new girl was sitting there. She offered me a bright smile.

'Can I help you?'

'No, thank you, I'm Sophie Angel. I'm a tenant here. Sorry not to have met you before, but I have been away.' It had taken longer than I thought to recover, and I'd spent the time at my parents' house, while the divorce inched forward. Theo constantly failed to supply the details of his financial situation that Ayesha Patel needed in order to split our assets and agree maintenance for our baby. But with the difficult part of my pregnancy over with and my body healed, I felt ready to move forward. I saw the interest register in the new receptionist's eyes. I was still news.

My name was still up there on the tenants' board in the familiar cursive script, but Theo's had been erased. He had gone to the new chambers that Lee had invited me to join, still insisting to his closest supporters that I had humiliated him by walking out on him to go to Gus. Polly, however, had told everyone who would listen about her affair with Theo, claiming to have been manipulated by him. She had also resigned from chambers. Gerald, much to my surprise, had taken my comments seriously enough to report Polly to the Bar Council. Enquiries into her uncle's affairs were pending from various police forces.

Apparently, Theo told Gerald that he felt that we couldn't both remain after such a scandal, but that it was he who should leave, because I needed the stability of a familiar environment. Such a nice man, his supporters said. Another rumour was that Gus had convinced Gerald that these days it was important to be seen to be defending the woman in a situation where two people could no longer work together. Gus had come up with several Latin aphorisms that had made Gerald consider the matter carefully. Or, it was also whispered, the new chambers Lee had invited me to join were potentially really rather good. Theo had spotted an opportunity and jumped. Whatever the explanation, I was relieved. I didn't want to change chambers. Now Theo's name was gone from the board, it was almost as if he had never existed.

As I climbed the stone steps up to the first floor, I could hear the usual frantic clamour coming from the clerks' room. Lee heaved himself out of his seat and came out into the corridor. 'Hello, Miss.' He cleared his throat. 'Er… I called that one wrong, Miss, I don't mind admitting it. That Mr Frazer is always such a convincing bugger when he wants to be.'

I nodded. 'He certainly had me fooled.' It hurt me to smile and say the words, although they were true. I still missed the way Theo laughed, his incisive way of dismantling an argument and the softness in his eyes when he watched me. But, above all, I was angry. At Theo, and also at myself for believing in him.

'It's what makes him such a bloody good brief.' Lee shifted uncomfortably. 'But I've got your back from now on, Miss. You're a bloody good brief yourself, and we're lucky to have you. Anyway, I've got a nice little GBH for you. Your bloke's bitten off his wife's ear. Still, there may be a run in it. There's two sides to every story. Woolwich, not before two. Thought you might a appreciate a little lie in.' He paused, his eyes drifting nervously down to my now obvious bump. 'Good to have you back. Now, where is that useless git, Tony?' He shoved the papers into my hands and bustled off swearing under his breath.

I went on up the stairs, and stepped into the coffee room, catching a glimpse of myself in the mirror over the sink. The scar on my forehead where I had hit my head against the stairs was fading and was now just a thin pale line, half hidden by my hair.

'Ah, Sophie!'

I jumped at my name and turned to see Gerald poised uncertainly in the doorway, balancing a coffee cup in his hand.

'Gerald.' I smiled at him – an English smile, my voice expressionless.

'Just most terribly sorry about all this dreadful business, terrible, terrible… Well, we can put it all behind us and let bygones be bygones, eh? *Improvidus, apto, quod victum.*' He peered at my blank expression. 'Improvise, adapt and overcome, don't you know?'

'*Vali na serogo seryy vsyo svezyot.*' I smiled sweetly at him.

'What?'

'Blame the wolf, it can bear anything. It's a Russian saying.'

He looked perplexed for a moment, then rallied. 'How are you? You look awfully well. We've missed you around the place. And if there's anything you need, anything at all, just ask.'

'Thank you, Gerald, I know I can always count on you.' He had the grace to blush as he scurried away. I took my papers up to my room and stuffed them into my bag. Gus grinned at me over the familiar pile of papers, as I made a space on my desk and fired up my laptop.

'Are you going tonight?' he asked.

I nodded as I logged onto my email. There was a reception

at six-thirty in Middle Temple Hall to welcome the new silk we had taken on to replace Theo. It was also an excuse to let solicitors know I was back in circulation.

Already the world was forgetting about the scandal of the charming QC with the wife and the mistress, both in the same set of chambers. There was more concern about a defence barrister who was stalked by one of her own clients, with a ripple of unease about how easily he seemed to have got into my home. But, above all, I needed to work and to create the patterns of what would be my new life.

Daylight was fading as I left chambers and the lamps around the Temple were flickering on one by one. A soft drizzle had started to fall. The square by Temple Church was unusually deserted. My steps echoed on the wet flagstones. I thought about Henry Hanbury, once again, and Eva Scott, both victims of an underfunded, creaking system that had left a dangerous rapist out on the streets to strike again. I walked on over the cobbles of Middle Temple Lane to where a pool of warm light spilled out of the door to Middle Temple Hall. It stood half-open and welcoming, as it had for hundreds of years.

I was home. This was where I belonged.

Book Club Questions

1. The book starts with a quotation by T.S. Eliot about a journey. How is this reflected in the book?
2. Were Sophie's parents justified in keeping the truth about her uncle's death and her role in it a secret for so long?
3. How far do you think that early childhood experiences influence our personalities and choices as adults?
4. In the story, the crumbling and underfunded Criminal Justice System fails Eva. Do you think that people don't really care about this until they themselves become victims or are wrongly accused of a crime?
5. Do you agree with Sophie's assertion that jury trial protects the citizen from the state?
6. Is the right to a fair trial being damaged by social media?

Acknowledgements

Many thanks to everyone at RedDoor, Clare Christian, Heather Boisseau, Anna Burtt, Laura Gerrard and Lizzie Lewis.

Also to Posy Gentles, Marion Doyen and Hugo Charlton for their encouragement and advice.

If you would like to learn more about the challenges faced by the criminal bar, *The Secret Barrister* by Anonymous is highly recommended.